The Locket

Hope you enjoy the book

Published by

Corrxan Inc.

1135 Hunterston Road NW

Calgary, Alberta, Canada

T2K 4M9

ISBN # 978-09948242-1-9

Publisher's Note

This book is a work of fiction. Names, characters, places and incidents either are the product of the author's imagination or are used fictionally, as with the use of actual historical figures and events. Any resemblance to actual persons, living or dead, business establishments, events or locales is entirely coincidental. The publisher does not have control over and does not assume any responsibility for author or third party web sites or their content.

thelocket.corrxan.com

To my Grandma Gilbert,
who instilled in me a love of reading
at a very early age.

Part 1

1

November 7, 1918
South of Sedan, France

He saw color.

It still seemed unreal to him. Captain Robert Rainey had become used to the grayness of the front lines after four years of war. That narrow strip of France reachable by artillery from both sides had been pounded into a quagmire. He remembered the ground, the sky, the ruined buildings in the distance, the dead trees, the sandbags, the uniforms, absolutely everything being gray. But that was behind him now. This battlefield had color.

OK, the color was mostly brown, being it was November and all. The air was cold enough to see his breath. Another winter was coming. The American forces he was with had advanced ten miles through the Hindenburg Line. They were out of the stalemate area, through the Argonne forest and approaching the gates of Sedan. The normal landscape he was passing through right on the battlefield raised his hopes that the war would soon be over, hopefully before it snowed. But the never-ending sound of artillery in the distance interspersed with occasional rifle and machine gun fire close enough to be dangerous to him continued to play its deadly song, reminding him that the fighting wasn't over yet.

It had been a long, hard couple of months, advancing against a determined foe, but it appeared that the Germans were slowly giving out. Captured soldiers were becoming younger or older. Rainey was beginning to believe there wasn't a healthy man alive in Germany between the ages of nineteen and fifty. The French Army, however, didn't look much different. Although Allied forces were advancing, which was something very new in this war, they were still piling up an enormous casualty list.

Rainey ducked and crawled towards the next mound of dirt. He was crawling among the craters occupied by units of the 28th US Infantry Regiment. They had been reported to be holding this section of the line, where a German counterattack was suspected. Rainey had volunteered to go find them. The newly appointed regimental commander, Colonel Hammond, had only taken over command the day before and was looking for someone to go out and find his men.

Rainey peered over the mound and saw someone he recognized moving towards a crater about fifty yards in front of him. It was Sergeant Kennard. He reached back and stroked the bottom of the scabbard that held his sword on his back, his good luck charm. His fingers ran over the small crest on the end, feeling the outlines of the square and compass arranged in masonic formation. He felt the wave of peace that he always felt when touching the crest. Then he jumped up and ran in a crouch towards Kennard.

John Kennard was a mountain of a man, seeming as wide as he was tall, making him easy for Rainey to spot. With the big sergeant's twenty years in the regular army, young Lieutenant Jeremy

Clarke was lucky to have him. Kennard would lead Rainey to Clarke. And that would be his last stop on this little excursion into the war zone.

He felt a bullet whiz past his right ear, making him instinctively dive to the ground about five yards short of the crater he'd seen Kennard plunge into. As he lay there, he could hear voices from the hole. Clarke was getting a report.

"Ammunition?"

"As usual, we let them do all the shootin'. We were too busy runnin'."

"I'd still rather have the machine gun." Clarke was talking about the French Hotchkiss machine gun that was part of an American infantry platoon's armament. It was heavy and required a three-man crew to move effectively. While the Browning Automatic Rifles that were also part of Clarke's firepower were effective in attacks and good for short bursts, the Hotchkiss was a better defensive weapon.

Rainey slowly crawled forward, listening as Clarke continued. "I want to create pockets for crossfire, so let's get out of some of the forward shell holes. You know, jagged front line. Make use of what trees are still standing. Don't know what command wants to do next, so we may be here awhile. Check the flanks as well, see if anyone we know is out there."

"I'll get on it."

Rainey had reached the lip of the crater when Kennard came up to the same point. "Sir," was all Kennard said as he moved past. Rainey slid into the crater and stopped to survey the scene. For a crater it wasn't very big, perhaps four feet deep and twenty feet across. Apart from Clarke up on the far edge, another two soldiers were huddled to his left digging, trying to connect shell holes into a quick trench line.

"There you are," he said to Clarke. "I've been through six or seven of these holes looking for you. I was half expecting to crawl into one and find Germans." Rainey never used slang terms for the enemy. He had too much respect for them.

"Don't worry," Clarke replied. "They're not that close. About fifty to seventy-five yards that way." He pointed north and looked at Rainey. "You brought the toothpick. Expecting trouble?" he asked.

Rainey's sword was an ancient Japanese blade thirty-two inches long with a twelve-inch hilt and a small circular guard elaborately engraved with dragons. The scabbard and hilt were adorned with a number of small tokens and coins.

"Anywhere the Germans can shoot at me is trouble," replied Rainey, reaching down and stroking the scabbard's tip crest again.

Leaning his back against the shell hole's sloping edge, he glanced over at Clarke, whose eyes showed no sign of fear. He had a new line across his cheek since the last time Rainey saw him, compliments of a piece of shrapnel. "Well, Lieutenant, as usual, you are in the very position intelligence says is a target for the coming German counterattack. I'm here to warn you about it."

Clarke chuckled. "Typical. Always me and my men."

"I'm sure they're not just picking on you," Rainey replied. "They're targeting the whole regiment. I've been up and down the line giving the same warning."

He looked down into the shell hole where the two soldiers were digging. They continually looked up at the rim of the crater, as if expecting German soldiers to suddenly appear. Rainey had noticed a very similar scene in the other craters.

"Sure wish that machine gun would get up here," Clarke said.

"It's on its way," Rainey answered. "I found them back about a hundred yards. There's only two of them now, so they'll be a little slow. There are snipers about. In the meantime, keep an eye on our friends over there. They're getting some artillery lined up."

Clarke sighed. "I was starting to wonder if we made a mistake moving this far forward."

"Nah," replied Rainey, looking around the crater. "You found yourself the best hole in the ground for a hundred yards."

Clarke shrugged. "I remember some roomier ones back there."

Rainey laughed. "That's the rich industrialist's son talking. You're living down in the dirt with us plain folk now."

Kennard slid back into the hole and crawled back to Clarke's side. He curtly nodded to Rainey as he pulled out his notebook, opening it to a page with a hand-drawn map. "Sir, this line here is the top of the ridge. I've placed our line as such here, here and here." He pointed to X's on the map. "Each point is close to squad strength. I made contact with Lieutenant Ronald on our left, so they're in position. I still have to go out and see if Lieutenant Bennetti has made it up on our right yet, but it looks like most of the company is up on the line. Everyone's digging. The trench line should be reasonably prepared within the hour."

Clarke nodded. "I remember the days when we could make use of the German trench we'd just taken. Thank you, Sergeant. Go check our right."

"Yes, sir," replied Kennard, closing his notebook. "One more thing, sir. Young Bradley is getting one of his feelings again."

Clarke sighed as a small chill passed through Rainey. He had learned over the past several months that Bradley's feelings were never wrong. He didn't know how the kid knew what he did, but it was a little disturbing. He was just glad Bradley was on their side.

"No rest for the wicked," Clarke said. "Let's hope Bennetti is where he should be." Kennard nodded and headed off towards the line's right flank.

Clarke opened his left breast pocket and took out a silver locket, tarnished from months at the front. The plain oval shape was unremarkable; the thin chain dangled from his hand. He opened it to see the image of his sister Elizabeth, smiling back at him. In a world of photographs where everyone posed very seriously, Elizabeth had smiled. The smile made her high cheekbones more prominent. Her long hair was done up as was the style in New York, exposing the curve of her neck before it disappeared beneath the collar of her blouse.

"How is Lizzie?" asked Rainey, his eyes fixed on the locket's picture.

"Got a letter from her yesterday. Still struggling for control of the steel mill. Business is good as long as we keep blowing things up over here. Dad's still missing in Russia. And apparently, some Yale dandy has put his mind to courting her. Hasn't impressed her, though. Still a chance for you." Clarke handed the locket to Rainey, a ritual that had started months ago whenever they found themselves together before battle.

Where the locket itself was Clarke's good luck charm, a link with home, Rainey had become attached to the picture. It somehow gave him peace among the chaos surrounding him. It made him believe that he would survive the war and that something worthwhile was waiting for him afterwards. He even had thoughts that maybe he was falling in love with Elizabeth just from the picture. He knew it was silly, but the feelings gave him peace. In the process, a strong bond had formed between the experienced Canadian captain and the young American lieutenant.

"I have mentioned you in my letters, you know," Clarke said.

Rainey smiled, breaking the picture's hold on him and handing back the locket. "Lieutenant Clarke. Are you trying to marry me off to your sister?"

Clarke laughed. "It's not like you don't know what she looks like, and I can tell you like what you see."

Rainey turned his face away, hiding his embarrassment. "What would she want with an old war dog like me? I'm sure some rich tycoon will show up and sweep her off her feet with his talk of balance sheets and output figures."

Clarke placed the locket back in his pocket. "Not very likely. She's very good with those details, but doesn't get excited about them."

The two of them lay there quietly, thoughts of Elizabeth clear in Rainey's mind. What on earth had made him even hint at marriage, even if it was a joke? What bothered him more was that his thoughts were both happy and disturbing at the same time. He'd never felt this way about anyone before, let alone someone he had never even met. And the feelings were distracting him. People were trying to kill him here.

Clarke spoke, bringing Rainey back to the war. "You still keeping tabs on your old regiment?"

The Princess Patricia's Canadian Light Infantry had been Rainey's home for most of the war. However, after Passchendaele, the regiment's colonel saw a change in Rainey and decided this captain needed a change as well. Then the newly arrived American 1st Division asked the British for officers with combat experience who spoke French or German. The colonel came just short of ordering Rainey to take the transfer. The move had been good for Rainey, putting him back among fresh and confident troops and an army structure less restrictive than the British system.

"They're up closing in on Mons by last report. The Germans seem just as tired and worn out up there as we're finding here."

"So are we finally winning?" Clarke asked.

Rainey smiled. "For us, winning will be us still standing when the shooting stops."

Clarke looked around. "Or hiding in a hole?"

"Yeah, that will work too," Rainey replied. The two turned toward a commotion at the back of the crater. A man was hauling the platoon's machine gun with him, crawling through the dirt.

"Now there's a sight for sore eyes," Clarke said. Both slid across the crater to help the man. "Private, you alone?"

"Yes, sir," he replied, mud and blood mixed on his face. "Corporal Gibbons bought it. Sniper about five minutes ago. The stand and ammo are about five yards back."

Clarke waved to the other two soldiers in the hole, directing them to go get the extras needed to fire the machine gun effectively. Rainey realized the man was wounded as well. "That's a nasty head wound. Should go get that looked at, soldier."

"I'm OK, sir. Stings a bit, but it just grazed me. Not as bad as it looks."

Clarke gave Rainey a look. "You planning on staying a while?"

Rainey smiled. "You know how much I enjoy firing a machine gun." He began manhandling the gun towards the shell hole's forward edge. "Come on, Private, I'll need you to feed me."

The private smiled. "Yes, sir, be my pleasure." He set to dragging the gun stand to where it was needed.

"You're Private Cavanagh, right?"

The private smiled though the mud caked on his face. "Yes, sir."

Rainey smiled back. "You guys can all look alike in the middle of a battle."

"So do the officers," Cavanagh replied flatly.

A shell whistled overhead, exploding twenty yards behind them. "That was a big one," mumbled Cavanagh.

"I'd say a 155," Rainey replied. Another shell passed over them. "Guess we'd better hurry. Hand me your spade," Rainey yelled. He yanked the machine gun up, pausing just below the edge for protection. Grabbing a spade from Cavanagh, he furiously dug a small firing platform for the tripod into the side of the shell hole.

Clarke pressed himself against the dirt for better protection from the shelling. The men at the bottom scrambled up beside Rainey with the ammunition boxes and then followed their lieutenant's example. The noise soon became deafening as round after round landed among the entire regimental line. Keeping his head down, Rainey dug without pausing so the machine gun would be ready before the main attack began.

His thoughts were now focused squarely on the war.

2

April 28, 1919
Long Beach, NY

Sitting on the veranda, Elizabeth Clarke closed the file on her lap. She glanced across the yard at the ocean. She had always liked the time spent in this house as a child with her brother and father. Returning to Long Island made her think about her father again. She had not heard anything from him in almost two years. She could only assume he was still in Russia, even though Clarke Steel Company no longer had any business there. He had stayed on as a quasi-diplomat at the request of the State Department because of the connections he had made over the previous decade. But soon he stopped sending letters and the State Department wouldn't tell Elizabeth anything.

A breeze blew her hair across her face, bringing her back to business. She brushed it back and reopened the file. The large furnace project had been approved. The day-to-day details could now be left to the chief engineer. She had never seen him smile as big as he did when she told him the furnace refit was a go. She smiled, remembering how she played the quiet girl at the board meeting, asking precise and leading questions until the board had decided that the furnace project was their idea. She hated the complete lack of respect she received from the men on the board, but she knew how to manipulate and play them off each other.

Her musings were interrupted again by the galloping footfalls of a horse coming toward the house. She glanced up expecting to see her brother reining in the horse as they approached the courtyard gate, but Jeremy was still pushing the horse full bore. Elizabeth became alarmed when she realized Jeremy was riding Chester, who abhorred jumping. It was a chore to get him to jump even a small creek.

Elizabeth dropped her papers to the floor and ran to the porch railing. "Jeremy, slow up!" she yelled.

Jeremy would have none of it. Chester, on the other hand, had other ideas. It's amazing how short a distance a horse needs to go from full tilt to a complete stop. Jeremy became airborne, luckily clearing the fence and going into a roll as he hit the ground. He came to a halt just short of the big maple tree in the yard.

Elizabeth pulled up her skirt and ran down the porch stairs, dropping to her knees as she reached where Jeremy lay. "Jeremy," she said, out of breath. "Are you all right?"

Jeremy moaned, then began to chuckle. "I'd forgotten Chester isn't a jumper." Chester watched him from over the gate with what seemed to Elizabeth like a questioning look.

She slapped Jeremy on the chest and stood. "Damn you," she said. "A year of being shot at and now you're trying to kill yourself right here at home."

Jeremy gave Elizabeth a sharp look. "I'm feeling bored. What's wrong with a little excitement?"

Elizabeth sighed and sat down next to her brother. "It's more than that and you know it." She glanced at the sky, hoping for some explanation for his state of mind. "I know you've only been home for two months, but you should start thinking about joining the company. I need you to take charge in the boardroom so I can get things done easier and faster."

Jeremy looked at his feet.

"Well," Elizabeth continued, "What do you think? Even Chester thinks you should."

They both looked over at Chester, who nodded and snorted.

"See?" Elizabeth said.

"He's not nodding 'yes,'" Jeremy replied. "He's nodding that he wants back in the barn."

"Jeremy."

"OK," he said, throwing his hands in the air. "I'll go into the city with you next week."

"Thank you," Elizabeth said, relieved.

They both turned to the sound of an automobile approaching the house. Getting up, Elizabeth saw the car circle around before it passed behind the house.

Jeremy chuckled. "Is that another poor suitor unaware he's about to get his ego badly bruised?"

Elizabeth looked down at her brother and smiled. "They know better than to arrive unannounced. Go put Chester back in the barn." On her way toward the house she glanced back to see Jeremy still sitting on the ground. The little silver locket was in his hand, the one she had given him when he left for the war. She made a note to ask her brother why he still carried it all the time now that he was home.

She arrived in the front hall to see a man in his early forties handing his gloves and top hat to the butler. He was six feet tall, very thin and had the most nondescript face she had ever seen. He was dressed formally, like a banker. He was pulling his watch out of his pocket when he noticed Elizabeth come into the hall.

"Good morning," the man said. "You must be Elizabeth Clarke."

"I am," Elizabeth replied firmly. "And who, may I ask, am I addressing?"

"Of course. Where are my manners? Arriving unannounced and all. My name is Charles Appleton."

"How do you do," she answered. "And what brings you out here today?"

"I am with the State Department. I have news of your father."

Elizabeth's chest tightened. She brought her right hand over her heart. "Is my father all right?"

Appleton smiled. "Don't worry. He was just fine the last time I saw him. He sent me here on a mission that requires your brother's talents."

Elizabeth lowered her hand tentatively. Then she frowned. "My brother's talents?"

"Yes," replied Appleton. "Is your brother home at the moment?"

"He's just putting away his horse. He'll be in presently." Elizabeth raised her arm to show Appleton in. "We can wait for him on the veranda." Passing down the hallway, she continued. "You've been with my father in Russia?"

As they passed through the library out to the veranda, Elizabeth signaled to the butler to make refreshments. Out on the veranda, they sat down on matching teak armchairs and Appleton began. "Yes. Your father and I have been working together for about three years now. I can't tell you what he's doing or done, but I can tell you that he's fine by last report and will be coming home soon. Right now, he needs your brother to carry out a mission for him in the utmost secrecy."

Elizabeth nodded suspiciously. "What kind of mission?"

Appleton shook his head. "I'm sorry, Miss Clarke. I can discuss it only with your brother."

"If it involves my father," she said, "it will involve me."

"Your father didn't say you would be involved."

Elizabeth frowned, holding down a tinge of anger. She had learned to let that sort of condescension go as she'd had to bear it several times in the boardroom. It was never a good idea to counter it right away. Best to plan carefully.

The butler came in with a tray of iced teas and small cakes and placed them on the table. She thanked him as he left. She took a moment to formulate her plan. "Jeremy will be a while with the horse. Fifteen minutes, perhaps. In the meantime, what can you tell me about the situation in Russia?"

Elizabeth steered the conversation artfully, but came to find Appleton much more astute than the members of her board. He did give her up-to-date information on what was happening in the revolution, but nothing past what she could have gotten from the daily newspapers. Appleton was skilled in answering evasively and seemed to know what Elizabeth was angling for. But when she asked for personal information about her father, Appleton had good answers, indicating that he did know him.

"So, in the end, there are between four and seven sides fighting amongst themselves in the revolution, depending on who you talk to," Elizabeth said.

"That's about right," replied Appleton. "It can be difficult to keep track sometimes."

"I can imagine," said Elizabeth.

"So is my sister amazing you with her mind?" Jeremy asked as he rounded the corner onto the porch.

"Yes. She is quite unique." Appleton got up from his chair and extended his hand. "Charles Appleton. State Department."

"State Department," said Jeremy, stopping suddenly before taking Appleton's hand. "You here about father?"

"Yes," replied Appleton. "He asked me to discuss with you a mission that he would like you to undertake."

"A mission?" Jeremy scowled and tilted his head. "What kind of mission and why me?"

"Those answers I must tell you in private."

Jeremy looked down at Elizabeth, who glanced up with her eyes wide, as if to say, *Don't you dare dismiss me.*

"There aren't many big decisions I make without my sister's counsel," Jeremy said. "She acquired the brains in the family. I'm just a lowly soldier."

Appleton glanced back and forth between the two Clarkes before answering. "I'm sorry. I can only divulge the details to you, Mr. Clarke. Your father was very specific."

Elizabeth glared at Appleton. "That does not sound like our father. What kind of mission could it possibly be that would require only Jeremy's skills?"

Appleton's head slowly pivoted towards Elizabeth, his face not showing any change whatsoever as he said one word. "Military."

Nothing happened for several seconds as that word seeped into Elizabeth's consciousness. Then she stood up suddenly. "If you will excuse us for a moment, Mr. Appleton." She grabbed Jeremy by the arm and dragged him into the house. She led him to the study and closed the door.

As she turned from the door, Jeremy crossed to his father's desk and turned on the electric lamp. They stood there, silently looking at each other for a moment before Jeremy spoke. "I know what you're going to say. We really don't know who this man is. I take it you did a reasonable interrogation before I got there?"

Elizabeth stepped farther into the room. "I believe he has actually come from Russia and he knows Father. He appears to be familiar enough with him. But that doesn't mean we can trust him."

"What I don't understand," said Jeremy, "is why Father would insist only I be privy to the mission? He knows as well as I do you're the smart one and I'd confide in you."

Elizabeth nodded knowingly. "That may have more to do with Mr. Appleton than Father's instructions."

Jeremy frowned. "I don't follow."

"Father wants a military mission undertaken. He only needs to tell Mr. Appleton to contact you. You, on the other hand, would make use of all resources at your disposal, like me. Mr. Appleton wouldn't need to know that."

Jeremy leaned back on the desk. "So this could be legitimate. What do you want to do?"

Elizabeth turned away, worries racing through her mind. "Military means war. I am not pleased that this will send you back into a war zone."

Jeremy moved to her and placed his hands on her shoulders. "Those are the skills Father is looking for. I'm a soldier, Sis. It's what I'm trained to do and I'm told I'm quite good at it."

"I'm sorry," replied Elizabeth, looking down sadly. "I worry about you. I worried during the whole time you were in France, reading about all those horrible things in the papers. I don't want you to go back to that."

"It may not involve that. We won't know anything at all if I don't give Appleton a chance to speak."

Elizabeth nodded. "You're right. We should at least hear his story."

"Then I'd best get to it. I'll take him for a walk along the beach for privacy."

* * *

That night after dinner, Elizabeth read over the notes Jeremy had made about his meeting with Appleton. The two of them had been down on the beach for two hours. Once Appleton had returned to New York, Jeremy was eager to tell her about the mission. But Elizabeth knew it would be better if some time passed for him to reflect before presenting it to her. She asked him to sit down and write out a report, including what Appleton had told him, word for word if he could remember, and what he thought was needed to make the mission a success.

The report turned out to be twelve pages, written in Jeremy's fine, small script. Elizabeth sat at her father's desk in the study, Jeremy sitting across from her with a boyishly excited look on his face. Elizabeth glanced up. Obviously, she thought, Jeremy's excitement about the mission had not waned in the slightest over the course of the day. Writing the lengthy report seemed to have fueled him to even greater excitement.

It was very detailed work. The mission involved taking a small military unit through Russia to a city called Chelyabinsk. There, they would retrieve their father and something referred to only as "the package." They would have to get him and it out through Vladivostok, where American troops were stationed. Jeremy was needed to lead the unit. Appleton had explained that trust was a rare commodity in Russia and with Communism being an international phenomenon, Jonathan Clarke thought it best that the unit be led by someone he knew and trusted. The report included no other reference to "the package." The rest of it detailed men, equipment, training and logistics using military jargon that was unfamiliar to Elizabeth. The whole exercise of reading Jeremy's carefully written pages made her more and more tense. It did involve Jeremy going back into a war zone. But was it for Father? Was there another agenda hidden behind Appleton's nondescript eyes? It was all fraught with danger.

Elizabeth placed the papers on the desk and looked up at her brother. For a moment, in the low light, he looked like he was 10 again, full of spit and vinegar and looking for trouble. She looked down at the report. This had not been done by a 10-year-old child. This was the work of an experienced planner well versed in all things military. It was a feasible blueprint for the mission.

She looked up again. "So, you want to go?" she said flatly.

"Yes." He said it without hesitation.

She picked up a page from the report. "You can get all this?"

"No," he corrected her. "That would be your job. Didn't you read the last sentence?"

Elizabeth shuffled the papers and picked up the last page. Clearly written in a larger script than the rest of the report was "Elizabeth will be in charge of logistics and financing."

She put the page down. "I don't know anything about buying weapons or shipping troops."

"Do you know about buying machine parts and shipping steel products?"

"Jeremy, it's not the same."

Jeremy leaned on the desk. "Observe. Learn. Dominate."

Elizabeth leaned in close to Jeremy's face. "Don't try and use my motto against me."

Jeremy backed away. "You taught it to me. Why can't you apply it here? I'm sure ordering and shipping anything is basically the same process. You find what you want, buy it and put it on a ship to where you want it to go."

"It's not that simple. You can't just go out and buy guns and bombs and . . ." She picked up a page with a list of equipment on it ". . . whatever a trench mortar is." She slapped the page back down on the desk. "People will notice and wonder who I want to start a war with. And booking a ship to send out a small army? I'm sure the government would have something to say about that."

"Appleton is with the State Department. I'm sure he could get clearance."

"We don't know who Mr. Appleton really is."

Jeremy smiled. "You're smart, Lizzie. I'm confident you can find out about him and figure out how to do everything else quietly. And I'll be bringing in some expertise to help you evaluate the weapons."

Elizabeth looked sternly at him. "And how am I supposed to hide the fact I'm spending a lot of company money on weapons and the like from the board of Clarke Steel?"

Jeremy laughed. "Seriously? From that bunch of old curmudgeons? They're more worried about what's being served for lunch at the Waldorf than how much steel you made that day. And I believe those are your words, not mine."

Elizabeth sagged. She knew he was right. She could sell Clarke Steel and most of the board wouldn't know it until the next board meeting. She was just throwing up obstacles because the whole idea of this mission scared her. She wasn't ready to let her brother go off to another war at the behest of some man she had never met before. She looked down again at the pages under her fingertips. It even mentioned the coming sale of steel pipes destined for Rumania in June. Jeremy had obviously been paying some attention to the business.

She picked up that page. "You have me coming to Rumania to arrange payment for horses and wagons. Just how am I supposed to find time for that? I can't be leaving the company business for a jaunt across the world."

Jeremy smiled. "I knew you wouldn't even trust me with money. But weren't you thinking of going to Paris to work with that Davidson character on some potential business? Doesn't Europe need rebuilding?"

Damn, she thought to herself. *He has been listening*. Miles Davidson had just left after the board meeting to return to Paris where the world was meeting for peace talks. Davidson had been making good contacts and suggested that Elizabeth could be useful in "charming" some business their way. That was the way Davidson had put it. Elizabeth figured it would require something more like flirting.

"That's Paris, not . . ." she picked up the page again, ". . . Constanta."

"Miles said the real action will take place once the peace negotiations are done. That will be sometime around July. You'll have plenty of time to get there."

They looked at each other, Elizabeth sternly, Jeremy smiling. She knew she wasn't going to win this tonight. There was no reason to say no now other than her fear for her brother. Perhaps later, as they investigated possibilities, something else would come up.

"Go find your experts," she said. "I'll do some investigating, both on our Mr. Appleton through my contacts at the State Department and the logistical aspects." She silently said a little prayer asking that something throw a monkey wrench into the whole thing. "In a week or two, we'll review what we have learned and reevaluate."

Jeremy almost jumped out of his chair. "Great. This is going to be fun, Lizzie. Just you wait and see." He turned and hurried toward the door. His hand on the knob, he stopped and turned around.

"This is what I do, Lizzie," he said seriously. "I'm good at it. I can bring Father home. You don't have to worry so much."

That did not ease Elizabeth's misgivings.

3

May 1, 1919
Washington, D.C.

It was three days later when Elizabeth took the train down to Washington, D.C. to visit her contact at the State Department. She made the appointment supposedly to talk about her upcoming trip to Paris, but when she got there, she pushed him to get her Appleton's personnel file. It took some doing and a little cash, but Geoffrey Carver had feelings for her and she played that card decisively. Now she was sitting in a reading room with a file stamped with the name Charles Appleton on the cover.

The file was awfully thin for a career diplomat. Entering service in 1897, Appleton's first assignment was Havana, arriving there before the Spanish-American War. There was virtually no information on what he actually did there. In 1903, he was assigned to the American Embassy in St. Petersburg. Other details included his language skills (he spoke several languages, including Russian) and a photograph that was at least fifteen years old. Elizabeth thought it must have been taken just before he left for Russia. Though considerably younger looking, she still recognized the same nondescript face of the man who had come to visit three days before.

She found little else about what he had done in Russia, either. A short note mentioned a young woman he had saved from Russian guards in front of the Winter Palace during Bloody Sunday in 1905. There was a reference to a report about a man named Anton Kolochov of the "Okhrana," whatever that was. And there was the order assigning Appleton to work with Elizabeth's father starting in 1916, followed by a note about both men going missing in late 1917. The last addition to his file was a page stating Appleton's unannounced arrival at the State Department offices five days ago, and his request to put off his debriefing for a month, citing "personal reasons." He had then checked out a number of maps of Russia from State's map room. A slip from the map room's librarian, four days old, was the file's the last entry.

Elizabeth closed the folder and gazed at the cover. *Who was Charles Appleton?* She looked up and saw Carver walking towards her. She got up and held out the file.

"Thank you, Geoffrey," she said. "Wasn't much there, but it confirmed what I really wanted to know."

Carver took the file and looked quickly around him before speaking. "The man is an enigma. And he has clout. No one else who had gone missing for two years would be able to beg off a debriefing for a month."

"What section of State does he work for? There wasn't a title or anything like that in the file."

Carver looked over his shoulder again and lowered his voice. "There are a few men here at State with files like this. It's the only indication that they work for us at all. We call them 'Ghosts.' We think they do the kinds of things our government can't be seen doing."

A chill went down Elizabeth's spine. "Like what?" she asked, not really wanting to know the answer.

Carver shook his head. "I don't know and don't want to. Charles Appleton is the first Ghost I've ever seen and he scares me. He seems so normal and friendly, but everyone around him looked scared."

"He must report to someone."

"If he does, I don't know who it is. It worries me that you are showing an interest in this man."

Elizabeth gently, and reassuringly, placed her hand on his arm. "Thank you for your concern, Geoffrey, but I should be all right. He's working with my father."

* * *

During the taxi ride back to the hotel, Elizabeth mused over her meeting with Carver. *Poor Geoffrey*, she thought. *He's been pining over me for years now.* Carver had been fresh out of Princeton when he joined State and began working with her father on his Russian business dealings. Elizabeth was only seventeen when they met and he was smitten by her right off the bat. This wasn't the first time she had played on his feelings for her to get information and it probably wouldn't be the last. And each time, the little pangs of guilt she felt went away quicker.

Besides, what she had learned about the mysterious Charles Appleton had been worth it. It surprised her somewhat to feel relief that her father was working with such a man. Jonathan Clarke was a shrewd, intelligent businessman, but she had no idea how he would handle himself during a violent confrontation. Having someone like Charles Appleton around, who scared the living daylights out of people, would make him safer. At least she had found out that Appleton was with State, even if it was in a "sort of" capacity.

Next on her agenda was to look into acquiring surplus war material. It was the day after Appleton's visit when she remembered a memorandum that had come across her desk about a month before. Much of the war materials could not be sold off because of their dangerous nature. Elizabeth thought all weapons were dangerous, but apparently rifles and pistols were fine. It was the heavier items that needed destroying. Large caliber and automatic guns, cannons, those mortars that were on Jeremy's list. Most, if not all of their parts were made of steel, and Clarke Steel could be paid to dispose of them in their steel furnaces. It would be easy to divert a small portion of the weapons away from the furnaces. She had arranged a meeting tonight with an old friend of the family, who was the assistant secretary of the Navy, to talk about getting a contract. First, though, she was to meet up with Jeremy and his friend, Sergeant Kennard.

Arriving at the Willard Hotel, Elizabeth went straight to her room to freshen up. She was expected for lunch downstairs at noon. When the time arrived, she entered the Pompeiian Room and spotted Jeremy over by the French doors leading out to the back patio. Seated with him were two men, one about the same size as Jeremy and another man who was very large. Neither of these men were dressed appropriately to be in the Willard and got scornful looks from other tables and the staff.

As she approached the table, Jeremy got up and held out his hand to her. He was dressed superbly in a modern-day jacket, crisp crease in his pants and a new tie she had bought for him in New York. "My," said Elizabeth. "I haven't seen you this dressed up in ages. You look . . ."

"Like a dandy?" Jeremy shrugged. "After a year of rolling in mud and dodging bullets, it seems a little frivolous to me." He turned to the men at the table. "Let me introduce you to Sergeant Kennard and Corporal Bradley."

Elizabeth held out her hand to Kennard, but Kennard didn't know what to do. She lowered it and took the seat Jeremy held out for her. "Sorry," she said. "I should know better considering all the workers I deal with at the mill. But when at the Willard . . ." She spread her arms wide to take in the restaurant. She glanced over at Bradley, who stared blankly back at her. Not even his eyes moved. She found that a little disturbing and quickly turned back to Kennard.

"I'm sure your first name is not Sergeant," Elizabeth said pleasantly.

"It's John, ma'am," answered Kennard. "I was Lieutenant Clarke's platoon sergeant in the war."

Even though all three men were out of the army, the formality of rank still permeated their relationship. Elizabeth never liked be called ma'am, but it was obvious she would have to accept it from Jeremy's army buddies. They meant it as a sign of respect. She glanced back and forth between Kennard and Bradley, sensing Kennard's nervousness of being in the Willard and Bradley . . . she couldn't sense what the young man was feeling. He was a total blank.

"These two men will supply expertise and security for you during your meetings about weapon acquisitions," Jeremy said. "I trust them explicitly. They know their guns, are well trained and I'll feel better if they are there with you."

"I don't need security," said Elizabeth. "I'm meeting with Franklin."

"Roosevelt?" asked Jeremy.

Elizabeth nodded. "Yes. There's a program to destroy surplus weaponry and we have a steel mill. I should be able to get all your heavy weapons through the program. And since we'll be paid to get rid of the weapons, it solves some of our hidden financing problems."

"That's excellent," Jeremy exclaimed. "I knew you could figure out an angle."

Elizabeth leaned forward and put her hand on Jeremy's arm. "Quiet. This is Washington. There are ears everywhere."

"Sorry," answered Jeremy. "Do the machine guns fall under this program?"

"Yes."

"What about the small arms? Rifles and pistols?"

"Those are being sold off, along with your requested rations and other supplies. I will have to put in place a number of blind trusts to make sure we can hide where all our purchases are going. It'll be too noticeable if we buy two hundred rifles in a single purchase. I will be dealing with some unsavory characters for this process, so security will be an issue at that time." Elizabeth nodded to Kennard.

"How about ammunition?" Jeremy asked.

"Ammunition for the small arms is readily available. It is handy that all the guns use the same cartridge except for the Colt pistols, so we'll buy it in installments. But for the heavier guns, it won't be so easy."

"Why not?"

Elizabeth frowned. "From what I was able to gather, the army puts it in holes in the ground and blows them up. I don't know how I can divert any to us."

"I can take care of that," Kennard said. He turned to Jeremy. "Remember Sergeant Corelli? He's still in and involved in munitions disposal."

Silently, Elizabeth sighed. That was one of the snags she secretly hoped could end this exercise. It was a little disheartening, as she was finding out how easy it was to get most of what Jeremy had put on his list. But she promised him that she would try her best and only a legitimate roadblock would stop them.

"There is one other item you had on the list that I'm finding troublesome. These automatic rifles you wanted. The Army is not letting those go out to the public."

"That's understandable," Jeremy said. "Sergeant, how many do we need?"

Kennard started counting off on his fingers. "Each fire team needs one, two per squad, four squads to a platoon, four infantry platoons. So, a minimum of thirty-two."

"Do you know anyone here involved in international arms sales?" Jeremy asked.

"What are you thinking?" Elizabeth asked.

Jeremy grinned. "What if the Rumanian government ordered up some BARs and they went out with our steel shipment?"

Elizabeth looked doubtfully at Jeremy. "Does Rumania even have an embassy here?"

"I was thinking more along the lines of Geoffrey Carver at State," Jeremy answered. "He works on government approvals of international deals, doesn't he? That's what he did for Father."

Elizabeth paused for a moment as she thought through what she would have to do to get Carver to approve a fake business deal. "That's a little outside his job description for me."

"Come on, Lizzie. He passes you information all the time. He really likes you."

Elizabeth shook her head, "It is one thing to get a look at a file or get some information. It's quite another to do something illegal."

"But he will do it for you," Jeremy pushed. "You can set it up to look legitimate and he won't look too closely if it comes from you. And I'll check to see if there is a Rumanian embassy in D.C."

Elizabeth was doubtful. "How important are these rifles?"

Kennard answered. "Very important, ma'am." Jeremy nodded in agreement.

Elizabeth was getting uncomfortable. She was used to controlling conversations like this, but she was out of her element here. She knew very little about weapons and Jeremy was pushing hard. She wanted to end the meeting now without committing to anything.

"I have just seen Geoffrey this morning," she started, "getting information on our visitor. I can't go in again so soon with a ploy like that. It needs to be planned carefully."

"Well, we have a month," said Jeremy. "I'm sure you can arrange something before we want to ship out."

Three days in and Elizabeth could tell that Jeremy was committed to the mission. It was not going to be easy to get him to accept any mission-ending roadblock. "I'll work on it," she said. "So, let's order some lunch and Mr. Kennard can tell me some stories about you in France."

Her eyes glanced over at Bradley. He hadn't moved, his face blank, his eyes fixed on her. She wasn't even sure she had seen him blink since she sat down. A very strong feeling of fear germinated in her mind.

This man was definitely from outside of her world.

4

May 6, 1919
Manhattan, NY

Christopher Street was dark and quiet. The hum from the electric street lights, mixed with some jazz music spilling from a dance hall, was the only background noise. The street was deserted, this particular block not having any speakeasies or clubs. A man stepped out of the shadows, his coat collar up, his fedora pulled down. He checked both directions to be sure no one was watching, then quickly crossed.

At the door of a tenement building he knocked three times, paused and then knocked once more. Simple signals were the best. A small peephole opened and an eye checked out his face. It closed abruptly, followed by the sounds of locks being disengaged. The door swung open. A single kerosene lamp on a table was the only light.

"Good evening, Comrade," the man inside said.

"Is the coordinator in tonight?" said the visitor.

"Yes, he's up in his office. You can go right up."

The visitor handed over his coat and hat and ascended to the second floor. In the cramped room, a low light emanated from an electric desk lamp. The coordinator sat behind a nondescript desk, busy writing notes. When he looked up, a slow smile spread across his face.

"Comrade, it has been a while."

"Too long," said the visitor.

"Can I get you anything? Tea, a beer, some whiskey?"

The visitor sat down in a large armchair in the corner of the room. "I see you don't agree with those capitalist prohibitionists?"

The coordinator smiled. "If they could be successful, but they will just make a new profitable business for criminals. How are things in Baltimore?"

The visitor placed a cigarette between his lips, struck a match and slowly brought it up to the cigarette. He inhaled slowly and deeply, held the smoke in his lungs and slowly exhaled. The smoke drifted towards the ceiling in a slow swirl. "No one seems interested in revolution. Even returning soldiers that can't find work don't have time for our message. It's still too soon after the war. America was too . . . 'untouched' by it."

The coordinator shifted uneasily in his chair. "It is a good message. It needs to be pressed hard. There are many people here in New York who . . ."

"Are rich dandies rebelling against their parents," the visitor cut in. "There's too much optimism about the future in America. Along with those fool anarchists mailing bombs, it's hard to operate at all."

The coordinator leaned forward, his fists clenching in anger. "Then why are you here, Comrade?"

The visitor's face remained stern. He leaned forward in his chair. "I have found out about a counter-revolutionary plot from

America aimed at our comrades-in-arms in Russia."

The eyes of the coordinator widened with disbelief. "Go on."

"I have been contacted by an old war associate. Apparently, a Lieutenant Jeremy Clarke is mounting an armed expedition to Russia."

The coordinator scoffed. "A lieutenant. How serious could that threat be?"

The visitor continued. "His father is Jonathan Clarke, of Clarke Steel. I've read that they have done a lot of business in Russia before the revolution. The last news story I read said Clarke Senior is missing in Russia right now. So, for what other place would his son be raising a small army?"

"So the boy wants to rescue his father. I still don't see the importance."

The visitor shook his head. "You don't need a small army to rescue one man. There is something else. Something that must be very important to the situation over in Russia for a rich American to want to get it out."

Leaning back in his chair, the coordinator took in what he had just heard. "I've never seen you chase anything that wasn't significant in all the time I've known you. Can you get on this expedition?"

The visitor smiled. "Already accepted."

"What can you tell me about it?"

"Nothing much right now. I am meeting my contact at Penn Station in two days. Nine a.m. You should have someone follow me. From there, I can see about smuggling out information. I don't think I'll be free to wander away as I please once I'm there."

The coordinator cocked his head to one side. "You've thought this through pretty completely. You were sure I would let you go."

"It would be in the best interest of the revolution that I do," the visitor replied.

"Very well," the coordinator said. "I'll send a message to the Comintern about this expedition. I will also find you some contacts in Europe and Russia." He pulled a photograph out of his desk. "Look for this man at Penn Station at seven a.m. Make a discreet contact. We'll take it from there."

The visitor stood up. "Good." He handed back the photograph. "I'll look for your man."

The coordinator stood and shook the visitor's hand. "Good luck, Comrade."

5

June 3, 1919
Long Beach, NY

It had all come together rather quickly. There they were, 216 men, all lined up in parade order in the field facing the summerhouse's back porch. Jeremy Clarke stood at the top of the stairs surveying his new company. Elizabeth and Corporal Bradley stood to his right, Sergeant Kennard and Appleton to his left.

Elizabeth had discovered that all of the men felt the same way her brother did. With the war over, they had been unceremoniously decommissioned out of the army and sent back into civilian life. But they had changed and America had not changed with them. When Jeremy and Sergeant Kennard went out to seek recruits, they found many men ready and willing to step back into the army life. To build their company, the recruiters kept to soldiers they knew were loyal and professional.

This morning's parade was the last one. Next they would be packing up to leave for the ship Elizabeth had arranged to take them to Rumania. As she stood there, her mind went over some of the company's statistics that had been important to her logistical duties. Four infantry platoons, each of four squads with two four-man fire teams each. The platoons were led by Senior Sergeants Gilbert, Canning, Garcia and MacGregor. A corporal led each squad. One artillery support platoon, also set up in four squads, was headed by Sergeant Corelli. The logistics platoon included twenty-six men commanded by Sergeant Sutton. They were in charge of moving and feeding the company. A small medical team of six was headed by a former captain from Boston named Brendan O'Hanlon. And lastly the command team, consisting of Jeremy, Appleton, Sergeant Kennard and Corporal Bradley.

The next list came to her mind automatically. Two hundred fifty Springfield M1903 bolt action rifles, bought in lots through seven blind fronts. Two hundred fifty M1911 Colt semi-automatic pistols, using a different set of seven blind fronts. Two 37mm Mle1916 trench guns, twelve mortars and thirty M1918 Browning heavy machine guns secretly split away from shipments enroute to the steel mill. And thirty-five Browning Automatic Rifles purchased through a ruse that used Miles Davidson in Paris to request the purchase for the Rumanian Government. The Rumanian diplomatic mission in Washington was not well established. Elizabeth had found it easy to circumvent the few Balkan diplomats when dealing with Carver at State.

Finally, the ammunition. The rifles, machine guns and BARs all took the same cartridges and she had acquired 100,000 rounds. An additional 20,000 rounds of Colt pistol cartridges were also on hand. It seemed an excessive number of bullets considering that the mission called for avoiding combat as much as possible. Appleton had said they could probably talk their way out of many confrontations, but Jeremy wanted to be safe, not sorry. Elizabeth didn't know how many 37mm gun rounds, mortar rounds or grenades Corelli had sneaked off his army base, but Jeremy seemed pleased with the numbers.

There was one other item that Appleton had requested and Elizabeth had not even told Jeremy about. Although trading machine guns for passage and information was the mission's plan, Appleton had told Elizabeth that at times machine guns wouldn't work for trade. The mission needed a supply of a universal currency. She knew what he meant. Gold. Although she didn't like leaving control of the gold to Appleton, someone she didn't fully trust, it was a small price to pay for the mission's success.

Elizabeth had made only brief trips out to the Long Beach house while the men were assembling and training, and those were to see to cash payments for deliveries. For the people she used as the blind fronts, cash on delivery was the nature of the trade. She handled the company's acquisitions from the Manhattan house where she could also keep an eye on the steel company's business. Because of this, she never got to know any of the men, although she seemed to be a star attraction every time she stopped by the camp. Men will be men. She also gained some weapons knowledge by watching some of the more mundane military activities during those brief visits. The most intensive training the men undertook was how to ride a horse. Many of them had never ridden before. Jeremy had her pitch in with that training when she was there.

Elizabeth turned her mind to focus on the parade. All the men wore uniforms without unit insignia. This would make quick identification of the company difficult in Russia.

"The company is ready for inspection, sir," Kennard said. "The men would appreciate it."

"Very well," Clarke replied. "Lizzie, if you'd care to join me. You might find this interesting. Mr. Appleton, you are invited as well."

The inspection went quickly, with Clarke stopping to chat with only a couple of the soldiers. There was an electric feeling that Elizabeth felt while walking through the ranks. Each soldier stood proud. She had the sense they were all excited to start the mission, all willing to follow her brother wherever he led them. She sensed their loyalty to her brother. One evening, about a week earlier, she had gone for a walk through the camp and overheard the men telling stories of their battles. They spoke in tones of great reverence like they were quoting the Bible, their listeners enraptured by the stories. That was when she began to understand her brother's experiences and why he had returned from France a changed man.

"Sergeant Kennard, we leave tomorrow," Jeremy said. "Get the equipment packed up so the men can have the rest of the day off. Equipment goes out first thing in the morning, the men right after that. When you've dismissed the men, come back to the dining room. We'll be going over the plan's details again."

"Very well, sir," Kennard replied.

"The men look great. You did an excellent job."

"Thank you, sir." Kennard snapped a salute. Jeremy returned it. Kennard spun smartly and walked off to dismiss the men.

They gathered in the dining room fifteen minutes later, Kennard showing up last. "We can now get started," Clarke said. "Report on the men, Sergeant."

Kennard went over his report in an efficient and military manner. The men were anxious to get going, all training had been completed satisfactorily, and all equipment except their personal items, tents and bedding would be ready for shipment to the New York docks by dinnertime. Clarke then asked Elizabeth for her report.

Elizabeth stated that the two ships set aside for the expedition would leave New York on time. One ship would have the actual steel shipment for Rumania. The BARs would arrive with the steel shipment, but would be loaded onto the second ship that would carry the company and all its equipment. Through the State Department she had been able to access a source for horses and wagons in Constanta under the ruse that they would be returning with the ships to New York.

Next, Jeremy called on Appleton. His report covered conditions in Russia and the likely major players in the areas they would traverse. The idea was to pass themselves off as supporting whatever group they ran across and avoid firefights and battles on the way. Rail lines were fairly intact since no faction wanted to reduce them to the point where they couldn't use them to move their own troops. A route following rail lines was plotted from Odessa to Ekaterinoslav, east to Tsaritsyn, up the Volga to Samara, and then east again to Ufa and Chelyabinsk. Once there they would meet up with Jonathan Clarke and take the package out on the Trans-Siberian rail line to Vladivostok. Once there, they would arrange for a ship to take the company to San Francisco.

Clarke looked up from the maps. "Charles, you said Denikin's Volunteer Army is the best trained and equipped. If he's started a successful campaign, we may end up running into him as early as Odessa."

Appleton nodded. "He probably won't bother going out of his way to Odessa. Moscow's his target. We will want to avoid him regardless. He'll conscript us for his march to Moscow and it won't be easy for us to slip away. Once past his forces, though, we would be able to cruise all the way to Tsaritsyn without much of a problem. There's not likely to be much military presence left behind him."

"Will you be able to get more up-to-date intelligence once we're in Rumania?" Elizabeth asked.

"I'm sure we can get some news on the situation from local papers once we're there," replied Appleton. "After that, I have some contacts across the Ukraine."

Jeremy tapped the table with his hand. "Then we're set here. Sergeant, are we going to be ready to roll out of here on schedule?"

Kennard nodded. "Yes, sir."

Jeremy turned to Elizabeth. "Lizzie, you'll be all right crossing Europe alone after you leave us?"

"Yes, brother dear," said Elizabeth. "I'll be leaving on one of the ships and it will drop me off in Naples. The train trip from there to Paris should be uneventful."

"Then we'll adjourn until tomorrow morning. Charles, we'll see you at the docks."

"But please stay for dinner before you go," Elizabeth added. She gave him what she hoped looked like a sincere smile. She hadn't had a chance to talk with Appleton much during the past month. Any opportunity to get information from him was worth taking if she was ever to dispel her mistrust of the man who would be guiding her brother across Russia.

"Yes, thank you," Appleton said. "You'll be staying here to-night?"

Elizabeth continued smiling. "I have shady truck drivers to deal with tomorrow morning."

Jeremy continued. "Sergeant, we have quite a spread planned for the men for their last day here. I'll be out shortly to oversee preparations once we've cleaned up in here. But tell the men the sooner they can pack everything up, the sooner we'll feed them. A little incentive never hurt."

Kennard smiled. "Yes, sir, you always know how to treat the men right." He saluted, turned and left.

The meeting broke up immediately, Jeremy rolling up the maps for placement in the safe, Appleton heading to his room to pack, and Kennard and Bradley returning to the troops. Standing by the table, Elizabeth stood watched her brother opening the safe. Something bothered her. Something was out of place. Then she realized that it was the glass paperweight. The round piece of glass with the green and red swirls in it had been a gift from her father, many years ago. It was on top of the safe. It should have been on the table beside the safe, holding down mail. She shrugged and after Jeremy locked the safe, she picked up the paperweight and put back on the desk.

As she walked towards the stairs, she passed Bradley, who was standing stiffly and looking out a window at the camp.

"What are you looking at, Corporal?" asked Elizabeth curiously.

Bradley kept staring out the window. "Something isn't right," was all he said.

* * *

The feast was extravagant. Many of the men proclaimed they had never had such a meal in their lives. Elizabeth had arranged the catering. Long tables had been set up and each man brought his army mess kit, with its thin metal fork and spoon, tin plate and mug. Pork, beef, vegetables, fruit and lots of wine and whiskey. After dinner, music came from an accordion and a fiddle that two men played by the light of a bonfire. And there was Jeremy, right in the middle, singing soldier songs along with the lowliest private.

Elizabeth smiled. Her little brother had grown up and this was his world now.

"Quite a group, aren't they?" Appleton said from behind her.

Elizabeth turned, holding the smile on her face. "They do seem to know how to enjoy themselves."

"Camaraderie is a very strong force in the military. Without it, units don't function and they get destroyed. Your brother is very good at establishing the bonds between soldier and officer, and between soldier and soldier. Not only do they trust him completely, they also trust each other. They will do well."

"For a diplomat, you seem to know a lot about soldiering, Mr. Appleton," Elizabeth replied.

Appleton looked up at the stars. "I've never been much of a diplomat."

Elizabeth looked up at him. That was about as good an opening as she was likely to get.

"You're not really a diplomat then, are you." It wasn't a question.

Appleton met her gaze, no indication of anything on his face. "I work for the State Department."

"Which section?" she asked.

"International Relations."

"Geoffrey Carver had never heard of you until about a month ago and he is in International Relations."

Appleton turned away slowly. "He's in International Business Relations. It's a different section."

Elizabeth frowned. Appleton could deflect that line of questioning all night. She'd have to try another tack. "Who is Anton Kolochov?" she asked innocently.

She was scared by the speed at which Appleton's head spun to face her. She saw a tense anger in his face and his eyes looked deadly. She had hit a nerve.

"How do you know that name?" he asked coldly.

Elizabeth regained her composure. "It's in your file. A very thin file, I might add."

Appleton's face softened and he slowly turned away from her again. "You are a very resourceful young lady."

"You are taking my brother into a war zone. I know he can handle himself fine there, but I need to trust you and I don't."

"Your father trusts me."

"According to you."

Appleton nodded and turned to Elizabeth. "Have you thought of any other reason I would have come here to ask your brother to lead a small army into Russia?"

That stumped her. She had been trying since this whole thing started to sort out any hidden agenda Appleton might have that would put her brother in danger. She couldn't identify one.

"I didn't think so," Appleton said when she didn't reply. "You are a very smart woman. I'm sure you would have figured out something wrong if this was more than I said it was."

And that was that. No more hoping for a snag. The company was going to Russia. Her attention turned back to the noise the men were making. Her voice took on a sad tone. "I just hope they can all make it back, even though I know that some of them won't."

"It's the life they've chosen, Miss Clarke. They know the risks and are trained to handle them."

Jeremy had been singing along, a bit off key, to roars of laughter from the men. As he ended a verse, he spotted Elizabeth and Appleton standing separate from the group. He shouted to all who could hear him, "Wait! Wait! My sister is an excellent singer. Come on, Lizzie, give us a song."

His words were slurred and Elizabeth almost couldn't understand him, but with every man now looking at her and shouting encouragement, she knew full well what he had said. She turned to Appleton, who said, "Sorry, I can't help you there. Good luck and I'll see you tomorrow." He backed into the shadows towards the house, his head dipped in a goodbye.

Elizabeth turned back to the men, who were still shouting encouragement. *I'm going to have to find a way to get back at Jeremy for this*, she thought. Smiling, she held up her hands to quiet the crowd, then almost floated towards them. "Private, you on the accordion, do you know 'Till We Meet Again'?" The private nodded and started a short intro to the song. Then, with no sound from the wind or the sea, Elizabeth began singing with an angelic tone, in sync with the crackling of the fire. The men's rumblings came to a halt as her voice and the soft accordion took over. She felt her voice touch the sky, lit up as it was with a million stars and a crescent moon.

> *Smile the while you kiss me sad adieu,*
> *When the clouds roll by I'll come to you,*
> *Then the skies will seem more blue, . . .*

When she was finished, she saw tears in every man's eyes.

* * *

It was two a.m. and a soldier walked his patrol beat on the estate's edge. In the trees, he noticed a cigarette's faint glow. *Good. My contact is here.* He walked up to a large oak and dropped an envelope. It was the latest report indicating when the company would be leaving and an update of the route they would take through Russia.

The soldier continued to the next tree, where he found another envelope. He opened it immediately to read the contents by his flashlight. It contained more contact names, code phrases and a note from the coordinator that granted him authorization from the Comintern to sabotage the expedition if he could. The envelope also contained a small lapel pin, consisting of a simple red circle. He was to wear it on his left breast pocket as identification for agents in Europe and Russia. The soldier smiled. *Better to catch young Jeremy Clarke in Europe where his connections can't help him.* He had already formulated a plan to stop the expedition cold, leaving Clarke in a jail and the company leaderless. They would have no choice but to head back to the ship and sail home.

He had no desire to harm any of the soldiers. He was one of them. Stopping Clarke didn't mean any of the men had to suffer. He folded the notes back into the envelope and put it in his pocket. Looking back toward the trees, he noticed, the cigarette had vanished. Shouldering his rifle, he continued his patrol as normal.

6

June 4, 1919
Pier 38, New York City

Elizabeth stepped out of the shipping office, all the paperwork now completed for the two ships bound for Rumania. The president of the XMS shipping company had come up through the ranks of smugglers and was quite content to turn a blind eye to the second ship for a price. Besides, with the war over, business was pretty slow. Any business was good business.

Something Elizabeth had seen from the office window disturbed her. Someone was watching the ships. Quickly moving down the side of the warehouse, she made it to the point where the men, in discreet pairs, were crossing the pier to the ship. She found two men there ready to go and quickly pulled them back.

"We're moving too fast. Tell Sergeant Kennard to increase the times between pairs of men." Before they could reply, she hurried farther down the pier to deal with the problem she spotted from the window.

A man leaned up against a crate, making notes. He was watching the comings and goings around the two ships. Medium height, thin as a rail and wearing an old suit and a derby, he was trying to look invisible. He had been watching for a while now. Long enough to notice a pattern, Elizabeth concluded: two men going up the gangplank, then two minutes later, two more men.

The man shifted his shoulders in his jacket and adjusted his derby, as it tended to slide down when he wrote his notes. Elizabeth watched him from a doorway. She noticed a loose brick on the ground. She made her decision. They needed to leave New York without any chance of being discovered until they had crossed the Rumanian border with Russia. This man was a threat and she would have to take care of him.

She placed the brick in her bag and quietly approached the man. "Excuse me, sir," she said. "I'm looking for my little brother. I think he's running away to join a ship and I have to find him. Mother will be so angry if I don't come home with him. Can you help me?"

The man turned, visibly surprised to find a beautiful young woman standing before him, a worried look on her face. A damsel in distress, which was what Elizabeth was trying to portray. He stumbled over his opening words.

"Uh, sure, yes, of course, I can help you," he stammered. "Uh, what does he look like?"

Elizabeth smiled sweetly. "He's about fourteen years old, about so high, and wearing gray long pants, a brown vest and a tweed cap. And his shirt is checkered." She was describing the last man she had seen getting on the troop ship.

"Actually, I think I did see him," replied the man. "I think I saw him getting on that ship right there."

"Really," said Elizabeth, great relief in her voice. "Which one?"

The man turned to face down the pier, pointing, "That ship right . . ."

Elizabeth quickly swung her bag as hard as she could at the man's head. She made contact right around his temple and he crumpled at Elizabeth's feet. The sight scared her. She was half relieved that she had hit him hard enough not to have to hit him again and half worried that she had killed him. She stood over him for a few seconds, staring, until she realized he was still breathing. Reaching into her bag, she pulled out the brick and let it drop to the ground.

The realization of what she had done now engulfed her. *What was I thinking?* She should have left this to one of the soldiers. There were still plenty of them around the pier. It was then she realized she was as married to the mission as everyone else. No more misgivings. They were going and nothing could get in the way.

Her mind started working with the problem of what to do next. First, how to move him. But then when he wakes up, he'd tell the authorities what had happened. Maybe she should kill him, but that thought scared her to no end. Besides, a dead body of some man found on the pier would raise questions, threatening the very existence of the mission.

"Ma'am?" came a voice behind her.

Elizabeth almost jumped out of her skin, spinning around in a fright to come face to face with Corporal Bradley's ever-blank face. "Corporal, you gave me a start. You should learn not to sneak up on people like that."

"That's my job," he replied matter-of-factly, like it should be obvious.

Elizabeth stared at him. A small pang of fear ran through her, followed by relief that Bradley was on her side. "Of course it is. I'm sorry."

Bradley leaned over to look at the man. Elizabeth now had help, but her mind was turning quickly trying to find a solution. The man couldn't be left here, but she'd be damned if they were just going to kill him outright. The solution came to her.

"Corporal, do you think you could get him on the ship without anyone noticing?"

Bradley's face didn't change, giving no outward indication that he was even considering her question. But he answered all the same. "Yes."

"Good," Elizabeth replied. "Get him on board and tie him up someplace out of the way. I'll want to talk to him once we sail."

"Yes, ma'am," said Bradley, holding out his Colt pistol.

Elizabeth stared at it. She wasn't afraid of guns. She had done quite a bit of shooting small revolvers with her brother during his time home from West Point and knew how to handle them, but the big, ugly Colt automatic was another matter. She looked up at Bradley for an explanation.

"In case he wakes up," Bradley said.

Elizabeth took the gun. Bradley promptly pulled the limp body into the alley behind a crate, then took off down the alley at a run. Self-consciously, Elizabeth placed the gun behind her handbag out of view and stood there, nervously trying to look casual. Her greatest fear was that the man would wake up.

It was only a few minutes, but for Elizabeth, it seemed like an eternity. With great relief, she saw Bradley come running back up the alley with another soldier. Without a word, each took an arm. Making it look like they were drunk, the three of them staggered out onto the pier towards the ship. Elizabeth watched from the alley, scanning back and forth to see if anyone was watching. The dockworkers sneered at the threesome, but nothing else.

She slipped Bradley's Colt into her handbag and turned back down the alley. Her turn to board the ship was not until five, and she still had a few errands to finish first.

* * *

"Miss Clarke," the private said. "Your guy is awake."

"Thank you, private. Is Corporal Bradley with him?"

"Yes, ma'am."

Elizabeth stepped through the cabin door into the hallway. "You can return to your duties."

"Thank you, ma'am."

She made her way towards the hold, wondering how she would handle this situation. She had been thinking about it since the ship had left New York, but really didn't know exactly what to do. She decided she would pick an option once she had talked to the man. She opened the engine room door.

She had changed her clothes. Gone was the long skirt, linen vest and spring hat. Her hair was pulled into a tail down her back. She wore a linen shirt, a short leather coat and brown jodhpurs with riding boots. "Mr. Paul Reinhardt," she said firmly. "I'm sorry about the circumstances, but it couldn't be helped."

Bradley had been through his pockets and found his federal Customs identification. He had taken the card to Elizabeth. Customs. Elizabeth wondered why Customs would be watching an outgoing ship. It would be something she'd have to ask Reinhardt.

"You know I'm with the government and will be missed," Reinhardt said.

Elizabeth smiled knowingly. "Not necessarily. You just have to disappear for a short while. Then you can return to your life back in New York after a nice little tour of Europe which, I can assure you, can be most enjoyable."

"You mean to tell me I'm being forced . . . on vacation?"

"Yes," Elizabeth answered pleasantly. "You could say that. And don't worry about your job. I have connections to make sure it's still there for you when you get back."

"Do I get an itinerary?" he said sarcastically.

Reinhardt's tone told Elizabeth that he was not some desk-bound bureaucrat. This was a field man. He would not intimidate easily. "No, you'll go where I want to go. I haven't decided that yet," she said with an air of innocence.

Reinhardt shook his head. "OK, how about a name? You know who I am, but I don't know you."

"My name is Elizabeth."

"And how about Mr. Friendly here?" asked Reinhardt, nodding his head towards the man sitting across from him.

"That is Corporal Bradley. You're going to see a lot of him during the first leg of our journey because it's his job to keep you out of trouble. I suggest you don't give him any."

Reinhardt looked across at Bradley. "Is he always like that?"

Elizabeth looked over at Bradley. "Yes, but don't let that fool you. He's been in combat and from what I've heard, you don't want to cross him." She hadn't actually heard that, but it sounded like a good thing to say to a man who could be trouble. "Now, I have a few questions if you don't mind. Why were you watching our ship?"

Reinhardt turned his head away from her. "I don't have to tell you anything."

"How about I tell you something first?" said Elizabeth.

Reinhardt turned slowly back to her. "I'm listening."

Elizabeth smiled. Her business negotiating skills came in handy even in this kind of situation. "You have stumbled upon a secret government mission. Security is very high and we couldn't have other agencies asking questions about it for the next two weeks."

Reinhardt looked doubtful. "Secret mission?"

Elizabeth was ready for that. She pulled out Appleton's State Department credentials and showed them to Reinhardt. "I'm sorry we didn't have time to explain the security requirements to you. We just couldn't leave you out there raising questions."

"So you hit me in the head."

Elizabeth pointed to Bradley. "The alternative would have been him and you'd be dead." She saw a flash of fear in Reinhardt's eyes. It was the effect she wanted. "Now, why were you watching our ship?"

Reinhardt seemed to be of two minds, but Elizabeth had continued to hold out Appleton's credentials for effect. Finally it worked and the Customs man spoke. "I was just on my way to Pier 42 when I noticed all the men getting on this ship. I stopped to take some notes to forward to the police. I thought maybe some criminals were trying to get away or something."

Elizabeth nodded, taking back Appleton's credentials and putting them in her coat pocket. "So you never had the chance to forward your notes?"

"No."

Elizabeth smiled. "Then there has been no security breach. Thank you, Mr. Reinhardt. I'm sure you are hungry. The corporal will untie you and escort you to your quarters. I'm sorry, it won't be a private room. You'll be sharing it with the corporal for obvious reasons. Our doctor will meet you there to check your head.

We must make sure I didn't do too much damage. Then, when you have freshened up, you can join me and the senior staff for dinner in an hour. We'll tell you more about the mission then, because it'll be more than two weeks before you can tell anyone anything."

Elizabeth turned to open the door. Reinhardt asked, "Can I contact at least one person?"

"Do you not understand the concept of security?" Elizabeth said firmly.

"I'm getting married in a month and a half. I can't be missing for a couple of weeks."

Elizabeth frowned. "I'm sorry. We can discuss that later." She closed the cabin door behind her.

7

June 5, 1919
Moscow

Anton Kolochov sat late at his desk just about every night when he was in Moscow. He spent half of his time with Red troops gathering intelligence, but enjoyed coming back to the peace of his office every now and then. He scanned papers on his desk with a speed and thoroughness that amazed his colleagues. His duties as deputy director of the RU, the revolutionary government's military intelligence arm, involved the very important aspect of identifying the military enemies of the state. And there were many.

His aide poked his head into the office. "Comrade, I've been given some information from the Comintern you might find interesting."

Kolochov looked up, perturbed by the distraction. "And what information would the Comintern have that could be deemed important?"

The aide stepped into the office and placed a file on the desk.

"You asked us to keep an eye out for any information that involved the Americans Jonathan Clarke and Charles Appleton. A contact in America sent this over. It took a while to make it to me, but I think you'll find it very interesting."

Kolochov's attention riveted onto the file. "Clarke and Appleton. I knew they'd surface sooner or later." He grabbed the file and opened it quickly, beginning to read. His aide slowly began to back out of the office.

"Stay a moment," Kolochov said curtly without looking up.

The man froze. Kolochov's reputation was brutal. Years in the Okhrana, the Tsar's secret police, chasing revolutionaries. Then changing sides at the right moment to become a high-level functionary in the Bolshevik regime. The man was a survivor.

He went through the file at his usual rapid speed. He read about the company, about Appleton with Clarke's son, about the agent in the group and that agent's contact criteria. And, most important, their destination. Chelyabinsk. *So that's where Clarke has been hiding. Too bad it is currently out of Bolshevik control.*

Kolochov looked up. "Is this all of it?" His aide nodded. "You make it known at the Comintern that *anything* else that comes through to them concerning this gets to my desk within the hour. Now, who is our man down in the southwest of Ukraine?"

"Tuchenko is operating out of Kiev."

Kolochov mused for a moment. "Close enough. Go find me a secretary. I'll have new orders for him." The man didn't move. Kolochov flung his hand out. "Go!"

The man jumped. "Yes, Comrade," he said, bolting from the office. Kolochov smiled. Fear was a great motivator. He got up and went to a map of Russia on the wall behind his office door.

He found Chelyabinsk. A long way to go from Rumania. He wondered why they preferred that route to getting past the American forces in Vladivostok. The mission must not be sanctioned by the US Government. He could send a few agents into Chelyabinsk to see what they might find. But no, he didn't want to show his hand to Clarke. Kolochov knew from experience that Clarke could sniff out a spy unit looking for him within a day or two. He would have to see if the Revolutionary Military Council had a timetable for retaking Chelyabinsk. He chuckled at the idea. The new Red Army didn't tend to use timetables. When they would reach Chelyabinsk was anyone's guess. So, what to do with this little American expedition?

Kolochov sat back down at his desk. Of course, the other question. What was Jonathan Clarke doing in Chelyabinsk that needed a two hundred-man escort? He might not learn the answer if young Clarke's expedition didn't make it.

He smiled. *Now that is a novel idea . . .*

* * *

During the dinner the night before, Reinhardt had been told a story about a secret US Government mission to Rumania. That story included very little detailed information. All his questions were answered with, "I don't know," mentions of security concerns and vague assertions that even the senior staff didn't know what the mission was about. They would all get more information, everyone assured their involuntary guest, once they reached Rumania.

With dinner out of the way, Bradley became Reinhardt's shadow as they returned to their cabin. Early the next morning, Elizabeth headed for the ship's bow to watch the sun come up.

When she was younger, she had always loved standing on the

bow of her family's sailboat with the wind passing through her hair. Now, before dawn, the sky was clear with an abundance of stars. She had never seen so many stars before, but their light was slowly fading as the sun began its climb over the horizon. The air was crisp, so she wrapped her shawl tighter around her shoulders. The hum of the ship was drowned out by the wind passing her ears, her long hair flowing behind her. She felt a real peace standing there, with nothing between her and the power of the sea and the night sky. Her fears about the coming month faded away.

Elizabeth sensed him before he arrived at her side. Her brother leaned up against the railing, looking out like Elizabeth was. He was there for a couple of minutes before he spoke.

"Remind you of the sailboat?"

Elizabeth laughed. "Yes, it does. How did you know?"

"I've only seen you this content when you were on that sailboat," he said. "Any other time, you had your head in a book or a financial report, or you were scolding me for bothering you."

"You were a little pest when you were younger."

Jeremy shifted to look at his sister. "I was trying to make you have some fun. You were always so serious about everything. And you still are. Apart from the sailboat, I've never seen you have any fun."

"I have fun," Elizabeth insisted. "I enjoy what I do."

"Lizzie," Jeremy said, "you're missing out on so much of life. Parties, adventure. Love. You're already twenty-six. When was the last time you had a gentleman caller?"

Elizabeth frowned at him. "Three months ago. You were there."

"That's a long time."

"With the mission, there hasn't been any time to think about any gentleman caller."

Jeremy sighed. "OK, how about one you didn't intimidate the hell out of or scare off after the first encounter so he never called back? I've only seen you flirt with men when they have information you want."

Elizabeth stopped herself when she realized he was right. She had treated the men who tried to court her like trash unless she could profit from what they knew. Irritated, she said, "So what's your point?"

Jeremy put his arm around her shoulders. "I don't want you to end up alone with nothing but a financial report and a boardroom that's scared of you."

"Yes, Father," Elizabeth replied sarcastically.

"Lizzie, I know I'm only your little brother, but I have to think of the family. If I don't come back, you could be all that's left."

Elizabeth spun under his arm, an angry look in her eyes. "You are coming back. I can see you need the army to be happy, but that doesn't mean you have to get yourself killed."

Jeremy shrugged. "In the army, there is a belief that there's a bullet out there waiting for you with your name on it. You can't avoid it, so there's no need to be afraid of it. You're careful, but you can control the fear, because when your time is up, it's up. My time might be up in Russia. No one knows where that bullet is hiding."

"That's pretty fatalistic."

"It helps with morale under combat conditions. If you can believe that maybe it isn't your time, you have a better feeling going over the top into machine guns."

"Who taught you that?"

"A certain very knowledgeable captain who helped me

through a lot of tough times."

Elizabeth turned back into the wind, gazing out into the ocean's blackness. "I'd like to meet that captain someday," she said, "and give him a piece of my mind."

They stood together as the eastern sky turned bright, the sun finally breaking the horizon. "I don't want you to go," Elizabeth said.

"I have to," Jeremy answered. He reached into his breast pocket and took out the locket she had given him in 1917. "I still have this. It will protect me."

Elizabeth looked down at the locket in his hand. "How is that supposed to protect you?" she asked skeptically.

"I don't know, but it did in much worse conditions than we're liable to find in Russia."

"I suppose that's part of how you control your fear?" asked Elizabeth.

"Yes," Jeremy replied. "Sergeant Gilbert has a silk neckerchief from his mother. Sergeant Corelli has a German bayonet that nearly impaled him. Sergeant Kennard carries a metal coin from a French officer for luck. And have you seen that big knife Appleton carries?"

Elizabeth giggled. "Yeah, that does seem to be a bit excessive. He said it was a bowie knife."

"That's not as excessive as that captain I mentioned. He has a Japanese sword."

"You've mentioned him in your letters," said Elizabeth. "Do you know what happened to him?"

Jeremy shrugged. "I suppose he went home to Canada. He was with me at the Armistice."

They stood there on the bow for a few moments, letting the

wind pass them by. Eventually, Elizabeth said, "I still don't want you to go."

They let a few more moments pass quietly, the mood somber. Then, "Reinhardt seems nice," said Jeremy, breaking the mood.

Elizabeth slowly turned her head to face him. "And engaged."

Jeremy laughed. "Minor obstacle. The only reason I haven't shot him and thrown him overboard is because I think he would make you a good husband."

"Jeremy!" Elizabeth scolded him.

"I could probably recruit him for you real easy like."

Elizabeth turned back to the ocean, sighing in resignation. "What am I going to do with you?"

"Nothing, as usual."

And they continued to stare out at the steadily rising sun and its blinding reflection, one excited, the other anxious about the coming adventure.

8

June 9, 1919
Gibraltar

Reinhardt ought to be secure in his shared cabin, Elizabeth figured. He had been sufficiently intimidated by his abduction, and by Bradley's eerie presence, that he ought to behave during their stop in port. In spite of herself, though, she found her thoughts drifting back to Jeremy's teasing remark about the Customs man as a potential husband. Reinhardt was attractive enough, after all. Disgusted with herself, she shook off those thoughts. She had too much serious work to do.

They had arrived in Gibraltar in the late afternoon. The ship was docked behind her sister ship, with the strong smell of fuel oil permeating the air. The men were kept out of sight in the hold so the authorities wouldn't ask questions. After four days of tossing seas, the men seemed quite content to snooze below deck in the harbor's calm waters. Jeremy, Kennard, Bradley and sergeants Gilbert and Canning were dressed as crew members to keep an eye on the docks. Appleton and Elizabeth went onshore to get up-to-date intelligence from newspapers. Elizabeth was also expecting messages by cable from Clarke Steel if anything needed her attention. There was only one message, clearing a budget item to her satisfaction.

As the sun dropped over the horizon, Elizabeth and Appleton returned to the ship. It was not lit up like the other ships in the harbor, keeping just the bridge lights on, a light at the gangplank and two deck lights. It occurred to her that keeping the ship dark actually made it stand out. She would have to mention that to Jeremy. Bradley stood guard at the top of the gangplank.

"Good evening, Corporal," she said. "Is Mr. Reinhardt in his cabin?"

"Yes, ma'am."

"Thank you. You have a good evening."

"Thank you, ma'am."

Appleton smiled as they stepped onto the deck. "Interesting fellow, that Bradley."

"I'll say," Elizabeth said. "Never says much and shows up out of nowhere just when you need him."

"That's kind of handy, isn't it?" Appleton asked. "I'm going to head up to the bridge. I'll see you later for tea?"

"Yes, I just want to go by and see Mr. Reinhardt."

They split company and Elizabeth crossed to the dark side of the ship, towards the gangway to Reinhardt's cabin. She knocked softly. No sound came from the room, so she knocked harder. Still no answer. She tried the door, which was unlocked. She opened it. The room was dark. She reached in to the wall switch and turned on the light.

Reinhardt wasn't there.

He had been told to stay in his room while in port, and he had agreed. Elizabeth's pulse quickened as she spun around and ran up on deck.

* * *

Rounding a corner, Elizabeth came upon Reinhardt, clutching the stern railing and looking back over his shoulder. "I'm . . . sorry," he stuttered. "I had to try." He was speaking to Bradley, who stood half a dozen paces away, eyeing him down the barrel of his Colt pistol, hammer drawn back.

"Corporal!" Running to Bradley, she placed her hands on the gun. "Corporal, I won't have him shot. Give me the gun."

Bradley instantly uncocked the gun and handed it to Elizabeth. This was so quick that Elizabeth almost dropped it. Bradley stood there, silent.

"You can go back to your duties," Elizabeth said softly. Bradley turned his head to face her, looked back at Reinhardt, then turned and headed away.

Elizabeth sighed with relief. "Mr. Reinhardt, that was very foolish. The corporal could very well have shot you if I hadn't turned up."

Reinhardt began to relax. "Well, if he was going to, he was sure taking his time about it."

Elizabeth looked perplexed. "Really? I'll have to ask him about that. But that does not excuse your attempt to escape. I thought we had an agreement."

Reinhardt was looking at the gun hanging in her right hand, down at her side and pointed at the deck. It appeared to Elizabeth like he was trying to make a decision. Then he did, quickly turning back towards the railing and climbing up on it.

"Paul!" Elizabeth yelled, raising the gun and assuming a professional shooter's stance. The Colt was heavy in her hand, but she wasn't going to miss at this range. "Get down from there right

now. I'm warning you, I will shoot you." In her mind, she wasn't
sure if she could or not.

Reinhardt paused for a moment. Without turning around, he
said, "I don't think you can. Goodbye, Miss Clarke." He swung
his left leg over the rail.

Elizabeth pulled the trigger on instinct, her stance taking the
recoil evenly. Still, the gunshot surprised her. The black hole that
appeared in the center of Reinhardt's back mesmerized her and,
as if in slow motion, Reinhardt's body launched itself off the railing and disappeared from sight. The last thing she noticed was the
small wisp of smoke rising from the Colt pistol in her hands. She
focused on that as she tried to understand what had just happened.
When it became apparent to her what she had just done, everything began to get blurry. She collapsed to the deck.

* * *

Elizabeth woke up looking at the ceiling of her cabin. She
could see Jeremy sitting on her bed with Appleton by the door.
Dr. O'Hanlon was packing up his doctor's bag. The haziness began to clear. "What happened?" she asked.

"You fainted," Jeremy replied.

"It doesn't look like you banged your head when you hit the
deck, little lady," O'Hanlon added. "You'll be fine with a little
rest."

Elizabeth quickly shot up onto her elbows. "Paul?"

Jeremy paused, as if afraid of what telling her might do.
"Dead," he said. "Don't worry, Kennard and Bradley took care of
things. The Brits have no idea what happened and are satisfied
with what we told them."

Tears began to well up in her eyes. "I killed him?" she asked
weakly.

The concern in Jeremy's face drew deeper, as he clenched his teeth and deep creases formed on his forehead. He nodded silently. Elizabeth sank back onto the bed and rolled over to face the wall. "I killed him," she said.

* * *

Jeremy looked to Appleton and O'Hanlon, not knowing what to do. Appleton opened the door and signaled Jeremy to follow him out. In the passageway, Appleton closed the door and faced Jeremy. "She's going to need some time by herself to work this through. A little traumatic, but she will eventually understand that Reinhardt had given her no choice."

"I hope you're right," Jeremy replied. "It's not going to be easy for her."

"No, it won't," Appleton said. "But in the end, she'll be stronger for it."

"She's been pretty strong all her life." Jeremy stepped past Appleton and headed off in the direction of the bridge. When he reached the deck, he looked up at the stars. He wished they could sail away from here right now. He began to think of his father, alone somewhere in Chelyabinsk, waiting for his rescue. And how this rescue had already significantly changed his daughter.

"I'm sorry, Dad," he said softly.

9

June 11, 1919
Mediterranean Sea

It was two days before Elizabeth came out of her cabin. She had been eating the food Bradley loyally brought to her three times each day. On the third morning, she appeared in the captain's mess for breakfast. Jeremy looked up as she entered. As the door closed behind her, he noticed Bradley standing in the passageway.

"Hi, Lizzie. Sit down. I'll get you some coffee."

Elizabeth sat while Jeremy got the coffee. Kennard brought her eggs and bacon. She thanked them both and then proceeded to eat without saying anything else. Jeremy, Kennard and Appleton all sat and ate in silence as well.

When they were finished, Elizabeth finally spoke in a deadpan voice. "I have reconciled with myself the events that took place in Gibraltar. I would appreciate if no one talked to me about it, as I have put it behind me."

Across the table the three men just nodded. None gave any sign of wanting to say anything.

Elizabeth slowly got up from the table. "I'm sure you three

have important work to do so I will leave you to it." She looked directly at Jeremy. "Did you assign Corporal Bradley to watch over me?"

"No, I didn't," Jeremy stated. "He kind of assigned himself."

Elizabeth's shoulders sagged. "I was afraid of that," she said. "Could you please give him some other orders? I don't like him being my shadow."

Jeremy thought about that for a minute. Elizabeth's state of mind seemed very fragile. He preferred having Bradley close to her while she worked through her guilt at killing Reinhardt. Elizabeth could try to lose Bradley on the ship somewhere. *Good luck doing that*, he thought. Either way, he would have to make Bradley be more discreet. Considering the man's talents, that should not be a problem.

"Send him in," Jeremy said. "I'll speak to him."

"Thank you. I'll see you at lunch." Elizabeth turned and left the room.

There was a moment of silence after she left before Jeremy spoke. "That was a little unnerving. I really wish now she could have trusted me with the money to buy the horses and not come along."

"Each person handles different things in different ways," Appleton observed. "I would say the fact that she came out of her cabin is a very good sign."

The door opened and Bradley entered. He snapped a salute and stood straight as an arrow.

"At ease, Corporal," Jeremy said. Even at ease, Bradley stood rigid. "You have taken an interest in my sister. Perhaps you can tell me why."

Bradley didn't answer right away, which spoke volumes to Jeremy. *Am I finally going to see into the inner workings of the mind of Corporal Bradley,* he thought?

"She may hurt herself, sir," Bradley finally answered.

Jeremy agreed with that, but continued sternly. "Be that as it may, she is being disturbed by you always being there. Can I ask you to keep an eye on her more discreetly? I know you can do that."

"Yes, sir," Bradley said.

The ship's captain entered the mess. "Would you three join me on the bridge? I have something I need to show you."

* * *

According to the reports coming in from Italy and other ships, the storm was severe. The captain had suggested they head for a port and wait it out, but it was moving too quickly and the ship would be caught out anyway, so they decided to sail on.

As the storm got closer, Elizabeth stood at the bow, watching the clouds slowly roll in from the port side. The ship was already pitching up and down as the waves got larger. On the horizon, she could tell, rain was falling in sheets. That horizon looked closer every minute, marching towards her like some malevolent crusader destined to strike her down for her crimes. And she would face it and accept her fate.

The wind suddenly shifted. Even at the speed the ship was going, she could tell the wind had changed, blowing in at high speed from the dense clouds off the port bow. Almost on cue, the ship began to turn, ever so slowly aiming her straight into the storm. *I'm coming,* Elizabeth thought. *I'm not afraid. Do your worst.*

It was a strange sensation, facing down nature's wrath with no fear. She had never felt this strong before. It was exhilarating. The bow's pitching turned more violent and rain began to beat into her face. Firmly gripping the railing, she scowled at the storm, then starting yelling insults. The wind seemed to anger as its force increased. The bow was pitching even more now and each time it came down, Elizabeth could feel her feet begin to lift off the deck. A large wash of spray came over the bow, soaking her and almost loosening her hands from the rail, but she screamed into the wind. "Is that the best you can do?! Come on, I'm ready for you!!"

An even greater force enveloped her, but where it came from was totally unexpected. It was like someone was grabbing her from behind and yanking her hands from the railing. But she didn't fall. Spinning around, she came face to face with the blank stare of Corporal Bradley. He was attached to a long rope rippling across the deck. She yelled at Bradley, "What do you want?!"

Without a word, Bradley threw Elizabeth over his shoulder. With the balance of a mountain goat, despite her screaming and flailing, he slowly worked his way back across the deck. His grip was strong and all Elizabeth could do was move her legs and pound Bradley's back with her fists. It did no good. Bradley ignored her blows, gingerly pulling on the rope with his free hand, stepping and moving with the ship's motion until he slipped into a gangway and off the deck.

When they reached Elizabeth's cabin, she was exhausted and lay limp over his shoulder. Dripping water, Bradley laid her on her bed and then stood upright, still swaying with the ship's movements, looking down at her. Elizabeth stared back, her fury spent. "Why did you come get me?" she asked.

Bradley's blank stare never changed. "It's my job, ma'am." They looked at each other silently for a moment, then Bradley quickly turned and left the cabin. Elizabeth lay still for a moment, wondering if Bradley had actually wanted to say more but couldn't. Although his blank expression was the same as always, she thought she had seen a little more sadness in it today.

* * *

Up on the bridge, Jeremy and Appleton watched the spectacle on the deck below them. Jeremy was ready to run out himself when Bradley came into view, doggedly making his way to the bow. Once Bradley had made it back to safety with Elizabeth over his shoulder, Jeremy moved for the door, but Appleton grabbed his shoulder. "Give yourself a little time before you go barging into her cabin."

Jeremy's anger was evident. "She's trying to kill herself. I'm not leaving her alone for a second."

Appleton shook his head. "If she really wanted to kill herself, she would have jumped. I believe she was looking for penance."

"Pretty dangerous place to ask for forgiveness, don't you think?"

A small smile arose on Appleton's face. "That's the point. Where were you when you were looking for penance for all the terrible things you did in the war?"

Jeremy thought of the dangerous horse riding he had been doing, which Elizabeth scolded him for. Appleton was right. "OK, I'll give it half an hour, but I understand what she's thinking and can handle it from here."

"No, you don't," said Appleton. "Who was the first man you killed?"

Jeremy looked puzzled. "I don't know. Some German soldier."

"Did you know him personally?"

"No, of course not."

"And what was he trying to do at the time?"

"Kill me."

Appleton raised his eyebrows as recognition crossed Jeremy's face. "So it's nowhere near the same," Jeremy continued. "By the time I got to actually think about it, I'd killed dozens of men over several days of battle."

"And it was your job to kill," Appleton added. "You were trained for it."

Jeremy came to the full realization that Elizabeth had been totally unprepared for the act of killing Reinhardt. For Jeremy, killing wasn't what weighed on him from the war. It was memories of the destruction and the fear that haunted him. For Elizabeth, it was personal. It bore down into her very soul and asked the question, "Are you worthy of life yourself?"

Jeremy turned back to the bridge's forward windows. He hung onto the railing as the ship pitched up and down. As he looked at the storm's fury, a tear came to his eye. The tightness in his chest became tighter as he realized that he was totally unable to help his sister through her crisis. She had to deal with it alone.

10

June 20, 1919
Constanta, Rumania

They had weathered the storm well. Four days later, they reached Istanbul and put in for more fuel. It was another four days before they reached the port of Constanta as they were stuck in Istanbul for two days waiting in the queue to get fuel and supplies. During this time, Elizabeth slowly began to feel like herself again. She had insisted that Bradley be assigned to her and spent the time trying to get to know him, which wasn't easy. His first name was Tom and she began calling him that. She felt that behind that blank stare she could see that Bradley had taken some blame for what had occurred with Reinhardt and how it had affected her, so she talked to him about it. Though good for her, it was generally a one-way conversation since Bradley barely said anything. However, just having him there was comforting.

No one else had spoken of the Reinhardt incident. Elizabeth had resumed her wandering about the ship, now with Bradley in tow. As the ships took on fuel oil in Istanbul, she spent the time curiously watching the refueling process.

No one left the ship. The Turkish Government was in turmoil dealing with a newly started revolution and the Allies breaking up their empire. Greek soldiers were reported to have landed in Smyrna a few weeks before. Best to stay on board.

The ships set sail the next morning, moving slowly through the busy shipping lanes of the Bosphorus and out into the Black Sea. At dawn the next day, the 20th of June, the port of Constanta came into view on the Rumanian coast, dimly lit as the sun rose over the eastern horizon. The long voyage was coming to an end.

The harbor looked like any other European port. Piers, cranes, ships, and the lane ways out of the docks, which were lined with taverns and inns. The smells of seaweed and sea salt were strong. What surprised Elizabeth was to see four three-mast wooden sailing ships in the harbor. Although she had seen similar vessels back in America, they were for pleasure or show, while these ships looked like they were still in the service of hauling freight. Some parts of the world were still behind the times.

The captain and Jeremy had gone ashore to see to the unloading. Everything was properly crated and labelled as machine parts, and everyone was dressed in their civilian clothes. All the men had been given directions to a rented warehouse on the city's north side and, again in pairs, they began to filter slowly off the ship. Kennard, Bradley, Appleton and Elizabeth went ahead to the warehouse to contact the owner's agent and pay the rent. The horses and wagons they had arranged to buy were supposed to be nearby.

The warehouse sat among several factories, some churning out smoke, but most looked abandoned. It was on the industrial area's eastern edge within sight of row houses and buildings that looked little better than cardboard shacks. At the warehouse, there was no one to be found. The local populace was either working in the factories or sitting at home. The building was dark. A padlock secured the large sliding door.

Noise was coming from a tavern down the block. "Any guesses that our contact is having a beer while he waits?" Appleton said.

"A good a place as any to start," Elizabeth said. The four headed towards the tavern.

"What was the name of the agent again?" Appleton asked.

Elizabeth took out a small notebook from her bag. "A Captain Runy. Sounds like he isn't Rumanian."

"No, probably not," Appleton replied. "Many ex-soldiers from different nationalities are selling their services to anyone willing to pay. This gentleman could be German, Russian, Turkish, or even an American."

The dingy tavern was no modern building by any stretch of the imagination. It appeared to date from the early 1700's when this area was a small rural village. As they approached the tavern, they heard a crash. A man came flying out the front door, landing in a heap. Laughter rang through the door before it slammed shut. The man in the street slowly tried to raise himself, but fell back after each attempt. Kennard looked at Elizabeth. "Miss Clarke, perhaps you should wait over by the warehouse with young Bradley."

Elizabeth put on a brave face. "I've handled steelworkers on a regular basis. You think I can't handle a rough tavern? Besides, with you and Tom here, I'm sure I'll be just fine." Deep in her heart, however, lingered a little fear of the unknown.

"No, it's not that, it's just that some things in there you might not want . . ." Kennard trailed off as his eyes met Elizabeth's. She was not going to let him win this argument. He stepped to the door and opened it. "Corporal, take point," he ordered, just as if entering the tavern was a battle maneuver.

Elizabeth followed Bradley through the door into a crowded room. A boisterous clientele was drinking heavily and talking loudly in a language completely foreign to her. Checking that Elizabeth was directly behind him, Bradley placed her hand on his shoulder and began clearing a path to the bar. One of the patrons bumped into Bradley and turned with anger in his eyes. But after one look at Bradley and what Elizabeth assumed was the towering vision of Kennard standing behind him, the man slunk out of the way. Appleton elbowed his way up to talk to the bartender.

Appleton greeted the man in Rumanian. Elizabeth could tell he was asking a question, which ended with "Captain Runy?"

The bartender's face was rugged with scars. He stared, unblinking, at Appleton until the American pulled out a few notes of Rumanian currency and placed them on the bar. The man's lifted his face and pointed toward the building's back wall. His other hand was quick as the money disappeared from the bar. "*El datorează pentru băuturi.*" His hand signals indicated to Appleton that Runy was running a tab.

Appleton turned around and surveyed the back wall of the tavern. Elizabeth followed his eyes. There, in a dark corner, was a man slumped back in his seat with his cap pulled down over his face. He wore a military tunic, British design. This was encouraging but by no means indicated he was British, but at least they had found him easily enough. Appleton turned back to the bartender. "*Cat?*"

The bartender gave him a figure, obviously inflated, but in US dollars it didn't amount to much. Appleton paid the tab and signaled for everyone to follow him through the crowd. Appleton, Kennard and Bradley formed a triangle around Elizabeth.

"Speaking Rumanian wasn't in your file," Elizabeth said to Appleton.

"There's a lot about me that's not in my file," he answered. "But I'll tell you a secret. That's about all the Rumanian I know."

They slowly wove their way through the crowd. Many of the men they passed smiled at her. Some actually made rude gestures when they caught her looking their way. She just rolled her eyes and they laughed.

When they reached the table in the corner, Elizabeth took a closer look the man and his military tunic. He wore insignia on the sleeves, rank insignia on the shoulder and a cap badge, which would indicate his regiment. It was all Greek to her, but she sensed Appleton knew.

"Finished looking me over," came a guttural voice in slurred English, but without a British accent.

Elizabeth scanned the table, her eyes stopping at the sight of an Oriental-style sword leaning up against the wall beside the man's chair. Something about the sword told her she should know this man.

"Sorry," Appleton replied. "You're American?"

"Close, but not quite." The man looked up and his eyes widened as they fixed on Elizabeth, first in confusion, then in recognition. "Lizzie?"

Elizabeth glared at him. "I beg your pardon, sir?"

Kennard broke the tension. "Well, sir, you're a long way from home."

The man's gaze shifted to Kennard. "Well I'll be . . ." the man bellowed, words still slightly slurred. "Sergeant Kennard and Corporal Bradley. God, it's a small world."

Appleton turned to Kennard, doubly perplexed. "You know this man?" Elizabeth could see a look of confused recognition on his face.

Kennard was smiling from ear to ear. "Yes, I do. May I introduce Captain Rainey." He faced Rainey. "Captain, this is Mr. Appleton and, of course, you know Miss Clarke."

Rainey looked back at Elizabeth. "Only from her picture." There was something about the way he looked at her that made Elizabeth uncomfortable.

"If you don't mind me asking, sir," Kennard said, "What are you doing in Rumania?"

Rainey laughed and raised his glass. "Well, Sergeant, I was in Paris with the Canadian peace delegation. I started helping a young man try to free Indochina from French rule based on *your* President's Fourteen Points. Next thing I know, I'm here guarding wheat."

"Wheat?" asked Kennard.

"Good Canadian wheat. Come on, sit down and tell me what brings you to this hellhole."

Bradley pulled out a chair for Elizabeth, but she didn't move right away. She now realized this was the man her brother had told her about in his letters. But that didn't mean she should let her guard down. She sat down slowly, not taking her eyes off Rainey. Bradley stood. Kennard and Appleton took the other chairs.

Kennard spoke to Elizabeth. "I'm sorry, Miss Clarke. I don't know if you know of Captain Rainey."

Elizabeth leaned back in her chair, arms crossed, continuing to glare at Rainey. "I do. My brother had mentioned him in his letters. And something about names on bullets."

Rainey sat up, eyes a little wider. Elizabeth intended for Rainey to feel her contempt. Rainey tried to deflect the scorn. "I must apologize for the decor, but then . . . I don't own this place." He glanced at Appleton. "You seem a little out of sorts."

Appleton shook his head. "Forgive me. You just remind me of someone else from a long time ago."

"Someone you like, I hope."

Elizabeth leaned forward. "Can we get down to business so I don't have to sit among this decor any longer than I have to?"

Rainey turned to Kennard. "You're here for the horses and wagons?"

"Yes, we are," Elizabeth said coldly, "and you will be dealing with me, not Sergeant Kennard."

Rainey kept his eyes on Kennard. "I can't believe you let her come in here."

"Miss Clarke insisted."

Rainey glanced back at Elizabeth. "Yeah, I can see that."

"Captain Rainey." Elizabeth broke into the conversation. "The warehouse; the horses; the wagons."

"Very well Lizzie, to busin . . ."

"And you are not in a position to call me by that name, Captain," she scolded.

* * *

Rainey felt a pain in his gut. He was being treated like a five-year-old child being scolded by an adult, but instead of getting angry, he actually felt five years old. The alcohol didn't help, either. Elizabeth just appearing out of the blue like this had unsettled him. He had obsessed over her picture during the war and now, here she was, acting abrupt and surly. This was not how he had envisioned their first meeting.

Rainey shook himself out of his funk, shaking his head to clear the cobwebs, and sat up straighter in his chair. *Damn it*, he lectured himself, *you're an experienced combat veteran, not some nervous romantic dandy.* "I'm sorry, it's just that your brother referred to you in that way during the war and . . ."

"And I'll have to speak to him about revealing that in public," Elizabeth replied. "Now, business?"

Rainey's attitude was beginning to shift fast, his stubborn streak starting to rise up. He sat up straighter in his chair. "Your deposit has cleared for both the warehouse and the horses and wagons. I am to accept the banker's notes from you today and give you a key to the warehouse. I will then take you over to the field where the horses are located. It's close by, too. After I deliver the banker's notes to the bank, I'll come back and assist in the transfer of the horses. I'll need about an hour to get to the bank and back."

"That is acceptable," replied Elizabeth, "with one small change. I will accompany you to the bank to make the deposit."

"You don't have to do that."

"I am not about to pass any sort of financial instrument to someone I just met."

"I'm sure the sergeant and the corporal can vouch for me."

"And if it was their money, then it would be their decision. But it's not."

Rainey was taken aback. The lieutenant had said his sister was a shrewd businesswoman, but he never expected to see her in action so up close and directed at him. "Very well, I just assumed that you didn't want to take the time . . ."

"You assumed wrong, Mr. Rainey," Elizabeth said. Her tone

was matter-of-fact.

Rainey's stubbornness level went up another notch. He blinked his eyes a couple of times. His vision was clear now, no sign left of the alcohol. He leaned forward towards Elizabeth "Do you allow anyone to finish a sentence before you cut them off?"

"Only when they are not making redundant statements." The flash of anger that crossed Elizabeth's face was there for only an instant for Rainey to see, but the fire in her eyes burned strongly. Rainey saw the flash, knowing he had hit the mark. She deserved it. *Hell, she was being rude.*

The pause in the conversation allowed Elizabeth let her face relax. She must be trying to get her anger back under control, Rainey decided. This was a business meeting, she was the astute businesswomen, and control must be maintained.

Rainey stole a glance towards Kennard, who he could see was working hard to hold back a smile. His eyes then darted to Bradley; he wasn't sure why, because the blank stare he got was exactly what he expected from the enigmatic corporal. His focus then settled on Appleton. Here was a man he didn't know, who looked like a bookkeeper, but his eyes betrayed something much deeper: a man who used his stuffy appearance as a cover for something else. Rainey had seen it before in men doing intelligence work. Right then, he knew the horses were not being put on a ship headed for the United States.

Rainey leaned back in his chair. "Fine. So you will accompany me to the bank. I can then bring you back here. In the meantime, I'll get the warehouse open. If you'll wait here a few minutes, I have a tab to pay before we leave."

"We took the courtesy of paying that for you," said Appleton. Rainey smiled. "Well, thank you. Let's get out of here, then."

He staggered a bit as he got up, but then rose to his full height, took a big breath and stepped out from behind the table. He reached behind his chair and picked up his sword.

Rainey noticed Appleton's eyebrows raised at the sight of the sword, but when he looked around, no one else seemed surprised. He expected a little bit of a reaction from Elizabeth, but she only glanced at it briefly. Rainey raised the strap over his shoulder so the sword hung on his back. "Come on, I know a back way out."

* * *

He had made it a point to lose his companion on the way to the warehouse. It wasn't hard. The private knew the way and had gone up ahead in the crowded streets. It was easy to make it look like they had just gotten separated in the crowd.

The address from his list was a bookshop on a narrow lane just off the main street. A small bell hooked to the door announced visitors. Four rows of back-to-back shelves ran down the narrow room, with very little space between them. For a bookstore, it was pretty dark. It was also empty except for a single person at the counter.

He passed between the rows to the counter. The small, balding man wore a sweater and a pair of circular reading glasses. He looked up. *"Buna ziua, vă pot ajuta?"*

The response was in English. "Do you have the works of Karl Marx in German? The English version isn't as fun to read."

The little man's eyes widened. Evidently he had never heard the code phrase before and was beginning to get excited. An agent of change was standing in front of him. The clerk scrambled to remember the response phrase. "No, I'm sorry," he stuttered in English, "but the Russian version is even more exciting."

The man smiled. "I have just a little job for you. There is a ship in port, called the Constance. I need you to arrange an investigation of its cargo. Can you do that?"

The shopkeeper paused for a moment, then smiled. "Yes, I know someone in the *polizei* who can have that done. He is a comrade as well. What should he be looking for?"

"That doesn't matter," replied the man. "Just start the investigation and have your friend arrest whoever he can after one p.m. Not before. I can guarantee he'll find something interesting."

"Consider it done," the shopkeeper replied. The man turned to leave. "Long live the revolution," the shopkeeper added.

11

Constanta was a busy port, which helped mask the transfer of over two hundred men off the ship. The trucks and wagons were slowly being loaded as a crane emptied the hold. Jeremy was taking inventory of everything. Browning machine guns labelled as engine parts. The 37mm guns listed as specialty pipe. The mortars passed as pipe sleeves, the rifles as tie rods. Food ration crates had lead liners to add weight to them; they were labelled nuts and bolts. Everything had its code and all was in order. The system had worked perfectly. *Elizabeth could try a new career in smuggling*, he thought.

On the gangplank he saw Sergeant Sutton sending two more soldiers, dressed in civilian clothes, onto the pier. Sutton came down the gangplank himself after a few minutes. He casually strolled to where Jeremy was overseeing the loading of a truck. "Everyone's out sir," he said softly into Jeremy's ear.

Jeremy just nodded, checked his list and then pointed to the front of the truck. "Go with this one. We've got one more truck to go and I'll be along with it. Got your map?"

Sutton nodded and headed for the truck. As he hopped in, the driver released the handbrake and jammed the truck into gear. Jeremy watched it leaving the pier before turning his attention back to the last load.

He checked his watch. It was 1:03 p.m., making him smile. It had gone like clockwork. Everything off the ship on schedule and no mistakes. The last two crates were Browning machine guns, which were slowly lowered into the middle of the flatbed. Jeremy helped the driver tie down the load, then strode off to the port authority office with the inventory.

The official gave the list a curious glance only, stamped it and handed it back to Jeremy. Jeremy smiled a thank-you and turned to leave the office. As opened the door, he noticed a policeman moving up to the front of the truck. Another one was heading up the gangplank. Something was wrong.

He reached into the pocket of his jacket and rubbed the Colt, sizing up the situation, but decided against action when it became clear there were seven policemen in the detail. This wasn't good at all. One man jumped up onto the flatbed with a crowbar and began cracking open one of the crates. It was time to find a way to disappear. At least the driver of the truck, looking frightened with his hands being held behind him by another policeman, had no idea of where he was supposed to be taking the crates. Jeremy lowered his gaze and stepped down, moving to his left, trying not to look suspicious. He walked right into another policeman.

"*Tu!*" he yelled. Jeremy didn't move. The man grabbed the documents from his hand. The entire shipment, all listed as machine parts and the like and destined for a company on the other side of Constanta from where the warehouse was, would be of no use to him, Jeremy thought. As far as he could tell, all they would have is him and two crates of Browning machine guns listed as engine parts.

The policeman looked up from the documents. *"Sunteti in stare de arest!"* which Jeremy figured meant "You are under arrest." He looked about for an escape route and was just about to make a dash for it when two more policemen with rifles appeared. On the open pier, he wouldn't get five yards before he was gunned down. There was no escape at the moment. He reached for his breast pocket for comfort, but found nothing. The locket was in his army tunic, on the way to the warehouse.

I knew it was going too well.

* * *

Two hundred thirty-six horses. Most were magnificent animals, attentive, with fire in their eyes. These were ex-cavalry mounts. The others held their heads lower, ears back, a blank look in their eyes. They pulled wagons. They were all colors: black, chocolate brown, white, gray, etc. All were grazing in a ten-acre field about a mile from the warehouse. And with 236 of them came quite a buildup of odor. Elizabeth took her time wandering among the horses, checking the odd hoof, another's teeth, another's hind quarters, seemingly oblivious to the stench. Bradley followed her as if a tether stretched between them. Rainey, Appleton and Kennard remained at the gate, watching her.

"Quite a collection," Appleton said, making conversation.

Rainey nodded. "The Rumanians, along with everyone else, found that cavalry horses were not good for much on the new battlefield. Most of these mounts are cavalry, but my contact was able to throw in a bunch of workhorses to get the total number up to your requirements."

"Motorized vehicles are becoming more reliable," said Appleton. "Horses will be totally replaced in warfare before long."

Rainey smiled. "Don't you remember? The Great War was the war to end all wars. Don't need armies and weapons anymore."

"Now you're being sarcastic, Mr. Rainey."

"Yeah, I suppose I am. Does Miss Clarke know horses?"

"Her family runs a stable of racehorses," Appleton replied. "A passion of her father's."

Elizabeth came out of the herd, Bradley still shadowing her. "Quite a few spirited specimens in the bunch. I'm pleased," she said. Her voice was all business.

"Glad I could be of service," Rainey replied. "If that's all, here's the key to this gate." Elizabeth signaled for Kennard to take the key. "So, now to the bank. I have a truck parked over by the tavern. How many are coming?"

"Just the corporal and myself," Elizabeth replied. "Mr. Appleton and Sergeant Kennard can commence with moving the horses."

"I know Kennard isn't exactly the wrangler type and it doesn't look like your other friend is either."

"They will be fine, Mr. Rainey," Elizabeth said. "And they are not alone. We have men who will do the 'wrangling' at the other warehouse."

Shut down the curiosity, boy, Rainey admonished himself. *They don't want me to know. Live with it.* "Well then, let's proceed. Miss Clarke, if you'll follow me. Sergeant, it was good seeing you again. I'll bring Miss Clarke back in about an hour."

"Thank you sir," Kennard said.

As the truck pulled out, Rainey looked back and saw Appleton speaking into Kennard's ear. The sergeant was looking intently at Appleton. As he spoke, both turned to look directly at Rainey's departing truck. *Doesn't look like they trust me very much.*

* * *

Jeremy sat quietly in the horse-drawn police wagon. During the ride to the station, his thoughts swirled. *How did they know?* But more important, *When did they know?* If they had been waiting for the ship to come in, there would have been no getting off the ship. The entire company would have been captured with all their supplies. The only thing that made sense is that the police were tipped off *after* the ship had arrived. That would mean someone inside the company was a traitor. But how would a traitor be able to tip off the police? For a start, he would have to know how to speak Rumanian.

Appleton. He was the only one he knew who could speak other languages. But that didn't make sense, either. Appleton would have had the contacts to have the entire company arrested. Hell, he could have stopped the mission by just not showing up in New York in the first place. What possible purpose could there be for getting only Jeremy arrested? It made no sense. It had to be someone else in the company and he had to find out who. His focus changed to finding a way to escape.

* * *

The ride to the bank was bumpy. The conversation was limited to directions. Elizabeth sat between Rainey and Bradley, who drove. There was no way Elizabeth would let Rainey drive when he was still feeling the effects of alcohol. The old truck was of early construction, perhaps 1905, she thought. She recognized it as a Ford design with familiar controls, similar to the vehicles she insisted on mastering around the steel mill. The truck didn't appear to have gotten much maintenance, either.

Elizabeth could tell that Rainey continually glanced over in her direction, pretending that he was just surveying the scenery. It was like he had never met an American before, but she knew that wasn't it. In his letters, Jeremy had spoken very highly of this man and mentioned Rainey's odd attraction to the locket Jeremy carried with him. Elizabeth had never thought too much about it, never figuring she would actually meet Jeremy's Captain Rainey. But here he was, seemingly fascinated by her presence. It was almost embarrassing.

Without returning his glances, she said, "Does my picture do me justice?" She then turned to see Rainey's face go beet red and his knuckles turn white. She smiled and turned to Bradley. He looked totally focused on driving.

They traveled in silence to the main square. Elizabeth and Rainey climbed the steps to the bank's heavy doors, leaving Bradley with the truck. Rainey said something in Rumanian to the man at the front desk, who stood and escorted them to a back office. They waited in silence. The tension Elizabeth felt from Rainey was amusing to her. She was used to acting intimidating or flirting in business, but she didn't have to do a thing here.

Rainey repeatedly checked his wristwatch, fidgeting in his chair, until the banker finally stepped into the office. "Ah, Captain," he said in a cultured, slightly accented English. "You are here to do the deposit? The deal went well then?"

"Yes, it did," Rainey said. "May I introduce Miss Elizabeth Clarke of Clarke Steel. Miss Clarke, this is Nicolai Tercescu. He will take the documents for deposit."

Elizabeth stood and held her hand out for a traditional handshake, but a slightly confused Tercescu hesitated, took her hand gently, turned it and then bent over to kiss it.

"An unexpected pleasure, Miss Clarke," said Tercescu. "It is always a good day when I get to meet a captain, or may I say captainess, of industry from the United States."

"Have you met American businessmen before?" Elizabeth inquired.

"It is rare, but I had the pleasure of meeting Andrew Carnegie in London many years ago."

"You've been to London, then."

Tercescu put his hand on his chest. "Oxford, Class of '97. When you are learning banking, learn from the best. I began my career with Barclays."

Elizabeth smiled at him. "I'm impressed. It also explains your excellent English."

"Thank you, Miss Clarke. I do not get to use it as much anymore."

Elizabeth brought the banking documents out of her bag. "Well, I'm glad to have given you the opportunity. Here are the documents for the sale of the horses and wagons and the warehouse rentals. The horses are splendid. Please thank the vendor for their excellent service."

Tercescu tilted his head and winked towards Rainey. "The captain has always served the vendor well over the last few months."

Elizabeth gave Rainey a look, a slight smile forming on her lips. She decided she couldn't just let the man off that easy. "Apart from finding him in a tavern, he has performed well." Tercescu mocked being shocked and turned to face Rainey.

* * *

The room remained silent for a moment. *OK*, Rainey thought, *score another point for the heiress, standing there with an amused look on her face.* "Nicolai, if that's all, we'll be on our way. I know Miss Clarke has another appointment to make."

Tercescu pulled out a document. "I will just need Miss Clarke's signature here and I will be able to convert the funds to your . . . your client's account."

Elizabeth sat at the desk to sign the document. "There. Thank you for your service. We will consider your services again for any future business we have in Rumania."

Tercescu bowed and escorted them out to the front door of the bank. "That is most agreeable. Again, it was a pleasure to do business with you Miss Clarke, and I hope that . . ."

The sound of gunfire from the square cut him off. People screamed and ran in all directions. Rainey stepped out the door. Elizabeth rushed to follow and saw four policemen with rifles running across the square towards the street opposite the bank. Rainey held her back from the door. "We'll be safer in here until the police clear the square," he told Elizabeth. "Wait . . ." Turning back, he saw, in hot pursuit of the police, Bradley with his gun drawn.

12

June 20 - 22, 1919
Rumania

Escaping from the police turned out to be relatively easy. When they reached the station, Jeremy made mental note of the town square, the building's doors and interior layout, and the stairs down to the cells. After being plopped into a chair in front of a detective who couldn't speak English, he was quickly led to the cells. The stairway was right by the front door facing the square.

Jeremy acted dejected, stopping every few steps and letting the guard push him forward. Every time he stopped, he counted to see how long it took the guard to push him forward. Scanning the cell area, he found no one else was there. *This is going to be easy.*

As they reached the cell door, he paused again. This time he waited for just a second, then quickly spun to his left. The guard's hand was pushing forward, but when it made no contact with Jeremy's back, the man fell forward and had to catch himself. His head came up, exposing his neck. Jeremy finished his spin by pounding his fist into the guard's throat.

The guard made a choking sound. His hands went to his neck

as he teetered sideways. Jeremy pulled the policeman's pistol out of his holster as he went down. Jeremy cracked the pistol butt onto the back of his head to knock the man out. For a moment he stood stock still and looked around. Nothing moved in the basement. He heard only the sound of the people upstairs going about their business.

Let's hear it for combat training, Jeremy thought. He glided quietly up the stairs. With any luck, he could just walk out the front door before anyone noticed him. He paused, calmly opened the door, and stepped towards the door to the square.

"*Tu!?*"

So much for just walking out. Jeremy turned and raised the pistol, aiming over everyone's head, and began firing. With screams and shouts, all dived for cover. Jeremy spun and bolted out the door into the square.

The gunshots had made people stop in front of the police station. As Jeremy burst out the doors, passersby saw the gun in his hand and panic ensued. He didn't stop, but tried to run with the crowd. He was about twenty-five yards from the steps when he heard a rifle shot. A woman running just ahead of him screamed and fell to the pavement. *They're shooting into the crowd.*

The entire square erupted into panic, people screaming and running every which way. Jeremy targeted an exit street in front of him, trying to stay with a crowd. More rifle shots. Just as he entered the street, he felt a hard punch to his left shoulder. It threw him forward, but he kept his balance and kept going.

He ran towards the end of the street, but knew the police were close. The pain in his shoulder was becoming unbearable. He was sure the bullet had shattered his collarbone, making him lurch to his left as he ran, killing his speed. But he had to keep moving.

Don't look back. Must make it back to the company and find the traitor.

He tripped on a cobblestone and almost lost his balance, but spun around to regain it, grunting in pain as his arm swung around for balance. Looking back down the street, he saw a policeman taking aim with his rifle, a puff of smoke coming from the muzzle. He had to dodge, trying to move to the right. But the bullet found him, this time in his upper chest. It spun him around again as he fell heavily to the cobblestones. As he lay there, he heard the police running towards him. He tried to move, but he had no energy. More shots were fired, but nothing hit him. *Why are the police still shooting at me?*

The sound of these shots was different. Familiar. Not that it made any difference. The wound in his upper chest was very serious. He knew it was bad. All he could do was lie there and hope the Rumanians would quickly give him some medical attention. Only one set of footsteps was approaching him now. He moved his head slightly to make out who the feet belonged to. A familiar face came into his line of sight, a face that was totally unexpected. A face of salvation.

Bradley.

Bradley kneeled down to Jeremy, quickly examining the wounds, and slipped his arms under his body. "Corporal," Jeremy croaked as Bradley started to lift him.

Bradley didn't reply, but moved back towards the square. Confusion reigned in Jeremy's head. He was heading back towards more police. It didn't make sense. Bradley wasn't stupid. Then he heard the truck coming up the street and Elizabeth's strained voice.

"Oh, my God! Tom, get him in the back." The truck stopped and another set of hands grabbed hold of him. He got a glimpse of another man, someone who shouldn't be there.

"Captain?" he whispered.

"Yeah, we can chat later," came the reply.

Jeremy closed his eyes as he was placed in the back of the truck. All he could do was listen.

"Sir!"

"I see them. Covering fire."

Two shots rang out.

"What are you doing?"

"I know how to drive this truck," Elizabeth said hurriedly.

Another shot. A bullet ricocheted off the side of the truck.

"Go. Go. Take a right, go three streets and then do a left."

The truck lurched forward; another bullet sounded like it hit the windshield. Return fire. They were moving. Moving to safety. Jeremy faded into unconsciousness.

* * *

Elizabeth drove furiously, as fast as the vehicle would go, careening around corners as Rainey instructed her. She had to get Jeremy to the warehouse and O'Hanlon's medical attention. Finally, the truck came up the street to the warehouse. Elizabeth honked the horn incessantly, causing the men to jump up and begin opening the large door. Slowing only slightly, she drove the truck inside and slammed on the brakes.

"Corpsman," Rainey yelled. Three men with medical kits ran up to the truck, with O'Hanlon right behind. Elizabeth watched from behind the truck, Bradley beside her holding her hand. Rainey turned and surveyed the warehouse. Horses were being saddled, wagons loaded, army uniforms put on, weapons checked, ammunition distributed. All paused for a second as the truck rolled in, then continued like any good army. *Someone is looking for a war*, Rainey thought.

Appleton rushed up to the truck. "What happened?" he asked.

Rainey shook his head. "Not really sure. We were coming out of the bank when there was an apparent escape from the police station. Turned out to be the lieutenant."

Appleton turned to O'Hanlon. "How bad is it?"

"Not good," O'Hanlon said. "Pretty sure he took it in the lung."

Kennard stood next to Appleton. Slowly, all movement in the warehouse came to a halt except for the medics on the flatbed. They worked hard trying to save Jeremy, but after ten minutes, O'Hanlon slowly looked up at Appleton. He shook his head. Elizabeth let out a short cry and buried her head in Bradley's shoulder. Rainey stepped up into the truck and knelt down beside the young lieutenant. His labored breathing was getting fainter with each gasp. Jeremy slowly raised one hand and signaled Rainey to come closer.

He rasped, hardly above a whisper. "Hello, Captain."

"Hello, Lieutenant."

Jeremy's head tilted to the left. "Where's Elizabeth?"

Rainey looked over his shoulder and signaled Bradley to bring Elizabeth up onto the truck bed. Tears were rolling down her cheeks. She gulped back her sobs. With her first sight at Jeremy's face, she started to break down.

"Lizzie," Jeremy began. "I need you to continue on with Captain Rainey. Captain, I need you to take command. Sergeant Kennard and Charles Appleton know everything and can brief you."

Rainey was silent for a moment, looking for clues from Elizabeth, then from Kennard and Appleton. All through the warehouse, he recognized faces. Faces from the war. Faces from the

28th. They were all on a mission; where, he didn't know. For what reason, he had no idea. But the lieutenant thought it was important. Rainey had a lot of respect for Jeremy Clarke. Looking back at Jeremy, he nodded his head.

Elizabeth cradled Jeremy's head, slowly rocking back and forth and sobbing. "Lizzie," Jeremy continued. "Find Father. Complete the mission." Elizabeth nodded mutely. Shock setting in, Rainey realized. "Captain?" Jeremy was addressing him now.

Rainey leaned forward. "Be careful. There's a traitor . . ." Jeremy gasped. Abruptly, he began to shake and cough, spewing blood from his mouth. In a moment, he settled down, the air slowly leaving his lungs. Rainey reached down and closed Jeremy's eyes. Elizabeth looked up at Rainey, an awful emptiness on her face. Then the realization set in. A loud wail came from her and she hugged her brother, hard.

Rainey waited a moment. Brother and sister. A strong bond abruptly broken. He wanted to reach out to her, but didn't know how, and knew it wasn't appropriate. She didn't know him. As he was thinking that, Bradley climbed into the truck bed. He sat down next to Elizabeth.

Rainey stepped away from the truck and towards Appleton and Kennard. "He wanted me to take command."

Kennard nodded and saluted. "Yes, sir. I'll inform the men." Before he could move off, Appleton grabbed him by the arm.

"I'm sorry, but the mission is finished. The lieutenant had to be in charge at the other end for our contact to even approach us. He insisted on family."

The wheels in Rainey's head started turning faster. *"Find Father."* That's what the lieutenant had commanded his sister. They were on a mission to find their father, who had apparently arranged to go missing and wouldn't come out of hiding without seeing a family member. Rainey nodded. "Very well. Do you need my help to get back on your ships?"

"That would be appreciated," Appleton said, resignation in his voice. "They were 'supposed' to head back to the US with the horses. Now, I guess they actually can."

"No, they won't. We'll be going on."

The three men turned to find Elizabeth standing over them, Bradley at her side, tears streaking down her face but a cold resolve in her eyes.

"Miss Clarke . . ." Appleton began.

"I know," Elizabeth said. "My father wants family. I am family. I will go on with you."

"Now, hold on there," Rainey said. "Russia is a dangerous place to go into."

"And I have a 216-man, well-equipped and trained bodyguard. I will be fine. Will you lead us, Mr. Rainey?"

Rainey didn't reply. He looked to Appleton and could see his mind churning, evaluating the option. "Sergeant, you can vouch for this man?" Appleton finally asked.

Kennard replied immediately. "Yes, sir. The men will follow him."

Appleton turned back to Rainey and nodded.

"Are you sure?" Rainey asked Elizabeth.

She fixed him with the same firm look.

"OK, I need a briefing. Now. And in one hour, a meeting with all the NCO's so I know who I'm dealing with. Sergeant, you arrange that."

"Yes, sir," Kennard replied smartly, snapping a salute and

moving off.

Elizabeth turned back and kneeled down next to her brother. She took his hand in hers and bowed her head. Bradley continued to stand like a sentinel over her.

Appleton spoke to Rainey. "Let's go outside where it's more private and I'll give you an outline of the mission."

"Don't trust me, do you?" Rainey asked.

"I never fully trust anyone, Captain," Appleton replied. "Consequence of the trade. But if Lieutenant Clarke and Sergeant Kennard consider you a good replacement, then I can rely on that judgment for now. The alternative is to abort the mission and I don't want that, either."

"Good. A quick summary will do for now. We can do the full briefing after we set up our first campsite. Looks like we're getting ready to move out of here and it's best we don't stay in Constanta tonight." Appleton raised his eyebrows. "The police are involved," Rainey continued.

Slipping aside into a corner of the warehouse, Rainey noted that all had returned to the way it was before the truck showed up. The company continued to prepare. The only difference, he saw, looking over his shoulder at the truck, was Elizabeth grieving over her brother, and the lone figure of Bradley, standing guard over the fallen.

* * *

It was the end of their second day out. They set up camp in the forest north of Tulcea, where the multiple campfires wouldn't draw too much attention. Rumania was at war, after all, fighting for its supposed fair share of Hungary. At least it kept the Rumanian Army occupied, so no one took a second notice of the small company making its way to the Russian frontier.

It had been an interesting two days. Elizabeth had been avoiding everyone, keeping only Bradley close, but she had joined the
mission for the duration. Now, her father was the only family she
had left. It was against Rainey's better judgment to bring her along,
but in the end, it wasn't his decision to make. Without Elizabeth
along, there would be no mission.

Rainey's first conversation with Appleton outside the Constanta warehouse had been an eye-opener.

"So, what are you people up to?" Rainey asked straight out.

"We're going into Russia," Appleton began.

"Russia. OK. What's the goal of the mission?" asked Rainey.
"From what I've been able to gather, we're on our way to rescue
the father?"

"Yes," Appleton said.

"And what else?"

Appleton didn't answer right away, so Rainey continued. "I
can't see the need for a small army to rescue one man. I could do
it with a team of about six if he was being held in a prison. And
from the stories the lieutenant has told me about his father, he
could probably get out of Russia by himself quite easily. What else
is there?"

Appleton's face never wavered. "I don't know."

"So Clarke Senior didn't tell you?"

"At the time, I believe he didn't know, either."

Rainey looked up at the warehouse's roof trusses, exasperated.
"Great. Into the middle of a civil war with no idea why. You clandestine types are always doing this."

"I'm a diplomat," Appleton said flatly.

"Yeah, and I'm the King of England," Rainey retorted.
"Where in Russia are we going?"

"The City of Chelyabinsk."

"And from there?"

"Out through Vladivostok."

Rainey rubbed his face with his hands. "So we're going across the entire length of the Russian empire."

"Yes."

"Do we have a timetable?"

"Only to be in Chelyabinsk by the end of August at the latest."

"And where exactly is Chelyabinsk?"

"Just on the other side of the Ural Mountains."

Rainey stared at Appleton for a moment, letting the information sink in. Then he turned to face the door into the warehouse. "You sure can pick 'em, Robbie," he mumbled to himself. He turned back to Appleton. "We'll talk again tonight once we've set up camp. We can go over the details then." He went in search of Kennard and a meeting with the platoon sergeants.

That first night, after the camp was secure, the company held a small service for Jeremy Clarke and buried him beside a large elm tree. Elizabeth stood, slack-jawed and glassy-eyed, while Rainey gave a short eulogy.

Later in the evening, Rainey got a more complete briefing from Kennard about the company's logistics and the route to Chelyabinsk. Rainey was impressed by the outfit's organization and training. He hadn't seen such logistical skills from the young lieutenant during the war, but he soon learned that, when combined with his sister's organizational skills, Jeremy had created a first-rate company, fully equipped and supplied and carrying an incredibly detailed plan. The plan itself was full of flexibility and contingencies. They were going to get where they were going come hell or high water.

The next day, as they rode towards Tulcea, Rainey would glance occasionally at Elizabeth to see how she was doing. She looked frumpy, dressed in her brother's uniform, the cap pulled down with her hair all tucked up into it. It had been thought best that she not stick out to anyone observing the company. The expression on her face never changed: sorrow. Since leaving Constanta, Rainey made no effort to talk to her. Now he sat by the fire outside his tent, staring into the flames. The day's duties done, he let his mind wander, churning over the last few days' events. Meeting Elizabeth at the tavern. Watching her move among the horses. The sheer driving skill she exhibited as they fled from the center of Constanta. The deep emotion she felt over her brother's death. It was then that Rainey realized all his thoughts were about Elizabeth. Nothing about the mission, nothing about anyone else. It felt so strange. What power did this woman have over him? And how long had this power been there? He could recall many times he would think of her before going on an attack, all based on a little picture in a locket. But those thoughts had never been this obsessive. He shook his head and went back to staring at the flames, trying to clear his mind of everything, when Appleton came by and sat behind him.

"I thought we were done," Rainey said quietly.

"I'd like to discuss what particular skills you may have that I should know about," Appleton said.

Rainey turned his head to look at him. "Like what?"

"Have you commanded a company before?"

"D Company, Princess Patricia's, at Sanctuary Wood, Vimy and Passchendaele. Don't worry, I know what I'm doing."

"Do you have any language skills?"

"I know Russian and Ukrainian," said Rainey. "There are a lot of Ukrainians where I come from."

Appleton looked surprised. "That will come in handy. My Ukrainian isn't that good. Now I have to emphasize the high level of secrecy the mission requires. The . . ."

"I have been on secret missions before. I know the protocol. It's not like I know anyone in Russia to tell secrets to. Now I have some personal questions for you since we're going to be working together closely for the next few months. How long have you been operating in Russia?"

Appleton hesitated before speaking. "Since 1903."

Now Rainey was surprised. "That long? You should know most of the players then."

Appleton nodded. "Even met Lenin once before he was exiled."

Rainey looked hard at Appleton. "Who do I remind you of?"

"Excuse me?"

"Back in the tavern. You said I reminded you of someone."

Appleton got up, looking a little uncomfortable. "It was a long time ago and not important. I'll bid you goodnight."

Rainey watched Appleton disappear into the darkness. *Typical spy.*

Part 2

13

June 26, 1919
Majaki, Ukraine

Clarke Company moved fairly quickly across the open expanses of Bessarabia. Clumps of forest among the rolling hills and steppe supplied firewood for camps and cover to avoid being seen. This was farm country. The area had been fought over by neighboring armies for centuries, but the last two days had been peaceful. Bucolic homesteads with few people sighted. Scouting patrols had little to report. Bridges over rivers and streams were all intact. Small towns were bypassed. It all seemed like a vacation to most of the men.

Elizabeth travelled in a daze. She had heard Jeremy's voice in her head saying, *Find Father*, and then got up to tell Rainey and Appleton that the mission would continue with her. After that, the days had gone by without her noticing much. Forty to fifty miles of riding with rests, Bradley always riding beside her, putting up her tent and cot for her; then sleeping, waking, eating and repeating the previous day's schedule.

But today, things were different. Even in her dazed state, she could sense something was amiss. Maybe it was Bradley riding closer to her than usual. Maybe it was the tension she sensed in the men as a whole. She turned in her saddle and looked back. The company was strung out on the road in two columns, everyone either with the wagons or on horseback. And alert.

One platoon was up ahead, on point, while another was out scouting. So far, everything was going according to plan, but everyone was uneasy.

* * *

Rainey reined his horse to a stop. The command group plodded by: Elizabeth and Bradley, Kennard and Appleton. As Kennard came even, Rainey jerked his reins and his horse aligned its pace with the sergeant's.

"Who's out there right now?" Rainey asked.

"Garcia, sir," Kennard replied. "He's due to meet us at the Dneister River. That's where MacGregor will head out with his platoon."

Rainey looked up at the hills to his left. "You still feel the shadow?"

"Yes, sir, and young Bradley is getting even more edgy."

Rainey glanced ahead at Bradley, whose head was pivoting back and forth like he was watching a very slow tennis match. His horse was also much closer to Elizabeth's, something that had not been as noticeable a day ago. He wondered whether he and Kennard actually sensed the shadow or were just attuned to changes in Bradley's behavior.

Rainey made the decision. "We may get met at the river. If not, we get across the bridge and make camp with our backs to the river and prepare a defensive perimeter. Go back and tell Mac-Gregor he won't have to go out. I'll want everyone close."

"Sir," Kennard said with a salute. He pulled his horse out of the column, turned and made his way to the rear.

"Expecting trouble?" asked Appleton, now riding even with Rainey.

Rainey looked up at the hills again. "I don't know, but we are being shadowed. I just hope we can make it across the Dneister before we run into anyone."

"This is Gregoriev's territory," said Appleton. "He's a Bolshevik, so we can probably talk our way past him."

"He's a thug," Rainey replied. "Rape and pillage is his way. And right now, the Bolsheviks are trying to kill him."

Appleton looked surprised. "That's not what my intelligence sources say."

Rainey grimaced. "Your intelligence was sound about a week ago. It's a rather recent turn of events and not very well known. I only heard about it myself the day before you came into port. The story is that Gregoriev ignored his orders to assist the revolution in Hungary. He's happy playing warlord here."

Appleton nodded. "I expected to be able to get passage in exchange for a machine gun or two."

"Not anymore." Rainey tapped his horse's hind quarters with his boots and moved forward in the column.

As he passed Elizabeth, she said, "I heard you talking. Is it bad?"

These were the first words he had heard her utter since her brother's death. Rainey looked blankly at her for a moment, wondering what her speaking might signify. Her eyes seemed more alive, something he hadn't seen since before Jeremy was killed. He shook his head, knowing he had to focus on other things that were more important at the moment. "Can't really tell. The shadow we picked up could be a reconnaissance unit for the local warlord. Or could be Bolsheviks hunting them. Won't know for sure until we're confronted."

"Can I do anything?"

"Keep your hat on and stay close to the ground. I'll assign someone to stay with you."

Elizabeth sat up straight in the saddle. "I have Corporal Bradley assigned to me."

Rainey shook his head again. "Sorry, I'll need him for other things that are more suitable to his skills than watching over you." Rainey scowled right away, realizing how that sounded. "That didn't come out right."

Elizabeth lowered her head. "No, it did not. I'm sorry to be a burden."

Rainey sighed. He just couldn't get anything right with this woman. "I'll inform you after I work out the details." He poked his horse again, prodding it into a light gallop, heading up towards the lead platoon. Gilbert had point at the moment and should be told of the change in plan at the river, but it was more an excuse to get away from Elizabeth before he said something else he would regret.

It was just after noon when Rainey reached the river valley's rim and looked down on the bridge with his binoculars. The Dneister was about two hundred yards wide here, spanned by a good solid modern railroad bridge of steel beams anchored on three concrete pillars placed in the river and two on each shore. On the other side, the provincial town of Majaki looked quiet, about a half a mile farther along the road, up on the valley's far edge. A forest spread up to the river bank north of the town; open steppe extended to the south.

Rainey could see Sergeant Garcia's platoon occupying both sides of the river. If an enemy unit was out there, they would want to meet the company here and use the bridge as a defense. However, the company had gotten here first.

Surveying the far bank, he began to spot key defensive positions he could use. The trees to the north could conceal his short-range artillery. The town would funnel an attack through the main street leading to the bridge, easily defensible. But the open steppe spreading out to the south was another matter. He would have to dig in most of his force there.

Moving the binoculars up, he began to sight the landscape behind the town. *Now if I had artillery*, he thought to himself, *where would I put it?* The land rose up slowly onto a low ridge, indicating the edge of the valley the Dneister had formed. A small forested area along the ridge could conceal artillery with a full view of the bridge. No other spot looked anywhere near as good. The only disadvantage was that if an attacker came from the south over the open steppe, its artillery would be isolated in the north. Not a problem if Rainey wasn't looking for artillery, but he was. As he watched the spot, a small glint of light shone at him. He smiled. Someone was looking back.

Another flash of light gained his attention, this time from the bridge. Garcia was signaling that all was quiet, but another message said one word in Morse code: *Hurry*. Rainey turned to Kennard, doing his own survey with binoculars. "Garcia says we need to hurry. I want the mortars and one 37 in the trees on our left. I want to place the other 37 by those bushes about a hundred yards downstream. If any shooting starts, we'll need that one moved to the bridge. Next, get the men to dig in about a hundred yards in front of the bridge, facing south. Place machine guns evenly along the line, but keep one crew over to the left to keep an eye on the town. And lastly, send Gilbert and one section to head up as discreetly as possible to that clump of trees on the ridge. There, that one, a little north of the town. They'll be looking for artillery."

Kennard smiled. Sections were a British Army term. "Sir, you're in the US Army here. They're called squads."

Rainey chuckled. He hadn't made that mistake since the battle on the Soissons-Paris road almost a year ago. "Well, since I'm in command, I can call them what I like. I'm sure you'll be able to translate."

"Yes, sir," said Kennard.

"Assign a couple of Corelli's artillery men to go with Gilbert. OK, let's get to it. Triple time." With that, Rainey kicked his horse and charged down the hill towards the river.

* * *

Elizabeth sat on her horse watching Rainey gallop to the bridge. Kennard was yelling orders and the whole convoy began surging forward, moving very quickly. But still she didn't move. She had a deep desire to contribute. For the mission. For Jeremy. But all she felt was that she was in the way. It was a strange feeling, one she had never felt before in her life. Even as a child, she never felt like she was in the way. She had always contributed in one form or another. But here, she had no idea how to contribute.

The last of the wagons and horses passed her in a rush, but still she didn't move until she started to feel very alone. There was nothing but the dust of the wagons and horses in front of her. Then a lone figure came out of the dust. It was Bradley, looking at her with his ubiquitous blank stare. This snapped her out of it.

She urged her horse forward into a gallop. As she passed Bradley, she yelled at him, "Don't worry, I wasn't thinking of running away." Bradley spurred his horse after her.

* * *

Down at the bridge, Rainey was getting his report from Garcia. He had spotted a column carrying green flags moving south along the river bank ridge, about a thousand men, he figured, with four armored cars and the rest cavalry. He'd also spotted four guns, which he estimated to be 75mm. The column was likely just over the ridge, still north of the town. Rainey calculated in his head that they would have about an hour at the most before they were confronted from the south or the town.

The armored cars bothered Rainey, as he'd never had to deal with any before. Appleton came up beside him. "I take it we're not facing Bolsheviks?"

Rainey shook his head. "Not likely. Green flags. That's got to be Gregoriev. They'll probably want to talk first, not knowing who we are, so what would make a good cover story?"

Appleton thought for a minute. "I guess it depends on how much time you're trying to buy."

"I'd settle for five minutes at this point."

"Then say we're Americans who have heard of the glorious Nikifor Gregoriev and have come to fight for the cause of Bolshevism. Might at least slow them down for a bit while they consider making us allies."

Rainey chuckled. "Yeah, I can sort of sell that." He watched Sergeant Gilbert hurrying off into the trees with a squad on horseback to find the guns. "If we find their guns, a thousand of them shouldn't be too much of a problem." He turned to Garcia. "Sergeant, your platoon will watch the bridge. Can I leave Miss Clarke under your protection?"

"I'll find a cozy spot under the bridge for her, sir," Garcia replied.

* * *

All around, as Elizabeth arrived across the bridge, she saw a flurry of activity. Men were putting on their helmets, digging shallow holes, placing guns, issuing ammunition, running here and there getting ready to defend the bridge. She started to feel lost again. Rainey hadn't said who he had assigned to her, but she spotted Sergeant Garcia at the bridge signaling to her. She rode to him.

"Elizabeth Clarke, reporting for duty, Sergeant. Where do you want me to hide?"

Without missing a beat, Garcia said, "Just down the bank a bit and up against the concrete support. You can feed ammunition up to the men."

A job! Elizabeth felt invigorated. She had learned to load bullets into gun clips during one of her brief visits to the company's training. She jumped off her horse, handed the reins to Garcia and started off to the river bank.

Garcia's stern voice stopped her cold. "Miss Clarke, the horses go over there. I'm not your groomsman."

Elizabeth went back to Garcia and took the horse's reins. "Sorry," she said, sulking off.

"And make it snappy, Clarke, we haven't got all day," Garcia barked. "And put your helmet on." Elizabeth spun, ready with a retort, but noticed a slight smirk on Garcia's face. He was trying to make her feel like one of his troops. She appreciated that and considered snapping him a salute. Instead, she just smiled back and ran with the horse.

* * *

The activity slowly wound down. All was in place. Holes had been dug; machine gun, mortar and gun placements set. The company was ready for defensive action. Rainey made a quick tour of the defenses. When he reached the bridge, he looked down the bank. There was Elizabeth, slapping bullets into clips. She looked up as she placed a clip into a neat row with about thirty others. She gave him a smile. He hadn't seen her smile since they had met, six days ago. Rainey smiled back, then caught Garcia's eye. Garcia nodded knowingly. She was doing fine, his nod indicated, and he'd take good care of her.

Rainey headed back to the command position. Binoculars up, he could see the forces lining up against him. As expected, they were forming up to the south. He estimated at least five hundred horse-mounted men and counted two armored cars. *There was supposed to be twice that number. Where is the other half?* Garcia had also reported finding a small bridge, not on the map, about ten miles upstream. He leaned towards the next foxhole. "Private, run back to the bridge and tell Sergeant Garcia to watch the west bank of the river in case we have company coming up behind."

The private jumped out of his hole and ran towards the bridge. Garcia would know what to do. He had successfully defended a bridge across the Meuse against a full German battalion with only two machine guns and seven men.

Now all Rainey had to worry about was whether Sergeant Gilbert had found the big guns or not.

14

As the two armored cars rumbled forward alone, Rainey lowered his glasses. Appleton, from a hole to his left, said, "I guess they want to start by talking."

Rainey looked behind him to Kennard. "Sergeant, two horses and Bradley. Give him a BAR. When I give the signal, have the 37's take those cars out."

"What will be the signal, sir?" asked Kennard, waving a hand signal behind him.

"I'll shoot the man I'm talking to."

As Bradley came up with the two horses, Rainey checked his Webley service revolver and returned it to his holster. He got up on his horse and reached back to rub the tip of his sword's scabbard as he always did before entering a dangerous situation. Together, they rode out to meet the armored cars, which had stopped about a hundred yards in front of the company. A man stepped out and stood in front of one of the cars, feet apart, his hands on his hips. Rainey held up his horse five yards short of the man. "Good afternoon. Wonderful day, isn't it?" he said in Russian.

The man's scowl didn't change. "Good afternoon for me, not for you. Who are you and what are you doing here?"

So much for small talk. "We've come from the United States to fight in the Great Revolution for the betterment of all mankind." *A little flowery, but what the hell, it bought time.* "We offer our services to the great Nikifor Gregoriev," Rainey added.

Puzzlement spread across the man's face as he tilted his head to one side. "Really. And what do you bring our Great Leader that he does not already have?" The man wanted an inventory.

Rainey looked up as if thinking hard, rubbing his chin. "Let me see," he began. "We have machine guns, mortars, horses, top fighting men, and the blessings of the State of Virginia." Rainey wasn't sure why he added Virginia, but it sounded good.

The man stepped forward. "Well, we do not need any more men, so you can start walking back to where you came from and leave your equipment behind. Comrade Gregoriev will be greatly pleased."

Rainey feigned hurt feelings. "But we came so far to fight for the Revolution."

The man had stepped right up and grabbed the harness of Rainey's horse. "The alternative is we just kill you all and take it."

Rainey felt that not enough time had elapsed yet. The man was pushing hard. "I'll have to go back and consult with my commander. I can't make that kind of decision."

"Then get off your horse and run to your commander," said the man. "I will hold on to that sword of yours to make sure you come back."

In the distance, Rainey caught the faint sound of rifle fire from the direction of the ridge where he'd sent Gilbert's team. The Russian's head shot to his right, looking towards the ridge. He knew something was wrong and reached for his pistol. Time was up. Rainey pulled out his Webley and aimed it at the man's chest.

"Piss off," he said in English and fired.

The shock on the man's face was absolute as he fell away from the horse. Rainey quickly raised his pistol and fired a couple of rounds at machine gunner on the first car, making him duck. Bradley, who already had the BAR aimed, brought it to bear and began pouring fire onto the other car, aiming for the machine gunner on its roof. He gotten off only about ten rounds and was sweeping towards the next car when both vehicles exploded. The horses reared up in surprise, almost tossing Bradley from the saddle. Rainey held on, feeling the heat from the burning hulks in front of him. The 37's had done their job, but had Gilbert done his?

They rode hard back to their lines. Rainey couldn't see anything up on the ridge. The rifle fire had stopped before he and Bradley had even begun to return from the wrecked cars. He swung the binoculars back towards the force arrayed against him. *You'd think they would look a little more upset after getting two of their armored cars blown up*, Rainey thought. But the force seemed unready to even instigate a charge at them.

They were waiting for the artillery barrage. Rainey looked around at his men. They were expecting it too, lying as low as they could in their foxholes.

What was going on up on that ridge?

The cannon roars gave him a partial answer. It wasn't really necessary, but Rainey yelled "INCOMING!" as loud as he could before ducking his head deep into the hole. The ground shook as two rounds landed some 250 yards in front of him. Then silence.

"Pretty poor shooting," Kennard grumbled. "I've heard of being short and long, but off to the left?"

Rainey was smiling. "It's Gilbert. He's telling us that he's got the guns."

The guns roared again as explosion after explosion now marched incessantly towards the enemy. Panic began to spread through their ranks as the shells started landing among them. Then the horsemen began an all-out charge towards the company in an attempt to get out from under the barrage. Shells stopped falling as the guns lost their target. Now with somewhat fewer than the five hundred men and horses they started with, they barreled down on the company positions. The men in their holes listened for the signal to fire, waiting as professionals did for the proper command, secure in the knowledge that their leadership was skilled. At about three hundred yards, the command was given.

Mortar rounds started dropping among the horses, throwing them and their riders into the air to land in heaps. The machine guns opened up, cutting a swath through horses and men. Horses collapsed forward as their momentum slammed them head-first into the ground, their riders pitching forward to be crushed under their animals, rolling over them. Coordinated, well-aimed rifle fire took rider after rider out of their saddles.

* * *

No charging horses made the company line. Several of the riders veered off towards the town and temporary safety. It had all happened very quickly. Elizabeth, a clip in each hand, could hear everything, but saw nothing. She felt she had missed out, undecided about whether that was a good thing or not. As things began to quiet down, she looked across the river. What she saw startled her.

"Sergeant!" she yelled.

"I see 'em, Miss Clarke," came the reply. Garcia was up on the bridge with binoculars.

She heard the artillery again and rounds started to slam into the far river bank.

"Get up here," he said, "sit behind this support beam and don't move."

Elizabeth scrambled up the bank, dropping the two clips into the box as she went past. From the top, she was able to survey the camp. Smoke rose from outside the perimeter. Bodies lay out there, man and horse, with some severely wounded horses attempting in vain to stand. It was horrible, yet she couldn't look away. An arm grabbed her and pulled her into the shelter of a steel I-beam.

"You can sight-see later," was all Garcia said. He handed her a pistol. "Just in case they get across."

Elizabeth's mouth fell open for an instant before she spoke. "Get across?"

Garcia half smiled. "You never know, but it's highly unlikely"

The exploding shells were landing a lot closer now than during the first volley. The noise was astounding. Elizabeth had to wonder how much worse it would be if they were being fired at her. Keeping her body tight against the bridge's rusty steel truss work, she slowly turned around and peered down the bridge. The enemy infantry were at the other end, trying to stay together as explosions were tearing them apart. An armored car got onto the bridge and started forward, firing a machine gun. Rounds ricocheted everywhere, one nicking the support beam in front of her. She ducked. A machine gunner and several riflemen fired at it, but it didn't stop. A crew was still hurrying to set up the 37 mm gun.

Behind the pillar next to her, she noticed the young soldier who had played the accordion and had been mesmerized by her singing on that last night they were stateside. Leaning out from cover to fire his rifle, his determined look suddenly changed to shock. Small explosions stitched across his chest, knocking him backwards. He landed at her feet with a thud. Elizabeth gasped. He lay there, eyes wide, unmoving. Elizabeth's shock and fear were quickly submerged by a growing wave of anger. That vehicle was killing *her* men. She got up, rolled out around the pillar, brought up her pistol and started firing at the armored car.

It was more than three quarters across the bridge when the 37 fired. It hit the car dead on in a deafening explosion. The car lurched up and slammed back onto the bridge deck, pitching onto its side with flames pouring out. The bridge was blocked.

The artillery rounds had stopped again. Past the burning vehicle Elizabeth saw the enemy beating a hasty retreat. From up the bank came another large group of horsemen in full charge. They plowed into the retreating enemy, cutting them down with pistols and sabers.

It all happened so very fast and now it was over. Garcia touched Elizabeth on the arm. "How you doin'?" he asked.

Elizabeth spun at him, raising her pistol. Garcia's hand was swift as he knocked the gun off to the side. Elizabeth stopped, eyes locked on Garcia's for an instant, before beginning to take in the scene around her. Her eyes stopped on the figure of the young private, four reddish-black holes aligned diagonally across his torso, like a rag doll tossed on the ground. A chill ran up her spine and her stomach churned. Sick to her stomach, she forced herself to settle down. She stepped over to the fallen soldier, kneeled down and closed his eyes, running her hand across his cheek. Noticing Garcia standing over her, she spoke.

"What was his name?"

15

Only one dead, with three slightly wounded but not out of commission. The company had performed well and come out of its first fight almost intact. Rainey was pleased.

Clean-up operations were under way. Appleton and a patrol went out among the dead and dying to lend aid and collect any useful items and information. No one went across the bridge. The unknown horsemen on the other side waited on their steeds. Garcia had no intention of letting them come visit without Rainey's authority.

As Rainey surveyed the scene with his binoculars, a soldier tugged his arm and pointed towards the town. Swinging his binoculars around, Rainey could see a group of horsemen coming out. Sergeant Gilbert and his squad were in the lead with another man he didn't recognize. The flashy uniform was unusual for a Bolshevik officer, but the rest of the men with him were dressed right. Appleton stepped up beside Rainey as Gilbert approached.

"Bolsheviks," he said.

"I guessed," said Rainey.

"You were right about Gregoriev."

Rainey nodded. Judging from what he could see, the Bolshevik unit wasn't much larger than the company. The armored cars alone would have decimated them in an attack.

The Bolsheviks stopped forty yards short of the camp, facing a guard with a machine gun and several riflemen. Gilbert directed his men to dismount and dismissed them into camp. He nodded to the Russian commander and the two rode slowly towards Rainey and Appleton. Rainey took a few swift glances around the camp, looking for Elizabeth. He spotted her with O'Hanlon, tending to the three wounded men. He was happy to see that she was still wearing her helmet and had her hair tucked up into it.

Gilbert brought his horse to a stop and saluted. Rainey returned the salute and turned to the Bolshevik commander. "Captain, this is Colonel Yuri Sergy . . ." Gilbert began, but he couldn't remember the Russian's name.

"Colonel Yuri Sergeyvich Krasenovsky, 14th Guards, at your service," Krasenovsky said proudly, with a slight bow.

"A pleasure to meet you, Colonel. You speak English," Rainey said.

"Yes, I had English nanny as boy. Nice to use again."

"Welcome. My name is Captain Robert Rainey and this is Charles . . ."

Appleton cut him off. "Charles Grady, United States State Department."

Krasenovsky frowned. "Is that sort of spy group?"

Appleton waved his hands. "No, no, diplomatic corps."

"Then why you use fake name? Is not your name Appleton?"

Appleton's face went pale as he stared up at Krasenovsky. His face gave no indication that the Russian was even vaguely familiar to him.

Rainey hoped he showed no sign that he was worried, but he

tensed up inside. Gilbert had placed his hand on his pistol. Rainey very slightly shook his head at him, making Gilbert slowly lower his hand away from his gun.

Appleton spoke slowly. "Aliases are useful during these troubling times. Where is it we have met before?"

Krasenovsky's face didn't change. "We never met. I saw picture in Cheka file."

"I see," Appleton said slowly. "Are you here to arrest me, then?"

Krasenovsky laughed. "With three hundred men on horse? Against your machine guns? Even I not that stupid. Sometimes, I given picture of people to look out for. Not enough Cheka to go around. Here, tracking Gregoriev pirates, saw you, thought good idea to catch them when spread out to attack you. Work well, no?"

Rainey stepped forward. "It worked very well. My thanks. We should talk further."

"Captain, my men hungry."

Rainey signaled to Gilbert. "Sergeant, go find Sergeant Kennard and see about feeding the colonel's men. Set them up on the north side of camp. And get Garcia to let their friends cross the bridge."

"Yes, sir." Gilbert saluted and rode off.

Krasenovsky watched the departing Gilbert a moment before dismounting. "Good man, Gilbert. Work guns well."

"I sent him up there with only two artillery men."

"I have eight," Krasenovsky replied. "Now have prize to take home."

"You're welcome to them," Rainey said. "There will be some spare horses around for us to split between us as well. Come, I've got some whiskey, Kentucky Bourbon. A little different from vodka."

Krasenovsky slapped Rainey on the back as they walked. "Nothing better than vodka, but I give this . . . Bourbon . . . a taste."

* * *

Elizabeth finished up wrapping the soldier's wounded arm. O'Hanlon had returned to watch her finish. "You could have been a nurse," he said.

"Clean and wrap," she answered. "Not that hard. Spent a lot of time cleaning up my brother . . ." She paused to fight back her emotions at the thought of Jeremy, then tapped the soldier on the shoulder. "There you go, Private. Report back tomorrow morning and we'll change the dressing."

"Thank you, ma'am," the soldier said. He reached down, picked up his rifle, and headed back to his squad mates.

"They tell me you did pretty good under fire," O'Hanlon said.

Elizabeth drew a pensive sigh. "You remember what happened on the ship?"

O'Hanlon's head tilted slightly to the right. "I do."

Elizabeth took a deep breath. "I felt terrible after that. His face still haunts my dreams, although they are fading. But here, it didn't seem to bother me at all that I wanted to kill whoever was in that vehicle. Now *that* bothers me. I'm afraid I'm becoming a heartless, cruel person."

O'Hanlon smiled at her. "Ah, lass, it's simple, really. You didn't mean to kill Reinhardt, so there is remorse. But when you kill someone who is trying to kill you? Well, that's an entirely different kettle of fish."

"How so? Killing is killing."

"On the ship, you did not fear for your life and there was a choice: let him go or shoot him. Here, you felt both fear for your life and anger. Combine those with no choice, and you don't feel too bad about coming out the other side alive."

Elizabeth thought for a moment. "But that doesn't explain the way Jeremy acted when he came home from the war." The emotional upheaval came and went again. She was finding it easier now to fight it back down.

O'Hanlon grimaced. "There were a lot more terrible things than killing someone going on in the war. Long bombardments turned soldiers into blithering idiots. The mud and desolation was very depressing. Lengthy waits between battles stretched into months of boredom. And being constantly surrounded by death, brutal death, with fellow soldiers getting dismembered by artillery . . . that takes a longer time to set in to the mind, but when it does, it can become permanent."

"Yet here we are," Elizabeth answered, "and everyone chose to come along rather than stay safe at home. That just doesn't make sense to me. I know they have a shared experience, but they don't need to go into another war to cope with it."

"Ah, that's another story again. You come home from the war changed. No one, not even your family, can understand what it was like. So they support each other. And, in some way, they miss the excitement."

"Did you miss the excitement?" asked Elizabeth.

O'Hanlon was silent for a moment. "I don't know. When I got home, I got involved in medical services for ex-soldiers. Very important work. But when I was approached to join your brother's expedition, I said yes before I realized I had. I had vowed never to participate in a war again. But here I am."

* * *

The Russian camp was a ramshackle, thrown-together sort of affair as opposed to the company's organized and professional camp. The men were hesitant around each other, but by nightfall, after feeding the Russians and undertaking a joint patrol into Majaki looking for supplies, a little camaraderie developed. Elizabeth stayed in her tent alone, out of sight, on Rainey's orders. She appeared to be getting ready for bed when Rainey pulled back the canvas.

"Miss Clarke, do you have a few minutes?"

"I have nothing but time," she answered flightily, "hiding out in my tent."

Rainey stepped in, not liking the tone. "I'm sorry about that," he said, "but it's better they don't catch on that we have a woman in our ranks."

"Why is that?"

Rainey thought about that for a moment. "Trying to keep the questions to a minimum. Women aren't supposed to be traveling with combat troops. You would become an identification marker of the company."

"As if Americans riding across Russia isn't distinctive enough."

"No one knows we're American until they talk to us."

"Just tell me the truth," Elizabeth insisted. "You feel better when I'm safely hidden."

She was right and he might as well admit it. "OK, yes, I feel better. I hope we won't have to hide you too much." He paused, not really knowing how to approach the subject he came here to discuss with her. He had questioned Garcia about her behavior during the firefight and he wanted to check with Elizabeth directly. And here she was, sitting on her cot, looking like it was just another day at the factory. That was a nice change from the sulking rider of the past six days. Even with her hair up and wearing a bulky oversized uniform, she was beautiful.

Elizabeth was looking out the flap of the tent. "The men and the Russians seems to be getting along pretty well. I guess that no matter where you go, soldiers were always the same. Trained to kill each other, but when meeting without a war, they get along famously." She turned her head to face Rainey. "Is there anything else, Captain?" she asked.

"Ah . . . no. Not really. It's just . . . ah, the day was . . . well, it must have been pretty upsetting for you . . . and . . . if you need anyone to talk to . . ."

Elizabeth was smiling. "Perhaps if you complete one sentence before starting the next," she teased.

That made him angry. "I just wanted to make sure you were OK."

Elizabeth frowned. "Sorry. It's a bit of a force of habit with me to take advantage of doubt."

"Then I'll have to try and complete sentences to your satisfaction."

"And I'll rein in the teasing. Now, is there anything else? I'm pretty tired."

Rainey shuffled his feet, coming back down from the hint of anger. "No, just wanted to add how I appreciated you pitching in today with the medical duties."

"My pleasure. Thank Sergeant Garcia for me for letting me help with the ammunition."

"Somehow, I didn't think throwing you in a hole and putting a private on top of you for protection was much of an option."

"But you wanted to, correct?"

Rainey looked down and shuffled his feet again. "Well, yeah, I kind of did."

"Captain," she said firmly. "I'm part of the company, too. I helped build it. I wasn't planning on coming this far, but since I have, I plan to continue to do my part. I'm not some fragile little flower you have to protect at all costs. I carried an ammunition crate today. It weighed a ton and I loved it."

"You did a little more than carry a crate," Rainey said. "Apparently you got angry at an armored car?"

Elizabeth's face went blank. "It was shooting at us."

"And you were shooting back with a pistol. How did that work out?" Elizabeth stayed silent. Rainey continued. "Remember, this expedition is over if you end up dead. So, in a sense, you are a fragile flower we have to protect at all costs."

"Of course," she said, feeling subdued. "But I'm sure my brother would not have been viewed as a fragile flower."

"He was in command with combat experience," Rainey replied. "You're not." He moved quickly to change the subject. "Now, what you saw today was pretty horrible. Are you sure you're OK?"

Elizabeth paused for a moment before replying. "I won't say it hasn't bothered me. But right now, I'm pretty sure I'm fine. Had a nice chat with O'Hanlon about it."

"Talking is good. If you have any questions, don't hesitate to ask me. Get some rest. We'll be getting an escort into Odessa."

Elizabeth lit up. "So the Bolsheviks think we're on their side?"

Rainey tilted his head to one side. "Not exactly. Apparently, Charles is on the Cheka's keep-an-eye-out-for list. Luckily for us, the Russian colonel doesn't seem to care. We'll get reported, so we'll have to see what happens."

Elizabeth frowned. "Charles is wanted? He's been out of Russia for months. How could he still be on their watch list?"

Rainey's demeanor turned serious. "I think they knew he was coming back." He paused for a moment, deciding whether to continue or not.

She caught the point. "What are you implying?" she asked seriously.

"I don't want to alarm you," Rainey said, "but I think your secrecy broke down before you left New York."

Elizabeth shook her head. "We were very careful."

"Over two hundred men, even vouched for, can still include a spy, or just someone who gets careless. Your brother thought it was someone in the company who is still with us now."

Elizabeth sat up straight. "He would have told me if he suspected anything."

"I'm sure he would have," Rainey replied. "I get the distinct feeling he had no idea until he was arrested in Constanta. He made sure to warn me. I don't know who to trust."

Elizabeth gazed off to nowhere in particular. "Something isn't right," she said quietly.

"What was that?" Rainey asked.

Elizabeth shook her head. "It was something Tom Bradley said." Her eyes opened wide. "The paperweight."

"You're not making any sense."

Elizabeth turned to face Rainey, worry etched on her face. "Someone was in the dining room, looking at our maps and notes."

Rainey's concern deepened. "They would have had to get the information out before you left New York." Rainey thought for a moment. "Picket duty. Did your brother have a perimeter guard at your New York camp?"

"Yes, every night." Realization crossed Elizabeth's face. "A guard could have handed information out of the camp."

"Yes."

"But how could that information make it to Rumania?"

"Communism is an international ideal," replied Rainey. "They have groups across the world all linked through an organization called the Comintern. I learned about it in Paris. Information could have easily made it here through that network. And someone in the company is tapped into it."

"Surely the command team is above reproach?"

Rainey shook his head. "I don't know what Kennard and Bradley have been up to since last November. And I don't know Charles at all."

Elizabeth's face screwed up in concentration. "I didn't know any of them prior to the starting of the company." She locked eyes with Rainey. "I didn't know you, either."

"I wasn't in New York."

"But you could have been put in place in Rumania."

Rainey thought about that for a moment. "True. But for what purpose?"

"To lead us into a trap?" Elizabeth suggested.

"Like the one we just avoided? You're seeing spooks around every corner now."

"Do you blame me?" Elizabeth asked.

Rainey sighed. "No, can't say I do." He backed towards the tent's entrance.

"What are you going to do?" Elizabeth asked.

"Go ask Appleton why the Cheka is looking for him."

* * *

Over in the Russian camp, one soldier had spent the entire afternoon and well into the evening observing the Americans. He'd been with the 14th Guards for only six days, but he was no ordinary soldier. He had been pulled from Kiev to make contact with an agent, part of the company, when it made its appearance. The Americans all looked alike, but his contact would be wearing a pin as a sign. This was to be used prior to the code phrase.

Felix Tuchenko moved along, smiling and nodding at Americans as he strolled through their camp, keeping a lookout for the pin. And there it was, the small circle of red on the left breast pocket. He found his man in an isolated place close to the Russian camp's perimeter, smoking a cigarette. Silently approaching, he kept his eyes the other man, who eyed him back. He stopped, just out of arm's reach.

The two stared at each other for a short moment before Tuchenko said in English, "Do you have the works of Karl Marx in German? The English version is not as fun to read." His excitement rose when he saw recognition flash in the American's eyes. He had found his man.

"No, I'm sorry," the American replied, "but the Russian version is even more exciting."

The two stared at each other for another moment. "Is it safe here?" Tuchenko asked.

The American took one step forward. "Good a place as any."

"What happened to Clarke? And who is this Captain Rainey?"

The American paused before continuing. "I made an attempt to stop the expedition. Lieutenant Clarke was killed trying to escape the police in Constanta. I figured everyone would just turn around and go home, but then this Captain Rainey came out of nowhere and assumed command. The lieutenant's sister is now along for the trip as well."

The Russian took it in before replying. "Tell me what you know of this captain."

"Not much," the American said. "He's Canadian. Was a liaison officer of some sort, attached to the American forces in France during the war. Knew the lieutenant, Sergeant Kennard and quite a few of the men in the Argonne. They seem to trust him as much as they did Clarke."

"I see. And Elizabeth Clarke is with the expedition now?"

"Yeah, she'll be the one in the baggy officer's uniform. Don't know why she had to come along. It wasn't in the original plan." The American looked around to be sure no one was watching. "My best chance at stopping the expedition without exposing myself was in Rumania. I have no idea what to try here."

"That is not problem," Tuchenko said. "We do not want it stopped." The surprised look on the American's face made Tuchenko smile.

"I don't understand," the American said.

"I do not know either, but those are my orders. We need from you notes on trip. Drop off at these locations as you pass." He handed the soldier a small map of the Ukraine, dotted with check marks along the company's planned route. "We see what can be done to make trip less . . . eventful. Will leave instructions at these same places to keep you informed of wishes should they change."

"And when we make it to Chelyabinsk?"

The Russian handed over a small notebook. "Do not know. If there is need for face-to-face contact, it will always be me. No one else. Understood?"

The American nodded.

"Good. I return to my camp now. Good luck." Tuchenko

walked backwards into the shadows.

16

June 27, 1919
Odessa

They rode in four columns, two of Americans on one side of the road and two of Russians on the other. Although they still tended to look suspiciously at each other, the relations built up from the previous night helped keep everything friendly. Rainey hadn't been able to speak with Appleton the night before, so he rode with him, letting Gilbert ride up front with Krasenovsky.

"OK," Rainey said. "You've been looking at me funny since we've met. Just tell me who I remind you of."

Appleton turned to Rainey. "Sorry. It's someone I knew about fifteen years ago. The resemblance is rather uncanny."

"Fifteen years ago, I was a school boy running around the Canadian prairies."

"So, you have no Russian relatives?"

"Russian?" Rainey exclaimed. "Not that I'm aware of. But I want to talk to you about something else. What are you doing on a Cheka watch list?"

Appleton chuckled. "I've been in and out of their country

since 1903. I'd be surprised if I didn't have a Cheka file."

"That's a file, not a watch list."

Appleton was silent. Rainey continued. "This could very well jeopardize the mission. Who's looking for you?"

"Nobody important, I'm sure." Appleton gave a light kick to his horse and moved up beside Elizabeth.

Yep, he's a spy, Rainey concluded.

* * *

They made Odessa by nightfall. Their patrols discovered no shadowing. When the city came into view, it looked deserted and quiet. Krasenovsky had advised them that once they entered the city, they would see some people, but normal day-to-day activity had been severely curtailed since the French left and Gregoriev had taken control. The Bolsheviks were slowly regaining control of the city, but some strong resistance remained.

"I must report in," Krasenovsky said. "If you want train, follow tracks. Do not know who controls station at moment."

"What are you going to report?" Rainey asked.

Krasenovsky winked. "Not sure, but I make good story for you."

"Thank you, Colonel." Rainey saluted. "Thanks for everything."

Krasenovsky returned the salute, spun his horse around and galloped to the front of his men, yelling commands in Russian. The entire column gave out a whoop and charged into the city, leaving the company on its own.

Rainey reflected back on the previous evening. Krasenovsky had asked what they were doing in Russia. The story about a fact-finding mission story was repeated and he accepted it without comment or question. He didn't seem to care. Rainey wasn't sure if that should make him feel secure or in danger. Krasenovsky was no fool, but maybe the job he had to do was around Odessa and where the company was going did not concern him.

Rainey turned his horse around to look down the double row of horses and wagons. "Sergeant Kennard, two ranks, standard format, you and me up front with the maps. We move out in five."

"Yes, sir," said Kennard, who immediately turned his horse and galloped down the row yelling orders. Elizabeth nudged her horse forward, coming alongside Rainey.

"Orders, Captain?" she asked.

Rainey smirked. "For you, keep your head down. I'll want you third horse down in the lead platoon."

Elizabeth tilted her head. "Why there?"

Rainey leaned forward. "Because snipers go for the lead or trailing riders. Third one down never gets shot at first."

"I see," Elizabeth said, worry on her face. "Third rider down it is. What happens if someone starts shooting?"

"Get off your horse and head for a building for cover. Corporal Bradley will come looking for you."

"Tom isn't staying with me?"

"I need him on point. He's very good at finding shooters before they start shooting."

Elizabeth nodded. "I thought so. Just wanted to confirm." She turned her horse around and went to find her position.

Rainey had to smile. He knew he should stop worrying about her so much. The fact that she didn't insist on being attached at the hip to Bradley was a very good sign. Deep down, though, he stayed worried.

Bradley reached the head of the column. "You have point," Rainey said. "Any dangerous sense and you tell me right away.

Scout out front about fifty yards from the column. Here's a map of the route."

Bradley nodded and nudged his horse forward. Looking back down the ranks, Rainey confirmed that the company was in good marching order, in parallel files. Kennard returned to the front. Rainey looked at the map one last time.

"We're alert and ready to go, sir," Kennard said.

Rainey's gaze rose towards the street that would take them to a main road. That road ended at the train station. He didn't like it. Too many places for a sniper to hide. He would have preferred to just follow the tracks into the station, but there was no way to stay hidden from anyone at the station that way. Bradley appeared down the street, waving. All was clear.

"OK, move 'em out, Sergeant."

Kennard looked back over his shoulder. "Company! Forward!"

The dual columns advanced as one, slowly moving forward into Odessa like a needle being injected into a sick patient. Time would tell if the company would come out the other side.

* * *

The march through the city was nerve-wracking, but peaceful. Any residents they came across gave them, and their foreign uniforms, suspicious stares. A few spit in the street as the company passed. Appleton mentioned that the French had not been very welcome, either. They signified foreign invaders that had kept Russia in the Great War, which was highly unpopular. Combined with the fighting that was still going on, the suspicions lingered like a pall of smoke.

It took them an hour to reach a park a few hundred yards from the train station. Silently, signals were given and a defense perimeter was set up in doorways, wagons parked to guard both ends of the columns and machine guns set up. Men climbed up the sides of the buildings to get up on the roofs, climbing on drain pipes and ledges. Once all was secure, the company settled down to wait.

Rainey spoke to Kennard. "We'll wait here for a while. Send out two patrols. I want a survey of the rail yards done, with intelligence estimates on the force holding it. Make sure Sutton goes along to look at the trains. We have an hour and a half of daylight left. I want reports back before then."

Kennard nodded and headed off to deploy the patrol. Elizabeth was busy distributing ammunition from one of the wagons. Appleton stood in a doorway, observing the rail yard gate through binoculars.

Rainey settled down on a doorstep. His map of the rail yard wasn't very detailed, but it would have to do. He wanted to get into the yard and among the trains undetected. Then, with Sergeant Sutton, he'd look at how to assemble a suitable train, defend it while assembling, and clear out enemy strong points as needed. With only company strength, clearing the entire area first wasn't practical.

He noticed someone standing over him. He looked up to Elizabeth, her figure silhouetted. All thoughts of the rail yards jumped from his mind, like a spring had been released and the thoughts catapulted into oblivion. He felt a complete sense of peace. Safe in a world gone mad.

* * *

"Hello," was all she said. Rainey didn't reply. She gazed down on him, this man her brother had trusted enough to take over the company's leadership, who had shown strong leadership skills so far, and yet seemed flustered in her presence unless she made him angry. She had never met anyone like him before, so like her brother, yet so different. So . . .

Elizabeth had forgotten what she had meant to ask Rainey. She couldn't have said how long they had been looking at each other. It was Elizabeth who suddenly broke the spell, becoming more aware of her surroundings when a lock of her hair came loose from her cap and fell across her face. She brushed it back and thought hard about why she had approached him in the first place. The reason resurfaced in her mind.

"Captain, are we going into the rail yards before dark?"

Rainey blinked, then exhaled. The moment had passed. "Just scouting parties. Once we know what's there, we may try an attack during the night."

"Who are you assigning me to?"

Rainey paused. Elizabeth could almost hear the wheels turning in his head. He obviously hadn't thought that far ahead. "Report to Sergeant Sutton. He'll be looking for a decent locomotive. You can stick with him."

"Yes, Captain."

As she was turning to leave, Rainey asked, "Can you call me Robert?"

Elizabeth paused. "No," she said. "Not yet." The small smile that appeared on his face made her feel warm inside. She knew what words were ringing in his head.

Not yet.

* * *

As darkness overtook the city, the company was on high alert. The patrols had returned and reported to Rainey with good intelligence about the rail yards. Although they did not know who held the station, they were able to identify strong points held by the force in the yard. Sergeant Sutton had led one of the patrols to survey the rolling stock. One locomotive had at least half of their needs already coupled to it. Add a couple of flat cars and a few box cars for the horses and they would be ready to go. Tracks in and out of the yard were in good shape. Rainey assigned Appleton to Sutton's platoon to read the Russian placards.

He was still in conference with the patrols when the alarm went up. Cavalry had been sighted coming in their direction. Rainey bolted to the defense perimeter, Kennard at his side. He heard the clip-clop of hooves on the cobblestones of the next street over, drawing closer every minute yet completely unrushed. Suddenly the noise stopped; only the clopping sound of a single horse continuing. The horseman appeared from around the corner, stopped, waved and resumed a slow trot towards them. It was Krasenovsky, with a big smile on his face.

"Hello, my friends. Ready to attack station?"

17

Krasenovsky informed Rainey that Gregoriev's forces held the station and that he had orders to take the place. With Krasenovsky's men, the plan changed. With just the company, all they could do was sneak into the yards, steal a train and hope they could get clear without too much of a firefight. The odds of success were not great. Now, with double the strength, actually taking the rail yard was a possibility.

The strongest target was the station house itself. The two-story building held several riflemen, a couple of machine guns and what looked like four artillery pieces of a 35mm caliber set for firing over sights. Two aimed over the square in front of the station while two faced into the yards over several tracks that had been left empty. Several teams of men were stationed in and around the rolling stock. Sutton said he figured the defenders had been there for a while with nothing to do. None of Gregoriev's men seemed too concerned about hiding. Sutton's patrol had been able to move among the freight cars and locomotives and spot defensive positions without getting too close.

Timing would be critical. The new plan called for Krasenovsky to fake an assault on the front gate. This force was given a timetable to start the attack, allowing enough time for Rainey's men to infiltrate the yards and get close to the defensive positions among the rolling stock. When the attack began, the company would take these defensive positions by surprise. Then, with the defenders' focus still on the square, the stationhouse could be surprised from behind, finishing the job.

As the command meeting broke up, Krasenovsky put his hand on Rainey's arm. After the others had left, Krasenovsky said, "Cheka does not know what you up to, but fighting for us here will keep them happy. However, someone else involved. Someone who can scare Cheka."

Rainey frowned. "Why are you telling me this?"

Krasenovsky smiled. "I think I like you, believe you not looking to harm Russia. What you do could benefit, yes?"

Rainey shook his head. "I'm not even sure what our objective is. Just get to where we're going and wait to meet someone. But rest assured, if I think it's something really bad, I'll stop it myself."

"I know you will," Krasenovsky replied. "So watch back. Do not know what they want with Appleton."

"Any idea who it is?"

"Tell Appleton: RU. Maybe he know."

Rainey frowned again. Krasenovsky gave him a knowing look. He shook Krasenovsky's hand. "Thanks. Let's go get me a train."

* * *

Elizabeth stood with her back flat against a boxcar, trying not to bang her helmet against the planks. Two privates were assigned to get her to the engine Sutton wanted to take. They had been slowly weaving among the boxcars for about fifteen minutes, moving slowly to their staging point. The lead private waved his hand as the signal to go. She crouched over and crawled under the boxcar, pressing her back up against its other side, her brother's Colt at the ready.

Her emotions were a mixture of fear and exhilaration. Her breathing came in quick gulps, and her head turned constantly, trying to see everything. Other than the two men with her, she only caught glimpses of the company members. At their staging area, a third-class carriage a few cars down from the engine, the privates took up defensive positions just inside each door in case a roving patrol came by. Elizabeth crouched on the floor between the benches to wait. It was so quiet. She wanted to talk to the privates, ask questions, but understood that she couldn't. She knew she had to focus on something in order to calm down.

As she waited, she started to become fascinated with her gun. Her mind started going through her lessons with Jeremy. She could actually hear his voice in her head. *The Colt M1911 is a very reliable weapon. When firing, hold it with two hands, held straight out in front of you. Let it become an extension of your arms. Spread your feet a little more than shoulder width apart. Now move your right foot half a step back for balance. Now, look right down the barrel. Bring it up a little higher so you don't actually see the top of the barrel, just the sight. Aim at something a little lower than where you want to hit to compensate for the kick. OK, squeeze the trigger very slowly . . .*

The first time she fired a Colt, it scared the living daylights out of her, but she was off by only an inch on a target twenty-five yards away. The Colt was a big pistol and kicked too much for her to be very accurate at any greater distance than that.

The sound of crunching gravel stirred her from her daydream. She had discovered that her breathing had now become regular. The window above her was open, letting in a cool, gentle breeze off the Black Sea. She glanced at the window and then to the private by the door. He quickly put a finger to his mouth, telling her to be silent. He had shut his door and had his back to it. The other private, at the far end, had scurried between two benches, out of sight. Elizabeth heard feet climbing onto the carriage platform. She pressed herself back as far as she could go. She held her breath at the sound of the doorknob turning.

"*Podoiti* . . ."

The doorknob ceased turning. Boots crunched back onto the gravel. Two men were out there, talking to each other as they continued their patrol. Elizabeth lifted her head slowly, peeking out from between the benches. The private was back at the far-end door, peering through a crack. He gave a thumbs-up behind his back to his team. All was well.

Elizabeth let out a sigh. Just then, rifle fire crackled in the distance. The frontal attack on the stationhouse was under way.

* * *

Rainey also heard the fight start. He had been thinking about Elizabeth, but the attack brought him right back to where he was. The targets of his current concern appeared startled by the sounds of the initial attack. There were seven of them, manning a machine gun on a flatcar and also armed with rifles. With their attention drawn away, Rainey and Kennard popped up with rifles and shot the two men at the machine gun. The rest of the team swung their rifles around, only to have three more members of Rainey's team pop up behind them and fire. The two survivors looked around furiously, with no idea what to do as Rainey and Kennard, fresh rounds chambered in their Springfields, popped up again and ended their confusion.

This scenario took place exactly the same way at nine places around the yards. The only worries left now were the roving patrols. No one knew for sure what these men would do once the shooting started. As it turned out, they all seemed to charge either for the stationhouse or for one of the locations the company had just taken. That made it easy.

The roar of the artillery firing shrapnel into the square rose over the din of rifle and machine-gun fire. Krasenovsky's force out in the square was doing its best to keep the stationhouse occupied without putting themselves in direct harm.

With a nod to Rainey, Kennard gave a signal to Krasenovsky, who was waiting with twenty of his men and horses out of sight of the stationhouse. They were in a position to make a lateral charge at the back of the building, reaching it before the bigger guns on the platform there could be turned on them. With a quick yell, they were off.

Rainey watched the charge as he ran towards his next staging post. He almost missed the man with a rifle stepping out from behind a boxcar. Rainey was quicker with his Webley revolver, placing a well-aimed shot into the center of the man's chest.

At the end of a line of boxcars, he was joined by Bradley and Gilbert. Their next target was something that hadn't been discussed at the command meeting, something only Rainey had heard from the patrols. In a shack in the middle of the yard, with a clear run to the stationhouse, sat an armored car.

Rainey wasn't sure why he had kept this information to himself. Maybe it was because its presence might have made Krasenovsky's team hesitant to charge the back of the stationhouse. Rainey's group had just gotten assembled when the wall of the shack fell forward and the car emerged. It rumbled forward, heading straight for the stationhouse. As it passed them, they jumped out, grabbing what they could to hang on to its sides. The surprised look on the machine gunner's face became a permanent fixture as Gilbert was quick with a shot into the man's forehead. Bradley shot the driver through his viewing slot, making the car lurch to one side. Rainey, now firmly on top looking down into the car's cabin, shot the two men inside. Bradley had by then reached the controls and brought the car to a halt. He turned around, aiming his pistol to find the two passengers behind him were already dead.

"Another present for Krasenovsky," said Rainey.

Now it was time to begin assembling a train.

* * *

The plan had called for Elizabeth and her escort to wait five minutes after the first shooting started before making their way to the engine. Like clockwork, the first private got up and waved them forward out of the carriage. Once down on the gravel, they began a slow trot alongside a row of boxcars towards the engine Sutton wanted. They stopped at gaps between the rail cars to check before cautiously moving through more open areas. All seemed to be going well.

The locomotive looked old compared to what Elizabeth had seen back in the States. It was small and black, with peeling paint and several dents. A long crease, looking like it had been applied by some immovable object the engine had run into, ran the length of its water tank. As they came level with the coal bin, a large, bald man with a sneering face stepped out of the cab. Quickly raising his pistol, he fired twice, hitting each private with a single round before they could bring their rifles to bear. Quite suddenly, Elizabeth was alone.

Everything seemed to go in slow motion. The first shot, the

gun swiveling for the second shot, and then swiveling again to be aimed at her. At the same time, her view included two arms, fully extended, with a pistol sight aimed squarely just below the center of the man's chest. She felt her right foot move back a bit. While her mind was wondering what being shot and killed would be like, two red splotches appeared on the man's chest, his body jerking twice. His face contorted into an agonized grimace. Silently, she wondered, *Who shot him?* His body stood there forever, fascinating Elizabeth with the slow dance as his gun left his hand, and he collapsed down the engine's ladder to the ground. The barrel of her gun followed the motion. She then noticed the small whiff of smoke rising out of the barrel she was still sighting down. Any doubts about who had done the shooting quickly evaporated.

She didn't move. She couldn't move. She was afraid the man could still jump up and kill her. Then a hand came to rest on her shoulder. She spun quickly, gun at the ready, finger starting to squeeze.

Sergeant Sutton deflected the gun upwards as it discharged harmlessly into the air. "Miss Clarke, are you all right?"

Elizabeth looked down at the two privates who had been ordered to protect her. One was lying face up, eyes wide in surprise, a red hole over his heart. The other was breathing heavily, gurgling as blood ran into the hole in his lung.

Her mind snapped into action. "I'm fine," she said curtly, kneeling by the living soldier at her feet. "Get me a medical kit."

But it was too late. The private took in a big gulp of air, only to hold it for a second before it released under its own pressure, creating the same sound Elizabeth had heard only once before. His body sagged. He was gone. The last thing he'd seen was Elizabeth's face.

She reached over and closed his eyes. She then did the same to his buddy. Around her, Sutton and his team were hurrying through the process of firing up the engine. Someone guided her to a safe corner of the locomotive's cab where she sat down and mindlessly watched the team work to get up steam.

She had killed again. Worse yet, two men had died to protect her. She felt guilt at not being able to protect them. Yet again, she hadn't even bothered to find out their names while they were alive.

* * *

The fighting in the stationhouse was hand to hand, but once the two guns aimed into the square were neutralized, Krasenovsky enjoyed a major superiority in numbers. Only about forty men stood against him in and around the stationhouse. The company secured the yards.

As the firing died down, Rainey surveyed the work of assembling the train, boxcars and two flatcars coupled to the three carriages. The company's wagons were being rolled onto the flatcars. Horses were being escorted into the boxcars. Rainey was installing two machine guns on the roof of the second carriage when he noticed Krasenovsky watching from the stationhouse doorway.

Rainey scrambled to the ground and trotted across the yard. Krasenovsky assumed an imperious stance, a small smile on his face. Taking the hint, Rainey stopped at the bottom step and saluted. Krasenovsky returned it.

"Good battle," the Russian said. "Not too many casualties on our side. Your men fought well." Indicating the preparations in the rail yard with his outstretched arm, he added, "Is rather orderly operation."

"We're just about ready to get under way," Rainey said. "That armored car over there is operational if you'd like it."

Krasenovsky scowled. "Did you know about it before attack?"

Rainey looked Krasenovsky straight in the eye. "Yes, but I knew we could take care of it before it got very far."

Krasenovsky maintained his glare for a moment, then his features softened. "I would not have told my men about it, either. Not good, looking over shoulder during battle." Then he laughed. "Safe journey, Captain. Perhaps we meet again."

Rainey nodded. "I hope so. People like you give the Revolution a good name."

Krasenovsky let out a great laugh from deep in his chest. "Perhaps you put in good word for me with Comrade Lenin."

Rainey came up the stairs to shake Krasenovsky's hand. "If I get the chance, I'll insist he promote you. Thank you for everything, and if we ever meet again, I'll tell you all about what we're doing here."

"Assuming you find out yourself," Krasenovsky said, deadpan. "*Dasvidania.*"

"*Dasvidania,*" Rainey replied.

18

June 27, 1919
Train to Ekaterinoslav

Rainey got a full report from Kennard on the train station battle. The company had lost four more men and two wounded. Two of the dead had been with Elizabeth. As he heard the story of how Elizabeth defended herself against the man in the engine, Rainey's feelings bounced between worry and relief. Worry that she had been left alone with an armed enemy, relief that she had taken the man down by instinct. Sutton said she had acted like a soldier. Perhaps Rainey didn't have to worry about her so much after all.

As the train rolled through the night, Rainey looked around the carriage. Elizabeth was sitting with Bradley, her eyes small slits as she began to drift off to sleep, Bradley attentive as ever. Sitting alone on another bench was Appleton. Rainey figured there was no time like the present. He sat down beside Appleton.

"Not a bad day," Rainey said. "Got a train and, apparently, the Bolsheviks' blessings to continue on."

"I suppose we talked a good game," Appleton said.

"So, no idea why the Cheka is showing your face around?"

"No idea," Appleton replied. "Jonathan and I haven't crossed paths with the Cheka for quite a while."

"How about the RU?"

Appleton's head snapped around. "What do you know about the RU?"

"I don't even know what it stands for, but you obviously do. And I'd say they know you, too."

Appleton sat back on the bench and looked out the window. Rainey waited for the conversation to continue, but Appleton stayed silent. Finally, Rainey got up and looked down at Appleton. "Someday, when we can trust each other a bit more, you can tell me about this RU thing. But I would suggest you make it sooner rather than later. Krasenovsky said that the RU seems to want to just keep tabs on you. And I think they may know where we're going. I find that very disturbing."

Appleton looked up. "How could they know?"

Rainey looked up the aisle towards Elizabeth. "Talk to Miss Clarke. She will have a story to tell you that you'll only believe if it comes from her." He turned down the carriage aisle and sat down beside Kennard.

"Sir?" Kennard asked.

Rainey didn't know how to begin. Kennard could be the traitor for all he knew. He started with an innocuous question. "How do you think Lieutenant Clarke got caught?"

Kennard rubbed his chin. "Purely by chance, I would think, sir."

"But a chance inspection would have occurred before the ship was unloaded."

Kennard turned toward Rainey, brows knit. "What are you getting at sir, if you don't mind me asking?"

Rainey looked hard into the sergeant's eyes. This man, who he'd fought beside, who he respected greatly, and who was a lifer in the US Army. As a lifer, what was he doing here? "Why are you here?" He said it aloud. "I thought the Army was your life."

"It is, sir," Kennard replied, "but when the war ended, I was pushed out the door like everyone else. Not all of us regulars got to stay on. I guess the Army thought I was getting too old. Offered me a training position and a year off before starting. I was twiddling my thumbs, getting extremely bored, when the lieutenant reached out to me."

"I would have figured they would have hung on to an experienced old war horse like you."

"You'd think," Kennard said. "I know I didn't have a say in the matter."

"Did that make you angry?"

"No, more disappointed."

"Meet any Communists who saw your disappointment and tried to recruit you?"

Kennard's face turned dark. "No," he said emphatically.

Rainey couldn't see any fear of discovery in the big sergeant's eyes. Quite the opposite, in fact. He felt comfortable continuing. "The lieutenant said just before he died that there was a traitor among us."

Kennard face went even darker. "I find that hard to believe, sir," he said with just a hint of anger. "Why don't you just say what you're getting at?"

Rainey saw anger in Kennard's face, not fear. That confirmed it. "Sorry, Sergeant, I had to check. I knew it couldn't be you, but I had to ask."

Kennard was still a little angry. "I can vouch for every man in the company."

"I'm sure you can," replied Rainey, "but do you really know what they have all been up to in the last six months? There's a lot of politics going on right now. Loyalties may be a little different now than when we were in the trenches and it was clear who the enemy was. I know that Communists would have been agitating with unhappy returning soldiers. They even tried to recruit me in Paris." He shifted his weight to face Kennard more directly. "Someone's agenda could very well benefit from us being stopped, even if they are not sure why we're here at all. For all we know, Appleton could be trying to screw us, although I'd have to ask myself why he would even bother to show up at the Clarkes' home if he didn't want us to succeed."

Kennard was silent. After a moment, Rainey continued. "Keep this between you and me for now. Don't want to alert the bastard that we're on to him. We'll keep our eyes and ears open. The guy will have to tip his hand eventually."

"Are you sure about this, sir?" Kennard asked, subdued.

"The lieutenant said there was a traitor. I can only conclude that something about the way he was captured told him that. It was less messy to just get the lieutenant arrested as opposed to the entire company. With the leadership gone, the mission would be scrubbed."

The muffled clacking of steel wheels on track was the only sound. Neither spoke for a while, just listening and digesting the theory that one of their own was plotting against them. "It is possible, I have to admit," Kennard said after another long silence. "He'll try again, won't he, sir." It was more a statement than a question.

"Oh yes," Rainey said. "You can bet on it."

"He'll go after you."

Rainey smiled. "I'm too hard to kill, Sergeant. You know that." Then an awful thought crossed his mind. "Elizabeth."

"He'd have to get past young Bradley to do her any harm," Kennard said calmly. "Besides, none of the men know why she had to come along."

Rainey put his hand on Kennard's shoulder. "Our traitor knows more than the rest of the men. From what I saw earlier, I probably don't have to say this, but assign Bradley to her permanently."

"You're right. You don't have to say it."

Rainey smiled again. "Get some rest. We'll talk more tomorrow." He got up from his seat and went to find an empty bench so he could get a little sleep himself.

* * *

Rainey slept fitfully, slowly rocking to the train's motion, coming out of deep sleep every time it stopped for water and then promptly dropping back in when it moved again. In his sleep, he had visions of Elizabeth. She was smiling at him, but always from a distance. She never said a word, just stood there smiling. Then, finally, he saw her approaching him. She looked different. Her hair was no longer down around her shoulders. She was wearing her brother's tunic, open and hanging down to her hips, exposing the big, loose shirt she had on underneath. The trousers were hefted to just below her breasts, held up by suspenders Bradley had sewn shorter for her. The trousers still bunched at her feet, not allowing the puttees to fit smoothly around her ankles. Rainey smiled, thinking she looked both beautiful and ridiculous at the same time.

Then she spoke. "I've done some fitting. I think I can make my own boots look military with the puttees."

Rainey frowned. This seemed odd for a dream.

"Captain?" Elizabeth said.

Rainey suddenly realized he was awake. "Good, good," he answered, a little flustered. "If we have to do some running, your brother's boots will get you killed."

Elizabeth gave a mischievous smile. "What were you dreaming about?"

Rainey shifted uneasily. "Nothing. . . . I don't remember."

She sat down beside him. "Thank you for your kind words at Jeremy's funeral. I'm sorry I haven't thanked you sooner."

Rainey blinked hard to clear his mind of the spell it was under. "That's OK," he said. "You were not in the best frame of mind. You're better now?"

Elizabeth smiled. "Yes, thank you."

Rainey looked into his lap, not sure what to say. He thought about Sutton's report on what occurred as the engine was taken. "You handled yourself very well back there," he said encouragingly, although the tone of his voice was wrong. He sounded more like he was talking to Elizabeth about a tennis match.

Elizabeth stiffened, but didn't turn to him. Her voice was cold. "You think so," she said matter-of-factly, a slight tremble in her voice, but the sarcasm was clear.

Rainey caught her meaning, helping him get back the tone he wanted to project. "You saw a danger, you reacted to it instantly, you removed the danger. Yes, I'd say you handled yourself very well indeed." He was now talking to a new soldier.

Elizabeth leaned towards him, anger showing in her voice. "I killed a man. How is that 'handling' myself?"

Rainey made an effort to make his face look cold and expressionless. "Better him than you."

* * *

Elizabeth stared into his eyes, which felt cold, unfeeling, and yet filled with a deep sadness she hadn't noticed before. Of course, she had never looked for anything in Rainey's eyes before. She began to wonder why she hadn't. From countless boardroom encounters, she had mastered the skill of determining where people stood by how they held their eyes. But there was something about Rainey that made her stay back, as if she feared what she might find if she delved too deeply into his soul. Now here she was, looking deep into his eyes. Rainey didn't turn away, but gazed right back. Elizabeth felt trapped, yet strangely calm.

To break the spell, she reached into her pocket and pulled out a small chain. "I'd like you to have this," she said, lowering the chain and its locket down towards Rainey. His eyes moved, seemingly transfixed by it. "I found it in Jeremy's tunic." She tapped the left breast pocket. "He didn't have it with him when he was arrested. I know how much it meant to him, and to you, during the war. So I think you should have it while we're in Russia. To keep you safe."

* * *

He heard genuine concern in her voice. It gave Rainey a warm feeling. She actually cared. He reached out and took the locket in his hand, quickly springing it open. There it was, the picture that had given him a reason to go on in the last months of the war. He gazed at it, lifted his head to look into Elizabeth's eyes, then back to the locket. "As beautiful as this picture is, it doesn't do you justice," he said, then realized that he had said it out loud. He quickly looked up at Elizabeth, whose face was a mixture of smile and apprehension, eyes wide, corners of her mouth slightly turned up. In the dim light, Rainey couldn't tell if she was also blushing.

He reached for her hand and gave her back the locket. "As much as I appreciate the offer, it's you who needs this lucky charm now. I'll be fine." He put his hand on the sword propped up against the wall.

"Oh, yes," Elizabeth said. "Jeremy mentioned you and your sword in his let . . ." Tears began to fill her eyes. Rainey reached to comfort her, but Elizabeth stood up, blinking away the tears. "I'm sorry. I will get control. I know you don't need a crying woman on the road."

Back in the darkness, Rainey saw, Bradley stood, silently watching. He signaled the corporal forward. As Bradley approached, Elizabeth held up her hand. She paused for a moment, then pushed on. "Just a quick question. How would I . . . take a bath if I wanted to?"

19

June 29, 1919
Ekaterinoslav

It took two days to cover the three hundred miles from Odessa to Ekaterinoslav, which included stopping regularly for water, running slowly to keep an eye on the tracks and stopping to fix the rails a couple of times. Either way, it sure beat being on a horse for three hundred miles. To a large extent, the land seemed mostly deserted. No one confronted them at any of the watering towers or asked for payment for coal. Elizabeth figured the people thought it wise to avoid a train full of armed soldiers.

Elizabeth had been able to sneak a bath during one of the stops. Rainey had not been very helpful, saying the men washed themselves regularly in rivers and streams. However, she obviously required privacy. In the end, it was decided she could wash in one of the water towers. Placing Bradley on guard at the bottom of the ladder (with a BAR in his hands to make a point), she went for a quick swim. She felt quite refreshed afterwards.

As the train proceeded across the Ukraine, Elizabeth began to notice more and more black flags. According to Appleton, they had crossed into Makhno's territory. Makhno the Anarchist.

The train had slowed to a crawl about ten miles outside of Ekaterinoslav as the evening descended. In the distance she heard artillery, the slow rumbles like short bursts of thunder. Through the car window Elizabeth saw smoke rising in several places. The city was under siege.

She moved down the carriage to where Rainey was signaling for Kennard and Appleton to follow him to the front. He was about to signal her as well, and broke into a smile when he saw her already moving towards him.

"How you doing?" he asked, worry in his voice.

"I'm fine," she said, waving it off. "What's going on?"

"I think we've found a front line," he said.

Kennard pulled out a map of Ekaterinoslav and its surroundings and placed it on the bench.

"Charles," Rainey said. "Why don't you start?"

Appleton nodded. "Reports we've collected on our way here suggested that Denikin and his army were moving forward fast. We were hoping we could get lucky and cross the Dnieper either before or after this city was fought over. Looking at the barrage taking place, I'd say the war is here now."

"So we have to abandon the train here?" Rainey asked.

Appleton nodded. "The only way to make it to one of the bridges now is on foot and horseback. We don't even know if either have been blown, but my guess is the main rail bridge is too big and too valuable to both sides to see it destroyed."

Rainey was engrossed studying the map. "And Denikin could already be on our side of the river and surrounding the place. Damn," he exclaimed. "We could be in for a long wait."

Elizabeth piped up. "We can cross enemy lines inside the city."

Rainey looked up at her, then over to Kennard and Appleton.

"We did talk about that possibility," Kennard said.

"So it wasn't Lieutenant Clarke's first choice, either," Rainey said, more statement than question.

When no one answered, he continued. "OK, let's hear it." His face betrayed his surprise when Elizabeth spoke up.

"We break the company into its platoons. Each one gets a map and a route laid out for them. Each one also takes a wagon or two. They make their way to a location, in this case, the bridge, to meet up. Small groups have a better chance of slipping through the streets than the entire company together."

Rainey looked at her. "This was your idea?"

Elizabeth stared back confidently. "Initially, yes. As Sergeant Kennard said, we needed this extra contingency."

Rainey turned his head toward Kennard. "The men are advised?"

"They've been told the drill and can work the plan if necessary," Kennard replied.

Rainey rubbed his face with his hands. "Damn risky. We need more information," he said. "But either way, we can't roll in there with a train. Sergeant, prepare the men to disembark. We're going to have to ride in on horseback. We'll take the train to about here—" he pointed to the map "—and then ride to the outskirts and see who we run into."

The carriage door opened and a private stepped in. "Sir, a mounted patrol has been sighted, moving towards us."

Rainey gathered up the map and handed it to Kennard. "Seems we've already run into someone. I suppose asking the locals might help with our lack of information." He turned to Appleton. "Charles, let's see who they are, what they know and how to talk our way past them. Miss Clarke . . ."

"I know," she cut him off with a smile. "Keep my head down."

* * *

The train came to a stop as the mounted patrol approached with evident caution. The two manned machine guns on the front carriage were enough to give anyone pause. The patrol consisted of seven riders only. Appleton and Rainey walked towards them, their hands out in reassurance.

Elizabeth watched from her window as the two men talked to the riders. After a minute, the riders started to lower their weapons. Rainey signaled the top gunners to turn their guns away from the patrol. Elizabeth could almost hear a sigh of relief emanate from the train, like the machinery itself had made the sound. They had passed muster.

The conversation took about five minutes. The lead rider then shook hands with Rainey and his little party headed off to resume its patrol. Rainey and Appleton trotted back to the train.

Rainey opened the door to the carriage and announced, "Well, gentleman, we have now officially become anarchists." A cheer rose from the men that turned into laughter. Rainey turned to Kennard. "We're going into town by train. We'll pass a checkpoint where we will likely pick up a passenger. We'll disembark somewhere in the south side of the city and be assigned an area to hold against an attack. We'll play it by ear from there. We'll need to pick out some routes to the bridge. Charles, Miss Clarke, will you join us?"

They assembled around the map again and waited in silence for Kennard. When he arrived, Rainey began. "Denikin is in the city. He was able to take the bridge before the anarchists could get enough troops to hold it. The Bolsheviks are here as well, but undermanned as well as trying to arrest Makhno, which seems a bit odd in the middle of a battle. Denikin will take the entire city eventually. A lot of chaos in there right now, which will work for us. Denikin's been slowly moving out from the bridge. He has well-spotted artillery, which so far has taken out any strong points his troops have run across. We'll have to see how fluid the front really is when we get there. Charles, your opinion on Denikin's forces and what's behind them?"

Appleton cleared his throat like he was a professor about to give a lecture. "They are professional, volunteers from the old Tsarist army with Great War experience, well led by men like Colonel Krasenovsky. Against the anarchists, they have been unstoppable. Behind them, however, is virtually nothing. We get free and clear on the other side of the Dnieper and we'll most likely meet no more than bandit gangs all the way to the Volga."

Rainey nodded. "OK, we set ourselves up in whatever defensive positions they give us. They're not very numerous, so they won't likely be looking over our shoulders. Then just before dawn, each platoon will leave at fifteen minute intervals. I want Garcia's out first with the shortest route since he's our bridge battle expert. Gilbert will go second. Sergeant, you head out with Canning's as the third one out and take command of the bridge until I get there. Charles, I'd like to assign you to Garcia's platoon for the language thing. Sutton and MacGregor's platoons will go out together, last, with me. We'll take any of the extra horses and run the river route. I'll want Bradley with me. Have Corelli's platoon spread out across the four groups so they all have some machine-gun firepower. And O'Hanlon can spread his medic team across the four groups, too. My main concern is getting the horses through because it's a long walk to the next possible train station. We'll be doing building-to-building movements and if we run into any of Denikin's forces, try to hide first. Talking is not likely to work here. The wagons each group will have won't make that easy, but there you go."

"Who am I with?" Elizabeth asked.

"I figured I'd take care of you myself this time, if you don't mind," Rainey said. "This will be a very dangerous trip, so I want you close."

She nodded the affirmative, hoping she looked business-like to Rainey.

"Any more questions?"

"Is taking the bridge at my discretion?" Kennard asked.

"Yes, by all means, but remember you have to hold it, too. If you can take it without them realizing you have it, that would be great."

Kennard frowned. "So you want me to be creative."

Rainey chuckled. "And you know you can be. Now get up front and tell Sutton to get this pony show rolling."

* * *

The train rolled up to the checkpoint just outside the city. The artillery hadn't been targeting this part of the city yet; the industrial area looked very much intact. Rainey rode up in the engine and quickly stepped off just before it stopped completely. He strode up to the man who seemed to be in charge and bellowed in his best Ukrainian over the engine's noise.

"We're here to fight. Where is your headquarters?"

The guard commander bellowed back. "Who are you?"

"Company of Americans, well trained, well-armed, come to fight for the Great Makhno and the Revolution. Over in Odessa, they told us to come here."

Information didn't travel very fast in Russia. The train would have beaten any courier from Odessa to Ekaterinoslav, so Rainey was betting on no one being the wiser and everyone happy to have more troops. The guard commander looked over at the train and decided, with a nod, that it was legit. He showed Rainey on his map where headquarters had been one hour ago, but his side was losing ground steadily. He couldn't guarantee it was still there.

Behind them, the company was disembarking on the double. During the last few hours, horses had been saddled in their box-cars and weapons cleaned and loaded. Getting off the train and onto the street, ready to go, would take only minutes. The guard commander assigned a soldier to accompany Rainey and Appleton to headquarters. Kennard would be in command until they returned.

From the sound of the artillery and the visuals on the rising smoke, Rainey figured he could find a clear path to the headquarters and caution was not necessary. Panic seemed to be everywhere as defending soldiers rushed here and there in no organized way. It reminded him of when the Germans made their breakthrough in the spring of 1918; the rear areas were in chaos, panicked soldiers trying to retreat faster than the Germans were coming on.

They reached a hotel to the south side of the city center in about twenty minutes. Inside, a large table strewn with maps sat in the middle of the lobby, the walls and ceiling still decorated fittingly as a fine dining hall suitable for the Tsar. Men were running here and there with scraps of paper. Rainey saw no sense of uniformity in the men or their actions, and felt the prevailing panic. Except for one man, standing behind the table. His full black hair brushed back, oval face with a moustache and a deep crease across the bridge of his nose, he carried a look of authority amid the chaos, even at his diminutive height. He looked up from the maps and saw Rainey and Appleton standing in the wide doorway.

Curiosity crossed his face, followed by a hand beckoning them to enter. With hats in their arms, the two of them approached the table.

"Have you come to arrest me?" the man asked in Ukrainian.

Rainey stopped a moment, confused, then remembered that the man in the patrol had mentioned the Bolsheviks had turned on the Makhnovists just a few days earlier. "Good afternoon," he began. "My name is Captain Rainey. We are a group of American anarchists who have heard great things about Comrade Nestor Makhno. We have come to fight for the freedom of Ukrainia. We have been sent to you. I have a full strength company of men, well-armed, well-trained and well-experienced."

The man stood staring at Rainey, as if unsure what to make of him. "Your Ukrainian is impeccable," he said. "How does an American learn Ukrainian so well?"

"Thank you. Many Ukrainians have immigrated to America," he answered with a smile. "Many to my very neighborhood."

The man laughed and held out his hand. As Rainey took it, the man's face went serious again. "I am Nestor Makhno."

"Comrade Makhno. It is a pleasure to meet you," beamed Rainey.

"You can forget the 'Comrade.' The stinking Bolshevik Trotsky would rather the Whites take over all of Ukraine than have us around. You may want to leave to fight another day. We are in the process of giving up the city."

"Oh, that's too bad."

Makhno shook his head. "Denikin has too many men and complete control of the bridges over the river. We can't stop him with what we have, especially since we seem to be shooting as many Reds as we are Whites. The Bolsheviks keep withholding supplies and tend not to fight except from their trains. A company, no matter how good, won't change that. Denikin has divisions at his disposal."

An idea popped into Rainey's head. "The bridges are key, correct?"

"Very key," said Makhno. "We managed to wreck a section of the Central Bridge, but the Amur Railway Bridge is still intact. Would have liked to destroy it, but I did not have the explosives necessary. It is big and built very well."

"We could get to it," Rainey said, just a little too quickly.

"And do what?" Makhno exclaimed. "It is too late for the city. And you would never get back out. We can blend in with the citizens if trapped. You stick out in your uniforms."

"Think of it this way," Rainey said. "With no bridge, Denikin slows down. He gets the city, but no way to proceed out of the city quickly without the bridge to bring his artillery across. He'll have to stay put for a while, giving you the chance to put some distance between you and him. As for us, we can cross the bridge, blow it, then make our way upstream or downstream to find a crossing and find our way back to you. If we can't, you've just lost a company of foreigners, no big loss. We're fresh and anxious to get into the fight now."

Makhno appeared to think it over. "You would do that? For us? It seems suicidal to me and I cannot order you to do this. It is not our way."

Rainey had heard of the Makhnovists' "democratic" nature. It played well for the company, as they would not be ordered anywhere they didn't really want to go. Hell of a way to run an army, though. "What information do you have of possible gaps in the White lines?" Rainey pressed.

"There are many of those, but no forces to exploit them."

"Point them out on the map."

Makhno pointed out seven possible gaps, explaining he had received the information within the past hour. "But there is no guarantee they are still there," he concluded. "Denikin might have a superior force, but not large enough to cover every route."

Rainey marked the gaps on his map and handed it to Appleton. "Batko Makhno," he began, remembering the unofficial title Makhno's troops had given him. "We're professionals. We can adapt out there better than any of your men. If anyone can make it to the bridge, we can. We'll cut it for you."

Makhno nodded knowingly. "Then go, and may providence be with you. If you get away, ask any loyal Ukrainian where to find us. They will show you the way. We will be retreating to the southwest."

20

June 30, 1919
Ekaterinoslav

The ubiquitous low rumble of artillery fire began again around four a.m. The city's north side was taking the brunt of it. It was a good wake-up call for Elizabeth, but she woke to find the company already up and getting ready to move. She hurried into her pants and tunic, wrapping the puttees as best she could in the dark. She stepped out of her tent to find Bradley waiting.

"Good morning, Corporal. Is the company ready to move out?" Bradley simply nodded and proceeded to take down her tent.

"Good morning, ma'am. Fine morning, isn't it?" she mumbled to herself. She did up the last button on her tunic and headed off to find Rainey. He was standing by a wagon where a machine gun was being set up. She saluted. "Reporting for duty, sir."

Rainey spun around, creases of concentration on his face, but they softened when he saw her. He saluted back. "Good morning, Miss Clarke. Fine morning, isn't it?"

Elizabeth broke out laughing. Rainey looked confused. "That

was exactly what I hoped Tom would have said to me about five minutes ago," she said.

Rainey smiled. "You should know better than that by now."

"I know. Where do you want me?"

Rainey looked back at the wagon. "Right up here. You can help with the machine gun. Just do what the gunners tell you."

And with that, the company split up and moved into the darkened streets of Ekaterinoslav.

* * *

With her helmet on, Elizabeth crouched beside the machine gun as the light of day crept in among the streets. The other soldier had given her instructions on how to make sure the belt fed the gun smoothly. She was part of the team now. Pistol at the ready, eyes concentrating on any unfamiliar movement, glancing back and forth like she had seen Bradley do. Like she had seen Rainey do. Like she had seen all the men do. She may have felt sweaty and dirty, but in her excited state, she could manage to ignore it.

And she was scared. The adrenaline pumping through her body also helped her keep the fear at bay, but she could almost taste it. At least she wasn't alone. She kept checking on Rainey as he moved quickly and cautiously down street after street. She could always spot him by the sword hung on his back. One and a half platoons, trying to move about seventy horses and two wagons, keeping them moving and quiet. From their wild eyes, Elizabeth knew the horses were more scared than she was, or maybe just not capable of masking it as well as she could. The men, on the other hand, looked totally professional.

By full daylight, they were along a riverfront road. The bridge was visible to the north of them about a mile away. The river road looked like it ran all the way there, but Rainey moved the group away from the river. It would be too easy to get caught there or seen from the other side. A few streets in, they had room to maneuver. Nothing was said by anyone; all communication was conveyed by Rainey's hand signals. Elizabeth was starting to figure out what each one meant.

They continued to move forward until the soldier fifty yards up front suddenly thrust his fist in the air and crouched to the ground. The entire group did the same. They stayed down for almost a minute while the front soldier crept to the corner of the nearest house and peered around it. He quickly flung himself back and up against the wall. Someone was there.

* * *

Rainey ran silently to the corner. Pulling out a small mirror, he eased it out past the corner to observe what was taking place there. What he saw didn't please him. Two armored cars and about twenty men were resting, talking loudly and drinking in a broad street about twenty yards from the corner.

Rainey lowered the mirror and leaned back against the wall. The soldier with him had a look of anticipation on his face, asking *What now?* His mind was spinning with possibilities until he decided to mount an attack. Trying to talk their way past had too many risks and would create too much of a delay, as did trying to sneak around them. Attacking had its cons too, but with surprise, a lot fewer of them.

Rainey looked back at the group. He signaled Sutton to take eight men with grenades and two BARs up onto the roofs. He then signaled MacGregor for the wagon with a machine gun. As his team found their way to the roofs, Sutton ran up to Rainey for a quick determination of the situation.

Rainey whispered, "Get set up and then drop grenades into

them. Get your best aimers to try for the two armored cars. We hear a boom, that's our cue to go in with the Browning. Then just throw as much fire down on them as you can."

Sutton nodded and made for a doorway. Rainey looked down the street to see the wagon being backed towards the corner as slowly and as quietly as possible. Soldiers were moving up behind the wagon so as to be in an ideal place to push it forward when the time was right. He saw Elizabeth on the wagon with the machine gun. She had the locket popped open, looking at her picture and frowning.

* * *

All was quiet except for some loud laughter from the White soldiers around the corner. Elizabeth put away the locket, slowly lowered her pistol to the floor and picked up the machine gun belt like the soldier had taught her. She was ready.

Several "whumps" and screams of pain reached her as the wagon quickly sprang out past the corner. A wave of panic struck her as she saw the White soldiers gathering themselves to fire back. Then the machine gun opened up. She watched as the bullets ripped into them. Mechanically, she fed the gun without even thinking about it. It was all over in fifteen seconds.

Turning, she saw Rainey standing beside the wagon. He looked over his shoulder and grinned at Elizabeth. The fear left her immediately. She dropped the belt, picked up her pistol and smiled back. Then she looked at where the White soldiers had been. The armored cars were both smoking hulks and dead men lay everywhere, sprawled at grotesque angles, blood stains on the pavement. An acrid odor she had never smelled before filled her nostrils. Two corpses were on fire, hanging out of one of the cars. She held back some bile and turned away.

"What do we do for them?" Elizabeth asked.

Rainey frowned. "Nothing. We don't have the time."

"So we just leave them there to rot?" As soon as Elizabeth said that, she realized Rainey was right. "Sorry," she continued quickly. "I know, under different circumstances we'd bury them."

"Yes, we would," Rainey replied. The look on his face made her think he wished they did have the time.

* * *

One street over, a lone Russian soldier slowly peered around the corner at the carnage that used to be his unit. Breathing heavily and shaking with fear, he quickly pressed himself back against the wall. *Who were these men?* He had never seen uniformed anarchists before. He took a deep breath to settle himself down, and then ran as fast as he could down the street towards his command post.

* * *

Kennard reached the bridge to find Sergeant Garcia scanning it with binoculars. There wasn't a lot of movement on it and the sentries were not numerous. Kennard brought his own binoculars up to scan the bridge as well.

"Have any trouble getting here?" Garcia asked.

"One pesky sniper, that's all," Kennard responded. "You?"

Garcia smiled. "Like a lovely walk through town."

They surveyed the bridge in silence. "Sure is a big one," Garcia mumbled.

Kennard lowered his glasses. It was a magnificent bridge, spanning the Dnieper River and over a mile long. Without demolition charges, it would be near impossible to bring down even one of its spans. That wasn't what concerned him. He had to figure out a way to take the bridge and hold it long enough to get everyone across. Appleton came up from behind.

"Well, there she is," Appleton said. "One of the longest bridges in the world, and we have to get across."

"Easier said than done," Kennard replied. Something caught his eye to the left. He raised his binoculars and saw a small band of men marching down the road towards the bridge, then swung around to the bridge again. "Garcia," he said, "how many sentries have you spotted?"

"I think four at each end," he replied. "Guess they figure it's pretty secure."

Kennard's binoculars focused on the troop of men marching again. He counted eight of them. A slow grin spread over his face. "Mr. Appleton, how would you like to help us switch sides?"

* * *

Bradley had point when they came upon a park. He had immediately stopped the platoons. Rainey trusted Bradley's senses when they warned of danger, even though neither one of them could see it. Rainey trotted up to the corner to take a look.

The park was spotted with huge trees. A church tower on the opposite side had a commanding view. If there was an observer, he would be there. Several streets converged onto the park. All looked empty, but something was bothering Bradley, so Rainey put his binoculars to his eyes and scanned each street. Nothing was within sight, but there was something about the walls.

Shadows. There were man-shaped shadows on the walls of two streets. He swung his binoculars up to the church tower. It was dark up there under the onion-shaped dome, but he could make out the muzzle of a rifle barrel sticking over the edge. They were waiting. It was an ambush.

"Feelings, Corporal," Rainey said.

"We've been shadowed for about five minutes, sir," Bradley

replied.

Rainey turned to face Bradley, surprised. "Fine time to start keeping things like that to yourself."

Bradley lowered his gaze. "Sorry, sir."

"Don't worry about it," Rainey said. "I already knew. I could tell when you started slowing down and looking around more." Bradley had gone back to surveying the park. "What do you figure now?"

"They're waiting for us here, sir."

That troubled Rainey. They knew the platoons were coming. Taking out those armored cars must have raised an alarm. The question now was what to do. They most likely were watching the other streets so going around wasn't an option. The bridge was just a couple of streets over. They were so close. It was paramount to get the horses across the park.

Rainey signaled Sutton and MacGregor up to the front. "They look like they're waiting for us," he began. "Sutton, take your people and back up and head down to the river with the horses. MacGregor, you and I will keep your platoon here and engage these guys so Sutton can make a dash for the bridge. Sutton, ride fast. When you get there, tell Sergeant Kennard we will be coming in under fire."

Sutton looked concerned. "How many do you figure you're up against, sir?"

Rainey shook his head. "No idea, but the horses have to make it."

Sutton nodded and ran back. Rainey turned to MacGregor. "The trees are the best cover. Spread your BARs evenly. Take half the men into the trees. Aim for the fourth street down to the right. That looks like a main road right to the bridge. Send a fire team up to this roof to keep their guys busy on the opposing roofs. They'll be on their own when making it to the bridge. I'll wait for a strong point to form and hit its flank with the other half of the platoon, then dodge into the trees to follow." He paused to let MacGregor nod confirmation. "Who's your sniper?"

MacGregor glanced over his shoulder. "Miller, front and center." A young private stepped up. "You're with the captain."

MacGregor nodded to Rainey and went off to assemble his men. Rainey started rubbing his scabbard when he glanced back and found Elizabeth right behind him. She was rubbing the locket.

"My brother wasn't kidding about getting fixated on this locket," she said.

Rainey smiled. "I want you to go with Sutton and make a run for the bridge."

"No."

Rainey was dumbfounded. "Excuse me?"

"I'm staying with you," she said.

Rainey sighed. "It isn't safe with me. We're the diversion. Go with Sutton."

Elizabeth lifted her pistol next to her face. "And the company can't afford to lose you. You should be going with the horses. Sergeant MacGregor can handle the diversion. I'll go with the horses if you do."

Rainey didn't have time for this. "I believe I'm in command here and I make those kinds of decisions. Now get your ass down that street and join Sutton."

Elizabeth didn't move, glaring at Rainey with obvious anger. Then her face softened and she said, "I don't want to lose you."

Rainey was taken aback. He was totally lost for words and had to look away for a second to recollect his thoughts. Was she serious? Was she playing some game to get her way? Or was she just concerned about the mission's command structure? Just before a battle was not an appropriate time for this. "Just. Go. Join. Sutton," he said, speaking each word individually and with emphasis.

Elizabeth stepped back. "Be careful," she said, then turned slowly and headed down the street.

Rainey watched her walk away, his mind reeling with her words. *I don't want to lose you.* He shook his head and finally turned back to the task at hand. Bradley had a peculiar look on his face, something like curiosity, Rainey thought. He had never seen the corporal even crack a smile before. "Never you mind," Rainey said. "Keep focused." Bradley's face went back to his standard blank.

And I'll keep focused too, Rainey told himself.

21

The men were up on the roofs, the horses and wagons were ready for their sprint, and the other side didn't seem to have seen them yet. Rainey noticed more movement of the wall shadows over the last few minutes. He felt they had a good chance. First on the agenda was the church tower.

Rainey tapped the sniper on the shoulder. "Private Miller, is it?" The private nodded. "OK, set up for the church tower. There's a sniper up there. When I give the word, take him out."

Miller had acquired a target and signaled to Rainey. It was a long shot, but Rainey preferred to spill out of their street without being in the sights of that guy up there. He hesitated for a second, binoculars focused on the tower, then slowly lowered his hand and touched Miller on the shoulder. The rifle barked once and Rainey saw a sudden movement in the tower's shadows, the rifle suddenly pitching forward and falling to the ground. *Nice shot.* Rainey yelled, "Go!"

MacGregor's team sprinted out of the street and into the trees of the park. Almost immediately, White soldiers began spilling out of two side streets farther up, firing as they went. Several men appeared on a roof and began to rain fire down into the trees, only to be suddenly silenced by the fire team on the opposite roof. The running gun battle had begun.

Using a standard leapfrog pattern, each fire team of four men moved bit by bit from tree to tree, two running, two covering. Rainey's team remained in the street, watching the enemy set up. He had forty-two men including himself to get across the park and he wanted to make the far side before the enemy was able to cut them off. So far, it was looking good. The open run to the park that the enemy had to cover had left them with several casualties from MacGregor's BARs and rifle fire. Rainey hadn't seen a single one of his men go down yet. However, the growing number of enemy soldiers began to concern him. It looked like his platoon, lightly armed, was up against a company-sized force.

Two enemy machine guns were being set up between Rainey and MacGregor. This was the strong point. It would be one point of a crossfire layout. Rainey pointed at the guns for his men to identify the target, then jumped up, firing his Springfield at the enemy position. His team followed, charging across the street.

The determined charge met its objective. The gunners were killed, unable to turn their guns to meet Rainey's charge on their flank. As his team swept by, two of them dropped grenades by the guns. Three seconds later, the explosions wrecked them. The team veered right into the trees.

Another machine gun opened up on the forward left, several bullets whacking into a tree Rainey had just dived behind. Toward his goal, he saw another machine gun being set up right in their path, with an open killing range of thirty yards between it and the trees. They were cut off from their exit. The only move left now was to begin heading down the park toward where Sutton would be crossing. As he looked, the last of the horses and the wagon went by. They were clear. Rainey yelled as loud as he could for the platoon to retreat in that direction. All he could do for the men on the roof was hope they got the right idea and followed, although he could see that the four men up there were still creating havoc.

He barely heard the first low explosion over the rifle and machine-gun fire, but the round got loud very quickly as it whistled in on the park. It exploded behind the platoon, giving them all pause before they beat a hasty retreat. Rainey understood what the enemy was doing. They hadn't actually bothered to penetrate into the trees, but stayed put mainly to keep the platoon in a pocket. Now with artillery from across the river, the White army would annihilate them. Rainey quickly looked back up at the church tower. A soldier was hanging out with flags, signaling the artillery.

Rainey looked around and spotted Miller on his right. "Private, the tower," he commanded.

Miller swung his Springfield around, set and fired. The signalman's body twitched violently and fell back into the belfry. Another artillery round came in and landed only ten yards from Rainey. He was saved by a large tree but saw three of his men go down. Another round was incoming. *This just won't do.*

* * *

As the last of the horses went by her, Elizabeth stopped to look at the beginnings of the action. She, too, saw that the enemy outnumbered the platoon. When the first artillery round came in, she knew they didn't have a chance unless they could cut out of the trees and into one of the exit streets, fast. A machine gun blocked their way.

Sutton rode back to her. "Miss Clarke, we have to keep moving."

Elizabeth turned to face him. "Sergeant, how many men are required to get the horses to the bridge?"

Sutton shrugged. "I don't know, maybe ten or twelve."

Elizabeth turned back to the battle. "Then send ten or twelve. The rest of us have to open an exit for the other platoon."

"We can send back another platoon once we make it to the bridge."

"Captain Rainey and his platoon won't exist if we wait that long!" she insisted.

Another artillery round landed among the trees as if to emphasize Elizabeth's statement. Sutton didn't argue any more. He turned to where his whole platoon was at a stop, waiting. "Binter," he yelled, "Your squad take the horses to the bridge. The rest, follow me."

Sutton charged his horse out into the street. His men followed, rifles and pistols at the ready. And right in the middle, Elizabeth was with them.

* * *

Rainey was running out of options. The artillery, at least, was aiming blind, its rounds falling dangerously close, but near the enemy, too. The machine gun between his men and the exit chattered noisily, keeping them pinned to the trees. It was then that he heard the screams of a cavalry charge. There was Sutton, going full gallop at the machine gun. The gunners had stopped firing and were desperately trying to turn the gun ninety degrees to meet the new threat. The charging cavalry was firing and Rainey saw one of the gunners go down. There was no time like the present.

He shouted over his shoulder. "Go! Go! Go!"

As a unit, the whole platoon got up and charged across the open area toward the machine gun. It had been turned, but its crew were run down by Sutton's charge. More enemy infantry moved toward the gun, taking shots at the horsemen. The trap had been broken and they had to re-establish it if they were to keep Rainey and his platoon from escaping.

* * *

The jolt of adrenaline Elizabeth felt during the charge was exhilarating. She fired a round from her pistol towards the Russians, but since she was in the middle of the pack, she was afraid of hitting one of her own men. She reached the machine gun, which one of the soldiers was turning a hundred eighty degrees, while Sutton and the rest of the horsemen formed a perimeter fire line, guns firing. Elizabeth jumped off her horse, turned it towards their exit street and slapped it on the behind. As the horse trotted off to the safety of the buildings, she turned and stepped up to the ammunition box beside the machine gun. The soldier grinned at her and pulled the trigger while she reached into the box and made sure the belt fed smoothly. Rifle rounds zinged by her, but she ignored them, concentrating on the ammunition belt. She finally took a quick glance to see what damage they were doing. Her helmet's chin strap slipped up onto her face, so she reached up to pull it down.

* * *

Rainey continued to run as fast as he could. He made the clearing just in time to see Elizabeth jump off her horse and start feeding the machine gun. Rainey charged towards her, waving his men on as he did.

Then, to his horror, he saw Elizabeth's head kick back, flinging her body backwards away from the gun, her helmet coming off in the process. She landed hard on her back, her hair flying loose. Rainey cried out, "NO!"

* * *

The shock of the force that hit her helmet was enormous. Before she could even fathom what had happened, Elizabeth was on her back, looking up at the sky and seeing stars. The rat-tat-tat of the machine gun continued to ring in her ears as she became aware of what was happening around her. She had a job to do and she couldn't do it lying on her back. She pulled herself up and got back to the gun belt.

* * *

Rainey was relieved when Elizabeth quickly got back up. Then he was angry. *What the hell is she doing?* As he reached the gun, he paused only long enough to grab Elizabeth and drag her to the street where the horses were waiting. "What are you doing?" she screamed at him. Another soldier right behind him got the hint and took over feeding the belt. Shells continued to fall among the trees, but the platoon was out.

Throwing Elizabeth on the horse, Rainey slapped its behind and it took off down the street to safety. He turned to find another horse. He yelled at the gunners to retreat, only to see them torn apart by a shell. He heard an armored car approaching. Both platoons were past him, some with two riders per horse, galloping away as fast as they could. Rainey leaped up onto his horse and took off as well. As he turned a corner, he could hear machine gun rounds ricocheting off the walls behind him.

* * *

Kennard had heard the battle in the distance before he saw several squads with most of the horses come tearing past at full tilt. He stepped out onto the street and signaled them right on to the bridge. Everyone but him was up on or across the bridge now, except for whoever was engaged in the battle. When the shells started screaming in from across the river, it didn't give him a good feeling.

It was another five minutes before the next set of horsemen came into view. Some of the horses were rider-less and many had two riders. Scanning the horsemen, he spotted Sutton, MacGregor and Elizabeth, and breathed a sigh of relief. As MacGregor came up, Kennard yelled, "Where's the captain?"

"He should be right behind us," MacGregor answered.

"OK, get yourselves across the bridge."

MacGregor looked up at the bridge. "What about the sentries?" he asked.

Kennard smiled. "You'll know when you get there."

He swung himself up on his own horse just as Rainey came thundering down the street. "I've got company," Rainey yelled as he approached.

Kennard yelled back. "We're all crossing, just waiting for you, sir."

Riding up onto the bridge deck, he flew by the sentries. "That's it, let's go," Kennard yelled at them as they passed. The armored car came within view of the bridge as the sentries mounted up and began tearing across the bridge.

Rainey looked over his shoulder. "Is that Garcia in a Russian uniform?" he asked Kennard.

"Yes, sir," Kennard replied with a grin. "I'll tell you about it later."

* * *

About a hundred yards across the bridge, Sergeant Corelli and a small team were waiting. Kennard and Rainey stopped while Garcia and his team continued on with the horses. "We've rigged a little something, sir," Corelli said. "Don't know how well it'll work. I've never blown up a bridge before." The armored car was up on the bridge deck, closing on the team with machine gun firing. Bullets were bouncing off the metal structure, causing everyone to dive for cover.

Rainey looked over at his demolition team. "Wait until the car is over the explosives. Can't have him firing at us from across the gap."

"Assuming we get a gap," said Kennard under his breath.

The armored car continued forward, accelerating to higher and higher speeds until it was over the area rigged to blow. Corelli muttered a small prayer and touched two wires together.

The explosion was deafening. Explosives from mortar rounds and opened 37mm high explosive shells all went off together, throwing a large cloud of dust and debris into the air. Everyone looked on expectantly, hoping to see a section of the bridge fall into the river. But nothing fell. Out of the dust cloud, the armored car sprang forward like a ghost. Then one of its wheels came off and the car sheared to the left, smashing high speed into the bridge's steel girders, coming to an abrupt halt. Rainey could see that the soldiers in the car were dead or dying. That was the good part. The bad part was that the bridge was still intact.

Kennard touched Rainey on the shoulder. "We'd better go sir," he said. Corelli was cursing in Italian and stamping his feet in anger when the bridge suddenly groaned. Everyone stopped to listen.

The dust was settling to reveal a contingent of infantry slowly advancing along the bridge. "Kennard, move 'em out."

Kennard didn't have to say anything. The team was already running as fast as they could, Kennard and Rainey in the rear. Single rifle shots rang out behind them, too far out of accurate range to worry about. The bridge groaned again and then a roar rose up as a forty-foot section of decking finally gave way and fell into the river.

The run across the mile of bridge took less than ten minutes. On the far shore, horses were waiting with a squad of men. They all mounted up as quickly as possible. Rainey passed by Corelli and slapped him on the back. "Good work, Sergeant." Then they raced off along the rail line after the rest of the company.

22

June 30 – July 1, 1919
Central Ukraine

They rode hard through the day. The horses were at a steady light gallop, heading east across the open steppe. No scouting patrol roamed ahead of them. The sun became hotter and hotter as the day wore on, but Rainey wouldn't stop past the few short breaks they took to rest the horses. During the rests, Rainey kept to himself, trying to avoid Elizabeth, fearing that he would explode at her for almost getting herself killed. He also wanted to punch Sutton, but that wouldn't accomplish anything positive, either.

The day seemed to go on forever. They continued on for over twelve hours. An hour into the ride, O'Hanlon had insisted on stopping to tend to the wounded. Rainey assigned MacGregor and his men to stay with the medical group and a wagon as most of the wounded were from his platoon. The rest of the company rode on. MacGregor would catch up when the company stopped to camp.

It was around eight p.m. when they finally came to a halt. A fair size stream ran through the steppe with trees filling the hundred-yard-wide valley the stream had made. A small village was about five hundred yards farther along the tracks. Rainey pointed to the trees, and the entire column pulled away from the rail line as if drawn by a magnet. Elizabeth sighed loudly, her relief at finally stopping plain for all to hear.

Rainey and a squad reconnoitered the woods for about ten minutes. "This will do," he said to no one in particular. He was in a small clearing by the stream and the trees were a little farther apart here. The area was large enough for the company to set up camp.

Rainey dismounted and led his horse the few steps to the stream, where the horse immediately began to drink. Flashlights came on as the men started to dismount, tying their horses to trees and starting to scrounge for firewood. Kennard rode up behind Rainey.

"Captain, your orders?"

Rainey turned. "We'll camp here. The horses watered and fed are the priority. We'll take a long rest here, until the morning of the day after tomorrow."

Kennard nodded. "Shall I send out a patrol to that village, sir?"

Rainey shook his head. "No. It's late. Let's settle in first. We can look it over in the morning. Usual picket duty. And send me Sutton."

Kennard looked at him dubiously, but Rainey waved him off. "He's not in trouble, I just need to hear the story."

"Very good, sir," said Kennard, reining his horse around to return to the men.

Rainey turned back to his horse. It was a fine animal, spirited, but docile from exhaustion at the moment. Stiffness was working its way into his joints as well. He began to stretch his limbs, trying to fight off the inevitable.

"I'm stiff too," came Elizabeth's voice from behind him.

Rainey turned to see Elizabeth still up on her horse, her hair frizzed out and blown back from hours in the wind. She looked exhausted, too; her face dusty, her mouth hanging loose and her eyes like slits.

"I thought it best to put as much distance as possible between us and Ekaterinoslav," said Rainey.

Elizabeth nodded silently. Rainey looked back at the stream. "Come on down," he said. "You can wash up a bit."

"I can't," said Elizabeth.

"Why not?"

"Well, right now, I can't seem to move."

Rainey chuckled.

"You find this amusing?" Elizabeth murmured.

Rainey stepped over to Elizabeth's horse. "I'll help you down." He slowly took her foot out of the stirrup and then reached up for her hand. As Elizabeth slowly began to slide towards Rainey, the horse took a step sideways at Rainey, making him fall backwards. Hanging onto Elizabeth's hand, he started to fall, pulling her with him. Elizabeth made a feeble attempt to grab the pommel with her other hand, but she didn't have the strength. Rainey hit the ground hard with Elizabeth landing on top of him, on her side. On impact, she let out a small cry of pain. They both lay there for a few seconds while Elizabeth's horse joined Rainey's at the stream.

"Guess she was anxious to get you off her back," Rainey said with a grin.

Elizabeth turned her head to look at Rainey. "I still can't

move."

He gazed into her eyes. She returned the gaze, her weariness seeming to melting away. Even after hours of riding, when she probably thought she looked like hell, Rainey still saw the face of an angel. He began raising his face to hers when a set of boots appeared in his peripheral vision.

He let his head fall back to the ground. "Corporal, help Miss Clarke up."

Bradley leaned down, placed his hands under Elizabeth's arms and swiftly lifted her to her feet. She let out a little yell. "Thank you, Tom," she said with a weak smile.

"Walk her around for fifteen minutes to loosen her up before you allow her to lie down and sleep," Rainey said.

"Yes, sir," replied Bradley, who proceeded to slowly lead Elizabeth away from the stream. She winced with every step. Rainey grinned.

He continued to lie there for a minute, feeling somewhat stiff himself, his eyes closed, listening to the sound of the men making camp and the water in the stream careening over rocks. The vision of Elizabeth flying backwards from the machine gun flashed through his mind. He quickly shook it off and reset his mind to duty. He had work to do. He stiffly got up and walked into the camp.

* * *

The night passed quietly under a clear, star-filled sky. Kennard had given his report. They had lost seventeen men in Ekaterinoslav, most of them from MacGregor's platoon during the mad dash across the park and two of Sutton's men who had been manning the Russian machine gun. O'Hanlon and MacGregor had arrived late in the night with the four wounded men they had stopped to care for. How many of MacGregor's platoon had only been wounded he didn't know, but everyone knew the company couldn't go back for anyone. That had been made quite clear back in New York.

Sutton's report was brief. He nervously stated that Elizabeth had insisted on the charge to bail out Rainey and the platoon in the trees. He had no idea she hadn't left with the wagons until they were gathering after the initial attack and he saw her run to the machine gun. Rainey said he'd talk to her about it, but deep down he knew he wouldn't. He couldn't guarantee that the conversation would stay civil. More time needed to pass first.

It had been the company's single biggest loss. Up to now, they had lost twenty-five men. On top of that, seven had minor wounds, still combat capable, and two had more serious wounds that kept them out of action. The losses were disconcerting. There was a good chance they would be crossing battle lines at least twice more before reaching Chelyabinsk. They could ill afford to engage in any unnecessary combat.

Rainey woke the next morning from a sleep disturbed by visions of the Sanctuary Wood, Vimy, Passchendaele, Cantigny, Soissons and the Meuse-Argonne, all mixed together. And some senior commander had kept appearing, saying "acceptable losses." A cool breeze was blowing through his tent and clouds were filling the sky. Rainey stepped out of his tent and looked up. A gust signaled a quickening of the wind.

Rainey saw Kennard with a squad of men, no doubt setting up the next picket. As the squad dispersed, Kennard turned to greet him.

"Good morning, Captain. Sleep well?"

"As well as any other night," Rainey said. "Anything new going on I should know about?"

Kennard shook his head. "All quiet. Just one note. Mr. Appleton wanted to go into the village with the reconnaissance team to collect intelligence. Said he knew the village elder or something. Miss Clarke wanted to go with him. I made sure young Bradley went as well. They left about an hour ago."

Rainey's brow furled. "She's in the village?"

"Yes, sir."

Rainey surveyed the camp. "At least Bradley's with her." He returned his gaze to Kennard. "OK, no change. We'll spend another night here and get everyone lots of rest. Tonight, send a mounted patrol out to see what's in front of us. We'll break camp beginning at 0500 and be on our way by sun-up."

"Very good, sir."

Rainey turned back to his tent. He picked up his binoculars and crossed the stream towards the edge of the trees to take a look at the village. Through the glasses he saw that it was small, with probably less than a hundred people. Watching the dirt road that entered the village from the forest, he saw no signs of life. The first house was about six hundred yards from where he was standing, beyond an open meadow. Rainey made up his mind: he would get his horse and go join the little expedition.

* * *

The village was rustic. Most of the houses had been built at least a few hundred years before. Elizabeth had never seen anything so bucolic. When the patrol first arrived, all she saw was closing doors and windows. The people must be suspicious and fearful. Considering what their country was going through, that was understandable.

Appleton had said he wanted to come into the village to see

an old friend. The patrol proceeded slowly on horseback through the narrow street until coming upon the village square. A brick fountain stood in the middle, once a beautiful structure, but over the centuries it had been worn down. Evidence of bullet marks testified to recent events. Empty rifle cartridges littered the ground. The patrol became very attentive, scanning the roofs and the doorways for signs of danger.

Appleton tied his horse to the fountain. Elizabeth did the same. The team began its survey.

"Pretty quiet, Charles," Elizabeth said.

"I'd say they had a little too much excitement recently," Appleton said. "Let's see if my friend is home."

He went to what looked like a small hall. Using the large ring knocker, he loudly banged on the thick wooden door. Elizabeth scanned the building, thinking something was odd about it. It looked somewhat like a church, but it was missing something. Then it came to her. No crosses were visible. She looked for any signs that might signify what the building was for. Finally, her eyes came to rest on a spot next to the door.

A small Star of David was carved into the brick. This was a synagogue.

A small hatch in the door opened and a set of eyes looked out at them. It quickly closed, followed by the sound of a bolt being drawn back. The big door swung open.

"Charles, my friend," said a diminutive bald man in a black suit. "I have not seen you in such a long time. Please, come in." He was speaking English.

Charles stepped back to allow Elizabeth to go in first, then looked back at Bradley, waiting by the fountain. He nodded reassuringly before going in himself.

The small man closed the door. "And who must this be, Charles?" he asked. "You normally do not travel in such company."

"Rabbi Greenburg, may I introduce Miss Elizabeth Clarke?" Appleton said grandly.

Greenburg's eyes widened. "You must be the daughter of Jonathan Clarke," he exclaimed.

Elizabeth smiled. "Yes, I am."

Greenburg fixed his eyes on Appleton. "I thought Jonathan's son was going to be traveling with you."

Appleton lowered his gaze. Greenburg looked back at Elizabeth. He must have seen something in her face. "I'm sorry, what happened?" He ushered Elizabeth to a chair.

Elizabeth sat down. "He was captured and killed in Rumania. We don't know all the details."

"So you are traveling in his place?"

Elizabeth shot a sharp look at Appleton. "Not to worry, Miss Clarke," Appleton said. "The Rabbi is from Philadelphia originally. I sent a message to him before I left your father to tell him I would be coming back through here with a member of the Clarke family. That is all he is aware of about our mission."

"And I'd prefer not to know any more than that." Greenburg sat down on a bench opposite Elizabeth.

"How long have you been in the Ukraine, Rabbi Greenburg?" Elizabeth asked.

"Oh, about seven years now," Greenburg answered. "Started out as an educational experience, but once the war started, I just sort of stayed around. The people like me, trust me, and I'm a link to a better place. The way I talk about the ol' US of A, I think the whole village wants to get up and move there."

"The village is Jewish?"

"Very."

Appleton spoke up. "What is the situation like now?"

Greenburg shook his head. "The White army had a little battle here six days ago. We lost five villagers in the crossfire. Been pretty quiet since. But the Don Cossacks have been running around raping and pillaging. Their pogroms are focused mostly on Jewish communities."

"Pogroms?" asked Elizabeth.

"It means government authorized violence, in a sense," Appleton explained.

"Don't sugar coat it, Charles," exclaimed Greenburg. He turned to Elizabeth. "They blame us Jews for some disaster and then come in and try and kill us all. That is a Pogrom."

"That's terrible," Elizabeth exclaimed.

"Unfortunately, now a fact of life," said Greenburg.

"Have Cossacks been here yet?" Appleton asked.

"No," replied Greenburg, "but we've heard terrible stories. We're hoping Makhno comes back."

"Well, I can let you know that Ekaterinoslav has fallen. Makhno's retreating south, giving Denikin a free path north towards Moscow. Apparently, the Bolsheviks are on their own in that regard."

Greenburg sighed and looked at the floor. "That is bad news. Makhno and the Bolsheviks don't care whether we're Jewish or not, just whether we oppose them."

"You support the revolution?" asked Elizabeth.

"I support anyone who doesn't try to shoot us." He turned towards Appleton. "From here to Tsaritsyn, you should only run into roving gangs of Cossacks. They appear to be in groups of one hundred or less. However, I've heard a Cossack named Ratinsky has assembled quite a force. A couple of thousand, all on horseback. No idea where he is at the moment. If they find you, they will try and crush you just for being here."

"As long as we only meet the small groups," Elizabeth said, "we should be all right." She looked to Appleton for confirmation.

"Best to avoid them altogether," Appleton said. "Any idea where we might be able to find ourselves a train?"

Greenburg shook his head. "There were some around. Bolsheviks use them almost exclusively. They pretty much took all the trains with them in their haste to leave."

Appleton nodded. "How about bridges? Are most of them intact?"

"I've reliable information that the rail line is clear all the way to Tsaritsyn. No one seems terribly interested in destroying bridges. The main ones over the Donets and the Don are still there. Once in Tsaritsyn, you can follow the Volga up as far as Samara or down to Astrakhan. I don't have information as to who controls Tsaritsyn. Last I heard it was the Bolsheviks, but a White army was going that way."

"If we could only get a train," Elizabeth said.

"Thank you for your efforts, Rabbi," Appleton said. "We'd like to be able to stay and visit, but, you know."

Greenburg laughed. "Oh, Charles. You cloak and dagger types are always in a rush."

An urgent banging turned all their attention to the door. Greenburg hurried to open the view slot, then opened the door. A frightened-looking man stood in the doorway.

"Cossacks!"

Greenburg turned to Appleton. "You must go now. Cossacks

are coming. I've got to get everyone to the forest."

Appleton and Elizabeth looked at each other. "Rabbi," Elizabeth said. "We aren't traveling with just the few men we came into town with."

"Oh?"

Appleton continued. "We have almost two hundred well-armed soldiers camped out in the forest. They can protect you, but you shouldn't just charge over there. Let us guide you."

Bradley was running to the door. "Miss Clarke, soldiers coming."

"We know, Corporal," Elizabeth answered.

"No, ma'am, coming now."

The sounds of horseshoes on cobblestones rang through the village. Bradley pushed everyone into the synagogue and closed the door just as six horsemen entered the square.

Elizabeth got Bradley's attention. "Our patrol?"

"Hidden."

The view slot was open wide enough for her to see what was transpiring in the square. Five of the horsemen had dismounted and were going to various buildings and breaking down the doors. People were being dragged out, screaming. A small boy bolted and began running across the square, trying to escape to the synagogue. A Cossack still on his horse drew his sword and started to run the boy down. Anger rose in Elizabeth. *This is not going to happen right in front of me.*

Sliding back the bolt, she pulled the door open, assumed a shooter's stance, raised her pistol and fired.

23

Rainey had just finished cinching his saddle on his horse when the screaming reached his ears. He quickly trained his binoculars on the village to see people running toward the forest. Then he heard the gunshot, followed by several others.

Oh, shit.

"Kennard!"

Kennard came tearing through the brush like a bull. Rainey turned to face him. "Get the machine guns and mortars set up in a defensive line. Don't know what we're facing, but better to be safe than sorry. And get Gilbert's platoon mounted up and to the village, pronto." He jumped up on his horse and spurred it into a gallop.

* * *

The Cossack took the round dead center in his chest, catapulting him backwards and then sideways off his horse. Everyone else in the square froze, then turned their attention to the synagogue, where Elizabeth stood in the door with her pistol. As the Cossacks began to recover from their surprise, Elizabeth fired again, and again. One more Cossack went down while the rest dodged for the fountain in the center of the square. A bullet smacked into the wall beside Elizabeth, surprising her and making her jump back inside the building. Bradley passed her, going the other way with his BAR. The rest of the squad appeared from their hidden places and picked off the remaining four Cossacks as they approached the synagogue. Caught in the crossfire, they went down like dominos.

The firing stopped. Slowly, Elizabeth stepped out to look at what she started. The young boy who had been running across the square clutched her leg. Greenburg stood beside her.

"Thank you," he said. "But I fear this was only a patrol. There may be more coming."

"Then we'd better get your villagers to the forest," she answered.

The villagers knew the drill. Once the firing had stopped, they poured out of their houses and streamed toward the forest.

Elizabeth looked back to the synagogue. Greenburg and Appleton stood in the door. "Charles, I think we should all get going. Is there anything you need to take with you, Rabbi?"

"Just my Talmud. I'll get it," he said.

She heard another horse coming in at full gallop from the direction of the forest. The villagers parted as Rainey stormed into the square. He spotted Elizabeth in front of the synagogue and hurried to her.

"What's happened?"

Elizabeth looked up at him. "Cossack patrol. We had to stop them."

"How many more coming?"

"We don't know."

Rainey looked down at the boy clutching Elizabeth's leg, face buried in her hip. "And him?"

"Don't worry," Elizabeth replied with a grin. "I'm not going to keep him."

* * *

Rainey smiled at Elizabeth as he steered his horse out of the square to the village's eastern edge. Passing the last house, he looked out over the steppe and saw a large dust cloud rising behind a fast-moving group of horsemen.

"Oh, shit," he murmured under his breath.

He wheeled around back into the village. Just about all the inhabitants had made their way out past the squad guarding the exit by the time Gilbert and his platoon arrived. Rainey rode to meet them.

"Let the villagers get out and then head back to the camp," he ordered. "We'll have to make a stand there. Tell Kennard to pull out every machine gun we have." He turned to where Bradley's squad waited, Elizabeth and Appleton in their midst. "They're only about a couple of minutes out, and there's a lot of them. Let's get out of here."

They all urged their horses forward and galloped to the forest. The village people had all crowded in behind the company, looking nervously around upon discovering this small army hiding in their forest. But anything was better than being caught by the Cossacks.

Gilbert's platoon had just made it back into the forest when the thunderous roar of hooves sounded from the village. From the edge of the trees, Rainey observed the Cossacks as they flowed through and around the little cluster of houses. They slowly spread out across the field. Rainey estimated that there were over two thousand of them.

Rainey spotted their commander on a huge white charger. He

wore a splendid old white Tsarist uniform with gold braid and all the trimmings. Rainey turned to Kennard, standing beside him. "We broke out *all* the machine guns, right?"

"Here, sir, you'll need this," Kennard said, handing Rainey a rifle as he moved off.

Elizabeth appeared beside him. "I'm sorry," she said.

"For what?"

"I shot one of them who was running down a child with his sword."

Rainey raised his binoculars. "Well, we wouldn't have been able to hide from that whole group, anyway. Best we got a decent warning and you got your own pretty little ass out of there."

Elizabeth was silent for a moment before speaking. "What can I do?"

Rainey was concentrating on the Cossacks, still forming up in front of them. *Damn, there are so many!* He lowered his binoculars and answered her. "Go find Charles and see if you can get as many villagers armed as you can. If these guys get into the trees, everyone's going to need a gun. Stay with them. They'll need some leadership."

Elizabeth nodded curtly and went to find Appleton. Rainey noticed Bradley watching him. He angled his head towards Elizabeth. Bradley moved off after her.

Rainey stroked his sword's scabbard. He hadn't thought he was going to need to do that today, but nothing ever goes as planned. "Corelli!" he shouted over his shoulder

"Sir!" came the reply from a distance behind him.

"You got range on the village?"

"Yes, sir!"

"OK, get ready to give them a hint of what they're up against!"

Then he stepped out of the trees.

Standing out on the field alone, staring down two thousand Cossack horsemen, wasn't something he'd ever thought he'd do in his life. He started moving his head back and forth in the universal sign of "no," saying under his breath, "You don't want to do this . . ." while calculating his chances of shooting their commander from here.

The commander slowly drew his sword. That was it. Rainey raised his rifle, lined up his sights just above the commander's head, and fired. At six hundred yards and a head wind, he was hoping to arc one into the man's chest. It took almost a whole second for the bullet to reach the Cossack line. It was bit off, blowing the commander's hat off. The bullet didn't drop like Rainey had expected it to. The man looked a little bit angrier now.

"CORELLI!!!"

Instantly, a faint "whump" signaled that the mortars were hurling their small bombs toward the formed-up cavalry. Rainey waited and watched. The explosions began right in front of the horsemen, then moved in among them. The "whumps" continued, with corresponding explosions all along the middle of the cavalry's line. Rainey thought the Cossacks would stay there forever to be slowly pulverized, but their commander called the charge. Almost in unison, he could see, the mass of horse and man surged forward.

This was it. Six hundred yards, likely to be covered in under fifteen seconds.

"Change ranges!" Rainey heard Corelli command. Corelli knew what was coming.

A mighty roar echoed from across the field as the Cossacks began their charge. Six hundred yards. No point in waiting.

"FIRE!"

He had no idea how many machine guns had been set up, but it was a lot from the sound of them. The loud chatter was accented with the mortar explosions and rifle fire. Rainey scanned the field. The Cossack commander was gone, no doubt shot out of his saddle, back by the village, in the opening barrage of machine gun bullets. Rainey raised his Springfield and began firing. The massive wall of ammunition poured into the field mowed down everything in its path. The middle of the cavalry line ceased to exist about thirty yards from the trees. That was too close, but Rainey was more concerned about the flanks.

He knew Kennard would have rounded the ends of the defensive perimeter for maximum protection of the flanks. "Corelli, take half of your men to watch the rear! Close up with the flanks!" The flanking Cossacks would try to encircle them, but the trees worked to the company's advantage. Rainey ran to take direct command of the right flank. He saw Canning holding his own among the horseman. His platoon was getting into hand to hand among the trees, Cossacks swinging their swords, Canning's men blocking with their rifles and trying to keep shooting. The four BARs on the flank were doing good work. Rainey raised his rifle and dropped a Cossack about to swing a sword at the back of Canning's head. Then he ran in to join the melee.

He turned to see a Cossack lift a pistol towards him. Rainey raised his rifle and pulled the trigger. He heard only a click. He watched as the Cossack discovered that his pistol was also empty. He threw it down, drew his sword and charged his horse at Rainey, blade pointed forward.

Rainey tossed his rifle aside. There was no time to get at his Webley pistol. He reached for his sword. He only had a second before the rider was on him. He raised the sword, easily blocking the Cossack's blade and spun quickly away from the horse. He spun so fast he was able to move his sword lower and put a deep cut into the man's leg through the boot. The Cossack let out a gasp as he tried to rein in his horse and turn for another charge, blood pouring from his boot.

Rainey was unclipping the Webley's holster when two pistol shots rang out just behind him. The Cossack jerked twice and fell off his horse. Rainey turned to see Elizabeth lowering her Colt. She reached behind her and grabbed two clips of ammunition from a bag carried by a villager. Bradley stood back, BAR at the ready.

Elizabeth smacked the clips into Rainey's chest. With a devious smile, she said, "Play Samurai on your own time."

The three then moved off, handing out ammunition to other soldiers as the last of the Cossacks were dealt with.

The machine guns had gone quiet. Their gunners were picking up their rifles and moving to the flanks as well, leaving a small skirmish line to watch over the slaughter out in the field. None of the Cossacks retreated. Even at the disadvantage they found themselves in, they continued to fight until they all died.

And it had all taken less than six minutes.

Rainey picked up his rifle and slapped a clip home. Breathing heavily, he kept spinning around, looking for any horseman still threatening, but there were none. He emerged from the trees to see what the field looked like.

The carnage was devastating. Men and horses lying dead or wounded filled the field. Rainey had thought he'd seen the end of this type of slaughter. His eyes began to blur. He could feel himself slipping from reality. Images of the Great War started popping into his head. The explosions, the machine guns, the barbed wire, the screams of the wounded and dying. The fear you could taste.

"Captain?"

The voice seemed far away, not part of the reality he suddenly found himself in. But his mind gripped hard onto it, trying desperately to leave behind the slaughter and fear.

"Robert?"

His vision began to clear. He was lying on his back, looking up into the face of an angel. His angel. He forced his focus onto the face.

Elizabeth.

"Are you all right?" she said, the worry evident in her voice.

Rainey got up on his elbows, shook his head and looked around. Many of the company were standing or sitting, glazed looks on their faces, as they dealt with what they had just done. They had not committed this kind of slaughter, on this kind of scale, in a long while. And they had never mowed down a cavalry charge like that, ever.

"I'll be fine," he said to Elizabeth.

"I thought you had been shot, the way you fell."

"I'll be fine," he repeated. He spotted Kennard on the edge of the woods, looking over the dead. "Excuse me, Miss Clarke, but I have some things I need to do." He got up, leaving Elizabeth to ponder what was going on.

Rainey joined Kennard to see a tear running down the big man's cheek. He put his hand on Kennard's shoulder.

"The Germans always retreated under that kind of fire," Kennard said, almost to himself. "Why didn't they retreat?"

Rainey tapped him on the shoulder a couple of times. "I don't know. But right now, you and I have to get our heads straight. I need a casualty report and we'll have to clean up the field, with the villagers' help."

Kennard lowered his head and nodded, then slowly turned to return to duty.

They were at it well into the afternoon. The company's men centered on digging a mass grave, completely focused on the work and not what it was for. They worked in silence; everyone, including Rainey, Kennard, the sergeants, Appleton and even Elizabeth wielded a shovel. The villagers concentrated on the horses. There had not been much fresh meat in these parts for quite a while, so both live and dead horses had worth.

When the Cossacks had all been laid in the grave, the villagers came by and spat at them. Elizabeth at first thought how disrespectful that was, but immediately remembered the Cossack drawing his sword and trying to decapitate a young defenseless boy in the village square just for running away. She was tempted to go spit herself. Rainey watched at her side.

The Cossacks were all dead. Every last one of them. Any that had been just wounded had continued to try to fight. They were old, young, proud. Elizabeth had seen one body of a Cossack who couldn't have been more than sixteen years old.

"We should have the hole filled up in under an hour," he said. "You can go get some dinner."

"I helped dig it, I'll help fill it in," she replied.

And she did. Elizabeth insisted on carrying her weight and being involved with the men. Rainey shoveled beside her until the work was done.

The company had losses too, although it all seemed uneven and unfair. Four of Canning's platoon and two from Garcia's, the flank platoons, had been killed. Seven were wounded, one seriously enough from a saber slash to the back that no one was sure if he'd make it through the night. Thirteen against over two thousand. It was so unbalanced. It was modern warfare.

* * *

As night came across the camp, Elizabeth headed for her tent. As she slowly fell asleep, the day's events played out in her mind. Suddenly, she smiled, as one memory came back to her crystal clear.

"They'll need some leadership."

Rainey had recognized her ability to lead. And lead she did. That was significant.

24

July 2-16, 1919
Eastern Ukraine to Tsaritsyn

Five hundred miles.

With a train, it would take a few days. On horseback, it would take forever. Elizabeth counted in her head. At an estimated forty miles a day, so as not to wear out everyone and the horses, it would be seven days making it to the Donets River. Tsaritsyn was two hundred fifty miles past that. Six to seven more days. She found that depressing.

The routine was the same. Each morning, they all rose before sun-up and prepared morning meals. Once fed, the camp was struck and the company loaded up the wagons and mounted their horses by 0800. Elizabeth was now totally indoctrinated into military terminology. They proceeded east following the rail line with short ten to fifteen minute breaks until around noon, stopping at an appropriate location where they took a one-hour break to water and feed the horses and themselves. Then they'd mount up and continue east until around 1800 hours when again an appropriate location was reached. Again, a one-hour rest period would take place during which Captain Rainey would get together with Appleton to see if they could reach the next good spot for a camp near a river or a lake. Invariably, the decision was made to try for the next stop and the company would mount up again and ride into the dark hours until they reached what was deemed a better camp.

For the first three days, the company travelled quietly. Very little conversation took place. Elizabeth found it all mind-numbing, but she was so tired that she just closed her eyes and rode on. On the fourth day, she started to hear snippets of conversation from the men around her, starting with complaints about the scenery never changing. She smiled, knowing now that the men had processed the Cossack battle and were returning to normal.

It was another two days before Elizabeth felt she could approach Rainey. "Good morning, Captain," she said as she rode up beside him.

Rainey looked a little surprised. "Going to ride up front today?" he asked.

"Yes," she answered. "I'd like to get a better view of what's in front of us."

Rainey chuckled. "Looks the same no matter where you look."

Elizabeth sighed. "I know. The men started making comments about it two days ago. How far before we see something different?"

"All the way to Tsaritsyn by the looks of the maps," replied Rainey.

Elizabeth groaned.

"Come on, it's not that bad. Haven't you ever been to Kansas?" Rainey said.

"Riding across it in the hot sun on a horse? No, can't say I have," Elizabeth said.

Rainey laughed.

"You seem to be better today," Elizabeth said.

Rainey looked at her, curiosity in his face. "What do you mean?"

"Since the battle with the Cossacks, you've been pretty quiet and you've kept to yourself." Elizabeth saw a very distinct change in Rainey's expression. "I'm sorry," she said hurriedly. "I didn't mean to bring it up . . ."

"It's OK," Rainey said. "I take it you've been finding the men a little bit more open now, too. We just needed a little time, distance and a chance to talk about it amongst ourselves. Sorry if you felt left out."

"I would think everyone would be used to that sort of thing after the war."

"There wasn't too much of that bold cavalry charge into annihilation during the war, after some initial stupidity in 1914. And none of these boys would have seen any of that coming at them. Some might remember a French cavalry charge at Soissons that didn't go well. Under the kind of firepower we put up, most forces would have broken and run back to the village, like at Majaki. The Cossacks were very brave. It's part of their culture. It also made them very stupid. When we started dropping mortar rounds onto them, they should have gotten the hint."

Rainey's face started going blank. Elizabeth reached out and touched his arm. "I'm sorry. Let's change the subject."

"OK," he said. "Let's talk about you."

Elizabeth was a little taken aback initially, but recovered. "What do you want to know?" she asked pleasantly.

"What exactly were you thinking back in Ekaterinoslav?"

Rainey spoke calmly. Elizabeth figured enough time had passed that this could be discussed without shouting and anger.

"You needed assistance. We provided it."

"Could you not do that again?" Rainey said. "You scared the shit out of Sergeant Sutton when he realized you had not gone on to the bridge with the wagons. When I asked him about it, he thought I was going to shoot him."

Elizabeth smiled, thinking about poor Sutton when he would have seen her at the machine gun. "Is 'scared the shit out of' an official military phrase?"

"I'm serious," Rainey said, more urgency in his voice. "Do we have to have that conversation again about you staying safe?"

"We can't afford to lose you, either," Elizabeth countered.

Rainey paused for a moment. It looked to Elizabeth like a thought had just come to him. Could he have been thinking of that moment back in Ekaterinoslav, she wondered? When she had told him *I don't want to lose you*? He focused on her again and spoke. "The company can go on without me. Sergeant Kennard would take command."

Elizabeth hadn't thought of that. "Then why put you in command at all?"

Rainey gazed out towards the horizon.

"No answer?" she asked. "Is there something about Sergeant Kennard that I don't know about?"

Rainey continued to look away. Elizabeth decided to file that away as a piece of important information to acquire later. For now, she changed the subject. "Tell me about your sword."

Rainey glanced back at Elizabeth. "My sword. Well, it's called a tachi. It's very old, been in my family forever and, like that locket you gave your brother, it's my good luck charm."

"How would your family come across a Japanese sword?"

Rainey shrugged. "Don't know the story. I do know that my great-grandfather carried it against Napoleon and against the Americans when they invaded Canada in 1812."

"So you don't know where he got it from."

"I suppose from his father, but I don't know what my great-great-grandfather did."

Elizabeth leaned back to look at the sword more closely. "What are all the coins and tokens for?"

"Again, I don't know. My father said I would learn all about them in due time. I figure they trace the history of the sword."

"I recognize one on the handle. It's a Lutheran rose."

"I didn't know you were Lutheran."

"I'm not, but one of our board members is and he has the same crest on a ring."

Rainey nodded. "That's interesting. So, what's it like to run a steel mill?"

So it went over the next few days. Once the column got moving, Elizabeth would ride up beside Rainey and they would talk to pass the time, covering everything from personal anecdotes and family to world politics and religion, but never about the mission itself. Neither knew more about it than the other and neither wanted to engage in speculation.

The conversations also developed a new respect that Elizabeth had for Rainey. And, she came to suspect, his respect for her. She found him to be much more worldly than she had expected from an average soldier.

* * *

It was late afternoon when Tsaritsyn appeared on the horizon. Rainey and Appleton had gone out on a patrol the day before to get a sense of who was in charge there. They found that the Bolsheviks had retreated north back on July 1. The city was in White hands. They also discovered that a British Mission had been set up there.

The company slowed its pace approaching the city in order to avoid any sort of panic. It reached a checkpoint about a mile from the city, manned by four men. The company halted a hundred yards from the post while Rainey, Appleton and Bradley rode up to it. The discussion was brief, with Appleton telling a story of having orders to meet up with the British Mission. The post commander waved them through without taking much time for thought.

The company continued to follow the rail line to the outskirts of the city, where they stopped and set up camp in a field. Rainey took Kennard with him to the British Mission while Elizabeth, Appleton and Bradley took a squad down to the river where the Volga boatmen could be found. They would need boats to take them north up the river.

The British Mission was in a ramshackle building that appeared to have been badly damaged during the attack from two weeks before. The front door was hanging from one of its hinges, several bullet marks were scattered across the wall, and a four-foot round hole in the wall exposed the main lobby to the outside world. Rainey addressed the two guards at the doorway with a request to see the Mission commander.

As they were escorted into the office, they came to attention and saluted. A colonel stood up and looked them over. He nodded at his first glance over Rainey's uniform, but raised an eyebrow as he inspected Kennard's. He frowned as his eyes pass over their shoulders and collars, devoid of insignia. He casually returned the salute. "Captain. Welcome to Tsaritsyn. My name is Colonel Mac-Intyre, head of the Mission here. Who are you and what brings you to my little corner of Russia?"

"Captain Rainey, Princess Patricia's Canadian Light Infantry, and Sergeant Kennard of the 28th US Infantry Regiment. We are on a mission for the American president."

MacIntyre looked Rainey over. The Colonel was only about five foot five, but his short cropped hair, wide face with a straight jaw, and general commanding attitude made him seem much bigger. "Americans. Never thought I'd find any of you blighters down around here." He sat down without offering a seat to Rainey or Kennard. "Perhaps you could expand on this mission of yours and what a Canadian is doing with Americans? And why have all your insignia been taken off your sleeves?"

So that's how this is going to go, Rainey concluded. "I did liaison work between the Americans and the French during the war. As I have Russian language skills, I was requested to assist. The Americans have several thousand troops in Siberia, along with a contingent up in Arkangel. Their president wants a wider view of the situation in Russia, especially with this new Volunteer Army down here that seems to be doing very well. As for the insignia, it was thought best we don't advertise who we are."

"So he sends a military unit to investigate things," MacIntyre said.

"Yes, sir," Rainey replied. "He didn't think a couple of bureaucrats could survive the journey alone."

MacIntyre laughed, his head snapping back. "And he'd be right. So, what do you want from me? I'll tell you right now, I don't have anything to offer."

"Nothing needed at all, sir," Rainey said. "This is more of a courtesy call, let you know we're around. Although, a little intelligence on the fighting going on down here would be appreciated."

McIntyre's secretary stuck his head through the door. "Sir, General Wrangel is here to see you."

MacIntyre waved to him. "Show him right in. Gentlemen, if you want good intelligence, General Wrangel is the Russian in charge here and he will have it."

* * *

It was after dark when everyone arrived back at the camp. Rainey had gained some good intelligence from Wrangel. They now knew where the front line was, which was somewhere among the hills about fifty miles north of the city. The bad news was that a fair stretch of the Volga's east bank was still under Bolshevik control, making it difficult to sneak up on the front line before dark without being seen. They would have to wait for dark about thirty miles from the front to make it past Bolshevik troops unseen. Rainey had also heard about Denikin's movements. "It appears we just missed some of his forces in Odessa. He's off to Moscow now as Makhno suspected."

Appleton nodded. "I'm more concerned that Wrangel knows we're here. Did he say anything in particular about us?"

Rainey shook his head. "No. He seemed quite pleased about the fact that Americans are taking an interest in the Whites. I hinted about more support in the future. Other than that, he was a pretty common aristocrat, arrogant prig and all."

"Good," Appleton said. "We should be able to sneak out of town before he takes an unhealthy interest in us. Miss Clarke, would you care to present the details of our negotiations with the boatmen?"

Elizabeth had been able to procure enough boats and barges

for the trip north all the way to Samara. At first, she was surprised that many of the boats used to haul freight were still pulled with tow ropes by men walking along the shore. The company would have moved faster staying on horseback. But Appleton was able to steer them towards a contact of his who introduced them to a group with wooden steam powered boats and barges. Some of the boats had side paddle wheels while others were fitted with more modern propellers. The barges were not very big, but they had sides to them to keep freight contained and there were enough of them to do the job. With little commercial traffic because of the civil war and only one side of the Volga being in White hands, there wasn't much for them to do. When Appleton showed a few of the gold wafers for payment, the entire fleet at the river wanted to be part of it. They had arranged to meet all the boats the following afternoon at a small landing a few miles north of the city where they could embark privately instead of under the prying eyes of the citizens of Tsaritsyn.

When the meeting broke up, Elizabeth lingered for a while, as did Rainey. Before either could speak, Bradley appeared at Elizabeth's side. With a knowing smile, she nodded to Rainey and left for her tent, Bradley with her. Standing alone, Rainey kicked himself for not ordering Bradley to give them a few minutes.

It was late, but Rainey needed a walk, so he took the opportunity to pace around the camp, trying to clear his mind. Soldiers were huddled in small groups around fires, generally in their squads and fire teams. Eventually, Rainey came upon the medical tent.

"Good evening, Captain," O'Hanlon said pleasantly in his Boston lilt. "Are we all bunked down for the night?"

"All is well," Rainey replied. "How are our patients?"

Six soldiers lay on cots in the tent and four more sat on chairs, all looking at Rainey. O'Hanlon looked them over one by one, giving a verbal report on each.

When he had finished, Rainey asked, "You good for supplies?"

"Yes, fine, but if we're going to stay here awhile, I could go out and see what I can scrounge up."

"We're shipping out in the late morning, so you'll have a little time. How are the rations?"

O'Hanlon turned and picked up a sheaf of papers. "According to Sergeant Sutton, we're good for another month. We've been supplementing the supplies with what we could find on the trail. Tonight, we have a rabbit stew. Once into Siberia, we believe, deer will be more abundant."

"Good," Rainey said. Now for what he really wanted to know. "How's morale?" Soldiers confide in officers who are doctors more than their commanders.

"They've recovered from Ekaterinoslav and the Cossacks. They are in good spirits. They'd love to stay off their horses for a while now, me included. That was a long trek across a lot of nothing."

Rainey smiled. "We'll be riding boats for the next few days."

"That would be wonderful," O'Hanlon exclaimed. "We can make up tents with some tarps and keep everyone out of the sun, or rain, dependent on the weather. We've been lucky so far. If it starts raining too much, we'll end up with a lot more sick soldiers."

"Thanks for the report," Rainey said. "The timetable is the same as always. We won't need to start packing up until about eleven, so they can have some free time." He turned to leave the tent.

"Is there something else you'd like to discuss in private?"

O'Hanlon asked.

Rainey stopped without turning around. "Like what?" He said it so quietly that O'Hanlon barely heard him.

O'Hanlon stepped forward and, taking him by the arm, led Rainey out of the tent. "About your changing relationship with Miss Clarke."

Rainey grimaced. Was it that obvious? "What have you heard from the men?" he asked, having no idea how the men felt about whatever relationship they may think existed.

"Nothing from that quarter," O'Hanlon said. "From the start, they didn't like Miss Clarke being on the trip, but she seems to have won them over. I'm just a little more observant than your typical soldier boy. You seem troubled, Captain. I can only assume it has to do with Miss Clarke. I've noticed it since Ekaterinoslav." When Rainey didn't respond, he continued. "I can tell it's bothering you. Command is pretty lonely at the best of times. You've been getting pretty chummy with Miss Clarke, which is fine since we've barely met anyone since the Cossacks. But I also remember the ride out of Ekaterinoslav. You pushed us all hard, but when you left me behind with the wounded so you could keep going, I knew distance from the city wasn't the reason, even if that was what you were telling yourself. I've heard the story about Miss Clarke at the machine gun."

Rainey met O'Hanlon's eyes. "You studied Freud or something?"

O'Hanlon smiled. "Him and another gentleman named Carl Jung. He has some rather new ideas on how the mind works, ideas that I like. If you need someone to talk to, confidentially, I'm here."

Rainey looked into O'Hanlon's eyes, full of calm and intelligence. "Thanks. I'll think about it."

25

July 17-18, 1919
Volga River

Next morning went without a hitch. Rainey was thinking of letting the men sleep in, but they were up at 0500 anyway. The army routine had been ground into them. They had all sorts of time to themselves, but were warned about wandering off too far. Around 1100, they started packing up so they could move through the town by 1300, following the rail line in two columns to reach the rendezvous point by 1530. Some of the boats were already there, each towing a couple of barges. They could see a couple of others farther downstream making their way toward them, the chuff-chuff-chuff of their steam engines adding to the rhythm of sounds. Rainey was impressed. It was quite the little fleet with more than enough room for everyone.

The barges were big enough to hold half a platoon each with their horses. Another barge took the wagons, heavy weapons and a team from Corelli's platoon. Embarking on the barges was carried out over the next hour and they were out in the river and moving upstream by 1700.

As the first day came to an end, there was no sign of battle, but they had not reached where Wrangel had said the front would be. That was another two hours away. Rainey, Elizabeth and Bradley travelled in the lead steamboat, but once they put ashore for a few hours to wait for darkness, they joined their horses on the barge.

Around 2330, the small fleet headed out to cross the front lines. The twelve barges were strung out in a row as close to the middle of the river as they could get. The entire company was lying down with their horses, trying to keep them from getting skittish. No battle *per se* was going on, but an artillery duel was in progress.

Artillery flashes and thunder were noticeable off to the west where White and Red forces pounded each other's positions. Some Red artillery was on the east shore, firing rounds over the company's heads. These flashes were the only light the bargemen could use to keep them in mid channel, although they had a large margin for error considering the river was over a mile across. With the Volga being so wide, the chance of them being spotted from either bank was fairly low. Even so, no one spoke, each man responsible for keeping his horse down and quiet.

Elizabeth was nestled between Bradley and Rainey, each slowly stroking his horse, which seemed to sense their human companions' stress and became a little skittish in response. Elizabeth cooed into her horse's ear to calm it. She noticed Bradley was imitating her cooing and not doing it very well. Elizabeth smiled. His horse was likely distracted enough by his normal state of calm. These were, after all, originally cavalry horses, so she expected them not to be too disturbed by the artillery. Rainey was whispering into his horse's ear. She could hear that he was telling it a story. She smiled and strained to listen, but Rainey was speaking too softly, so she went back to cooing.

* * *

All seemed to be going well, considering. It would take five to six hours to get through the dangerous area. Rainey wasn't worried about the men coping with the stress.

The number of shells screaming over their heads began to increase. The Red artillery had found some important target to zero in on, although how they could see it was beyond Rainey. He figured that they must be spotting the White artillery's muzzle flashes and were trying to take them out. A few minutes later, shells started screaming from the west bank to the east. The artillery duel quickly intensified, the screaming adding to the stress on the horses. At least they didn't have to be as quiet as before, Rainey thought.

The explosion over their heads startled everyone, just above and to the right of the lead barge. Elizabeth let out a brief cry. Her horse struggled, trying to get up. Rainey spun quickly and grabbed its bridle to calm the animal. As the horse settled, Rainey heard Elizabeth gasp.

"You're bleeding!"

Rainey scarcely noticed the shrapnel that nicked his thigh. He looked down quickly, then shook his head. "It's just a graze, nothing to worry about," he said to Elizabeth as she turned back to her horse. He saw a stain on her back. In a panic, he reached for her shoulders, spun her to face him and quickly began unbuttoning her tunic.

Elizabeth slapped his hands away. "What do you think you're doing?"

"You've been hit," said Rainey, going back for the buttons.

"No, I haven't," she said, slapping his hands away again.

"There's blood on the back of your tunic," he said, reaching again for Elizabeth.

"It's mine, sir," Bradley said from behind her.

Rainey's grim expression made Elizabeth turn toward Bradley. His side was bloody.

"How serious?" Rainey asked.

Bradley glanced toward his wound, showing no signs of pain. "Deep but not serious, sir."

"Go get it looked after. We'll take care of your horse."

Bradley nodded, raised himself into a crawl and moved off to find the barge medic.

* * *

Elizabeth looked anxiously after Bradley. "Is he going to be OK?" she asked Rainey.

"He'll be fine. Just nicked him."

"You didn't seem too anxious to get his tunic off," Elizabeth said.

Rainey looked at her coldly, sending a shiver through her body. "I could tell he wasn't badly hit from where the blood was. The blood on your tunic was pretty square in the back, which means if you had been hit, it was going to be a hell of a lot more serious."

Elizabeth felt foolish. "I'm sorry. I'm just not used to being undressed by a man."

Rainey's voice was still cold. "Get used to it." He turned back to his horse.

Elizabeth thought about that for a minute. If she did get a wound, she would be undressed by a man since she was the only woman in the company. She wrapped her mind around that prospect for a moment and decided it would be fine. Better just not to get shot, though.

It then occurred to her that they had been in Russia for almost a month now and had come under fire several times. Apart from the bullet that ricocheted off her helmet, she'd never been hit, but until now had never wondered what to do if she was. She leaned toward Rainey, resting her hand on his shoulder. "What is the protocol for dealing with wounds?" she asked matter-of-factly.

Rainey spun his head around, angry confusion on his face. "Protocol?"

Exasperated, she snorted. "If I get wounded, what do I do?"

Rainey shook his head. "If it's slight, you deal with it yourself. If it's serious, a corpsman will take care of you. If it's really serious, just lie down and wait to die."

"Thank you," Elizabeth said, hoping he'd caught the hint of anger in her voice. She turned to her horse, her back to Rainey. The artillery fire didn't let up. Was he really so cold? She wondered as she stroked the horse's mane. As eager as he'd been to open her tunic just a moment before? A shell landed in the water right behind Rainey, sending up a cascade that drenched Elizabeth. She shrieked as the cold water surprised her. She turned and saw Rainey, also wet, watching her with a sad look on his face. She smiled.

"I'm sorry," Rainey said.

"For what?"

Rainey stared silently a moment, his eyes blanked over. Elizabeth raised her eyebrows, knowing he was at a loss. But then his eyes focused and he answered.

"I'm sorry I snapped at you."

Elizabeth lowered her eyes, then brought them back up to meet his. Rainey inhaled sharply and looked like he was holding his breath. It was hard for her to be sure; the muzzle flashes from the artillery behind him were making her blink. Rainey's eyes were locked on Elizabeth. In these circumstances, she asked herself, shouldn't he be focused on leadership?

Elizabeth could sense that he was fixated on her. She had to admit this made her feel warm inside, but the warmth was mixed with a keen sense of danger. She leaned forward and made sure her voice cut through everything.

"You don't have to apologize. I know you are two men. The kind, charming, funny man I have liked getting to know. And the one who shows up during battles, who frustrates and, quite frankly, scares the shit out of me. Right now, you need to be the Battle Man. So I apologize for bothering you and will now leave you alone."

Another low-flying shell screamed over the barge. Rainey shook his head, his attention turning away from Elizabeth. He grabbed his horse's bridle and stroked its ear, eyes darting over the mass of men and horses on the deck.

Elizabeth's brow was furled in worry. Rainey had never been totally distracted during a battle that she could remember, but just then, she had caused it. She had so totally taken his focus away from everything. He had been panicked at the thought that she had been injured. She realized now how much he cared for her, and not just because she was required for the mission. But she also worried about how easy it was, and how dangerous to the company, for her to be distracting their captain. Elizabeth decided right then and there that she would stay away from her captain when the Battle Man was required.

The artillery duel faded away to the south as the barges slowly continued their journey. The boatmen had proved their piloting skills to the Americans. The chuff-chuff of the engines in the night was reassuring. Now everyone could relax and get some sleep.

* * *

On the shore, a Bolshevik commander held his binoculars to his eyes, watching the slow progression of barges heading north up the river. He could barely make them out in the darkness, but they were past him now and out of the battle zone. His thoughts were disturbed by his being ordered to let the barges past.

"Comrade Stalin," Tuchenko said. "Are they away?"

Stalin lowered his binoculars. "Yes."

"Thank you, Comrade," Tuchenko said. "The Revolution is grateful."

Stalin turned on him. "You tell Trotsky he owes me. I am not going to make it a habit of sneaking his little adventures across my battle lines in the future."

"I will," Tuchenko answered. "I am sure he will understand." He then turned to another man behind him, who was holding two horses. "Come, Colonel. We have a train to catch."

The two of them mounted their horses and rode away, leaving Stalin with his thoughts. *I will definitely file this away to use against Leon Davidovich when the time comes.*

* * *

As the two horsemen reached their unit, Tuchenko turned his horse. "Colonel Krasenovsky, get your men ready. It will be a hard ride to the railhead if we are to make it to Samara before the barges." He then rode off.

Krasenovsky turned and looked at the men in his command, who all watched him in anticipation. Although he didn't know for sure, he was pretty confident that the barges carried the Americans from Odessa. The man from the RU had arranged a train to carry his 14th Guards across to the Volga to watch for these barges. How the RU knew the exact route the Americans were taking and why they were allowed to continue on their journey he didn't know, but they were back in Bolshevik territory now. The Americans would be watched more closely.

"Mount up," he commanded his men. "We ride."

* * *

As light began to creep over the eastern horizon, the fleet put in to shore so the horses could be properly fed and attended to. Rainey sat up on a ridge with a view of the river, map in hand. Elizabeth saw him sitting as she stood on the shore with Bradley. "Tom, I'm going to sit with the Captain for a bit. You need to go see Dr. O'Hanlon. You've been wounded and I don't want you to be walking around like that." Bradley nodded and gingerly walked towards where O'Hanlon was setting up a medical station.

Rainey was folding up his map as Elizabeth approached. She sat down beside him and looked upstream. "How far do we have to go?" she asked.

"Quite a ways," Rainey replied. "We have to get past Saratov and make Samara. At the speed we're going, sixteen hours a day, stops at coaling stations, we should make Samara in four days."

"Then we try to find a train to Chelyabinsk?"

Rainey just nodded, continuing to gaze up the river. They sat quietly for a couple of minutes before Rainey spoke.

"Battle Man?"

Elizabeth started to giggle. She leaned into him, bringing her arm across his back and onto his far shoulder. He leaned back into her and started to laugh as well. They turned their heads to look at each other, the laughing dying down, the pleasant smiles slowly fading, but remaining just a hint in the curved corners of their mouths. Rainey's smile then faded completely as he gazed, un-blinking, into Elizabeth's eyes. *He's losing himself. Nothing else matters to him right now*, she realized. Rainey had become oblivious to every sound and sight. And it was all because of her.

Elizabeth gazed back, a mischievous smile starting to form. She understood what was going on. Rainey was in love with her. There was no denying it now. Before, she had never paid too much attention. Not until their conversations during the long rides before Tsaritsyn. But there had always been something, right from their first meeting in the tavern back in Constanta. Now, it was definitely different. His hard steel-gray eyes had never seemed so soft, his face so innocent-looking. And it struck her that the closest to this look that she had seen was the day they first met and he called her Lizzie. He had broken away from that look very quickly then, even under the influence of alcohol. She wasn't about to let him escape this time. Because now she felt the same way.

"So, are you going to kiss me or not?" she asked playfully.

She caught a shift in Rainey's eyes and Elizabeth's heart sank, thinking she had lost the moment, fearing that she had crossed an unspoken line that soldiers hide behind when they have soldiering to do. She desperately wanted him back and started to lean forward in an effort to drag his soul back to her. But then, the left corner of Rainey's mouth curled up, just like hers. He wasn't going anywhere. He was accepting.

His head started to move towards hers. Her heart jumped, wanting this so desperately. She closed her eyes, her lips began parting, anticipating the texture of his lips coming to join hers. The wait seemed like an eternity. Then she felt his body move. Her mind reeled in confusion. *Where is he going? He's supposed to be kissing me!*

She opened her eyes, lips puckered, head thrust forward, only to see Rainey getting up off the grass. She quickly righted her balance and was about to admonish him when she heard him speak.

"Status?"

Status? You were going to kiss me. What do you mean STATUS?

"We got by with everything intact. A couple of the men had been pushed into the river by their horses during the artillery barrage, but they're fine. Everyone's fed and we'll be ready to depart inside the hour."

Elizabeth turned to see Kennard standing just down from the top of the hill. "Morning, Miss Clarke," he said, nodding.

"Good morning, Sergeant," she replied a little curtly, trying not to sound frustrated or embarrassed.

"O'Hanlon taking a look at Bradley?" Rainey asked.

Kennard nodded "Doc says he's fine. Cut wasn't that deep after all. He's probably a little sore, but you can never tell with him. How about your leg, sir?"

Rainey looked down at his thigh, where a little bit of dried blood stained a tear in his pant leg. "Just a scratch. I wrapped it up as soon as we were out of the artillery. Doesn't hurt at all."

"That's good, sir," Kennard replied, "but I'd still feel better if Doc took a look at it. And the head boatman wants to discuss the next part of the trip with you," he glanced at Elizabeth, "if you have the time."

Rainey caught the glance. "I'll come down with you," he said. "Miss Clarke, please join us." He held out his hand to help her up, but she waved it away and stood up herself. She promptly strode down the hill ahead of them without a word. Rainey looked at Kennard, who made no effort to hide the amusement in his face.

"Do you have something to say, Sergeant?" Rainey asked sarcastically.

Kennard turned to follow Elizabeth down the hill. "No, sir. Nothing at all, sir," he said innocently.

26

July 20-23, 1919
Saratov to Samara

The stop in Saratov was uneventful. Too uneventful. The members of the local Soviet did not seem to be concerned about their arrival. In fact, it felt like they were expected and the locals were rather helpful.

Before re-embarking on the barges, Appleton took Rainey aside. "Something doesn't feel right."

Rainey nodded. "Like they were a little too friendly?"

"You noticed, too," Appleton said.

"I think it has the whole company wondering. First time we weren't met with suspicion. And Bradley has been rather focused on the west shore. I think we have a shadow again."

Rainey watched closely as Appleton's mind came to a conclusion. "Kolochov," he said softly.

"Who?" Rainey asked.

Appleton looked directly at Rainey. "A very dangerous man. He knows we're here. We'll talk during the next rest stop." He hurried towards his boat.

Rainey moved towards the lead boat, where the ropes were being undone from the dock. He leaped on as the propellers started to churn the water, moving the boat and barges out into the river again. When he reached the wheelhouse, Elizabeth and Bradley were already there. She must have noticed the worry on his face.

"You felt it too?" she asked.

Rainey nodded. "Yes. That was way too easy. The only thing they didn't offer us was the key to the city. Kind of makes you wonder what they were told about us." They stood silent for a moment. Rainey continued. "I have a meeting with Charles at our next stop. I want you there."

"Of course," Elizabeth said.

Rainey looked around at the boat crew. Even they seemed edgy, stealing glances at him and Elizabeth, no doubt wondering why they were so special to the Bolsheviks.

Leaving the wheelhouse, Rainey and Elizabeth sat on a bench in the stern. She leaned into him again, putting her head on his shoulder. They sat there for a long time, silently listening to the boat's chugging engine, Elizabeth looking through the wheelhouse's rear window at what appeared to be the side of Bradley's head, scanning to the west. Rainey turned his head, also scanning the shore.

He finally leaned over and kissed Elizabeth on the top of her head. Elizabeth smiled, but didn't move. Rainey finally placed his arm around her shoulder, something Elizabeth had been waiting for ever since they sat down. She snuggled in a little closer, feeling his body's warmth.

"Appleton thinks he knows who's tracking us," Rainey said.

Elizabeth raised her head from his shoulder. "Who?"

"Someone named Kolochov. Ever heard of him from your father?"

"No," Elizabeth said. "Father never wrote much about individual people. Just about Russians in general. There was a note in Charles's State Department file about a report he wrote on a Kolochov fellow, but not the report itself. Could be the same man. I got a sharp reaction from Charles when I mentioned the name back in New York."

"What did the note say?"

"This Kolochov person was with a group called the Okhrana."

Rainey nodded. "That figures."

"How so?"

He turned to her. "The Okhrana was the Tsar's secret police. When the monarchy fell, these guys would have been turned loose to fend for themselves. A lot of them would have ended up in the Cheka. This Kolochov fellow must have moved on to something called the RU."

"What's the RU?"

"I don't know. They must be a pretty new intelligence group of some sort. Colonel Krasenovsky mentioned them to me. And I think Charles is aware that Kolochov is RU."

Elizabeth sighed. She organized all this new information in her head and it all pointed to one conclusion. "They want to use us to flush my father out, don't they?"

"That's my guess," Rainey replied. "It explains us getting the train in Odessa and what we just saw in Saratov. It also explains why our traitor hasn't made any more attempts to stop us."

"So our traitor is a Bolshevik?"

"That's the only group with any kind of international organization that could pass information from the US to Russia. He probably got new orders somewhere early in the mission."

Elizabeth thought about that for a minute. "We had a lot of Bolsheviks around us from Majaki to Odessa. How do we play it?"

"Let's talk with Charles first. I have a feeling he knows this Kolochov fairly well. Did he ask you about our traitor?"

"Yes." She placed her hand on his cheek and tilted his head down to face her. "You owe me a kiss," she said.

"I do?" Rainey asked.

"From back on the hilltop before Sergeant Kennard interrupted."

Rainey smiled. "That was two days ago."

"Did you think there was an expiration date on that?"

"The whole company can see," Rainey said.

"And so can two hundred horses and I don't care," she replied. "You're not Battle Man right now." She reached up and kissed him. She was glad to find he was kissing back.

* * *

The small fleet stopped at a flat stretch of ground that rose slowly from the water's edge on the west shore. Rainey immediately called a command conference with Appleton, Elizabeth and Kennard. They moved away from the men by about fifty yards before speaking. Rainey had Garcia take a squad to see if they could find out anything about their shadow.

"Information we got in Saratov said the Bolsheviks are about to retake Chelyabinsk, but haven't yet," said Rainey. He looked at Appleton. "Let's start with this Kolochov fellow. Give us an idea of who we're dealing with. And this is no time to be stingy with information."

Appleton took a deep breath and started. "When I first met him, he was with the Okhrana. He's an opportunist, however, and a very smart one too. We suspected he started feeding revolutionary groups information about mid-1916 when he saw signs of the Tsarist regime falling apart. When the revolution started, I believe he moved to the Cheka with a number of other Okhrana agents. He seems to have a particular interest in me and Jonathan. He's been keeping tabs on me since way back in 1905. We were constantly avoiding his surveillance. In late 1918, he tried to have us arrested in Moscow, but we gave him the slip.

"He has no loyalty to anyone except himself. He looks to stay ahead of the game by linking with leaders he thinks will end up on top. And he's very good at what he does, so leaders see his value to them. When Trotsky started to organize the Red Army out of all the ragtag Red militias, I'm pretty sure Kolochov left the Cheka and signed on with Military Intelligence. That's known as the RU. Being a student of history, my guess is that he believes whoever controls the army will end up leading Russia after the revolution. Through his Cheka connections, he has a very large web of intelligence, including into the Comintern."

"And he wants to help us make it to Chelyabinsk," Elizabeth said.

"To flush out Jonathan Clarke for him," Rainey added.

Appleton nodded. "That makes sense. But not only to flush Jonathan out. He'll want to know why Jonathan needs a small army. Good thing we don't know that answer or Kolochov would have sent a division to pick us up."

"Why hasn't our traitor taken another shot at stopping us?" Kennard asked.

"He's probably been told to back off," Appleton said.

"We think he got new instructions at either Majaki or Odessa," Elizabeth said.

Kennard nodded. "There were a lot of Russkies around us there."

Rainey continued. "Charles, what are the chances your friend Kolochov is holding off the Red Army from taking Chelyabinsk until we get there?"

Appleton tilted his head, brows knit. "I don't follow."

"OK, let me word it this way. What are the chances of Jonathan Clarke coming out of hiding to make contact with us if the city is under Bolshevik control and your friend is actively looking for him?"

"Not good," Appleton answered. "So you think Kolochov could be holding up the attack until we can make contact?"

"Does he have that kind of clout?"

Appleton nodded. "Quite possibly, as long as it doesn't make the attack window too long. He has a direct line to Trotsky, who can delay battle plans if a valuable reason is given to him."

"Why wouldn't he just let the city be taken and then go in and find my father?" Elizabeth asked.

Appleton turned to her. "Because he knows he'll never find him. Your father and I continued to operate in Moscow for three months after the arrest warrant on us was sent out. Must have frustrated the hell out of him. He'll be more able to find your father in Chelyabinsk by looking for a small American army."

Everyone looked to Rainey, who was staring into space. Finally, he turned and addressed the people around him. "We don't know enough about his plan, but if he's planning on letting us into Chelyabinsk ahead of the Red Army, I say we take him up on his offer."

"He'll have a plan to make sure we don't get out," Appleton warned.

"Then we'll just have to be quick about it."

* * *

As the little fleet approached Samara, Bradley appeared to be having one of his feelings, keeping his eyes peeled on the river's east shore instead of the west. Rainey quickly noticed and started scanning the shoreline through his binoculars. For a time he didn't see anything, but then caught just a glimpse of a rider on a horse. A little while later, he saw that it was three riders. Later still, he counted eight. The shadow was no longer trying to hide.

Rainey tapped Bradley on the shoulder. "No point worrying about those riders now. Signal all the other boats to begin preparations for disembarkation."

"Yes, sir," Bradley replied, ducking into the wheelhouse for the signal lamp. Rainey followed him to speak to the boat's captain.

"How far to Samara?"

"We are about two hours out," the captain replied. "The city will come up on the right." Registering the look on Rainey's face, he said, "I can put you on shore just short of the city."

"No point with the horsemen out there," Rainey said. "Besides I want to meet whoever is expecting us."

The captain shrugged. "Your funeral."

Rainey left the wheelhouse to run right into Elizabeth's worried look. "Our shadow is being bold now?"

Rainey led her by the arm to the stern. "Yes, but if we do what they expect, and we will be doing that, we should be fine. They're just keeping an eye on us."

"I really don't like this," Elizabeth said.

"Nerves are good. It'll keep you on your toes."

"Yes, Battle Man," Elizabeth said, smiling. Rainey leaned down to kiss her, but she pushed his face away. "I will not be a distraction," she said firmly.

"It'll be two hours before we make Samara," Rainey replied. "I think I can afford to put Battle Man away safely for at least an hour."

"In that case . . ." Elizabeth said, her smile even wider now, and threw her arms around his neck.

A cheer went up from the barge behind them.

* * *

Two hours later the fleet approached the river docks, where Rainey noticed a small contingent waiting for them. He was surprised that it consisted of only twelve men, including what he could only assume was an officer.

"I need Bradley. You stay in the wheelhouse until we come back for you."

Elizabeth just nodded, the worry very apparent on her face. This was the moment they would all find out whether their guesses were correct. They would either find an easy path to Chelyabinsk or the mission was over.

Rainey signaled to Bradley and the two of them jumped onto the wharf. Bradley carried his BAR. They paused as Rainey looked over another boat already tied up, where Appleton stood on the deck appraising the welcoming committee. Appleton threw him a glance and made a sign of the letter "K" with his hand. Rainey understood. He stroked his sword's scabbard tip as he approached the soldiers and addressed the officer.

"Captain Robert Rainey, commanding the American Observer

Force," Rainey said in Russian.

"Your Russian is very good, Captain," the officer replied in English. "Welcome to Samara. I am Colonel Anton Pyotrovich Kolochov. Perhaps my friend Charles has mentioned me to you."

Without missing a beat, Rainey replied casually, "Yes, he has. He doesn't like you very much."

Kolochov laughed. "No, I suppose he does not. But he has never understood me."

"So how are things at the RU?" Rainey asked offhandedly.

Kolochov's eyebrows lifted. "You have heard of the RU?"

"Every army needs intelligence. Charles thought ex-Okhrana were more suited to the Cheka."

"As you said, armies need intelligence and the former Tsarist intelligence officers were horrible at it."

Appleton joined them, ending the initial sparring match of who knew more about the other. "Charles," Kolochov exclaimed, like he was greeting a long-lost friend. He gave Appleton a bear hug. Appleton didn't respond. "How good to see you again. How long has it been?"

"It's been a year since you last shot at me," Appleton said calmly.

"Ah, yes. But if I recall, you did shoot back. You should not have run away. I would not have taken my shot. Are you still carrying that huge knife of yours?" Appleton pulled back his coat, exposing the Bowie knife on his belt. "Always liked that knife," Kolochov said. He turned back to Rainey. "You must tell me the story behind the very unusual sword you are carrying. Perhaps over dinner. Bring Miss Clarke along, and Sergeant Kennard, and of course," waving a hand at Bradley, "Miss Clarke's guardian. My men will take your men to an area a few hundred yards from here where they can set up camp."

Rainey glanced at Appleton, who looked calm but couldn't hide a hint of his hatred for Kolochov. He had never seen Appleton like this before. "I can't leave my command until we are set up in camp. Perhaps later, say in two hours? And Sergeant Kennard will need to stay with the men."

"Excellent," Kolochov replied boisterously. "I will send my assistant to fetch you in two hours." He switched to Russian. "In the meantime, Sergeant Vladin here will show you the park. I look forward to dinner."

Kolochov saluted. Rainey returned the salute and they all turned to walk away. Rainey leaned over to Appleton.

"Think you can get through a dinner without killing the man?"

27

July 23, 1919
Samara

The table was filled with food of all kinds. A large candelabrum with lit candles sat squarely in the middle surrounded by several bottles of a clear liquid that Rainey could only assume was vodka. He thought it was quite a spread considering all the shortages he'd seen throughout the Ukrainian countryside.

In the room with Kolochov was only one man, wearing a German major's uniform. Rainey froze at the door upon seeing the German.

"Captain, I believe you know Major Dietrich?" Kolochov asked.

Elizabeth turned to Rainey. "What is it?"

"Oh, my God," Rainey exclaimed. "What the hell are you doing way out here?"

Dietrich laughed, crossing the room. They hugged each other. "I could ask you the same, Robert, my friend. It is so good to see you."

"When I stopped running into you after Vimy, I thought you

were dead."

"Reassigned to the Russian front," Dietrich said, "and then an easy posting as part of the occupation forces."

"Please," Kolochov said, spreading his hand towards the table. "Sit. Eat. Drink. Enjoy yourselves. Then we can talk about the world. I am anxious, Captain, to hear your views on how the new Europe will look after your time at the Paris Conference. And Miss Clarke, I would like to hear about your impressions of my Mother Russia."

Paris! How the hell did he know about me at Paris? Rainey began to wonder how much access to information Kolochov had.

Appleton hadn't moved from the doorway yet. Elizabeth gazed across the table of food and stepped forward to a place behind a chair. The intent was evident. Rainey nudged Appleton's elbow towards the end chair with its back to the door, nodding towards a side chair with a clear view of the door. Bradley took that seat, beside Kolochov. Dietrich took the chair between Bradley and Appleton while Rainey took the remaining position between Kolochov and Elizabeth. It was as if a giant chess game was under way.

Kolochov nodded and they all sat down. He proceeded to take up a platter of kielbasa and slide some onto his plate, passing it to Bradley. Dietrich did the same with the perogys, setting the scene for the rest of the party to follow suit. As the food was passed around, all sat in silence until everything was served.

Kolochov and Dietrich dived into their food first without hesitation. Rainey looked at Appleton and then Bradley, and getting no distinct message from either of them, stared a moment at his plate, shrugged and began to eat as well. The others joined in.

They had been eating silently for about ten minutes when Kolochov finally spoke.

Leaning over to Rainey and grabbing a bottle of vodka, he said, "So tell me, Captain. Where are you from in the Great US of A?" He poured some into Rainey's glass and then into his own.

Rainey thought for a second, chewing his food as he considered his answer. Dietrich would no doubt have told him something. The question may just be a test.

"I'm not American. Canadian, actually."

"Ah, yes. Peter mentioned that. Such a small world we live in. Who would have guessed that you would have run into Peter way out here?"

"We military types do tend to get around," Dietrich said with a smile.

"Yes, you do," Kolochov replied. "But not just military types. Is that not right, Charles?"

Appleton's stone face rose and stared Kolochov in the eyes. "Diplomats travel quite a bit," was all he said.

"Diplomats." Kolochov almost spat the word. "Honestly, Charles, are you still calling yourself that?" Turning his attention to Elizabeth, he continued. "Miss Clarke, I am sure Mr. Appleton has not told you much about himself.

"I know enough," she replied. "I have my own sources of information, including access to a report on you."

Kolochov's eyebrows rose. "Really? There is a report on me at the US State Department? I am flattered. No doubt written by Charles. I can assure you that if you want to know the real me, you must spend a month with me. You will find I am a rather boring office worker."

"Pretty flamboyant dinner for a boring office worker," Appleton mumbled.

Kolochov ignored him. "I take it you are on your way to see your father. May I ask why?"

Elizabeth showed no discomfort at this direct, shrewd question. Her prompt response told Rainey she had been prepared for this. "The company needs him home. Although women have made big strides over the last few years, my presence in the boardroom is not overly welcome."

Kolochov nodded his head. "I see. Perhaps a little revolution in your country could rectify your board's view on women." He began to laugh.

Elizabeth reached for a bottle of vodka and poured herself a glass. "I'm sure we'll get there just fine without resorting to shooting anyone," she replied, downing the vodka in one shot. She glanced at Kolochov, who looked impressed, and then at Appleton, who looked surprised. Rainey was surprised too, which Elizabeth must have realized when she caught his eye. She looked at her glass. "That is quite nice. Is it local?"

Kolochov leaned across Rainey towards Elizabeth. "I believe it comes from somewhere around Kiev. I am glad you like it." He leaned back in his chair as Elizabeth poured herself another glass. "But to the business at hand. I would like to offer my assistance in helping to find your father."

Appleton stepped in. "I'm sure you have more important things to do than to search for wayward American diplomats."

Kolochov glanced at Elizabeth. "There is that word 'diplomat' again. I find it odd that Charles had no problem getting out of Russia, but your father needs a small army. I could have easily arranged his departure."

"In a pine box, no doubt," Appleton replied.

Kolochov scowled. "Please, Charles. You should know me better than that."

"I know you all too well," Appleton said, not looking up from his food.

Kolochov turned back to Elizabeth. "Unfortunately, Charles has seen only the official side of me. Yes, I have done some terrible things for the Revolution, but I am secure in the knowledge that I am on the side of right. Once we have won, I can go back to my family life in Novgorod."

"You've been doing terrible things since well before the Revolution," Appleton retorted.

Kolochov smiled at Appleton, the cruelty apparent in his eyes. "Come now, Charles. You are not still angry over Natalia, are you?"

Rainey had never seen the look on Appleton's face before. Pain and fury. Appleton lowered his head and forcefully stabbed at a piece of meat.

Kolochov turned to Rainey. "But enough about why you are here. I'd like to hear how you and Peter met, Captain?"

Rainey had been eating quietly, casually taking in the conversation, trying to show little interest. He knew it was now his turn. "In a shell hole outside of Ypres. Spring 1915."

Dietrich smiled. "Yes, I remember. The attack on your regiment. We could not figure out who was still there shooting at us. Damned Canadians did not have enough sense to run when facing an entire division."

Rainey resumed his story. "I was stuck out in no-man's land coming back from a patrol. Since my side was shooting up a storm, they'd have killed me if I tried to keep going. So I played dead in a shell hole when this ghost from hell suddenly appeared and fell down beside me."

"Got knocked down by an explosion," Dietrich interjected.

"I glanced over, noticed his rifle was in two pieces and he wasn't moving, so I ignored him until he woke up a few minutes later."

Dietrich picked up the story. "So there I was, lying on the ground, the battle raging around me. I wasn't shot and didn't feel any bayonet. I saw my comrades running by in the opposite direction as the bullets were flying. We were still on the attack, but I felt considerably safer in the hole, so I decided to play dead too. Then I noticed Robert's sword and moved towards him to get a better look. When I touched it, Robert moved so fast I couldn't react."

"Rolled over, brought my pistol up and pulled the trigger," Rainey replied. "Fortunately for Peter, my gun was plugged with mud. We stared at each other for a few seconds and then both of us broke out laughing."

Dietrich continued the story. "The battle settled down, we introduced ourselves, talked about all kinds of things until it was dark, and then made our way back to our own lines. We gave each other souvenirs. I still have your cap badge, Robert," showing it to the table.

"And I still have yours," replied Rainey, pulling it out of his right breast pocket.

"But you met again?" Kolochov appeared fascinated.

"Yes, about five times," Rainey said. "It was almost like we were looking for each other every battle. Last time we met would have been Vimy."

"I was one of the last men off the ridge and Robert made sure

I made it out," said Dietrich. "My regiment was then rotated to Russia."

"I missed you at Passchendaele," said Rainey. "Would have made all that mud at least a little worthwhile."

"But how did you end up leading this group?" Dietrich asked.

Rainey hesitated. The look on Dietrich's face didn't tell him anything, but Dietrich ever so slightly nodded his head. He was following orders.

"I was posted as a liaison officer with the American Army," Rainey said, "because of my combat experience and I could speak French and German. Spent most of 1918 with them where I met Miss Clarke's brother. When this little expedition got put together, I was asked to lead when Lieutenant Clarke couldn't."

"Fascinating," Kolochov said. "It was a terrible war. But was it a just war, Captain Rainey?"

Here it comes, Rainey thought. Kolochov wanted to see if he could find a wedge to use between the company's command group. Rainey replied without hesitation. "Not even close."

"Really?" Kolochov asked. "I would have expected a different answer from the victor's side. Would have made for a great debate between you and Peter."

"I saw what it did to my brother," Elizabeth said. "Nothing could justify what he went through."

Kolochov looked around the table. "So we seem to all be in agreement. The Great War was not just. It follows that taking Russia out of the war was the right decision. I believe the current conflict here in Russia is just. We are freeing the peoples of Mother Russia from the tyranny of the Tsar."

Appleton could see where that was going. "Replacing it with another tyranny isn't exactly freeing the people."

Kolochov cocked his head to one side. "Tyranny in the beginning, yes, but tyranny is required for the Revolution to survive. Perhaps you should read Marx and then you will understand what we are doing in Russia."

Appleton smiled knowingly. "I am well acquainted with Mr. Marx's theories. The weaknesses in those theories lie in human nature. May I quote Lord Acton, 'Power corrupts. Absolute power corrupts absolutely.' History shows that ambition will always override good intentions."

Kolochov scowled. "You have so little faith in us, Charles. I firmly believe that our leadership will step down once our just war is over."

Appleton smiled. "No, you don't. Besides, don't they have to export the Revolution to the rest of the world first?"

Kolochov shrugged. "I suppose, but that should take only a few years, a decade at the most. The decadent capitalist systems will have fallen apart by then and we can raise the people against their oppressors."

"As if you believe that," Appleton remarked. Kolochov ignored him.

"So why has this civil war started?" Elizabeth asked. All eyes focused on her, but no one answered. "No one at this learned table cares to field that question?"

"It's complicated . . ." Appleton began.

"No, it really isn't," Rainey replied. "Democracy has never come out of the barrel of a gun. Britain took centuries to get where they are. France took two side trips into dictatorships before it stuck. Russia hasn't had any basis for democratic development. To think they could just transform into a democracy is very wishful thinking. This civil war is about trying to take power away from the aristocrats who have shown themselves to be incompetent and did nothing but show contempt for the Russian people, and those same aristocrats trying to take back their supposed God-given right to power. Throw in a couple of warlords thinking only about themselves and you get the chaos we've been marching through."

Rainey resumed eating; only the sound of his knife and fork working on the plate broke the silence. Kolochov leaned back in his chair. "Captain Rainey, I have to agree with you."

"Then you will agree that your civil war will also go further out of control with no democracy at the end of the road," said Rainey.

Kolochov continued eating, evidently giving himself time to find a way around that statement. Then an idea lit up his face. "The right leadership will maintain its sights on democracy. I refer you to the American War of Independence. The result was independence from England with a democratic system of government. And it happened under George Washington."

Rainey smiled. He looked over at Dietrich, who was also smiling and gave him a slight nod. "Yes, George made it happen because he wasn't interested in becoming the King of America, which is what his army offered him when the Continental Congress didn't pay them. If Washington had ambitions in that direction, democracy would have withered away. Whoever controls the army at the end of a conflict has political power if he wants it. Washington didn't."

Kolochov wore a shocked expression. "You have a command of American history I did not expect from a Canadian."

"They're big, they're powerful, and they live next door," replied Rainey. "It's a good idea to understand them, especially since they invaded us twice."

Kolochov laughed. "Well, my friend, perhaps we have a

George Washington-type leader here in Russia."

Rainey glanced back at Dietrich, who was still smiling. They had once had a similar discussion in a shell hole.

"I doubt it," Rainey replied. "Washington came from a somewhat democratic system. None of your leaders have."

"Robert, this reminds me of our discussions in the craters," Dietrich said.

"We're in better surroundings here," Rainey said.

Everyone at the table laughed, except Bradley, who had been eating throughout the conversation with one eye on the door. Kolochov finally noticed him sitting on his left as Bradley scraped the last bit of food off his plate. "And you, Corporal. What do you think of all this?"

Bradley looked up at Rainey, who nodded. Rainey had never heard an opinion of any kind from Bradley and so was just as curious as Kolochov appeared to be. Bradley turned his head to Kolochov. "What I don't understand is why so many people have to die for ideas that will never work."

Rainey looked at Bradley with shock. Appleton's and Elizabeth's faces betrayed surprise, too. That was the longest sentence any of them had ever heard from the man.

Kolochov looked around the table at each of his guests, his gaze coming to rest on Appleton. He shook his head slightly as if discarding one thought and settling on another. "Interesting point of view." He turned to Elizabeth. "Miss Clarke, this has been quite an interesting discussion. It is very refreshing to hear Charles tonight. I have never heard him speak so eloquently and passionately. He always had secret motives in his mind whenever we met. So, in the spirit of co-operation, I would like to assist in your expedition."

"As I said earlier, we . . ." Appleton began. Kolochov held up a dismissive hand, his gaze never leaving Elizabeth.

She shifted into negotiation mode. "And what kind of help can you possibly offer us?" she asked, a nonchalant tone to her voice.

Kolochov looked intrigued. "I have a troop train here in town that's headed for the front. We can make room for all of you and your equipment. And I can supply a letter of transit to assist you in passing through areas under our control as well as assign you a battalion as escort all the way to Chelyabinsk."

Elizabeth didn't even blink, but Rainey recognized her look that meant her mind was working overtime. *He just confirmed that he knows where we're going.*

"You seem misadvised as to our destination," Elizabeth said, "but I can see how the train and a letter of transit would be useful. The battalion, however, would attract too much attention. In return, what do you think we have to offer you?"

Kolochov leaned back in his chair. Rainey wasn't sure whether Russians played poker, but this fellow was acting like he held a winning hand. "It is obvious to me," Kolochov said, "that your father has in his possession something very valuable. Although I am sure he does not want it to fall into my hands, the fact that he doesn't want to give it over to my enemies is also clear, otherwise he would have done so by now. Therefore, since I cannot reach him, my next best option is to help ensure he gets it out of Russia."

"Your army is advancing," Rainey slipped in. "Why not just wait until you catch up with him?"

Elizabeth gave Rainey a look similar to what a parent gives a child who says something out of line. Kolochov smiled. "Risk. My enemies may find him first, and I am sure Charles has told you how skilled Jonathan Clarke is in avoiding capture when I am looking for him."

Appleton nodded knowingly. Silence fell over the table. This has to be alarming to Elizabeth, Rainey realized, but then thought with admiration that she had an excellent poker face, herself. Kolochov seemed all too well informed as to their exploits across the Ukraine. He didn't want to help. He wanted to follow.

"Your offer is enticing," Elizabeth replied. "I would like to take it under advisement until the morning, if I could, so I can confer privately with my staff." Rainey smirked. *So now we're her staff.* Elizabeth gave Rainey another of her *Don't be a child* looks.

"Very well," Kolochov said. "Join me for breakfast tomorrow at seven. We can discuss further terms and arrange for your group to join the train. It is planned to depart at noon tomorrow. It has been a wonderful evening and I thank you greatly for this opportunity to meet up with my old friend Charles. I must now retire as I have some other government business to take care of. Major Dietrich, if you would care to escort our guests back to their camp. I am sure Sergeant Kennard is getting concerned about them."

"My pleasure," Dietrich said.

Kolochov got up from the table. "Good night, and I will see you all in the morning."

28

"So, what are you really doing out here, Peter?"

Rainey, Dietrich and Elizabeth walked together, dropping back from Appleton and Bradley on the way back to the camp. Dietrich didn't answer right away. Rainey kept quiet, knowing that a response was coming.

"Let's go for a walk," Dietrich said. "We have much to catch up on."

Rainey stopped in his tracks and looked Dietrich in the eye. "I trust you, Peter, but not your associate."

Elizabeth had heard Dietrich's response and had stopped as well. "We need you at camp, Captain," she said formally, revealing a slight edge of fear in her voice, hoping he would take the out and follow her.

The three stood there, looking at each other like they were at a party and the conversation had run out. Elizabeth stared coldly and calmly at Rainey, her pleading visible only in her eyes. Dietrich did the same, with a little more pleading apparent in his face. More was going on than they knew, and Dietrich seemed to want to tell Rainey what that was.

Rainey turned to Elizabeth. "I'll be along shortly. Tell Sergeant

Kennard to mention it to the pickets."

She stood without moving, as if trying to will Rainey into going with her, before apparently admitting defeat, lowering her gaze and stepping back.

"Don't be too late," she said authoritatively, turning and walking away.

The two men watched her fade into the darkness, catching up with Bradley, who had waited for her. She spoke him. "Tom, I didn't know you had views on . . ." Rainey heard, before her voice faded out into the darkness.

Dietrich chuckled. "Are you in command, my friend, or is she?"

Rainey smiled. "She just worries about me."

"Like a wife?"

Rainey scowled. "No."

They walked along the edge of the town, following a lit path. Rainey got right to the point. "Well, what are you doing out here in Siberia?"

Dietrich looked around casually to make sure no one was within view or earshot, and then reached out his hand. Rainey took it and they immediately exchanged the Masonic handshake. Rainey smiled. "I'm so glad you wore your Masonic ring back in 1915. I would have killed you otherwise."

"I know," Dietrich said. "I will never stop thanking you for that."

"I must admit, I was a little worried about you tonight until the George Washington part of the conversation."

Dietrich released Rainey's hand. "I have to keep my Masonic roots hidden. Your muddy gun lie was appreciated. Bolsheviks are paranoid about allegiances to anyone else but them. As you might have guessed, I don't make a very good Bolshevik. But the General Staff thought I could put on a good show."

Rainey continued walking, not showing any response to Dietrich's words in case someone was watching. All they would see is two old friends reminiscing. "General Staff. I take it you mean the German General Staff."

"Yes."

"And you realize that it probably doesn't exist anymore, or that what there is of it likely has no memory of you being out here?"

Dietrich smiled. "That had crossed my mind."

"So, you're an agent with no home. Why didn't you just head home when the war ended?"

"Easier said than done," Dietrich replied. "I was getting pretty close to Kolochov and concluded that anything I could learn about the Bolsheviks would be invaluable to someone. Kolochov is pretty far up the Bolshie ladder. He has direct access to Trotsky."

"That I already knew."

"Did you know he's already looking internationally? He's using the Comintern to spread a worldwide intelligence network for the RU. And I am to be his key person for Germany."

With that, Rainey did stop. He looked squarely at Dietrich. "He trusts you that much?"

Dietrich laughed. "As much as he trusts anyone. But without having to report to anyone, it was easy for me to become fully immersed in my role. So now I am to coordinate Communist actions in Germany from behind the scenes. In a sense, it puts me in control of making sure the Bolsheviks do not get too strong a foothold in my country."

"You're going home?"

"I leave tomorrow."

"You're playing a very dangerous game, my friend," Rainey said.

They walked silently for a moment before Dietrich continued. "My intelligence could be dangerous if I gave it to whatever German government exists right now."

Rainey nodded. "Considering how chaotic conditions are now, it would very likely make it back to Moscow and they'd have you killed."

Dietrich continued. "I have to trust someone in the world. Can I trust you?"

Rainey didn't hesitate. "Of course you can. You're going to have to now that you've told me all this."

"I would like to send my intelligence to you."

Rainey stopped walking again and looked at his friend. "Me? What am I going to do with it?

Dietrich reached out and touched his shoulder. "I think we know each other very well. We have both seen the madness and uselessness of modern war and want to try to make the world better. Much of the world is in chaos and if a bit of well-placed intelligence can avert another war, I would want it placed regardless of who anyone thinks I'm working for."

"I don't run in those circles, Peter," Rainey said.

"Your Mr. Appleton does. Do you trust him?"

Rainey stood quietly for a moment, contemplating what his friend was asking of him. He was right. The United States will be the new world power democracy and Appleton was tapped into their State Department. "Trust is relative to men like Charles. I'll need some time to work things out," said Rainey. "You still have my family address in Canada?" Dietrich nodded. "Then send it there. I'll pick it up if I get out of Russia in one piece."

Dietrich smiled back. "You will, my friend. Men like us, we're survivors. Besides, you still have your sword to protect you."

Subconsciously, Rainey reached for and stroked the scabbard. "Famous last words," he replied. "If I hadn't shown up in Russia, what would you have done?"

Dietrich frowned. "I do not really know. Considering the alternatives, the Bolsheviks are not that bad for Russia. Perhaps I would just convert for real." Then his face turned serious. "Are you aware that you have a traitor in your unit?"

"Yes," Rainey replied without hesitation. "Do you know who it is?"

Dietrich was taken aback. "You know? Robert, you never fail to surprise me."

"What do you know about him?"

"Only that he exists," said Dietrich. "He will try to slow you down at a key moment in the future."

"Figured that," Rainey said, almost to himself.

"There's more," Dietrich said ominously. Rainey stood silently, waiting for him to continue. "My Russian isn't the best, but something is planned for before Ufa. Something about separating some of you."

He looked Dietrich straight in the eyes. "Thanks. I'll keep that in mind. So, no idea who my traitor is?"

"I am sorry, my friend," Dietrich said with a tinge of fear in his voice. "Kolochov insisted that even he not know the identity. His contact has been one RU agent and from what I know, there has been only one direct contact made, somewhere before you reached Odessa."

"Is that agent here?"

* * *

Out near the edge of camp, a shadow approached a soldier sitting on a stump, the red dot pin on his left breast pocket. He wasn't really guarding, but was able to take a short shift while the actual guard went to get some first aid. The soldier had come up behind the guard and knocked him to the ground and then offered to stand his post until the guard could get the gash on his arm treated. The guard had no idea the soldier's knife had made the cut.

The shadow moved closer. "Do you have the works of Karl Marx in German? The English version isn't as fun to read."

"No, I'm sorry," the soldier replied, "but the Russian version is even more exciting." The shadow came into the light. It was the same Russian from Majaki.

The soldier stood up. "Did you get my reports?"

The agent nodded. "We were only able to retrieve a few of them, but they were enough."

"That's fine," the soldier said. "Nothing much happened between Ekaterinoslav and Tsaritsyn except us slaughtering a Cossack cavalry regiment."

The agent's ears perked up. "That was you?"

"You heard about it, then?"

"Just that Ratinsky's Cossacks disappeared off the face of the earth shortly after your unit disappeared from Ekaterinoslav. They were twenty-five hundred strong."

"Now they're twenty-five hundred dead," the soldier said matter-of-factly. "Idiots charged into over twenty machine guns and mortars." The soldier shivered, remembering the attack. "Let's get to business. I don't know how long the guard will be gone. What am I to do?"

The agent stepped closer, lowering his voice. "We will be putting your unit on a train to the front and have made arrangements to get you into Chelyabinsk very late in the evening two days from now. What we need you to do is stay close to your command group from here on and find out where your group goes in the city. Once you discover where Miss Clarke's father is hiding, leave a note at this address near the train station." He handed the soldier a slip of paper. "And keep them there while we get it surrounded. We will begin the attack around four a.m. after you get there. Make sure your unit gets held up until we can cut off any escape route."

The soldier thought for a while, then answered. "I think I can do that. But don't be too slow. I can only slow them down so much without them wondering what I'm doing."

The agent smiled. "Not to worry. Comrade Kolochov has assembled crack troops to capture you with."

"And the men will be treated fairly and freed to return to the US?"

"Of course," the agent said. He then backed into the shadows and disappeared.

* * *

It was an hour later when the crack of a twig brought the soldier to attention, rifle at the ready. Gazing into the blackness, he could barely make out the figure some ten yards away.

"Protocol," he said.

"Patience," the figure said back in a familiar voice.

The soldier lowered his rifle. "Hello, Captain."

Rainey came out of the darkness to be illuminated by the fires of the camp. The soldier was the sniper from Ekaterinoslav. "Private Miller, isn't it?"

"Yes, sir."

Rainey smiled. Always good for morale to remember names. "All quiet out here tonight?"

"Yes, sir. Nothing out there but the wild animals," Miller replied.

"You hear them?"

"Yes, sir. Reminds me of home."

"Where's that?"

"Colorado, sir."

Rainey nodded. "You miss home?" Rainey asked.

Miller grimaced. "Yes and no. I love the wilderness, but I can get that anywhere. When I got home, people seemed scared of me and I missed my war buddies. Is that odd, sir?"

Rainey shook his head. "Not at all, Private. I think you'll find most of the men feel very much the same. That's why they're here."

"What was it like when you went home, sir?"

Rainey hesitated a long moment before answering. "I haven't been back yet. Been almost five years."

"I'm sorry, sir."

Rainey smiled. "Nothing to be sorry about. People get on with their lives and you come back to find yourself a stranger. I guess my experiences coming back from Singapore before the war showed me that. Even my family treated me a little differently. Haven't been anxious to experience it again."

"I actually know what you're talking about," Miller mused.

Something caught Rainey's eye. He touched a tear on the left arm of Miller's tunic, through which a white bandage showed. "What happened to your arm?"

Miller gave it another look. "I got knocked down in the dark by the sarge. He sent me to get fixed up while he watched my post.

I was only gone about ten minutes."

Rainey nodded. "Well, I'd better inspect the rest of the picket. Have a quiet night, Private."

"Thank you, sir," Miller replied.

Rainey slowly moved through the dark to the next picket position, mentally logging his conversation with Miller for future reference. It was probably nothing.

* * *

Elizabeth stood in the doorway of her tent, looking out among the campfires. Her mind was turning over the night's events. She knew she wouldn't sleep much tonight, so she finally decided to take a walk. Next to hers was the medical tent and she opened the flap to see O'Hanlon.

"Good evening, Captain. Quiet night?"

O'Hanlon's large body turned from the table. He tossed small bandages with blood on them into a bag to his right. "Ah, always a pleasure, Miss Clarke," he said in his warm lilt. "Quiet, indeed. Only a wee gash on Private Miller's arm to deal with tonight."

"How did he get that?" Elizabeth asked.

"Well, the story goes that he got accidentally knocked down by his sergeant in the dark while on picket duty. But I was thinking the cut was rather straight and clean for something that should have been caused by a rock or a branch."

Elizabeth smiled. "Well, then, Mr. Holmes," she said. "What does deductive reasoning tell you actually happened?"

O'Hanlon's big smile brightened the room. "Elementary, my dear Miss Watson. He was cleaning his bayonet or knife on his sleeve and cut himself by being careless. His sergeant came up at that time and sent him off to me to get fixed up."

Elizabeth cocked her head to one side. "Why would he concoct a story that his sergeant could dispute directly?"

The glint in O'Hanlon's eye sparkled brightly. "Because he fooled his sergeant into knocking him down. Therefore, the sergeant's story will concur."

"Ah," Elizabeth replied. "So in the end, they will both have the same story."

"Correct," O'Hanlon exclaimed, his finger pointing to the sky. "But the cut does not lie. It was clean, like by a blade."

"But, why would he bother?"

"He was playing with a knife when he should have been more attentive to his guard duties. He was trying to keep that fact from his Sergeant."

"Ah. Well, for sure he'll get the rope for trying to fool the Great Brendan O'Hanlon."

"I would prefer 'shot at dawn' myself."

29

July 24, 1919
Samara to Ufa

The train was ready and loaded. Several cars up front contained a battalion of Red Army soldiers while the rest held the company, its horses and supplies. Kolochov came around when it was getting close to leave to say his good-byes to Appleton.

"Charles," he said, holding out his hand. "Have a quick and safe journey."

"Anton Pyotrovich," Appleton replied, ignoring Kolochov's hand, "that sounded almost sincere."

Kolochov grimaced. "Come now, Charles. There was a time when we were good friends. Moscow in 1904, perhaps. You remember the nights on the town we had."

"We were spying on each other even then," Appleton answered.

"True, but we still had fun. Then, we were feeling each other out."

Appleton stepped into Kolochov's personal space. "Until Natalia. I'll never forgive you for that."

Kolochov's voice went cold. "She was an enemy of the state. You need to remember that you made her that way."

Appleton stared back into Kolochov's eyes. "Are you really a Bolshevik, or are you just betting on them being the winning side?"

Kolochov's cold, blue eyes never wavered, betraying nothing. "They took Russia out of a disastrous war and fed the people. The Tsar did neither. I am a Russian above all else. The choice was simple." Appleton stepped back.

Kolochov's jovial smile returned. "We will meet again soon." He turned and walked down the platform. Appleton gritted his teeth, his mind jumping between what Kolochov had said and the knowledge of how dangerous the man was.

"That looked friendly," said Rainey, coming up behind Appleton.

"It wasn't," Appleton mumbled and walked away.

* * *

Rainey was left alone by the train, watching the two old adversaries put distance between themselves. Appleton had briefed him about Kolochov, but it was from a very detached point of view. Obviously, there was some serious baggage between the two men, which Appleton preferred to keep to himself.

Dietrich appeared from between two trains, saw Rainey and smiled. Rainey strode towards him with his hand out. They greeted each other enthusiastically.

"Good luck to you," Dietrich said. "The hardest part will be getting past their lines, but I understand Comrade Kolochov has that covered."

"We'll be ready for anything," Rainey said. "Good luck to you. When do you leave?"

Dietrich slapped a carriage on the train next to Rainey's. "Due to leave about the same as yours. In Berlin in four days. They tell me that getting across Poland is the difficult part. There's still fighting going on between the Bolsheviks and the Poles, but some negotiations are going on that will allow me to slip through. Once across the frontier, I can become a German soldier again and will have no problem getting home."

The two friends stood there, smiling at each other. Rainey was lost for words for what to say next. Dietrich also said nothing. It was like they were back in a shell hole, promising to meet up again, knowing that it had only happened by chance anyway and that this could be the last time. But they always seemed destined to meet each other, and that made Rainey feel safe.

"I'm glad you survived the war," Dietrich said finally.

"I'm glad you did too," Rainey replied. "I actually missed you. If you ever land in Canada, I'll take you to Lodge."

Dietrich laughed, stepped forward and hugged him, patting him hard on his back. Rainey did the same. When they broke the embrace, Rainey saw a tear in Dietrich's eye and felt one in his own as well. There was nothing more to say, Dietrich backing away until he reached the stairs to his carriage, jumping on and disappearing inside.

* * *

The train chugged along as the daylight faded from the sky. The steady clickity-clack of the rails had a soothing effect on the men, including Rainey. Elizabeth was asleep up against Bradley one bench up from where Appleton sat in silence. Rainey sat looking out at the darkness, deep in thought. They still hadn't figured out who the traitor was. He had toured the picket line the night before, hoping to come across a clandestine meeting, but saw nothing. There was also the question of how Kolochov planned to get them into Chelyabinsk without letting them back out.

After considering this for a time, he got up and shook Appleton's shoulder. "Charles, we need to talk."

Appleton looked up at him and then at Kolochov's agents, sitting separately through the carriage. "Not exactly a good situation to discuss messing with their plan."

Rainey sat down beside him. "Then make it look like a casual conversation." And he laughed. "OK, first, there is our traitor. Who is he and what marching orders has he been given?"

"If he was given orders, it would have been last night," said Appleton. "Anything odd out on the picket line?"

"Just a private got himself a cut. His sergeant took his place and sent him to get patched up."

"That would have been Private Miller," Elizabeth said without raising her head or turning around. "O'Hanlon thought the cut was made with a knife."

"He told me he got the cut from a rock he fell on," Rainey said.

Appleton let out another laugh. Rainey joined him. "Who is this private's sergeant?" Appleton asked.

Rainey turned around with a big smile on his face. He nodded to the Russian agents who just scowled back at him. Past them, he noticed Sergeant MacGregor sitting with some of his men near the back of the carriage. It was the first time he had ever seen MacGregor travel in the front coach.

"He's in our carriage," Rainey said. Then almost to himself, he said "Separate . . ."

"What?" Elizabeth asked.

"Something Peter Dietrichs said to me before we left." Then

it dawned on him. "How many soldiers make a 'small army'?"

Appleton kept the smile on his face. "I don't follow."

Rainey found himself staring at the back of Elizabeth's head. "You said Kolochov would be able to find your father because he would only have to look for the company. How many men would be enough to make your father visible to him?"

Appleton's smile disappeared. "A platoon of Americans is enough to stick out."

"And MacGregor's in our carriage," Rainey said. "We really can't be sure he's our traitor. We only have a soldier's cut arm to go on."

Appleton and Rainey smiled at each other to cover their apprehension. It was Elizabeth who said it out loud. "They're going to shorten the train."

* * *

Rainey had let Kennard know that he wanted to meet Sutton and Corelli up on the company's second carriage's roof. He sat there now with the wind mixed with some smoke and cinders blowing past him, waiting. Two figures came towards him from the coach's far end. They sat down and huddled with Rainey.

"Got a job for the two of you that has to be done very quietly," Rainey shouted over the noise of the wind and the clacking wheels.

The two men just nodded. Rainey continued. "We need to wipe out the battalion in the front carriages and take over the locomotive before we reach Ufa. The Reds are in confined spaces. Corelli, we'll need grenades and BARs to hit all the carriages at once. You are also to take command of Sutton's platoon to do the job. Sutton, keep your best squad with you and when the attack starts, take over the engine."

"What about the Russkies in your carriage, sir?" asked Corelli.

"I'll take care of them. One more thing, sergeant. We think they are planning to uncouple the train behind this carriage. I need you to take a look at the coupling. Signal me if you can ensure the linkage is secure."

"Yes, sir," replied Corelli.

"Attack commences in forty minutes from now. Set your watches." They all glanced down at their wrists. "That's all. Good luck." They climbed down and back into their carriages.

When Rainey entered the carriage, he was confronted by the senior agent. "What were you doing out there?" he demanded in Russian.

"Getting some air," Rainey replied. "It's getting stuffy in here."

"Do not leave the carriage again without permission."

Don't worry, I won't. Smiling, he pushed past the man and took his seat, giving Appleton a knowing look. He then looked at his watch. Thirty-seven minutes.

Rainey's seat gave him a good view down the carriage to the back door. He kept his eye on the glass in the door. He checked his watch again. Thirty-three minutes. Back up at the door, he saw Corelli's face appear. Corelli gave him a thumbs-up. Rainey casually glanced at the watch again. Twenty-nine minutes.

Looking up, he met Elizabeth's face. She was looking at him in anticipation, not knowing what was going to happen, but knowing that something would. Rainey glanced out the window, thanking the Almighty that it was a cloudy day. No bright sun would cast shadows onto the passing landscape, shadows of men moving along the roofs of the carriages.

Another check. Twenty minutes. Elizabeth's eyes were also on his watch. Her eyes met his. From his lap, he flashed five fingers at her, four times. She nodded, ever so subtly. Rainey ventured a look at the Russians. They appeared attentive, but oblivious to what was going on. Fifteen minutes.

At the two-minute mark, Rainey slowly eased his Webley revolver onto his lap. Elizabeth did the same with her Colt. Appleton, sitting across the aisle from the Russians, slowly drew his Bowie knife from its sheath. All was ready.

Zero minutes. Nothing happened. Rainey held his breath. Had something gone wrong? The seconds ticked off. Ten seconds. Twenty. Rainey began to worry.

The explosions caught everyone's attention in the carriage. The senior agent leaped up into the aisle. Rainey rose just as quickly, bringing his pistol to bear and firing, catching the man in the forehead. As he moved his aim to the next Russian, Elizabeth had already spun around, stood and shot the man in the head. The soldier in the seat behind her ducked in surprise. The third Russian, sitting in the aisle seat, never saw Appleton's blade as it plunged deep into his gut. The fourth Russian had been riding one carriage back. He burst in, gun held high. Rainey was ready and shot him before he made it all the way through the door.

The noise from the front carriages lasted only about two minutes, consisting of more explosions and rapid BAR fire. When it went silent, the carriage door opened and Corelli stepped through with a big smile on his face.

"The operation was a success, sir. Complete surprise, no casualties on our side. Packed in so tight they could barely respond. Signal from Sergeant Sutton says we have the engine."

"You were late," Rainey said.

"Not according to my watch, sir," Corelli said innocently.

"How badly are the carriages banged up on the outside?"

"All of the windows were blown out, but from the outside, they should look pretty normal."

Rainey turned back and looked at the men in his carriage. There were some surprised looks, and some were smiling. Mac-Gregor's face showed nothing at all.

"OK. Spread the men throughout the carriages. We have to make it look like this train is full of troops when we pass through Ufa. As we pass through the station, everyone to the windows. Have them wearing the hats of the Bolsheviks." He grabbed Corelli by the arm. "Good work. How about the coupling back there?"

"There was a small bomb. It's lying on the tracks now, a few miles back."

* * *

In the distance, the buildings of a city came into view. Ufa, gateway to Asia and to the pass through the Urals. Rainey had clambered up to the engine and tapped Sutton on the shoulder, indicating that he should slow the train. They would have to stop for water. He glanced at his watch. It had been six hours since leaving Samara and it was getting dark. As the train began to pull through the town, it became apparent that a war was on. Ufa was the main supply depot for the Bolshevik army in this region. Everywhere in the streets, war supplies were piled up and armed soldiers looked suspiciously at the train as it moved past them, despite the red flags at the front of the locomotive.

The station was filled with trains being loaded with supplies for the front. Their train was directed to the track closest to the station house. Rainey looked down the side of the train to see his soldiers hanging out the windows, all wearing caps from the Red

Battalion.

The train slowly rolled through the station and up to the water tower for refilling. His nerves were taut for the minutes it took to top up the locomotive's water tank so they could keep going. An official-looking man appeared at the engine's cab where Rainey was standing and asked for papers. Rainey, dressed in the clothes of the senior agent he had shot, handed over the papers he had found in the man's vest pocket. The official looked them over for a few minutes, nodded and handed them back.

"Safe journey."

So far, so good, Rainey thought. The water spout was swung away from the train and Sutton opened the throttle. The train inched forward, easing out the far end of the rail yard before Rainey indicated to Sutton to increase speed. No one came out yelling for the train to stop.

* * *

In their carriage, Appleton sat with Elizabeth as the train began to pull out. "And that was Ufa," Appleton said, partly to himself.

He turned slowly from the window. Rainey entered the carriage, grinning. He plopped himself down in the seat opposite Appleton, then reached into his front pocket and pulled out some papers, handing them over.

"Are these Kolochov's orders?" Appleton asked.

"Yeah," Rainey replied. "Those are passes for the train and instructions for someone outside of Chelyabinsk to get us into the city."

Appleton opened them up and began to read. After a while, his eyebrows went up. "These are signed by Trotsky."

"Yeah. Makes you feel real important like, don't it?"

Appleton gave Rainey a steady look. "Do you think this will work? They may be expecting fewer men."

"You said Kolochov doesn't leave much to chance," Rainey said. "From those, you can see that they were going to blow the coupling just before Ufa. Then we would ride to this point and meet up with a patrol that can take us through the front lines. Assuming Kolochov's penchant for secrecy, the patrol probably does not know how many of us there are."

"The orders also say 'Comrade Karinin' would be in charge," Appleton noted.

"I guess that's me," Rainey said. "I just impersonated him rather easily."

Appleton nodded. "Well, it's not like we have another option, but let's hope whoever we meet outside Chelyabinsk has never met Comrade Karinin."

Rainey grinned. "Yeah." He looked down the carriage. "Sergeant MacGregor, send up Private Miller."

Miller stopped and saluted. "You requested me, sir?"

Rainey reached for his sword and hung the scabbard on Miller's back. He set his cap on the private's head. "There," he said. "Just in case our friends we are to meet have been told about a captain with a strange sword. For the next little while, you're me."

Part 3

30

July 25, 1919
Chelyabinsk

The train exited the pass through the Urals about four hours after passing through Ufa. It began to slow as it reached a forest that indicated the point on the map where the patrol was supposed to be met. As the train squealed to a stop, five horsemen appeared out of the trees to the south. They were heavily armed and did not look friendly.

Rainey slapped Miller on the back. "Don't worry, Private. Just step down from the train and stand there with Mr. Appleton. I'll be going to talk to them."

"I'm not worried, sir," Miller replied. "There's more of us than there are of them."

Rainey was still wearing the leather jacket, vest and cap from the senior commissar, with order papers in his hand for the patrol. He reached over to rub the sword's scabbard on Miller's back for good luck and then stepped down from the carriage. Miller and Appleton followed. Rainey continued to the horsemen alone, stopping about five yards short.

"I have orders from Colonel Kolochov for you to lead us into Chelyabinsk, quietly," Rainey said in Russian.

The leader held out his hand. Rainey stepped forward and gave him the orders, standing quietly while he read them. The man glanced down at Rainey several times during the course of the next two minutes, then folded up the paper and tucked it into his coat.

"We go now," he said.

Rainey nodded and returned to the train. The horsemen turned and disappeared into the forest. Rainey signaled to Appleton that all was fine. Miller turned to the train and yelled, "OK, Sergeant Kennard. Let's get everything unloaded here, pronto."

Miller turned back around to find Rainey right behind him. "Sorry, sir," he said sheepishly. "I couldn't resist."

Rainey grinned at him. "Just as well. You're going to have to continue playing me until we leave our friends in the trees. Just be careful."

"Yes, sir," Miller said, bringing up a salute. Rainey caught his arm part way up. Miller looked at his arm and back at Rainey, nodding knowingly. "Careful . . ."

The company had loading and unloading trains down to a fine art. They got all the wagons, horses and equipment unloaded in fifteen minutes. Kennard and Miller inspected everything in a military style. Some grins and sly whispered comments followed Miller as he went by.

Elizabeth spoke to Rainey. "The private does you well."

"He's being a little pompous, if you ask me," Rainey replied.

Elizabeth grinned. "I think he has just the right amount of pompous."

Rainey turned to her. "And I'm playing the evil Bolshevik, so you shouldn't be hanging around me."

When she realized he was serious, her grin faded. "You're right." She looked into his face and saw something that seemed to scare her. Had she sensed his own doubts and fears? She turned and walked away.

Rainey watched her leave, a deep sinking feeling in his gut. He could have said that better, kinder. But people could be watching from the trees. He sat down on the carriage's step, uncertainty seeping into his consciousness. He reached back to stroke the scabbard of his sword again, only then remembering it was on Private Miller's back. His hand settled on the rusting steel step, slowly supporting his weight as he began to sag to his left. He felt lost, full of doubt and didn't know why. Then a presence appeared beside him.

He looked up to see Elizabeth standing there. She held out her hand. In it was the locket. "Until you get your sword back," she said softly. As he took it, she turned and walked away again.

Rainey stared at the locket in his hand. He caressed it with his thumb, the way he'd seen Elizabeth's brother do all those many months ago. He finally snapped it open and gazed upon the picture of Elizabeth, smiling back. He could feel confidence coming back into him. She would always be there for him and he would do his job as a professional.

His sword and the locket were just objects, but it amazed him how much power these objects had in his mind.

* * *

They emerged from the forest to the east of the city, the railroad tracks passing through the clearing and continuing on east. The Red commander turned to Rainey and stretched out his arm as if to say *There you go.* He then turned around and melted back into the forest with his men.

Appleton joined him. "No sentries. If we can sneak into town this easily . . ."

"So can the Red Army," Rainey said. "I'll get Sergeant Kennard to set up patrols here to keep an eye out. This will be a natural choke point to be used against us when we make our exit. What's the best way to find Clarke?"

"Head for the train station. He'll be keeping an eye out for us there."

"He'd better find us quickly." Rainey looked back at the column. He put his hand up to signal "Forward" when Appleton stopped him.

"Can't be entering the city dressed like that," he said.

Rainey looked down at his clothes. "Oh, yeah." He turned to Private Miller. "Private, it's time for your demotion."

The streets were quiet. No one challenged them all the way to the train station. Rainey had Bradley next to him as an early warning system, but the corporal showed no sign of sensing anything dangerous. Still, it was all too quiet, even for the late hour. For a city that was supposed to have an army in it, he saw almost no signs of that being true. Rainey caught himself rubbing the sword scabbard a little too much. He brought his hand back to the reins.

When they reached the rail yard, a young soldier at a guard post stepped into the street and stood in their way. The sound of a train starting up emerged from the yard. Rainey stopped the column and moved his horse forward a few feet.

"I need to speak to your commander," he said in Russian.

The guard replied, "*Nerozumím ruské.*"

Rainey had no idea what language that was. He looked back at Appleton for help.

"I think it's Czech," Appleton said.

"And how is your Czech?"

Appleton shook his head. "Never learned it."

Rainey turned back to the guard, figuring he'd try German. "Me see your commander," he said with appropriate hand signals.

The guard nodded, lowered his rifle and went back into the guard shack.

It was ten minutes before two men in officer uniforms walked quickly up to the gate. Under his cap, Rainey could see that the older, senior officer had a patch over his right eye. He stopped at the gate, placed his hands behind his back and stared at Rainey. The younger officer took a step farther.

"What do you want?" he said authoritatively in Russian.

Rainey gave the man a salute. "Sir, we are looking for passage to the east. We are a professional fighting force and will fight by your side in exchange for passage."

The man leaned to his left to look down the column of horsemen and wagons. "Who are you?" he said as he straightened back up.

"We are an American observer force," Rainey said. "We have been traveling across Russia to gain information on the war here."

The older officer spoke up in English. "Hmmpf. Have you come to the conclusion that they are all crazy yet?"

Rainey smiled. "Just need to find a way of saying that in official government language."

The man laughed out loud. "OK, American. However, we have one train left here and we are leaving in next half hour. We have no room for you."

"Sir, how many troops are left to defend the city?"

"No idea. We Czechs have been abandoning this city for the last three days. Best option is for you to head out east now."

Rainey nodded. They knew the Red Army was close. "If we head out now and find one of your trains with room, who should I ask for, sir?"

"General Syrovy," said the man. "But you will probably be shot first for approaching the train."

* * *

Jonathan Clarke looked down from the second story of the house halfway down the block from the rail yard gate. He'd been watching since the column came up the street. Through his binoculars, he could see Appleton near the front, but the man in command was not his son. He scanned the people at the front more closely. There was a large man with sergeant stripes on his sleeve and a small-looking officer behind Appleton. He focused on the officer. The uniform did not fit very well. Hair was visible through the binoculars, sticking out from under the man's cap. When the officer's face turned towards his location, he quickly raised his binoculars for a closer look. He lowered the binoculars as the sudden recognition reached his mind.

Elizabeth? What the hell is she doing here?

"Is that your little army?" said a small voice behind him.

Clarke turned to see the boy standing beside him, holding on to the windowsill for support. "Yes, it is," he said. "We'll be heading east soon," although he wasn't so sure just yet.

"May I have the binoculars, please?" the boy asked.

Clarke handed them over and turned from the window. "I'll be back in a little while."

"Is that your son with the sword?" asked the boy, looking down into the street.

Clarke stopped at the doorway. "No, it is not."

"I want to meet him."

"That would not be wise."

"I don't care."

Clarke had been cooped up in this house for months with this boy and this was the first time the boy had challenged him on anything. "Why do you want to meet him?"

The boy didn't answer, but continued to look out the window through the binoculars. Clarke turned and headed down the stairs. He slowly opened the front door to see the column in the throes of turning around and moving towards a park near the station. Appleton and the two officers remained on their horses in the street, looking around.

It is Elizabeth. Clarke made the decision and stepped out the door. Elizabeth noticed him first and rode to where he stood.

"Hello, Father."

"I barely recognized you, my dear."

"I'm not supposed to be noticeable." She swung down off her horse and hugged him. "I'm so glad we found you."

Appleton and the other officer rode up. "Hello, Jonathan," Appleton. "Glad to see you're still here."

Clarke looked up at the second man. Taking the cue, Appleton continued. "This is Captain Rainey. He's been leading us across Russia."

Clarke took a long, close look at Rainey, then back to Appleton. "How many in the unit?"

Appleton turned to Rainey, who nodded to him. "We've lost a few along the way, but we're at least two hundred strong."

"One hundred ninety, to be exact," Rainey stated.

Clarke ignored him, turning to Elizabeth. "Where is your

brother?"

Elizabeth hesitated for a moment before replying. "We lost him in Rumania."

"What do you mean 'lost him'?" He saw the tears forming in Elizabeth's eyes and understood. His son was dead. He took a step back from her, his arm reaching out for the pillar on his right to steady himself. Then slowly, his head came up, his eyes boring into Appleton.

"You risked my daughter's life bringing her across this God-forsaken land?"

"You insisted on a family member," replied Appleton, "and Elizabeth insisted on coming."

Clarke stepped forward. "I don't care what she insisted on. Without Jeremy, the mission was to be aborted and I would have dealt with it at my end."

"We're here now, Jonathan. May I suggest we keep going?"

Clarke continued to glare at Appleton for a moment longer, then shifted his gaze to Rainey. "How did you convince this gentleman to lead you?"

Before answering, he noticed, Elizabeth looked to this Captain Rainey, who was looking pretty serious. Grim, in fact. She turned back to her father. "He knew Jeremy in the war. Jeremy trusted him. I trust him."

Clarke didn't shift his glare. "You're dismissed, Captain. Charles, Elizabeth, follow me."

"No."

Clarke stared at his daughter. "No? You don't have a say in this, young lady."

That got Elizabeth's back up. "The captain has been a trusted and very professional commander for this whole mission. He needs to know what the next phase of the plan is."

"And some information is of a very sensitive nature. It would be best, for him especially, not to know it."

"It's all right," Rainey said. "I have duties out here. Mr. Clarke, there isn't much time and we have no train to use. We need to move out shortly. We're going to rest the horses for an hour and get going." He turned his horse around and back towards the men.

Clarke saw the scowl on Elizabeth's face as he turned back towards the house. He held the door open for them as Appleton dismounted and climbed the stairs.

"Don't you ever refer to me as 'young lady' again," she said quietly as she passed her father. Such insubordination from her would have landed her a smack from him. But right now, he knew that would only make things worse. She wasn't afraid of him.

Appleton stopped beside Clarke. "She's grown up a lot since you last saw her."

"I raised her to be tough and smart," Clarke said. "I'd be disappointed to find out otherwise."

* * *

The boy lowered his binoculars as Rainey reached the far side of the street and began issuing orders. The soldiers all started to move towards an open area beside the rail yard and just down the street from the house. The boy was smiling. He had gotten a good look when Rainey was closer to the house.

"The Great Celt has come to save me," he said softly. Unsteadily, he made his way from the window back to the bed. As he finally got comfortable, he heard footsteps on the stairs. The door opened and Clarke entered with a man and a woman in an army uniform. The woman smiled. The other man looked shocked.

"Hello," the woman said. "My name is Elizabeth Clarke. Jonathan is my father."

"Jonathan," the other man said, still looking surprised. "You do know who this is, don't you?"

"Of course I know," Jonathan said flatly. "Your Highness, this is Charles Appleton with the United States Department of State."

"Your what?" Elizabeth demanded, turning to her father.

"Miss Clarke," Appleton said, "meet Tsarovich Alexis of Russia."

31

"Actually," Clarke said, "he's the Tsar. Nicholas abdicated and since Nicholas never got out of Ekaterinburg, it pretty much became official."

Everyone stood quietly, contemplating the implications before them. "So now what?" Elizabeth asked, breaking the silence.

"Now we get out while the gettin' is good, as the saying goes," Clarke said. "The Czech Legion is abandoning the city. There are virtually no effective forces to fight the Red Army when it arrives. Would have been nice if you had shown up a few days earlier."

"Wouldn't have made a difference. The attack would have started by our first morning here regardless," Appleton said.

Clarke looked surprised. "How do you know that?"

"We got here because we're part of Kolochov's plan to find you and whatever you've been hiding," Appleton said. He looked towards Alexis. "Won't he be surprised."

"Part of Kolochov's plan? I don't understand."

Elizabeth touched her father's arm. "There was a spy in New York. Kolochov knew our route, but not why we were coming for you and he wants to know that. So he's helped us get this far. But he also has a trap planned to keep us here."

"Then we have to leave immediately," Clarke said.

"Captain Rainey is preparing for that as we speak," Appleton said.

"But the men and horses need rest," Elizabeth said, "if only for an hour. We won't escape very far with tired horses."

Her father looked worried, especially after the mention of Kolochov. "How could he have a spy in New York?" Clarke asked

"That's a discussion for another time," Appleton said.

There was a knock on the door downstairs. Clarke moved quickly to the window to see who it was. "It's that captain you picked up. I thought I told him to stay away." He pulled out a pistol and headed for the door.

"No!" Elizabeth shouted, grabbing her father's arm. "I will take care of him." She ran down the stairs to the door and opened it, smiling at Rainey. "Couldn't stay away, huh?" she asked.

They hugged each other and moved into the house. "I forgot I still had this," he said, holding out the locket. "Got my sword back, so I thought it best to get this back to you."

Elizabeth took the locket in her hands. "Thank you," she said. "I know my having this is a great comfort to you."

"Are you the Great Celt?" said a small voice from up the stairs. Elizabeth and Rainey looked up to see Alexis standing behind Clarke and Appleton. Clarke quickly spun around and pushed the boy back into the room.

"I need to see the sword!" Alexis yelled as the door closed behind them. Appleton stood at the top of the stairs with a puzzled look.

Rainey asked Elizabeth, "Is that who I think it is?"

Elizabeth stammered. "Who-who do you think it is?"

From behind the closed door, Alexis continued to shout about "the Great Celt" coming to save him. Appleton started down the stairs.

"You weren't supposed to see him. Perhaps you should tell us who you think that is," he said.

"His picture with his family was all over the newspapers about a year ago," Rainey answered. "He's supposed to be dead."

"You have a very good memory," Appleton said.

"Just for faces."

"But how does he know you?" Appleton asked.

"No idea. This is my first trip to Russia."

"Why would he be calling you 'the Great Celt'?" Elizabeth asked.

"Again, no idea," Rainey replied. "Perhaps we should go up and ask him."

The door to the upstairs room opened and Clarke stepped out to the landing. "Charles, bring up the captain's sword, please." He answered the confused looks by adding, "He wants to see the sword."

"I know who he is," Rainey said, moving to the stairs. "I'll bring it to him."

A pistol appeared in Clarke's hand. "Charles, just the sword."

Appleton put his hand on Rainey shoulder. "Please, Captain."

Rainey paused, no doubt wondering how his sword could be significant to Russian royalty, Elizabeth thought. Taking it off his shoulder, he handed it to Appleton. Appleton nodded and carried it up the stairs. Elizabeth took Rainey's hand.

"Is your father always so nice?" Rainey asked.

Elizabeth put her head up against his shoulder. "He's been here hiding out for months. I can understand his suspicion. Please don't provoke him."

"That was never my intention," Rainey said softly.

Elizabeth sighed. "You are very complicated, Captain Robert Rainey."

"No, I'm not. But apparently my sword is."

After a moment of silence, the door opened and Appleton came to the top of the stairs. If possible, he looked even more puzzled than before. "You can come up now."

Rainey exchanged a look with Elizabeth, and together they climbed to the second floor. They found Alexis sitting on the bed with the sword unsheathed, examining the blade. Clarke sat in the corner, a worried look on his face and his gun still in his hand. Alexis looked up at Rainey and grinned.

"Come in, fine sir," Alexis said in English. "Tell me your name and rank."

Rainey stepped into the room. "Robert Rainey, captain, Princess Patricia's Canadian Light Infantry, your Highness." He made a slight bow.

The boy's eyes lit up. "So it is true. You know the story?"

"I'm afraid I don't, your Highness."

"Don't call me 'your Highness.' I am just Alexis here. Come closer. I want to show you something."

Rainey sat on the bed beside Alexis. The boy moved the sword's hilt in front of Rainey and pointed to a small golden disk embedded near the guard. It carried a crest, much like all the other disks that ornamented both hilt and scabbard.

Alexis looked up at Rainey excitedly. "Do you not know what this is?"

"I don't know what most of them are," Rainey replied.

Alexis frowned. "You should know your family history."

"Not being royalty, I don't have people keeping track of it for me."

"But you are noble," Alexis pushed. "You descend from the great House of Raynykov."

Rainey looked dubious. "OK," he said slowly. "I know my ancestors got around, but they only passed the sword on."

Alexis pointed to the gold coin again. "This is the crest of Grand Prince Ivan the Third. Ivan the Great. 'The Great Celt' came from the south and saved the Grand Prince from death. Then he helped him gather the lands of the Rus that would one day become Russia. In return, 'the Great Celt' was given lands to establish the Raynykov line, forever loyal to the Tsars of Russia."

Elizabeth was fascinated, seeing Rainey in an entirely new light. He looked about the room, acknowledging her admiring gaze. Clarke's expression hadn't changed. Appleton still looked puzzled.

"Well, I'm not Russian," Rainey said, "and I don't know of any Raynykov clan."

"Would that be because 'the Great Celt's' third- or fourth-born was given the sword and sent on his way?" Elizabeth said. She remembered what Rainey had told her about his family traditions concerning the sword.

Rainey took a moment before replying. "That would follow family tradition, but would also date back to at least . . . when?" he asked Alexis.

"Ivan the Great began his reign in 1462," Alexis stated.

"That's going back a bit," Appleton said.

"And now you are here to save me," Alexis said excitedly.

"Hold on there, son," Rainey responded. "That's not why I'm here."

"Actually, it is," Clarke said, breaking his silence. "He's the last of the Romanov line, rightful heir to the Russian throne."

"Which no longer exists," Rainey snapped back.

"That has yet to be decided," Clarke said coldly, his gun twitching in his lap.

"How much is he worth, Father?" Elizabeth asked.

Clarke frowned at this, but said nothing. Appleton frowned as well. His eyes widened, telling Elizabeth he was coming to the same realization she had.

"Tell us, Jonathan," Appleton said. "How much is out there and where?"

Clarke said nothing, mutely confirming the real reason for the mission.

"Oh, my God," Rainey exclaimed, spinning on Clarke. "We marched all the way across Russia, losing good soldiers, including your son, just so you could get your hands on some Russian gold?"

"Not me," Clarke spat. Pointing at Alexis, he continued. "I was totally unaware of his existence until I became involved in this operation. It was only then I considered the implications. There are large gold reserves that were placed in British and French banks by the Russian Government during the war. This was collateral for munitions and supplies. A good portion of that is owed to American businesses, but the banks have frozen the assets."

"And how much is owed to Clarke Steel?" Rainey asked.

"None of it is," Clarke said. "I closed all my dealings in Russia by 1916."

"But if you produce a Romanov heir," Elizabeth said, "you could unfreeze the assets."

The room went silent again. Money. It was all about money. Rainey clapped a hand over his mouth as if he were about to be sick. Alexis sank down onto the bed, shoulders slumping. The excitement had vanished from his eyes.

Rainey got up. "I have to go."

Clarke raised his pistol. "No, you can't now."

"Father!" Elizabeth shouted, stepping between him and Rainey.

Clarke hesitated, but did not lower the gun. "You'll have to stay here. I don't know if I can trust you to keep quiet."

"Father, put the gun down."

"Jonathan," Appleton said. "He has to go to organize our escape."

"I'll be quiet," Rainey said. "I know that if knowledge of Alexis gets out, it will jeopardize our chances of getting out of Russia. Quite frankly, any public announcement that Alexis is alive, in or out of Russia, will put him at grave risk."

Elizabeth knew her father could offer no counter to Rainey's interpretation of their situation. He slowly lowered his gun. "Go, Captain."

32

Rainey reached Kennard and immediately asked where Sergeant MacGregor was. It was time to talk to the man. Rainey still wasn't sure he was the traitor, but nothing else past the knife cut on Miller had popped out at him since the mission began, and by this point the traitor would be doing something on Kolochov's orders. He was directed to a particular area across the park where MacGregor's platoon was set up. The first person he saw there was Private Miller.

"Private, where's your sergeant?"

"He said he went to see Sergeant Corelli, sir," Miller said.

Rainey moved on to Corelli's platoon. Corelli looked confused, saying he hadn't seen MacGregor since they had reached the park. Now Rainey had cause for concern.

"Get some of your men together and find him," Rainey ordered.

"What's going on, sir?"

"Just find him."

* * *

MacGregor had not left a note at the address he was given. When he discovered the plan to separate a large section of the company from him and the command group, his priorities changed. It was never his desire to hurt any of the soldiers, but this country they were travelling through was full of complications and betrayals. His only goal now was to find out what Jonathan Clarke was hiding and deal with it.

The window was unlocked, making it easy to slide it open without needing to shift his weight on the ledge. The window slid quietly until the last inch, where it made a scratching noise. MacGregor hefted himself up through the window and onto the floor. As he picked himself up, the floor creaked and he heard a small voice from the dark.

"*Tho tam?*"

MacGregor struck a match and lit a candle he found by the window. The darkness dispersed to show a small bed, a few chairs, a table and a boy.

"Well, hello laddie," MacGregor said. "And who might you be?"

"Do not come any closer," Alexis said authoritatively in English. "The Great Celt will kill you."

MacGregor stopped, quickly looking about the room. "The what?" He shook his head. "Captain Rainey sent me to protect you."

"Then why did you come in through the window?"

MacGregor pulled out his knife, keeping it hidden from the boy's view, and proceeded slowly towards the bed. "The Captain didn't want the others to know he was assigning a special guard for you. Just keep quiet while I check the door."

"The door is over there."

MacGregor raised the candle. The kid was smart. He was almost at the bed. He looked over at the door. "Oh yes, there it is."

He lowered the candle and made one more step towards the bed.

The door crashed open. MacGregor spun to see the silhouette of a woman, long hair hanging down past her shoulders, holding something in front of her. The small flash and the gun noise coincided with a severe pain he felt in his stomach. The candle fell to the floor.

* * *

Rainey was briefing Kennard about MacGregor when they heard the gunshot from the house.

"Oh, shit," he said under his breath, bolting across and down the street toward the house. Another shot was followed by several more in quick succession.

He bounded up the steps to the front door and without slowing down, put his shoulder into it. The door gave way to the force. He regained his balance and took three steps at a time up the stairs. Clarke and Appleton huddled on the landing, peering into the room. Rainey pushed past them.

On the floor, a single candle lay on its side, casting a ghostly light on the scene. Alexis was sitting up in his bed, horror on his face. Elizabeth stood over the prone body of MacGregor, several bullet holes in his stomach and chest. Her Colt was still pointed down at him, two hands on the grip. A small wisp of smoke rose from the barrel. Rainey slowly moved towards her.

"Elizabeth . . ."

The gun fired again. A small jerk in MacGregor's body showed it had hit home. Everyone jumped, Alexis letting out a tiny yelp.

Rainey brought his hands up to her shoulders, slowly sliding them down her arms to the pistol. She was crying as he took the gun gently from her hands. The Colt's slide was back, indicating she had fired every round in the clip. Rainey held it behind him for Appleton to take, then slowly spun Elizabeth around to face him. She buried her face into his chest, crying full on now. Rainey wrapped his arms around her and held her, making small soothing noises.

Appleton headed out the door, leading Clarke out with him. Rainey and Elizabeth stood in the flickering light for a while, not moving, Elizabeth's sobs slowly fading.

"Thank you," Alexis said weakly.

Elizabeth came up from Rainey's chest, wiping her eyes and sniffing. "You're welcome."

"You all right now?" Rainey asked, a tremor in his voice betraying his worry.

* * *

Elizabeth gazed up into Rainey's gray eyes. She had just killed a man. A man responsible for her brother's death. A man that put her very life and that of everyone in the company at risk. The intense anger she felt as she repeatedly fired the gun had terrified her. She felt she needed saving now and knew she was looking at the man who could save her. "Yes," she whispered. "I'll be fine." She pressed her face into his chest again. "I'll be fine," she repeated.

Rainey spoke to Alexis. "You get some sleep now. You're safe and we'll be leaving soon."

"Please stay at the house," Alexis asked.

Rainey nodded to the boy as he led Elizabeth from the room. At the head of the stairs, he looked down to see Bradley standing in the doorway, Clarke glaring at him.

"Anyone out there with you, Corporal?" Rainey asked.

"No, sir." *

"Then get up here and take Sergeant MacGregor away."

Bradley ran up the stairs and into the room. Alexis recoiled at the sight of another soldier he didn't know, but Rainey nodded at him from the landing that it was all right and he relaxed. Bradley hefted MacGregor's body up onto his shoulders and carried him out of the house. He didn't look once at Alexis.

"Tell Sergeant Kennard we roll as planned," Rainey shouted as Bradley went through the front door. "I'll be back before then."

He turned his attention back to Elizabeth, kissing her on the forehead. Her eyes were still red from crying, but she smiled up at him.

"I don't want to be alone," she said.

"I'll stay downstairs with Charles and your father. We roll in thirty."

Elizabeth looked over her shoulder at the other room across the landing. "No, stay with me."

* * *

As soon as the door closed, Elizabeth attacked Rainey's clothes with gusto, fingers rapidly working the buttons on his tunic. Rainey stepped back in surprise. "We only have half an hour," he said.

"I don't need half an hour," Elizabeth said, in desperate whispered tones. Rainey got into the action by pulling Elizabeth's shirt open. The clothes fell one piece at a time as they crossed the room and moved onto the bed. They came together in heated passion, Rainey moving his hands over her hips and breasts, his lips finding hers, drinking in all he could of her essence. Elizabeth rolled both of them over, slamming her body onto his. Her right hand reached for his stiff member, gripping it hard and then guiding it into her. She let out a gasp as he thrust himself into her; her head came back as Rainey pulled on her hair, his lips onto her left nipple.

Their bodies moved together in a rhythm of heated passion. Everything else was forgotten. Where they were, what they had done, what the plan for tomorrow was, all forgotten as they lived only in the moment. The pent-up emotions that they had worked at keeping under control were let loose, culminating in his explosion into her.

The energy expended was high, so when they finished, both were exhausted. Elizabeth fell onto Rainey's chest, panting heavily. As her breathing settled down, she rolled off his chest and pressed tightly into his side.

"I love you," she whispered.

"I love you too," he whispered back.

"I know," she said with a quiet giggle.

Rainey lay there awake, eyes closed, reveling in his love for Elizabeth before his mind returned to the job of getting out of Chelyabinsk alive.

Elizabeth's mind evidently regained its focus, too.

"Are we going to get out of this?" she asked.

"We're going to damn well try," he replied. "We have a good chance."

The sound of a shell screaming in focused his attention immediately. Too close. Rainey, after years in the trenches, had learned to judge distance from the sound of artillery. This shell landed about three hundred yards away. He wasn't sure in which direction since he heard it mostly through the open window, but he bet it was targeting the rail yard. As his eyes snapped open, he could see the hanging light fixture over the bed slowly swinging back and forth. He looked at his watch. 3:12 a.m. They hadn't even gotten their half hour.

"Elizabeth, get up and get dressed. Now."

Elizabeth didn't need to be told. She was already vaulting out of the bed and reaching for her clothes. Another shell landed, shaking the room. It was hard to see in the dark, but the trail from the door to the bed was unmistakable. She started for the door, picking up each item of clothing and hurriedly pulling it on. The passion had been replaced by fear. The shelling of the city went on, with each explosion ringing a greater sense of dread into her head. At the door, the last thing she picked up was her cap, smacking it on to her head without worrying about her hair. She thought she must look awful, but taking the time to freshen up was not an option. She still had to pull her boots on. Rainey was already opening the door to the landing.

Appleton was at the bottom of the stairs. "They're concentrating fire on the station. The Czech train is already clearing the yard."

Rainey didn't figure Kolochov would have given them enough time to acquire a train. "Is everyone together and ready to go?"

"They're already assembling in the street." From outside came the crackle of sporadic small arms fire.

The decision was made. Clarke passed Rainey, leading Alexis, who was wearing a large hat. "Get Clarke and Alexis on a wagon," Rainey yelled. "Sergeant Kennard will assign you to the lead platoon."

Rainey bounded down the stairs and saw Bradley running towards the house. "Corporal, Miss Clarke is still upstairs," Rainey yelled. "You make sure she gets out of here." Bradley didn't even pause to salute, taking the steps three at a time.

Rainey glanced out at the assembling troops. It looked like chaos, but somehow organized. The barrage had not moved off the rail yard yet and he could hear the train rumbling away toward the east.

Kennard came up at a run. "Just about ready to roll, sir."

Rainey nodded. "Follow the tracks east. Corelli and one of his squads and MacGregor's platoon are to report to me here with all the firepower they can carry. Put Canning in charge of the platoon. They'll need machine guns, mortars and a 37 on a wagon. Take all the horses except for what we need for the wagon. When you reach the outskirts of town, leave a squad with horses for us. We'll be coming out at a full run."

Machine-gun fire, mixed with various other small arms, was getting closer. The Red Army wasn't even waiting for its own barrage to let up. Rainey looked up at Kennard. "Sounds like the Reds sneaked in during the night like we did. You're in command until we meet up again."

Kennard saluted quickly and ran back to the column, yelling Rainey's orders as he went. Rainey turned to see Elizabeth and Bradley running from the house toward two horses, saddled and ready to go. He nodded to Bradley and raced to where Corelli, Canning and their men were congregating.

* * *

As she mounted, Elizabeth turned to Bradley. "Tom, what's the captain going to do?"

"Rear guard," Bradley said.

"And what are we to do?" she pressed.

Bradley's blank look changed very subtly. "Escape?" he asked.

"I won't leave the captain behind, Tom. You have to promise me we'll not leave him behind."

"He knows what he's doing," Bradley said.

"So did my brother, and he never got out of Rumania." Bradley remained silent, so Elizabeth continued. "I know rear guards are considered expendable, but I will not consider Captain Rainey expendable by any stretch of the imagination. I want you to assemble a small team, a squad that will be available to go in and extricate the rear guard if it becomes cut off. Can you do that for me?"

"Who will command?"

"You will."

Bradley paused before speaking again. "I've never commanded."

"Then I will," Elizabeth answered.

"You've never commanded," Bradley countered.

Elizabeth was exasperated. "I've run a multi-million dollar company. I think I can handle a squad of twelve men. Not a whole . . ."

As she was speaking, she noticed Bradley shifting his weight forward on his horse. A shell landed in the street only twenty-five yards away. Bradley barely moved, but Elizabeth had to fight to control her horse as it reared up and almost tossed her off.

"Tom," she said, "I think we'd better get going."

33

"Keep them pinned down!" Rainey yelled at the gunners. He didn't like the situation. More infantry were assembling at the cross street. This was going to be tight.

"Sergeant," he yelled. "Get moving! Go! Go! Go!"

Kennard was up on his horse, directing the last wagon into the street. As the wagon was finally moving in the right direction, he leaned over and slapped the horse nearest him. It bolted, at first dragging the other along until it got the idea. Soldiers scrambled to hop on the wagon as it went by.

As the bulk of the company rolled away, Rainey yelled, "Fall back!" Covered by rifle fire, the machine-gun teams grabbed their guns and began running down the street towards the mortar positions. One machine-gun team stayed behind, covering the retreat. Mortar rounds helped keep the Red troops back. The retreating men ran halfway up the next block and set up again, the lagging machine-gun crew now scrambling to join them. The teams guarding the cross streets grabbed their gear and ran back to the next cross street. Rainey made it to the next block as well, bullets whizzing by him in increasing numbers. He dived into a doorway for cover and instinctively reached for the sword scabbard.

He looked down the street. The attackers seemed to be waiting for something. Then he saw it. An armored car rolled around a corner and up the street, machine gun clattering. Rainey asked himself where he had put the 37 when he heard it fire. The round hit the car dead on the front, cutting through the thin armor plating and exploding inside the car. It jumped, tilted and landed on its side, its ammunition firing off wildly among the Red troops. Another break.

"Fall back!"

Again, the teams made the move exactly like last time. Another street, another hundred or so yards. The company was away so Rainey figured one more jump and they could abandon the heavy guns and just bolt for where horses would be waiting. But the sound of horses behind him gave him a chill. He spun around to see a Red cavalry unit, about thirty horsemen, assembling in the street to attack him from the rear.

"Watch your backs!" he screamed.

The mortar team was the closest. Forgetting their mortars, they unslung their rifles and took aim as the cavalry unit began their charge. The mortar team, only eight men, didn't stand a chance. They were cut to pieces by sword and bullet. Corelli was the only one able to slip away, taking shots at the horsemen from behind a stairway. It all took only a few seconds and the Red cavalry were reassembling to attack again.

* * *

Elizabeth hung back with Bradley and the squad he had assembled. Riding at the company's rear, she was able to see the Red cavalry unit appear between them and Rainey's platoon just as the company was turning out of sight.

"Corporal," she quickly told Bradley. "That doesn't look

good."

The squad held up in the street. Bradley looked to Elizabeth for an order. She looked over each individual soldier in the squad, watching for fear, hesitation about her leadership, anything that could cause problems in an attack. She smiled. They were professionals. There would be no problems.

"Check your weapons," she said.

Bradley had gotten them all BARs. Firepower was key here. Elizabeth pulled out her pistol, checking to make sure the clip was full. She checked her men again, then reached up to her breast pocket to feel the locket.

"Let's go, gentlemen." And with that, they spurred their horses and, with a blood-curdling yell, charged towards the rear of the Red cavalry.

* * *

The cavalry behind Rainey had his platoon pinned and infantry was moving up on his flanks. He furiously spun around looking for a hole to get out through. There was none. The sound of firing BARs and charging horsemen screaming at the top of their lungs focused his attention on the rear. The enemy were falling from their horses, bodies jerking from bullet impacts. And through the decimated cavalry he saw a squad pounding down on them on horseback, Bradley and Elizabeth in the lead.

"God-damn-it woman," he said under his breath. But he recognized an escape route when he saw one. Spinning around, he yelled, "THAT'S IT! RETREAT! GO! GO! GO!"

* * *

Elizabeth jumped down from her horse and followed Bradley to a street corner. Her squad followed. Looking down the side street she found it empty. Elizabeth signaled and, as a unit, the squad ran to the far corner and took up a position against the corner of a building, near the slain mortar crews, to cover the retreat. The rest of the rear guard ran by, past their dead mates, with just a glance to acknowledge them. There was no time for sentiment.

"Keep an eye out down the side streets," Elizabeth said. She began searching through the running men, trying to spot Rainey.

* * *

The gunners left their machine guns and ran to the rear as fast as they could. Corelli stopped by the 37mm gun that had been taken off the wagon. "Leave it!" Rainey yelled. With a sad look on his face, Corelli turned and joined the retreat. Just about everyone had passed Rainey. He took one last look down the street. Several of his men lay there, unmoving. He could see that one of them was Sergeant Canning. Smoke and fire still billowed from the destroyed armored car. A mass of men was coming up the street.

It was definitely time to go. He yelled for the last group defending the corner. "FALL BACK! LET'S GO!"

He turned and began to run. The horses would be about half a mile away. His boots pounded on the cobblestones, watching the backs of the men as they barreled down the street in retreat. *I think we're going to make it.*

* * *

Elizabeth heard Rainey yelling the command to fall back. "Let's go," she told Bradley. As she leaped up to run, an armored car turned into the side street and bullets tore into the squad. Three men went down right away while the rest bolted across the street. Bradley grabbed Elizabeth and, using himself as a shield, ran across the street after the others. Elizabeth felt panic rise in her throat, running as fast as she could alongside Bradley, whose firm hand gripped her arm.

Then they seemed to slow down. Bradley's body jerked three or four times and began to sink to the street, dragging Elizabeth down with him.

"TOM?" she screamed.

Something punched her in the left shoulder and then again on the left side of her chest. She hit the cobblestones hard, banging her head as Bradley landed on top of her, knocking her helmet off. The pain was unbelievable. She could feel herself losing consciousness, seeing only Bradley's standard blank stare, gazing down at her. *If it's really serious, lie down and wait to die*, she thought as the darkness closed over her.

* * *

Rainey didn't hear Elizabeth's scream, but he began to realize that she was somewhere with the rear guard now. He began looking around wildly, trying to spot her while continuing to run. He caught up to another soldier. It was Miller. "Miller, have you seen Miss Clarke?"

"No, sir," Miller said between breaths. "Not since her attack."

Rainey began to slow. She must be up ahead, but doubt filled his mind. He didn't know. He slowed to a walk and looked behind him.

"Captain, we have to keep going!" Corelli said as he ran past.

His mind clicked over. They were in retreat. War zone survival instincts kicked in. He forced himself to turn and run, moving up the street at a full gallop. *Bradley is with her. She'll be fine*, he thought

They found the horses at the city's edge and quickly mounted up. He could see the rear of the company's column five hundred yards ahead, stopped. This was the choke point. He scanned the trees on both sides, looking for an ambush, but couldn't see anything in the dark. Then the column started to move forward. The front of the column should be in any kill zone by now. Kolochov would almost certainly make sure someone was here to stop an escape. But there was no gunfire.

Rainey began scanning the men with him. He recognized Miller and Corelli, but none of the other shadowy figures looked anything like Elizabeth or Bradley. He brought up his hand and stopped the group.

"Where is Miss Clarke?"

No one answered and he knew for sure that she was not among them. A slow burning fear arose in his mind. She was still back in the city. He had lost her in the battle. His stomach sank and he felt sick. He couldn't lose her. Not now.

"I need some ammunition, a rifle and a Colt," said Rainey.

Miller looked perplexed. "There's lots on the wagons, sir."

"I'm not going to the wagons."

Miller looked him in the face, hard, and started to hand over clips of pistol ammunition.

"I'll need a second Colt too," Rainey said flatly. Corelli handed him his pistol.

"What are you going to do, sir?" Miller asked.

Rainey didn't answer. He stuffed every pocket and belt pouch with clips and loose bullets, then checked his Webley revolver to make sure it was full, too. "Sergeant Kennard's in charge until, if, or when I get back. If he asks where I've gotten to, tell him I'm ordering him to get the company out of Russia and not to worry about me. I'll be fine."

Corelli looked doubtful. "Sir, we're not supposed go to back for any . . ." Rainey's cold stare stopped him. "Yes, sir" was all he could say.

Rainey turned and started back into Chelyabinsk.

34

July 26, 1919
Chelyabinsk

The darkness was complete. Elizabeth thought she was dead. She heard soft music from a violin playing in the distance, the odd sound of small arms fire, and occasionally men speaking Russian. It all seemed fantastic as she slowly ascended out of unconsciousness. She could feel the bed she was lying on, the sheet over her, her pants and boots still on. And then the pain. It started as numbness in her left shoulder, building to a point of pain that made her desperately want to return to the darkness. But her mind would not have it. She had to know what was going on because this definitely wasn't heaven.

She commanded her eyes to open. Light began to pierce the darkness and the sounds she was hearing became more focused. Her eyes finally flickered open, giving her a view of a ceiling. A familiar ceiling. Her eyes moved to the light fixture, to the walls. It was the same room where she had made love to Rainey. Maybe she was all right. She sensed someone else was in the room. Gazing around, she spotted a man rising from a chair in the corner and coming to her bed. He looked strangely familiar, but she couldn't place where she knew him from. He was dressed in what looked like an old Russian officer's uniform.

"You are awake," he said in Russian-accented English. "How you feeling?"

Elizabeth rolled her head to the left to look at her shoulder. It was all bandaged up. She also realized that she was not wearing a shirt under the sheet. "Where's my shirt?" she demanded quietly.

The man chuckled. "Gone, all torn up. I sent for new one."

With her right hand, she lifted the sheet a little to look down at her other point of discomfort. Her left breast looked heavily bruised. She pulled the sheet up close around her neck.

"I know you," she said.

"You remember," the man said in surprise. "We not speak, but I remember nurse from Odessa."

Nurse? Odessa? Her mind flew back almost a month before. In the same Tsarist uniform as now, riding a large black horse. He was a colonel. But what was his name?

"Forgive me, Colonel," she said while she searched for a name. "It's been quite a month." All she could remember was that it was a long name.

The man smiled broadly. "And you not familiar with Russian names, no? Then I reintroduce. Colonel Yuri Sergeyvich Krasenovsky, 14th Guards."

Elizabeth smiled weakly. "Yes, of course. I remember now."

"Comrade Kolochov thought it wise you wake up to familiar face." Krasenovsky pulled his chair closer to the bed and sat down. "Your wound not too serious. Need rest for while. Shoulder take long time to heal."

"I was also shot in the chest," Elizabeth said, confused.

Krasenovsky held up the silver locket, which looked like it had caved in on one side. "You very lucky. This stop bullet."

Elizabeth stared at the locket, slowly spinning on its chain. Jeremy, Rainey, and now her. The locket had saved her. She reached out and took it from Krasenovsky and pushed it into her pants pocket. Her mind instantly went somewhere else.

"Did the company get out?"

Krasenovsky smiled and nodded. "With little help from me." He put his index finger to his lips. "But do not tell Kolochov. He think I kill them all."

Kolochov. A spike of fear rose in her throat. "Where is Kolochov now, Yuri?"

"He downstairs," Krasenovsky said. "I get him?"

"No," she said too quickly. She took a breath. "I'd like to rest a while yet before talking with him."

Krasenovsky nodded knowingly. "He not nice man."

"No, he's not." Elizabeth scanned his face, looking for signs of insincerity: the way he held his eyes, the furl of his brow, some kind of nervous twitch.

"But I have to report you awake," Krasenovsky said. "I come back." He got up and went out the door.

Elizabeth lay there, thinking about Rainey, if he had made it out, was he thinking about her, did he even know she was alive. Then she remembered Tom Bradley. He had used his body to shield her from the machine gun. He had died saving her. Poor Tom. Tears welled up as she remembered his ever-attentive presence throughout the mission. He had always been there to protect her. She felt so small compared to that, guilty for having made him part of the backup charge. She wished he was there with her now, freeing her from what was sure to happen soon.

The door opened and in walked a little man with a bold nose, squinty eyes behind round spectacles, a large forehead and a scowl on his lips. Elizabeth recognized him from newspaper clippings. This was Leon Trotsky. A rising sense of dread consumed her. If Trotsky was interested in her father, Alexis must be so much more important to the revolution than any money he could access. She understood now how important it was to keep Alexis's existence to herself. Perhaps it would have been better to have died out there in the street, she thought.

Kolochov and Krasenovsky stood by the door while Trotsky stepped up to the bed and looked down on Elizabeth. "So, this is famous American you tell me about," he said in broken English.

"Yes, Comrade Trotsky," Kolochov replied. "Daughter of Jonathan Clarke."

"Hmmfp," Trotsky grunted. "Find out what Clarke was hiding. She no tell, shoot her. She tell, shoot her sooner." And with that, he turned and stomped out of the room.

Elizabeth turned to Kolochov. "Is he always that abrupt?"

"He is a busy man," Kolochov said, stepping up to the bed. "I am sure Charles told you that Comrade Trotsky is my superior. He is out seeing the troops, but he also has a great interest in what your father has been up to. As you heard, my orders are very clear. I am sorry that it has to end in your death, but it could be much less painful if you just answer a few questions."

"And miss out on all your refined torture techniques?" Elizabeth retorted.

Kolochov slowly circled the bed. "I see your brush with death has not dampened your spirit. But spirit can only carry you so far." He stopped and leaned over her left shoulder. "In the end, you will tell me what I want to know. And you will wish you had just told me earlier and gotten a quick, painless death."

His hand lowered to her shoulder, pressing his thumb into the bandages right over the wound. Elizabeth winced, but remained defiant. He slowly increased the pressure, watching the pain wash over Elizabeth's face, tears running down her cheeks until, finally, she gasped loudly.

He let go and stood up straight. Elizabeth reached over and gripped her shoulder, taking short gasps of air, but continuing to stare boldly at Kolochov. He smiled sinisterly back at her. "That was just a small taste."

"Really?" Elizabeth said through gritted teeth. "I was expecting to see at least some sort of torture equipment."

Kolochov's smile dropped. "That attitude will get you nowhere."

"You mean it will get *you* nowhere," Elizabeth replied. "Me, it comes naturally when I face stupidity."

Kolochov moved so quickly Elizabeth didn't even see his hand move. He slapped her hard with the back of his hand across her cheek. She let out a cry, but quickly spun her face back in defiance. She felt the heat of anger rising in her face. She wanted to kill him as much as that Cossack officer she'd shot in the Jewish village. But now was not the time. She rubbed her cheek.

"You hit like a woman," she said.

A short, bitten-back laugh emanated from Krasenovsky. Kolochov's head snapped up to scowl at him. He promptly returned his attention to Elizabeth. "I see I will have so much fun breaking you. And you will break."

A quick stab of fear tore through Elizabeth as she held her breath, but this faded quickly. Anger and defiance were all she had and she planned on using them. "We'll have to see then, won't we?" She couldn't think of anything more painful than that bullet in her shoulder.

Kolochov sighed. "You have one hour to decide your fate." He turned on his heel and left.

"He was so much more pleasant over dinner," Elizabeth mused aloud. She looked up at Krasenovsky, who had a sad look on his face. "Don't worry, I'll be fine."

"No, you will not," Krasenovsky said. "I know men like him. Very bad. They enjoy what they do."

"Well then, I'll just have to get myself out of here." Elizabeth began to rise out of the bed, only to have a stab of pain drop her head back on the pillow. "But maybe I'll just rest here a while."

Krasenvosky moved to the door. "I must return to regiment. I come back, see you soon." He opened the door to leave.

"Bring me back that shirt," Elizabeth said as he closed the door behind him. The room was silent now, leaving her with her thoughts. Thoughts full of fear and foreboding now that her anger had no visible target.

* * *

All was quiet on the street now, late in the morning. Fighting continued somewhere to the north. Rainey had picked up a Red Army cap along the way, storing his own in a saddle bag. He reached the corner where the slaughter had occurred to find his men still lying there, stripped of their boots, pants and weapons. In the middle of the street lay Bradley, face up, staring up at the sky. But no Elizabeth. If she had died with Bradley, she would still be there on the street. His heart jumped with this knowledge.

Rainey knelt by Bradley's body and closed the dead man's eyes. A sense of loss came over him. He and Bradley had seen a lot together. He picked up the body, threw it over his shoulder and found a vacant lot to bury his friend, saying a small prayer over the grave.

He tied up the horse so he could move less conspicuously on foot. As he turned to leave, his thoughts returned to Elizabeth. Where would she have been taken? He heard a door close. It was the house near the depot where Clarke had been hiding. A man in an old officer's uniform stepped out and walked down the street away from him. Something about the man was familiar. Rainey figured that if anyone could tell him where prisoners might be, an officer could.

He hurried toward the officer, then backed off a bit when another man, in a long black coat and fedora, emerged from the same house. The officer turned to speak to the man in black, showing Rainey his profile. Rainey couldn't contain his surprise.

Krasenovsky?

He couldn't believe his luck. The two men continued down the street, Rainey following at a safe distance. After ten minutes, they reached a building that looked like a hotel. Krasenovsky went inside while the other man continued on. Rainey saw his chance.

Inside the hotel, Rainey suddenly realized that he looked out of place. The lobby was full of officers with only a few enlisted men. Rainey would have to move fast before someone asked what he was doing there. He spoke to the man at the front desk.

"I have a message for Colonel Krasenovsky."

"He just came in," the clerk replied. "He went into the lounge."

The man pointed. Rainey, following his finger, cautiously pushed open the door to the lounge. He spotted Krasenovsky at the bar and maneuvered through the crowd. He was talking to another officer as Rainey came up behind him.

"The other half of the city will be a problem. The Whites have barricaded in and around the government buildings," Krasenovsky said. "They will be hard to dislodge."

"We'll get the rest of the army up to deal with that," the other officer said.

"But that won't be until tomorrow."

"Well, Yuri Sergeyvich," the officer said, "I must be getting back to my battalion. We have orders to watch part of the perimeter tonight and seek out weak spots for tomorrow."

"And my orders are to work on those government buildings," Krasenovsky replied. "I'll no doubt see you there."

The two officers downed their drinks and shook hands. The other man departed. Krasenovsky turned back towards the bar and signaled for another drink. Rainey stepped to his side. He glanced at Krasenovsky, who didn't look too happy.

"Problems at the front, Colonel?" Rainey said in quiet English.

Krasenovsky slowly lifted his drink to his lips, not acknowledging Rainey at all. When the glass came down, he mumbled, "Somehow I knew you here somewhere."

That was an odd thing to say. "I just have a little unfinished business," Rainey said.

"Yes, I know," Krasenovsky replied. "*Dzyevooshka* Clarke."

Rainey's head jerked around. "You know where she is?" he demanded, softly but forcefully.

Krasenovsky took another drink, not replying.

Rainey pressed on. "What is it you want, Colonel?"

Krasenovsky continued to stare at the bar. Several seconds passed before he spoke. "There is nothing I want. But I help you anyway."

Rainey's heart leapt. "How is she?"

"Serious wound in shoulder. She hard to move. Much pain. But problem is man called Kolochov about to start, what is word, inter-o-gation?"

Rainey grabbed him by the shoulder. "Where is she, Colonel? I have to get to her now."

"I show you," Krasenovsky said and led Rainey into the lobby. "I must wait for my sergeant."

"Your sergeant?" Rainey exclaimed. "Why?"

"He bringing new shirt for *dyzevooshka*."

Rainey didn't understand. Krasenovsky smiled. "She has no shirt. And my excuse to get alone for you."

Rainey nodded. "You knew I'd come."

"For her, yes. In Odessa, I saw how you looked at her."

God, Rainey thought, *it was noticeable even back then?*

"She not really nurse, correct?" Krasenovsky asked.

Rainey grinned. "No, she's not."

"Kolochov wants her father and what he was hiding. I tell him father dead, but he still wants to know what he was hiding."

"No doubt," Rainey said. He looked down the street. "I can't exactly tag along with you and your sergeant."

"You know house you stayed in while here?"

Rainey nodded. It was the house he had seen Krasenovsky come out of. "Which room?"

"You wait for me," Krasenovsky commanded. "It now RU headquarters. You never get in and out alone. I will signal you."

Rainey nodded. His gut said he could trust this Russian, but Elizabeth's life depended on it. That was a whole new equation when more than his own life lay in the balance. Krasenovsky was right, though. If Kolochov was there, Rainey wouldn't very well be able to walk in without being recognized.

"I'll meet you there, then," Rainey said. "But which room, in case you don't get there?"

"Top of stairs, door on right."

The irony struck Rainey. It was their room. But something else came to mind. "Do you know if my men made it out?"

Krasenovsky smiled. "I ordered to stop them. I escort instead. They are fine."

Rainey frowned. "Doesn't that put you in a difficult position?"

"Not if I say they all dead and buried." He raised his coat and showed Rainey Appleton's Bowie knife. "And have a little proof. Kolochov was happy and will not double-check for few days."

* * *

Tuchenko watched from the street as Rainey exited the hotel. The British cut of the uniform and the Japanese sword on the man's back were unmistakable. This was the leader of the Americans. Krasenovsky had reported they were all dead. So what was he doing here, talking to Krasenovsky? A minute later, one of Krasenovsky's sergeants arrived, carrying a shirt, and went into the hotel. He exited a minute later and returned the way he'd come. Krasenovsky then stepped out of the building with the shirt.

Krasenovsky walked back towards the RU house shortly after the American had crossed the street and headed in the same direction. Tuchenko moved out of the shadows of a wall and followed. The gnawing feeling he had always had about Krasenovsky now seemed to be confirmed.

35

Elizabeth was dozing when the door opened. Her eyes fluttered open to see Kolochov followed by two men and a cart carrying something she didn't recognize. The throbbing of her shoulder reinserted itself into her mind, bringing her totally awake.

Kolochov stood at the foot of the bed, watching her. She focused a stare back, knowing he would say something eventually. The two men with the cart said nothing. Kolochov finally broke the silence.

"Electricity is a wonderful thing. It can bring light to a dark room, heat to a cold place, and power to new inventions. It is this power that is transforming the world."

"Tell me something I don't know," Elizabeth replied. "We've had Thomas Edison over for dinner several times. Is there a point you are trying to make?"

A slow smile spread across Kolochov's face. "Electricity also has a dark side. It can deliver pain and death. If used properly, just pain."

Elizabeth took a closer look at the two men and their cart. "Oh, good," she said flatly. "You've brought one of your torture toys."

Kolochov laid his hand on the cart. "Actually, this little device was designed by the Okhrana, the Tsar's secret police. Our Cheka have found many of the Okhrana's methods quite useful. Information is easily extracted when the subject desires death over pain."

"Is this your way of blaming someone else for what you are about to do?" Elizabeth asked.

"Just some background," Kolochov said. "I need some answers from you and want you to know that you will give them to me."

Elizabeth sighed. "You have yet to pose a question. Perhaps you could try that first."

Kolochov picked up a wire from the cart, observing it with feigned interest. "No, I think you need a taste of this before we start." He placed the wire back on the cart. "Wire her up," he said in Russian.

"So much for the honor of the Bolshevik cause," Elizabeth said quietly.

"No matter the political cause, it cannot survive without people like me to defend it against its enemies."

Elizabeth glanced up at him. "Is that how you justify your enjoyment of torturing people?"

Kolochov smiled. "I do not justify it at all. I freely admit it."

The two men stepped forward. They applied straps to her hands and feet to hold her in place. Starting with her feet, they removed her boots and socks and placed a clamp on each of her big toes. They did the same with her hands, putting the clamps on her index fingers. Finally, they pulled away the sheet that covered her and placed a clamp on each nipple. Wires from each clamp ran to a box on the cart. Elizabeth lay motionless, knowing she didn't have the strength to fight. Fear was building up in her throat.

"This isn't necessary. Just ask your questions. You may find I don't have a problem answering them," she said. She tried to sound calm, but heard her voice betraying her panic.

"Oh, I think I will," said Kolochov. A faint smile showed that he had noticed the fear in her voice.

"And I thought you were a gentleman," Elizabeth said, glancing at the wires attached to her breasts.

Kolochov laughed. "Let us be honest, Miss Clarke. You never thought that. But perhaps we could start with a question, just to humor you. Where was your father hiding?"

"Right here, in this house," said Elizabeth. "He had the room across the hall. But you know that already."

"Yes, I do," Kolochov said.

"Then ask me something you don't know," said Elizabeth.

"Very well, what was your father hiding?"

That was revealing. Kolochov didn't know what the 'package' was. Elizabeth had to delay him as long as possible.

"I don't know."

Kolochov's fist banged on a large button, sending a brief charge through the wires. Her entire body jerked once. Her head snapped back, fists and jaw clenched. The electricity made all her nerve endings scream in pain. She gulped in air, trying to regain her focus. As soon as the charge hit her it was over, but her body now trembled uncontrollably.

She rolled her head so she could see Kolochov. "Was that the taste?" she asked through trembling lips.

He smiled. "Yes. Next time, I'll hold the button down longer. Now again, what was the item your father was hiding?"

Elizabeth stared at Kolochov. Maybe she could make something up that was believable, but to make it believable, she would first have to endure more. It would be so much easier if she could just die right then.

"I don't know," she whispered.

Kolochov's hand slowly reached for the button. Elizabeth braced herself for the charge, her eyes never leaving his.

"So defiant," Kolochov said. "And such a waste." He pressed the button and held it down.

* * *

Rainey was waiting in a darkened doorway across the street when the scream met his ears like a bolt of lightning. It was Elizabeth. He couldn't wait for Krasenovsky's signal. He had to move now. Throwing his rifle over his shoulder alongside the sword, he pulled out his Webley and one of the Colts and charged toward the guard in front of the house.

The guard had been watching him. When the screaming started, the man looked up towards the second floor window. When he turned back toward the street, Rainey was almost on him, a pistol in each hand.

The guard never had a chance. One well-placed round in his chest forced him against the wall, where he collapsed. Without breaking his stride, Rainey flew to the broken front door and kicked it open.

* * *

Elizabeth kept shaking violently even after Kolochov released the button. Her eyes full of tears, she gasped for air, her flesh tingling, the pain lingering. Sweat poured out as if the electricity was boiling her. She strained against the bonds that tied her to the bed, but they wouldn't budge. She was in hell.

"Now again, what was your father . . ."

Kolochov's words ended abruptly at the sound of a gunshot from outside. He turned to the window and as he took a step in that direction, the downstairs door crashed open.

The two technicians looked up, wide-eyed. "Go see what's going on," he barked. More shots rang out in the stairwell. Both men drew their guns and ran from the room.

Kolochov turned back to Elizabeth. "Now, Miss Clarke, where were we?"

Through the shaking, Elizabeth smiled. She knew someone was here for her.

* * *

Coming through the door, Rainey went into a roll and came up with pistols ready. Right in front of him was a startled soldier, trying to bring his rifle to bear. Rainey fired one shot from the Webley into his forehead. He pivoted to his left where, he remembered, was the entrance to a sitting room. A man at a desk was raising a pistol. A round from each pistol took him out. Rainey quickly moved up the stairs.

A bullet buzzed past his ear into the plaster behind him. Another shot clipped his thigh. He ignored the pain and began firing wildly up the stairs, then heard a grunt. One of his shots had hit the man on the landing, who toppled forward and tumbled down toward him. A second man dodged into the room across the hall. Never stopping, Rainey reached the top, fired at the door on his left and found the door on the right closed and locked.

Other soldiers appeared below and fired up the stairs. Rainey ducked as bullets slammed into the wall above his head. He aimed his pistols, but before he could fire, the soldiers all crumpled, hit suddenly from the side.

* * *

Tuchenko appeared in the front doorway in time to see Krasenovksy coming out of the sitting room with his gun up. Tuchenko had no chance. Krasenovsky shot him in the head, point-blank.

Rainey raised himself up, nodded at Krasenovsky, then fired two rounds at the door latch, splintering the wood. Rainey kicked at the door.

Inside, Elizabeth screamed again. Rainey slammed his shoulder into the door as hard as he could. He fell inside as the door flew open. He rolled, again, coming up in the far corner with both guns up.

What he saw froze his mind. Kolochov stood over a cart, pressing a large button. A buzzing sound emanated beneath Elizabeth's screams. She lay on the bed, yelling and sobbing, back arched, body convulsing, naked from the waist up, with wires running from her body.

Rainey's hesitation was almost fatal. Without releasing the button, Kolochov raised his gun and fired. Rainey ducked in the nick of time and rolled towards the next corner. Kolochov kept firing until a dull click of an empty magazine told both men that he was now defenseless. Releasing the button, he bolted for the door.

Rainey fired off two rounds that missed. Elizabeth lay quiet, unconscious on the bed, soaked in sweat. Rainey rushed forward to remove the clamps from her body and release her restraints. He listened for her heartbeat. She was alive, her heart beating very fast. He pulled the sheet up over her naked torso and pulled her onto the floor. Dragging the big dresser away from the wall, he hauled Elizabeth behind it. He pulled the magazine out of the Colt to see only one round remained. Making sure he had one in the chamber, he slammed a fresh clip into it. Next he reloaded the Webley. He unslung the rifle to get it ready to fire and placed the second Colt on the floor beside him.

He looked back at Elizabeth. Her breathing was becoming regular. He checked her heart again; it was slowing down to normal. He wanted to hold her, make her realize she was now safe, but that would be a lie. He hadn't thought past getting to Elizabeth. There was no escape plan.

Rainey could hear Kolochov shouting orders downstairs. "I want them alive. Now get up there and get them." Wanting them alive gave Rainey the advantage. The floor creaked as a soldier stepped lightly into the room. Rainey rose quickly, fired one round into the man's chest and dropped back behind the dresser. Several rifle shots plowed into the dresser.

"Alive, you idiots, or you'll wish you weren't," Kolochov shouted.

"He's barricaded himself, Colonel," answered a soldier on the landing.

Rainey pressed his body to the floor, looking under the bed for a clear view to the doorway. One soldier was against the wall, his feet visible. Rainey aimed closely and fired. The bullet struck the man's right foot. He let out a scream and crawled away from the door out of sight. Now all was quiet.

Nothing happened for two minutes. Rainey remained prone, watching the door. He heard a creak by the window. He popped up to find a soldier hanging onto the wall outside. He shot the man in the chest, pivoted and dropped to the floor as two more soldiers appeared in the doorway, firing. Rainey took cover under the bed again and shot the feet out from under them. Both cried in pain and fell back.

"Captain Rainey," Kolochov called out. "As you can see, there is no getting out of that room. If you surrender now, I will treat you as a prisoner of war."

"So you can wire Elizabeth up again?" Rainey spat. "I don't think so. Besides, I've seen how prisoners of war are treated. Bullet to the head is pretty standard, isn't it?"

"Come now, Captain," Kolochov continued. "We are both civilized men . . ."

"You have a lot of gall calling yourself civilized."

"We do what we have to for the Revolution."

"Oh, sure. Blame the Revolution for your sins."

* * *

Kolochov stood quietly at the foot of the stairs, apparently lost in thought, when Krasenovsky stepped through the doorway.

"Having a little trouble, Comrade Kolochov?" Krasenovsky asked.

Kolochov stomped over to the colonel. "You told me they were all dead. Your American friend is holed up there with his bitch."

"I cannot be held responsible for one man getting clear of my ambush," Krasenovsky said. "The Americans all looked alike to me in the dark."

Kolochov stepped up into Krasenovsky's face. "You dare to lecture me? Get up there and get him out."

Krasenovsky lowered his eyes, stepped around Kolochov and put his foot on the first step. As he did so, he marked in his mind where everyone was standing. With one hand, he pulled out his pistol. With the other, a grenade.

"I want them alive, Colonel," Kolochov said.

Krasenovsky nodded. He moved slowly up the stairs. "Captain, how are you?" he said in English.

No response.

Krasenovsky stood behind the men on the landing. "I only want to speak with you. If you come out, I will guarantee safety."

"I'll only come out shooting," Rainey said through the doorway.

Krasenovsky smiled. "I know. Perhaps I can arrange another way." He unobtrusively pulled the pin from the grenade and began to count in his head. When he figured it would go off just one second after he tossed it, his arm arched, heaving the grenade down the staircase. Shouts of shock were drowned out by the explosion. Krasenovsky fired his pistol directly into the backs of the three soldiers on the landing.

"You come out now," he said.

Rainey heard the noise and heard the cries. But was it all real? Slowly, he came up from behind the dresser, pistol at the ready. Krasenovsky was standing in the doorway, a dead soldier visible behind him.

"You really don't like Bolsheviks," Rainey said.

Krasenovsky shook his head sadly. "Bolsheviks fine. Do not like Kolochov. Now we must hurry. And here." He threw a shirt onto the bed. "I promise her shirt."

Rainey holstered his gun and grabbed the shirt. He propped Elizabeth up to clothe her. Krasenovsky crossed the room and began pulling on her socks and boots. Rainey noticed that her wounds had begun to bleed again. "We'll need some new dressings."

"I can get downstairs," Krasenovsky said. His boots clattered down the steps, Rainey following close behind, carrying Elizabeth piggyback so he still could shoot forward. Rainey stepped over several soldiers and saw the carnage the grenade had caused down below. But Kolochov was missing.

Krasenovsky emerged from the sitting room with wound dressings in his hand. "Have horses down street," he said.

"I can't thank you enough," Rainey said.

"No thank needed. I like to do something good for change."

His pistol up at the ready, Krasenovsky cautiously stepped out the front door and looked around. All seemed quiet. Rainey followed, carrying Elizabeth. Moving up the street, Krasenovsky kept an eye out for other soldiers. They found three horses where Krasenovsky said they would be, so Rainey hoisted Elizabeth up onto one and tied her feet to the stirrups. He mounted that horse as well, steadying himself by holding onto Elizabeth's inert body. He grabbed the reins of the other two horses and turned to say goodbye to Krasenovsky.

The gunshot surprised him. Krasenovsky was charging Kolochov, clutching his shoulder, reaching him before Kolochov could fire another round. The two Russians fought hand-to-hand in a dance of death. A pistol fell to the ground about three feet from both, who struggled to reach it. Rainey was about to jump down when Kolochov grasped the gun. Krasenovsky yelled, "Captain, go!"

The bark of a BAR startled Rainey, who saw rounds spitting into the dirt near Kolochov's feet. Rainey spun around to see Private Miller on a horse, charging down the street, firing the BAR from the hip. Kolochov bolted for the house. Krasenovsky ran in the opposite direction. Rainey spun his horse and raced away, the reins of the other two horses tight in his hands. Miller turned his mount and followed when Rainey galloped past him.

36

July 26-27, 1919
Chelyabinsk to Kurgan

Miller had helped by grabbing Rainey's horse on the way out of town, giving them five horses total. They rode hard out into the Siberian wilderness until they came across a shack used by rail linemen. Elizabeth was still unconscious as he pulled her down off the horse and carried her inside. Miller stayed outside to keep watch. Laying her on a cot, Rainey opened her shirt so he could change the dressings. The wound had stopped bleeding, but it needed to be washed. Rainey poured the little water in his canteen over the wound until he had none left. He would have to refill at the first stream they came across.

After he'd cleaned and dressed the wound, Rainey went over the contact points where clamps had been applied to her body. Small, dark burn marks were visible at each point, but nothing appeared to be too serious. The deep bruise over her heart made him wonder what had caused it. He clothed her, then sat back in a chair and watched her slowly breathing, the only indication she was alive. Watching Elizabeth, he knew she had a spell on him. He loved her very deeply. And he would never forgive himself if she didn't wake up.

Rainey found the locket in her trousers and rolled it in his hands. The damage explained the bruise on her chest. Rainey stared at it, transfixed for a few moments. Then he stood and slid the locket back into Elizabeth's trouser pocket. It had saved her. She still needed it.

He stepped out of the shack. "So, Private, do you always disobey orders?"

Miller kept his eyes on the horizon. "Just thought you could use some extra help, sir."

"This wasn't your business."

"I made it my business. You need Miss Clarke and the company needs you."

"The rules are that we can't go back for anyone."

"Those rules include Miss Clarke."

He was right. Rainey rubbed his face with his hands. He just couldn't be mad at the private. "Did you at least bring some food with you?"

Miller turned back to the little building. "Of course, sir." He lifted a bag from his shoulder and tossed it to Rainey. "The finest field rations Lieutenant Clarke could buy."

Rainey opened a tin, devouring it quickly to lessen the hunger pains. He hadn't eaten all day.

"Is Miss Clarke going to be all right, sir?" Miller asked.

Rainey looked back through the doorway at her on the cot. "I don't know. She's alive, but in pretty bad shape."

They stayed in the shack for only fifteen minutes. Dusk was coming and he wanted to make camp far enough into the wilderness to stay hidden. It would take two or three days to catch up to the company. Rainey put Elizabeth onto a different horse and re-tied her feet in the stirrups. Riding behind her like before, he urged the horse into a slow trot, following the railroad into the forest.

* * *

It was getting dark. The wind was whipping up into a frenzy, with gusts hard enough that Rainey had to hang tightly onto Elizabeth to stay on the horse. Thunder claps came more frequently as the storm slowly overtook them. A light rain was falling when Rainey spotted what looked like an overhanging rock formation among the trees. It would give them some sort of shelter.

They were venturing, alone in the Siberian wilderness with a couple of pistols, a BAR, and little food or shelter. Rainey was extremely hungry at this point, but he was more concerned that Elizabeth was still unconscious. Riding into the trees, they found that the overhanging rock would make a suitable shelter. Rainey brought Elizabeth down off the horse and laid her, sitting up, against the rocks. He took off his tunic and wrapped it around her shoulders, sat beside her and pulled her close.

Miller was taking all they had off the horses and moving it under the overhang. He led the horses up against the rocks to keep them out of the wind and tied them up. He then settled down with the BAR, keeping an eye on the tracks through the trees.

"You take a nap, Private," Rainey said. "I'll keep watch."

"I'm all right, sir," Miller said.

"That's an order."

A look at Rainey told Miller that he meant it. He lowered the BAR, curled up and closed his eyes. Within seconds, he was sound asleep.

Rainey scanned the forest towards the rail line. They sat hud-dled against the rock for two hours as the storm raged around them. The storm finally moved off, leaving a heavy, steady rain falling straight down. Rainey pulled Elizabeth's legs up tight against her body to keep them out of the rain. He was warm enough himself. Slowly, he couldn't help himself. He slept.

What he noticed first the next morning were the birds. Rainey slowly opened his eyes to see the sun shining brightly through the trees. The rain had passed. It was then he noticed that Elizabeth was missing, his tunic now draped across his body. He snapped his head back and forth looking for her when he heard a gunshot, followed by a loud "Owoo." The report registered in his head as a Colt automatic. He reached for the Colt he had been carrying, but it was gone. He jumped to his feet and looked in the direction of the sound, his hand now on his Webley revolver.

Miller also jumped awake, grabbing the BAR in one smooth motion and pointing it in the direction of the gunshot. There, about fifty yards away, was Elizabeth, gingerly rubbing her wounded shoulder and walking away. She bent down to pick up the rabbit she had shot. Turning to head back to the camp, she saw Rainey and Miller. Raising her rabbit in triumph, she smiled.

Rainey was ecstatic. She was awake. He pinched himself to make sure he wasn't dreaming. When Elizabeth made it back to the rocks he reached out to hug her, but she stepped back.

"Shoulder," she said.

"Sorry."

"You have a knife? I'm starving. Good morning, Private."

"Good morning, Miss Clarke," Miller replied.

Rainey handed her his knife, then stood staring. She bent over and, moving gingerly to favor her injured shoulder, began skinning the rabbit. She stopped for a second and looked back.

"Never seen a wounded girl skin a rabbit before?"

Rainey shook himself out of the spell. "Here, I can do that."

"No, no, no, no," she said, shielding the rabbit with her body. "I shot it. I clean and cook it. But you could at least build a fire."

Miller immediately set down his gun and went out to collect firewood. Rainey prepared a site for the fire. All went about their tasks silently. Rainey rigged a crude spit over the fire and refilled his canteen. Elizabeth slow-roasted the rabbit. When it was done, the three ate slowly in silence, sharing the canteen and glancing at each other frequently.

When they were done eating, Rainey leaned back and broke the silence. "Where did a rich girl like you learn to gut and cook a rabbit?"

Elizabeth smiled. "Our estate on Long Island is full of rabbits. I've been able to do this since I was seven. Had to keep ahead of my little brother."

Rainey laughed. "I could never see Jeremy as a little brother. He was such a good officer."

Elizabeth's expression turned serious. "We were pretty close as children. But he was closed to me when he came back from the war. I really don't know what he was like there, apart from what you've told me."

"One of the finest officers I ever came across in France," Rainey said.

"Private, did you know my brother?"

"No, ma'am," Miller said. "I was with the 325th Regiment."

"How's your shoulder?" Rainey asked.

She rotated her arm slowly. "Still sore, but not bad."

Rainey got up. "I'll make a sling for you. Then we'd best be going. We'll never catch up to the company if we lie around here shooting rabbits for food."

Elizabeth grinned. "That wouldn't be too bad."

It was Rainey's turn to become serious. "And Kolochov is probably out looking for us. Private, get the horses."

"Yes, sir," Miller answered.

Just hearing the name seemed to send a chill through Elizabeth. Rainey noticed her stiffening. "Are you sure you're all right?"

Elizabeth nodded. "Just remembering that rather unpleasant episode from yesterday. It was yesterday, wasn't it?"

Rainey nodded as Miller brought the horses around. Handing one set of reins to Elizabeth, Rainey said, "I'm glad you're awake."

She leaned into him and kissed him long and slow. "I'm glad I woke up beside you."

Miller stood grinning at them. Elizabeth gave him a look. "And what's your story, Private? I'm sure the captain would have planned my rescue to be a solo act, especially since it was against a company directive."

Miller threw up his arms. "Why is everyone so concerned about me breaking a rule?"

* * *

A lot of traffic had been following the railroad east. Rainey could see the tracks of horses, wagons and men in the muddy dirt for miles. Rainey set a good pace, pushing the horses, making short stops and rotating among the five mounts. Elizabeth's fatigue showed, but she put on a brave face and refused to ask for more rest. Miller stayed about half a mile back as rear guard, catching up whenever they rested.

About fifty miles short of Kurgan, it became too dark to continue. The clouds had gradually cleared since last night's rain storm. The moon and the stars were bright. Rainey found a spot up a small, wooded hill to make camp. He helped Elizabeth off her horse and sat her down next to a tree. She immediately closed her eyes and fell asleep. Rainey smiled down at her. He took off his tunic and laid it over her shoulders. Now his concern switched to the fact that he was starving and would have to scavenge for food and water.

He found a narrow stream trickling through the woods, gathering in a small pool. The water was exceptionally clear, and with a quick taste, he decided it was fine and filled his canteen. While doing so, he was startled by a noise to his left. A pheasant had jumped onto a rock, watching him. Keeping very still, he hoped that curiosity would bring the pheasant closer. It did. The bird finally jumped down off the rock and took tentative steps towards him. Just as the bird was about to peck at his sleeve, Rainey's hand shot out and grabbed the bird by the neck, breaking it in one swift movement. The bird went limp in his grasp.

Looking around, he decided that the clear spot by the pool made for a better camp. The pool looked very inviting to clean the dust off him. Elizabeth would probably appreciate a bath herself, he thought, not to mention the fact that her wound should be washed and redressed.

With the bird defeathered and cooking over a small fire, Rainey went back to get Elizabeth. Miller had caught up by then and was watching Elizabeth. She was still asleep where Rainey had left her, breathing softly.

"I can see why you went back for her, sir," Miller said quietly. "She looks like an angel sleeping there."

Rainey smiled. "It's more than that. She's smart, strong, and I don't repel her."

Miller chuckled. "Oh, come on, sir. Really? She's had something for you from day one." Rainey gave Miller a skeptical look.

"OK, maybe day fifteen."

Rainey crouched down and laid his hand on her right shoulder. She let out a little grunt and raised her head, but didn't open her eyes.

"Come now, darlin'," Rainey said. "Dinner is almost ready."

Elizabeth smiled, eyes still closed. "And what is Chez Robert serving this evening?"

"Pheasant," Rainey said.

Elizabeth's eyes opened. "Pheasant. I'm impressed."

Rainey leaned back to sit. "And I have an extra bonus for the little lady tonight."

"Did you find a can of beans out there, too?"

Rainey laughed. "No, we just have pheasant and whatever Private Miller has left in his food pouch. But we also have a nice, clear, clean pool of water."

Elizabeth brightened. "You mean . . ."

"You can have a bath," said Rainey. "I should wash your wound again too, make sure it's healing nicely."

Elizabeth gave him a sniff. "You could probably use one as well." She looked over at Miller.

"Yes, Miss Clarke," Miller said, resignation in his voice. "I'll be watching for anyone coming up behind us."

"You can wash up when we're done," Elizabeth said.

The pheasant was good. They didn't leave a speck of meat on the bones, the bare carcass discarded into the fire. Miller moved out towards the rail line to keep away from the pool during bathing time. A few feet away, Rainey's and Elizabeth's clothes were hanging from branches of a tree, damp after being washed. The pool was about two feet deep and eight or nine feet long with a smooth rock bottom. It felt good against her skin as she leaned back onto Rainey's chest, his one arm wrapped around her while the other stroked her wet hair. The water was cool and refreshing. Rainey had paid attention to her shoulder wound. Although it looked extremely ugly, surrounded by large brown and blue bruises, it was healing well.

Elizabeth closed her eyes and reveled in the sensations. The cool water on her body, the cool breeze on her face, the safe feeling of Rainey's arms, and the feelings she was obviously raising in him. "I'm going to have to do something about that, aren't I?" she said, playfully swinging her bum across his manhood.

Rainey kissed the back of her head. "One can only hope, but I'm not expecting anything."

Elizabeth snuggled in closer. "Private Miller won't wander by, will he?"

"Not if he knows what's good for him."

Elizabeth leaned back a little more. "But first, you'll have to tell me more about yourself, like, how many languages do you know?"

Rainey thought for a second. "Honestly, I've never counted."

Elizabeth giggled. "Well, you should sometime. How come you know so many?"

"My family just seemed to be able to pick up languages pretty quick," replied Rainey. "Many different languages spoken in and around where I grew up. We have a lot of immigrants from Eastern Europe."

Elizabeth nodded. "Lots of different languages in New York, but I never learned any. How about when you were a kid? I'll bet you were a real troublemaker in your youth."

"My father was pretty high up in the North West Mounted Police, so I knew all the police. Got away with an awful lot, but it's not like I was a criminal or anything."

"Just having fun?"

"For the most part."

"Then what?"

"At seventeen I entered the Royal Military College. My knack for languages and my rather unorthodox infantry skills got me an appointment to Sandhurst in England. Spent a year there and was then shipped off to Singapore for a year."

"Where you probably learned Chinese."

"And Malay and Tamil," Rainey said with a smile. "Singapore has quite a variety of languages."

"And then the war."

"And being shot at for four years."

"There must be a woman or two in your story," she said slyly.

"Or two," he replied coyly.

"Who were they?"

Rainey shook his head. "Sitting here with you like this, I'm not about to mess up the mood by talking about other women."

Elizabeth lifted herself up and turned around to face him. "I see. Well, maybe I could encourage you a bit." She moved forward and kissed him on the lips, and slowly lowered herself onto him. His hands came up onto her back, stroking gently. She brought her right hand up to his face. She winced momentarily as she put her weight on her left shoulder, but shrugged off the pain. They moved together with a slow, rocking motion, the swirl of the water creating a rhythm with their bodies. They kissed deeply and continually. His hands started moving everywhere; her legs, her back, her buttocks, her arms, her breasts, and through her hair. He wanted to touch her everywhere, envelope her, consume her. She pulled her face away to gasp for air as they came together. They gazed into each other's eyes, the light of the fire dancing across their irises.

"I love you," he said.

"Then tell me about your other women," she answered with a smirk.

37

July 28, 1919
Fifty miles West of Kurgan

The sound of horses jogged Rainey awake. Curled up with Elizabeth, he swung his hand around and instinctively grabbed hold of his Webley pistol before he was even fully awake. The sun was up. He chided himself for oversleeping. The horses were slowing down from a light gallop. Rainey slowly raised himself up to look toward the railway to see about thirty horsemen coming to a stop, just about where they had left the tracks the night before. Some of the horsemen were dressed casually, others as Red soldiers. And one face sent a chill down his spine.

Kolochov.

Rainey glanced over to his horses. They were tied to trees, standing in plain view. There was no hiding now. He had three pistols and a rifle against thirty men. Their capture would automatically mean eventual death. He remembered seeing Elizabeth hooked up to the electroshock machine and promised himself that she would not go through that again. He quickly checked the pistols and his ammunition supply.

Where is Miller?

"Elizabeth," he whispered, lightly shaking her damaged shoulder. "Wake up, my love. We have company."

Elizabeth winced in pain, groaned and opened her eyes. The sounds of the horses and low voices in Russian quickly brought her out of her deep sleep. She lifted her head to look.

"Oh, God," she exclaimed softly.

"They've spotted the horses," Rainey said. "Come on. We've got to get ourselves lost in the bush."

Grabbing only the canteen, the pistols and the sword, the two ran in a crouch away from their horses. They were spotted right away. A few rifle rounds were fired in their direction.

"Good morning, Captain," Kolochov's voice bellowed. "I'm so happy to have found you. Miss Clarke and I have so much more to talk about."

The pursuers dismounted quickly and formed into a skirmish line. They began advancing slowly into the bush, rifles at the ready.

"Remember," Kolochov ordered. "Wound, do not kill."

This bit of forest backed up to a swamp. There was nowhere to go. Holding Elizabeth's arm, Rainey directed her behind a mound covered in brush.

"Here," he said, handing her a Colt and laying the Springfield rifle beside her. "I'll be back."

"Where are you going?" she asked, panic in her voice.

"To even the odds a little. Anyone you don't know comes up to you, just shoot him."

Elizabeth looked around. "Where's Miller?"

Rainey smiled at her. "I don't know, but I'm sure he's around here somewhere." His smile couldn't hide the fact he wasn't that confident about Miller.

"Captain," Kolochov's voice rang out. "There is nowhere you can go. Let's say you just surrender and we can head back to Chelyabinsk right away. I promise you a nice cell with a comfortable cot."

Rainey circled silently through the brush. In their effort to spread a wide enough net, he found the skirmishers weren't keeping each other within easy sight. He chose a target and found a spot to lie low in, waiting for the man to approach, slowly drawing his sword from its scabbard. The man was almost on top of him when he sprang up and sliced open his throat. As the man fell backward, Rainey grabbed him and lowered him slowly to the ground. Returning sword to its scabbard, he picked up the man's rifle and took his place in the skirmish line.

* * *

Elizabeth kept an eye out in front of her, head pivoting back and forth as she had seen the company's soldiers do. The gun was out in front of her, feeling bigger and heavier than she remembered a Colt to be. She heard a twig cracking. She focused her attention on the direction of the sound. Movement of some brush caught her eye. She brought the gun to bear. The figure of a man appeared, in a crouch and walking tentatively.

* * *

The gunshot and a scream indicated that Elizabeth's position had been found. The skirmish line broke up as the men moved toward the sound of the gunshot. Rainey picked up his pace, approaching the next man in the line. Bringing up his newly acquired rifle, he slammed the butt into the man's head as he ran past him. He heard the Colt bark again before he saw a man raising his rifle and taking careful aim at Elizabeth. Rainey swung up his rifle and fired, catching the man in the shoulder. Quickly working the bolt, he shoved another round into the chamber just in time to register a surprised look on another man's face five yards to his right. He quickly swung the rifle and fired right into the man's face. Gunfire was thickening now as he became a target. A bullet whizzed by his ear. Elizabeth was returning fire as he dived behind the mound to join her.

"Don't kill them!!" Kolochov yelled.

The firing stopped. Rainey was breathing heavily as he checked his leg.

"You're bleeding," Elizabeth exclaimed.

"No time to deal with that now." He grabbed her pistol, ejected the clip, slammed in a new one and handed the gun back to her. He placed two more full clips on the ground next to her. "Any pause in the action, take the opportunity to reload the gun. And keep your eyes looking out there as much as possible."

Elizabeth nodded and swallowed hard. She swung her face back to the line of battle. Rainey chambered another round into the rifle and brought it to bear in the same direction.

"Captain," said Kolochov, much closer now. "You are a resourceful and talented soldier. But you must realize the futility of your position. You will only die here if you continue to resist."

"Better here than strapped to your little toy," Elizabeth shouted. Rainey heard no more hints of panic in her voice. Kolochov's voice must have helped her find the magic elixir, the emotion to banish fear in the face of death.

Anger.

She glanced calmly over at Rainey. "If we're about to get captured, you shoot me. In the head."

"What?"

Kolochov's voice carried over the soggy ground. "Miss Clarke,

I assure you that will no longer be necessary."

"You heard me," she told Rainey.

Rainey looked into her eyes. Cold, angry eyes. She was serious. There was no going back to Chelyabinsk for her.

"I love you," Rainey said, almost without realizing he was saying it.

"I love you too," Elizabeth replied flatly. Her eyes went back to searching for targets.

Rainey did the same. His mind reeled with the thought of losing her. He couldn't live without her, and looking at the situation they were in, he probably wouldn't have to. This was it. He had found the love of his life just in time to die with her. It wasn't fair. And so the magic elixir started to pump through his veins, too. They would fight fiercely. When it was all said and done, ballads would be written about the two lovers fighting against incredible odds in Siberian wilds, extracting a terrible vengeance and dying in each other's arms.

Then his professional mind kicked in.

Whoa, where did that come from? Focus on the job at hand, buddy boy. We're not in some romantic novel.

He watched the bushes move in front of him. They were closing in, most likely for a full-out charge once they were close enough. Rainey put down the rifle and took out the other Colt and his Webley. He could handle hand-to-hand combat, but Elizabeth, wounded shoulder or not, wouldn't stand a chance. Rainey contemplated shooting Elizabeth in the head, but there was no way he'd be able to do that.

The shouts began as all the pursuers jumped up at once and charged forward. They were within fifteen yards of Rainey and Elizabeth. The pistols started to bark. But there were just too many. As the attackers neared, Rainey stood up, reaching for his sword, ready to fight hand to hand.

The sound of automatic fire surprised everyone. It came from Rainey's right. He watched all the men in front of him take hits, pitching sideways. He instinctively moved to his left to cover Elizabeth, sword held high. But additional rifle fire from the left was taking out those men. When the last one fell to the ground, right beside Elizabeth, the firing stopped as suddenly as it had started.

Silence overtook the scene. Rainey and Elizabeth still held their weapons at the ready, their heads and eyes moving in quick little jerks so as not to miss any movement.

"What just happened?" asked Elizabeth.

Without taking his eyes away from scanning the bushes, Rainey said, "That was Miller over to the right. I don't know who's on the left."

"Which means?"

"I have no idea."

The brush rattled to the right. Rainey spun to see Miller step out, the BAR aimed at where the other shots came from.

"Cutting it a little close, weren't you, Private?"

"Sorry, sir," Miller said. "I got spotted and they sent a couple of guys after me. Had to circle back around and got held up by the swamp."

"Captain, are you all right?" came a voice from the left in Russian-accented English.

Rainey smiled as he reached down to touch Elizabeth's head. "It's all right." He called back. "Yes, Colonel, we're fine."

"Who . . . ?" She began to ask when a tall Russian officer stepped into view. "Oh, my God."

Krasenovsky was standing in a clearing with a few men. His

left arm was in a sling, but he stood tall and proud, like the first time Rainey had met him, pistol in hand.

Rainey's astonishment must have showed. Krasenovsky laughed. "No, Captain, I am not ghost. Comrade Kolochov very poor shot."

"Am I ever glad to see you," Rainey said, hurrying to meet him. "You have no idea how glad."

Krasenovsky surveyed the dead lying about. "I get idea."

"Why did you come after us?" Rainey asked.

"Kolochov want me dead now. Could not let him tell anyone."

Rainey smiled. "No, of course not."

Krasenovsky glanced over at Miller. "You were in street back in Chelyabinsk."

"Yes, sir," Miller nervously replied, BAR still trained on the Russians

A noise behind them made them turn. Pushing Kolochov ahead of him, Krasenovsky's sergeant came through the brush. "I found this shit trying to get away."

Rainey saw red, but quickly brought his rage under control. Krasenovsky stepped up and slapped Kolochov across the face with the back of his good hand. "Captain, myself and young lady have decision to make about you."

Rainey grimaced. "I say, let's send him back to Trotsky, where I'm sure he'll be shot for incompetence."

Kolochov stood up straight. Rainey thought he saw a glimpse of fear in his eyes. "I have much power among the Commissars. I can do a lot for you if . . ."

Four quick rounds from the BAR stitched a pattern of reddish black dots across Kolochov's torso. His body flung itself back and landed hard. He didn't move after landing. Everyone turned quickly to see Elizabeth holding the BAR, smoke rising from the barrel.

"My vote is kill him now," she said, the fire of rage burning bright in her face. She handed the BAR back to Miller. "Shall we go?" she said, as if nothing had happened. She lightly rubbed her sore shoulder and started walking back to where the horses were.

The men watched her trudge off into the bush. Krasenovsky nodded. "She like most American women?"

"No, Colonel," Rainey said. "She's one of a kind."

"Too bad," Krasenovsky mumbled to himself in Russian.

38

Krasenovsky and his men reversed course back to Chelyabinsk. He felt safe now that Kolochov was dead and Trotsky had mentioned that a position in the RU would suit him well. Obviously, Kolochov's position was now open, not to mention Tuchenko's. Rainey wished him good luck. Before he left, Krasenovsky handed Rainey Appleton's Bowie knife.

"I am sure he would want back," he said.

"I'll make sure he gets it," Rainey replied.

Rainey, Elizabeth and Miller mounted up and continued east along the tracks. Miller rode much closer behind Rainey than before, now that no immediate threat remained behind them. Rainey and Elizabeth rode side by side in silence for several miles. Rainey checked every now and then to see if her expression had changed. She was looking angry for more than an hour before her features finally softened and he thought it was safe to talk to her.

"How are you doing?" he asked lightly.

"I'm fine," she said, not looking at him.

Rainey shifted in his saddle uneasily before continuing. "Want to talk about it?"

Elizabeth turned to face him. "Talk about what?"

"About what happened back there."

Elizabeth looked forward again. "What's there to talk about? They tried to capture us, we killed as many as we could, Yuri showed up and saved us."

"I'm talking about after that."

Elizabeth's head turned again, a flash of anger clearly apparent to Rainey. "I'm sure the world will not miss Comrade Kolochov."

Rainey took a big breath. "You had a pistol. You didn't have to take a BAR to him."

Elizabeth looked away again. "I thought it was appropriate."

"You were filled with rage. You still are. It can consume you if you don't deal with it."

Elizabeth's head snapped around. She glared at Rainey, boring holes into his head with her eyes. "I felt all kinds of emotions back there. Fear. Panic. Love. Rage. All in a span of thirty seconds. The rage is what got me through it, so if you don't mind, I'd like to hang onto it for just a little while longer. At the moment, it feels comfortable."

"I just want you to come back to me," said Rainey.

* * *

Elizabeth stared back at Rainey. She couldn't figure out how to respond to what he had told her. Where had she gone? She was still the same Elizabeth Clarke . . . wasn't she? Doubts rose in her mind. Thoughts of the boardroom and her outlook on life back in New York, and the terrible things that had happened in Russia all meshed together in her brain. She wasn't the same person. How could she expect herself to be? Hell, she had killed a man in a vengeful rage. He wasn't trying to kill her at that moment. She would never have been able to do that back in New York. The realization of her change struck her like a stone. A tear ran down her cheek. She had to look away from Rainey.

"I'm a cold-blooded killer now," she choked. "I don't know how to come back."

"The best sign that you're not is thinking you are and becoming upset by that thought," Rainey said.

"How do you deal with it?"

Rainey look like he was about to answer when he stopped short. A moment later, he shook his head and said, "You probably won't believe this, but I've never been that enraged before. You learn quickly that in a battle, rage can get you killed as easily as fear. Fear freezes you. Rage makes you feel invincible, which of course, you're not. Anger is controllable. Rage is not."

Elizabeth sat quietly for a moment. "How about when you busted into the house to rescue me?"

"You were still conscious then?" Rainey asked.

"Last thing I remember was shots being fired in the room," Elizabeth said. Then she smiled. "You know, you're right. You *can* tell one type of gun from another by its sound."

Rainey chuckled. "Glad you took something constructive away from the experience."

Elizabeth frowned. He was avoiding the issue. *He can't just change the subject.* Rainey looked away quickly as if embarrassed by what he'd said.

"You didn't answer my question," Elizabeth said, "about what you were feeling when you entered the room."

Rainey rode in silence, for half a minute before he spoke. "Panic," he said.

"Panic?"

"Of losing you."

* * *

They were still too far away to identify without binoculars, but the dozen or so riders were moving fairly fast out of the east. There was nothing but low shrubs anywhere near the tracks, so hiding wasn't an option. All they could do was ride on to meet whoever they were.

It took another ten minutes before the two groups were in range for identification without binoculars. The man leading the group looked familiar. His uniform was familiar. Rainey smiled.

"It's Gilbert," he said. "They weren't supposed to stop and send anyone back."

Gilbert was waving as they approached. When they came together, Gilbert reined in his horse and snapped a salute.

"Good morning, Sergeant," Rainey said, trying to hide back a smile. "Have you been authorized to be running around back here against my orders?"

Gilbert was clearly too happy to suppress his grin. "Sorry, sir, but Sergeant Kennard is in command. We're just out on patrol checking our rear area now that we have some time on our hands."

"Why does he have time?" Rainey asked.

"The company's outside of Kurgan. Sergeant Sutton found a beat-up locomotive and is fixing it up. We have until 1800 to make it back or we're walking to the Pacific."

They had found a train. That was good news. "How far to Kurgan from here?"

"About four hours ride, sir."

It was almost noon. "Let's take a break here for half an hour. We're due."

"How are my father and his charge?" Elizabeth asked.

"Both doing fine, ma'am. The boy seems less sickly with the fresh air and all. And your father will be extremely pleased to learn you're all right, not to mention everyone in the company."

* * *

They were riding through a large group of retreating White soldiers and approaching the outskirts of Kurgan when they heard the locomotive whistle. The moving mass lifted their heads together at the sound. Gilbert looked back at Rainey, smiled and waved his hand forward. The entire group broke into a gallop, the horses straining after the long ride. No one wanted to miss the train, including the horses.

As they got around the town, they could see the train moving ahead of them, approaching the main tracks. It was moving slowly but steadily eastward about a mile ahead. The camp would be only another mile past that. They had made it.

The train came to a halt beside a small copse of trees where the company had taken refuge. Rainey's group rode up at about the same time. Kennard marched smartly up to Rainey's horse and saluted.

"Glad to see you're still with us, sir," he said. "Gilbert bring you up to date on what we're doing here?"

"Yes, he did," Rainey replied. "I see Sutton got the engine going."

"Yes, sir. Said it might make it to Omsk if we don't push it," Kennard said. He looked over Rainey's shoulder. "I see you found Private Miller."

"More like he found me," Rainey replied. "I know he needs some disciplinary action, but then so do you for sending a patrol back for me."

"Well sir, you always turn up eventually," Kennard said.

"Not always." Kennard just raised his eyebrows at this.

Rainey looked over the train. One engine, a tender and six

boxcars. It wasn't much. A team had mounted two machine guns per car already. They would have to leave horses behind, but not all of them. The wagons would have to be abandoned, as well.

"I want to keep at least two squads' worth of horses. Is our inventory the same as it was in Chelyabinsk?" Rainey asked.

"Apart from what the rear guard expended, our ammunition supply is the same," Kennard said.

Logistically, what would we need for the remainder of the trip? Rainey mused. It should be pretty clear sailing east now, especially if they could get in with the Czechs. Although the one 37 mm gun they still had could come in very handy, it and its ammunition took up too much weight and space. The same went for the mortars. A couple of extra machine guns would still be useful for trade if necessary.

The logistics settled in Rainey's head. "Keep three extra machine guns past what's on the boxcars. Ditch all mortars and the 37. All extra rifles can be left as well, but I want all the BARs we have to stay with us. I'll let you tell Corelli about his guns."

Kennard frowned. "Thanks a bunch, sir."

A small crowd was moving towards the defensive line set up between the train and the town.

"We'd better get moving quick," Rainey said. "Where are Appleton and Clarke?"

Kennard pointed to a makeshift medical station. Rainey could see O'Hanlon looking over Elizabeth. She was sitting in a chair, Jonathan Clarke hovering behind her. The medical tent was the only one still up.

"Time for departure?" Rainey asked.

"Fifteen minutes from now, sooner if necessary" Kennard replied.

"Make it sooner. Carry on," Rainey said, hurrying toward the medical station before Kennard could salute or respond. As he approached, Clarke looked up and smiled, stepping out to meet him.

"Captain," Clarke said. "I can't tell you how much I appreciate you bringing my daughter back to me safely."

"I didn't do it for you," Rainey said before he could stop himself. Clarke's confusion was clear on his face. Rainey quickly changed the subject. "How's the kid doing?"

"Much better," Clarke said. "Charles is in with him now."

Rainey then got straight to the point. "What happens in Omsk?"

Clarke hesitated for a moment. "I will make contact with the American mission and arrange for our exit via Vladivostok."

"Once we're back in the States, the men will be free to go? No harassment from the government?"

"That I can deal with better once we make Vladivostok. I'm a thorough planner, Captain Rainey. I don't foresee any problems at the moment."

"And then what happens to the Tsarovich?" Rainey asked in a softened tone.

Clarke's face didn't change or miss a beat. "Who?" he asked.

Rainey smiled. "Never mind." He turned to Elizabeth, crouched and took her hands. "How's my girl?"

She looked exhausted, worn out, but there was life in her eyes. "Brendan said you could have done a better job on my shoulder." Her shoulder was wrapped in clean bandages, hiding the wound and the ugly black and blue bruises.

Rainey sighed in mock indignation. "He did not. He knows

better than to say a disparaging word about his commanding officer. I'll have him digging out latrines."

Elizabeth let out a soft giggle, but was clearly struggling to keep her eyes open. "Soon, we'll have you napping on the train," Rainey said. "I'll have the boys make you a hammock in the first boxcar. And I want you to sleep. I'll wake you if anything exciting happens."

Elizabeth closed her eyes. "If you don't, you'll hear about it from me later."

* * *

Everything was packed up. The horses they were taking with them were put in the last boxcar, extra equipment in the next to last. Everyone else piled into the four remaining. The first boxcar became the command and medical space. Appleton and Rainey were the last to get aboard. As they stood at the open door, watching for any organized attempt to take the train from them, Rainey slid the Bowie knife into Appleton's hand.

"Yuri Sergeyvich wanted you to have this back, with his thanks."

Appleton smiled broadly and brought the knife up close to his face to examine it closely. "Kolochov knows about this knife and that I would never part with it. It was the perfect trophy."

"But you did part with it."

"For the company, yes I did. It was difficult. I never thought I'd see it again. When did you see the colonel?"

"He helped me escape with Elizabeth and avoid being recaptured by Kolochov."

Appleton grimaced. "He's not going to stop coming after us."

Rainey smiled knowingly. "Oh, I don't think anyone's going to hear from Comrade Kolochov again." He jumped up into the box-car and reached out his hand to Appleton. "You'll have to tell me the story behind your knife someday."

"It's a long way to Vladivostok," Appleton said. "I'm sure we'll find the time."

The train started moving, past the masses of demoralized troops lining the tracks. Rainey scanned their faces, all of them looking up at the departing train with despair in their eyes. No drive, no leadership, no hope.

The Whites have already lost.

39

July 29, 1919
Kurgan to Omsk

The sun broke over the horizon around seven that morning. Sergeant Sutton only felt safe getting the engine up to about twenty miles an hour. The coal seemed old and a bit damp, the sounds of metal straining against metal were continuous and the pressure gauge in the cab was broken so he had no way to monitor the boiler.

After a few hours had passed, Rainey began getting restless. As he moved among the men, he started to get an odd feeling. Something felt wrong. He really missed Bradley's sixth sense now.

He was back in the second box car when Kennard approached him. "You're not happy, sir?" It was more like a statement than a question.

"Something," Rainey said, shaking his head. "Something isn't right."

"I know," Kennard said.

Rainey looked up suddenly. "What?"

Kennard took him by the arm and led him to the big open

door. He pressed his mouth to Rainey's ear. "You've been relieved of command."

Rainey was shocked, but it made sense. The guarded looks from the men, the sergeants trying to avoid him. "Who . . . never mind. I know who." He moved past Kennard and headed for the ladder to move up to the first boxcar. As he got to the ladder, Kennard grabbed his arm.

"Sergeant!" he yelled over the noise of the train and the wind.

"Sir!" Kennard shouted back.

Rainey stood face to face with Kennard so he wouldn't have to yell so loud. "Were you given any orders about me?"

Kennard's face changed. "Yes, sir."

"And they were?"

"I voiced a protest in your name, but I have also been ordered not to discuss them with you."

Rainey was flabbergasted. "Excuse me?"

"I'm sorry, sir. In the end, we take our orders from the American government . . . and... you're not American." Rainey stared at Kennard, stunned. Kennard quickly continued. "I don't like it either, but there you are."

Rainey could see that Kennard was extremely uncomfortable. "Don't worry about it, Sergeant. I'll get it sorted out." He patted him on the shoulder and moved toward the ladder again, but Kennard did not let go of his arm.

"I'm sorry sir. You can't go over there."

Rainey stared back into Kennard's cold, dark eyes. "And why not?"

"As I said, I cannot discuss my orders with you." Kennard was deadly serious, moving his free hand slowly towards his pistol for emphasis.

"Sergeant," Rainey said tentatively.

The man was severely torn between loyalties, Rainey knew. That meant it would be dangerous to push the issue. "Very well, but I want you to make sure Elizabeth is aware of the situation. Can you do that much?" Kennard didn't even blink. "Come on, Sergeant. You can at least do that. She'll cover for you."

Kennard lowered his hand from his gun and released Rainey's arm. Rainey found an empty corner of the boxcar and sat down. There was nothing more he could do now.

"You outcast too, sir?"

Rainey looked over to see Private Miller sitting beside him. "Yes, and it would be in your interest to keep your distance."

"Not likely," replied Miller.

Rainey shook his head. "What do you mean?"

"I was brought into the company by Sergeant MacGregor."

Rainey caught the inference. "How many others?" he asked.

"Just me. I had no idea he was spying on us and he never asked me to help."

"It's OK, Private. None of us knew. Won't stop the 'guilty by association' verdict, though."

Miller sat down beside Rainey. "I knew the Sarge pretty good. I never remember him being political and he would not have done anything to put a soldier's life in danger."

"Probably why he only targeted the lieutenant. But the conditions that soldiers returned to after the war were fertile ground for the Communists."

"You sound like you're talking from experience," Miller said.

Rainey thought back to his days in Paris right after the war. A small Communist group had tried to recruit him upon hearing of his distaste for the politics of the peace talks. Teaching violent revolution immediately disillusioned Rainey, but he had learned how they thought and about the Comintern.

"Yeah, you could say I do," he said quietly.

Rainey's mind whirled back to the present. To Clarke, he was a liability. He knew who Alexis was. What would Clarke do? How far would he go to protect the secret?

* * *

Elizabeth had been dozing in her hammock. She woke when Kennard moved past the tarp set up to separate the front half of the boxcar from the medical team. The lanterns' dim light cast a warm glow. Appleton and Alexis were huddled around a make-shift table of crates. Clarke was sitting by himself.

"What is it, Sergeant?" Clarke snapped, as if he considered Kennard's presence an annoyance. He didn't look up from the documents he was reading.

"Captain Rainey is aware of the change in command, sir," said Kennard.

Elizabeth discreetly turned her head to observe the conversation. Clarke was looking up at the tall sergeant from his seat. His face sagged with resignation. "You know what to do."

"No," Appleton said from where he was sitting. "Jonathan, he saved your daughter's life. You owe him."

"Charles," Clarke replied, "there's no point rehashing old arguments. I don't like it either, but the secrecy and security of this mission demands it. Rainey now knows I don't trust him so there will be no loyalty from him once we reach Omsk. He needs to be silenced."

Silenced. Elizabeth did not like the sound of that. Her hand moved to the pistol that was resting beside her.

"You should never have passed the word through the company that he had been relieved of command," Appleton continued. "He wouldn't have been able to discover it then. Even Sergeant Kennard warned you about that."

Clarke looked sternly at Appleton. "It seemed appropriate since he went missing, and I have no intention of putting him back in command now. I have to have command and you know it. And the men had to know it in case of disputes. There was no question of that."

Appleton lowered his head into his hands. "It was unnecessary."

"It was my responsibility to the mission," Clarke said.

Elizabeth brought the gun up and cocked it. The cocking noise froze everyone. Slowly, everyone's head turned to face her. She held the Colt with two hands in front of her, sitting up as best she could in the hammock. The clacking of the wheels on the rails was the only audible sound, accompanied by the boxcar's slow swaying movement.

"Elizabeth, put that thing away," Clarke said.

She clenched her jaw and narrowed her eyes. She moved the gun's barrel toward her father, then looked over at Kennard. "What do you know to do?" she asked him in a low voice.

Kennard looked to Clarke, who shook his head slightly, and then back to Elizabeth. No one spoke for a moment. Kennard took a slow step forward.

"Miss Clarke," he began. "Your father is in command and has ordered, for security reasons, that the captain be shot should he pose a risk to the security of the mission."

Clarke scowled at Kennard, but reached out with his hand towards Elizabeth. "Now give me the gun and let the sergeant do his job."

Elizabeth cocked her head towards Kennard. "Since when is murder part of your military duties?"

"He follows orders," Clarke said.

"But is he not bound to ignore unlawful orders?"

"Don't quote military law to me," said Clarke. "We are not in normal circumstances, so normal rules do not apply. Now give me the gun."

Elizabeth didn't know what to do next. Kennard was about to go off and kill the man she loved. It didn't matter that he would hate doing it, she would kill him if he tried to leave. The gun's muzzle shifted towards Kennard. "Sit down, Sergeant. You're not going anywhere."

The movement was enough. Clarke shot forward and grabbed the barrel, twisting it downward in a single motion. The gun went off as he wrenched it from Elizabeth's hands, the bullet harmlessly embedding itself into boxcar's wooden floor. She cried in pain as her hands were twisted. She began to cry.

"I'm sorry, Elizabeth," Clarke said, standing over her. He handed the gun to Kennard. "Now go carry out your orders." Kennard took the gun, but didn't move.

"Sergeant?"

Kennard handed the gun towards Clarke. "Your daughter is right, sir. Murder is unlawful and against the rules of the Geneva Convention for the treatment of prisoners."

Clarke stood up and stared down Kennard. "And you are part of an unauthorized military unit. You're basically a mercenary. Under those conditions, the Geneva Convention doesn't apply. Are you really willing to test me with your freedom when we get stateside?"

"I will not have anyone killed because of me," came a small voice. Slowly pulling himself to his feet and rewrapping his blanket over his shoulders, Alexis stepped forward into the light.

"I'm sorry," Clarke said, "but it is necessary for your safety."

"My safety? Or the safety of money I have access to? I believe I will take that risk for such brave men. Just discarding them after their usefulness is completed is wrong. It will not inspire the rest of your men to follow you."

Clarke shook his head. "I have command. I don't need to inspire them."

The boy pushed back. "You may have command now, but without inspiration, your command will be lost."

"You don't know what you're talking about," said Clarke.

"But I do," Alexis replied. "My family's fate is proof of what the loss of respect and inspiration can lead to."

Clarke glanced at Kennard to see if some sort of recognition crossed his face. None did. He turned back to the boy. "That type of loss takes years. I only need their respect until we're all back in the States."

"You will not get to the States if I do not allow it."

Elizabeth gazed admiringly at Alexis. He was standing as tall as he could. Clarke slowly got up from his seat, trying to intimidate the boy. "Allow it? What are you talking about?"

"My authority in Russia is absolute."

"Your authority was absolute. Now it is non-existent."

The boy didn't move. "You misunderstand. Once we arrive in Omsk, I believe if I make my presence known, absolute authority will be given. So, right now, I will not have anyone killed because of me. Especially the Great Celt."

Elizabeth fell back in her hammock, laughing. A fourteen-year-old boy was out-maneuvering her father.

"I must say, he does outrank you, Jonathan," Appleton said with a smile.

"Oh, be quiet, Charles," Clarke spat. Elizabeth got back up and looked at her father, smiling at him. After a moment, Clarke gave a heavy sigh. "Very well. Sergeant, stand down. But you, young man, must follow my orders explicitly if we're going to get you out of the country secretly. And that means avoiding contact with anyone outside of this room." He turned to face Kennard. "And Sergeant, do I have to reiterate the extremely high level of secrecy required of you?"

"No, sir," Kennard snapped.

"Then retake your post."

Kennard handed the Colt back to Elizabeth with a wink, turned and pushed through the tarp. Elizabeth wiped the tears away and faced the boy who had saved the man she loved. "Thank you, your Highness." She scowled at her father, who turned back to his documents without any sign of a reaction.

Alexis put his hand on her shoulder. "I must do what I can to help those who have risked their lives for me. It is only right. Now lie down and rest. Nothing bad will happen." Elizabeth lay back in the hammock, pondering the feeling of calm generated by the words of a fourteen-year-old boy.

* * *

Kennard returned to the second car to find Rainey still sitting in the corner with Miller. Rainey saw him out of the corner of his eye and brought his hand to his gun. The small smile on Kennard's face, however, gave him pause. This was not the look he expected if Kennard was coming to kill him.

"All's well in command?" Rainey asked, standing to face Kennard. The men around him began to back away to give the two of them room.

"Quite frankly, sir, I have no idea what's what over there," Kennard replied. "And I don't want to know. What I do know is that you had best steer clear of the first boxcar, including when we arrive in Omsk."

Rainey nodded. "Fine. I don't have a problem with that." He looked into Kennard's face to see a questioning look staring back at him.

"No, I can't tell you about the kid," Rainey said. "Clarke will want to shoot you then, too."

"Someday, sir?"

Rainey nodded. "Someday. You might want to make sure the talk among the men is kept from the topic."

"They don't know anything."

"Won't stop them from speculating," Rainey said. Then he leaned forward. "Did you originally get orders to shoot me?"

Kennard smiled mischievously. "Sorry, sir, that's top secret."

40

August 3, 1919
Omsk

The engine was losing power, lurching forward in spurts and irritating everyone on board. Sutton did his best, but one of the drive cylinders had sprung a steam leak which was non-repairable. With all the stops, track repair and slow running, it was not surprising it took a little over three days to make Omsk.

As they waited five miles from the city's outskirts, Kennard stopped where Rainey and Miller were sitting. "Sir, Mr. Clarke would like to see you."

Rainey got up and followed Kennard to the first boxcar. At the tarp, Kennard took possession of Rainey's Webley pistol and his sword before allowing him to pass.

"Captain," Clarke said. "Thank you for coming. We have some things to discuss."

"Like what?" Rainey asked intently.

"There are security issues to consider," Clarke replied.

"I'm listening."

Clarke sighed. "I don't think you are aware of how sensitive this mission is."

Rainey gave a meaningful look at Alexis. "I think I have a pretty good idea."

"And I am concerned about your opinion of it."

Rainey thought for a moment before answering. "Honestly, I don't like the idea that men died so you could get your hands on Russian gold, not that it makes much difference. I don't think you have a hope in hell of getting those British and French banks to let go of any gold just because you have Alexis here. That doesn't mean we should throw the poor boy to the wolves either."

Clarke looked hard at Rainey before answering. "I can accept that. There are wolves on all sides of this conflict. Do you believe his best chance is with us?"

"Yes, by far."

Clarke nodded. "Then I will return command back to you, but of the men only. I will retain overall command of the mission."

"My command was always just the men," answered Rainey. "Strategic command of the mission was in Charles' and Elizabeth's hands. In combat, they did what I told them. In mission goals, I did what they told me. Charles made most of the calls on how we should approach each situation since he has experience in this theatre."

Clarke locked eyes with Rainey. "I'm sorry, Captain. Over the last few years, I've become accustomed to military leaders being political."

"Then you've been around too many generals, sir," Rainey said flatly. "I'm just a lowly captain running a company."

"Exactly," Clarke spoke up quickly. "But what I need from you, Captain, is for you to acknowledge my overall command of the mission and make that apparent to the rest of the men."

"I don't have to. That was automatic. You could have saved yourself a lot of trouble just by realizing that."

"Perhaps," Clarke replied.

"Robert?" Elizabeth's faint voice drifted over to Rainey. He moved to the hammock.

"I'm here, darlin'," Rainey said, stroking her hair. Her eyes flickered open, squinting into the darkness as his face became her focus. She smiled, reaching up to touch his face, her hand feeling the roughness of the stubble on his cheek.

"You need a shave," she said.

"I'll get one in Omsk."

"Are we almost there?" she asked.

"Soon," Rainey answered. "You rest some more. I'll come back when we get there."

Elizabeth raised her head to see her father, then looked back at Rainey. "I'm so glad to see you," she said.

"Me too," Rainey replied.

She reached into her breast pocket, pulling out the locket. "We're safe now. You should have this back," she said, holding it out to Rainey.

"No, my love," Rainey replied. "Not until we're on a boat and out of this country."

* * *

It was very late in the evening as the train slowly wheezed up to a guard station on the city's edge. The guards were skittish, wary of possible Red infiltrators coming from the direction of Chelyabinsk. No forces on horseback or foot had made it this far yet. Appleton and Clarke made a concerted effort to get past the guards, but had to settle for a note to be forwarded to a Major Slaughter of the American Mission.

It was about three a.m. when a truck pulled up next to the guard station. The noise awoke Rainey, who had been snoozing in the engine cab. Two tall men got out of the truck. Rainey recognized the American uniforms. He watched Clarke striding past the engine to meet them.

"Sergeant, watch the engine," said Rainey, who handed his rifle to Sutton. He jumped down from the engine and quickly closed the distance to Clarke, falling in step beside him.

"You are not needed here," Clarke said sharply.

"All the same," Rainey replied, "I'd like to meet the man who is going to help us on our way. There will be some logistics to discuss, which I am better acquainted with."

Clarke stopped and turned on him. "You don't trust me, do you?"

Rainey held his ground. "And that surprises you?"

They glared at each for a moment, then Clarke resumed his walk. "Very well, but speak only if spoken to." Rainey fell in beside him again.

"Major Slaughter," Clarke said. "It's good to see you again."

"Jonathan Clarke," Slaughter replied. "And where have you been for the last year?"

"Long story, Major, but I'll be happy to brief you fully in due time. Right now, time is of the essence. We need to keep heading east.'

Slaughter looked around, seemingly ill at ease. "I have no control over the railroads." He looked toward the train. "How many of you are there?"

Clarke nodded to Rainey, who took the hint. "One hundred sixty-six, plus four civilians including Mr. Clarke."

Slaughter looked Rainey over from head to foot, noting that

his uniform was not American. "And you are?"

Rainey came to attention. "Robert Rainey, Captain, Princess Patricia's Canadian Light Infantry. Currently assigned command of Clarke Company."

Slaughter looked back at Clarke. "You have a Canadian commanding your little expedition?"

"It wasn't planned, Major. It's just how it turned out."

"I take it this expedition was not approved by anyone in the United States government?"

Clarke was not fazed. "I'm sure you can vouch for me."

Slaughter looked over at Rainey again and then back to Clarke. "I don't know if I can or not, but you arriving gives me another headache. Ambassador Morris and General Graves are due to arrive here in another day or two."

"Best we get out of here before official Washington shows up," Clarke said quickly.

"That would be easier said than done," Slaughter said. "The rail line east is crowded, slow and treacherous. I can't just send you on your merry way."

"No one has full control of the Trans-Siberian?" asked Clarke.

"There is a railroad commission, but their control is in name only. The Czechs have the most control. Every few miles is a warlord, Czech battalion or a Jap unit looking to make trouble. No telling how Graves will even make it through to here. Our only advantage is that no one wants to get on our wrong side." Slaughter stepped back. "I'll get you authorization to make it into the station on an outside track. There you can set up camp. Come by the Mission in the morning to discuss what happens next. Until then." He stuck out his hand. Clarke took it and shook. Slaughter looked over at Rainey, who saluted. Slaughter returned the salute, spun and headed back to his truck with his aide.

"A rather no-nonsense officer," Rainey said. "I like him. Military intelligence?"

"He's going to get us out of Russia," Clarke replied. "You'd better like him."

Rainey had questions about Slaughter, but knew he wouldn't get any answers out of Clarke. As they walked back to the train, Clarke gave Rainey another hard look. "Remember, everyone stays clear of the first boxcar."

"I remember," Rainey said.

As they stepped back towards the train, Rainey noticed a man in a fine long coat and a wide-brimmed gray fedora standing by the corner of the guard house, watching them with a particular interest. His first thought was the Cheka, as he was dressed much like the man Krasenovsky had shot in the house in Chelyabinsk. Rainey acted like he didn't notice, but filed the event away in his mind for future reference.

* * *

As the sun started to broach the horizon, clearance was granted for the train to enter the rail yard. Sergeant Sutton barely got the engine moving at all. It crawled at a walking pace onto the assigned track before a loud noise announced that the engine was done. The camp sprang up quickly, spreading out around the train. Kennard had set up pickets and ordered everyone else to get some rest. As the morning drew on, the camp remained quiet. Rainey was alone in his tent and had gotten only a little sleep before the sun's rays reached through the crack of his tent and played a warm beam across his face. It was then he sensed a shadow of someone standing over him. He rolled quickly and brought his pistol to bear on the target.

Elizabeth jumped back with a little gasp. Rainey lowered the gun. "You should know better than to sneak up on me," he scolded her.

"I'm sorry," Elizabeth said. "I'm hoping one day you can sleep without a gun under your pillow."

Rainey smiled and sat up while Elizabeth sat down beside him, wrapping her good arm around his shoulders, wincing as she embraced him.

"It still hurts, eh?" Rainey asked.

"Just a little," Elizabeth said. "I don't notice it much anymore."

Rainey brought his arm up and around her and she nestled into his chest. They sat there quietly for several minutes, listening to the sounds of the rail yard.

"Are we going to make it home?" Elizabeth finally asked.

"That's up to your father now," Rainey replied. "I've got my fingers crossed."

"He's a good man, Robert. Deep inside, he has a strong moral core. I think just being in Russia during this chaos has made him have to bury that core deeper."

Rainey rubbed her back. "You'll have to excuse me for being suspicious of a man who initially wanted me killed, and trying to force a good friend of mine to make the attempt."

"It was Alexis who saved you," Elizabeth said softly.

"What?"

Elizabeth looked up into his face. "He spoke up and threatened to expose his presence here in Omsk if you were killed."

Rainey sighed. "I'll have to thank him later."

Another shadow crossed against the tent's sunward side. Rainey's hand rested on his pistol, but in his mind, the large shadow could only be one man.

"Captain," Kennard said from outside the tent.

Rainey got up, leaving Elizabeth on the cot. He stepped out into the warm sunshine, squinting at Kennard while his eyes grew accustomed to the light. "Report," he said.

"Mr. Clarke is heading to the American Mission. He has asked myself and Sergeant Sutton to accompany him. Mr. Appleton has been left in charge of our special passenger and has asked if you would join him in the boxcar."

"Is that what we're calling him now?" Rainey asked.

"As good a name as any, sir. We prefer not to talk of him at all."

"Dismissed." They saluted each other and Kennard headed off. Elizabeth had come out of the tent and stood with Rainey. From about fifteen yards away, Rainey noticed Private Miller looking at him sullenly.

"What do you think Charles wants?" Elizabeth asked.

"I have no idea," Rainey replied. "But first, I need to do something." With a wave, he summoned Miller, who collected his rifle and trotted over.

"Sir."

"Miller, with Corporal Bradley gone, I need a new batman …orderly. You'll find the duties do not include the regular 'clean my uniform' kind of stuff, but I could have used a little help putting up my tent last night. Are you interested?"

Miller's expression changed to excited. "Yes, sir. Thank you, sir."

"One of your main duties is to make sure nothing happens to Miss Clarke here when I'm not around. Is that clear?"

"Crystal, sir." Miller looked over at Elizabeth and smiled.

"Dismissed," said Rainey, who headed toward the first boxcar. Elizabeth followed him, frowning.

"Why did you have to tell him that?"

41

The conversation remained light and well oiled with bourbon. Appleton told the story of his Bowie knife, given to him by Theodore Roosevelt himself. Roosevelt had taken it off a Spanish officer he killed on San Juan Hill. He gave it to Appleton as a thank-you for the information about the disposition of Spanish forces on the hill. Appleton also told non-confidential stories about his time in Russia, including some adventures with Clarke.

"I imagine Kolochov took a verbal beating for missing us on that day," he said jovially.

"No wonder he spat when you called yourself a diplomat at the dinner," Elizabeth said.

Appleton's shoulders sagged. "Fine, yes. I will admit that I am a spy." He raised his glass. "Here's to the State Department for letting me have some fun."

"I thought you were called a Ghost," Elizabeth said.

Appleton's face went very serious. "Where did you hear that?"

She smiled knowingly. "We all have our secret sources."

Rainey leaned forward. "So I guess you trust us now, having told us all this."

"I haven't told you anything, really," Appleton said. "Not one important secret."

"I see," Rainey said with a smile. He looked over at Alexis. "Well, son, it's your turn. Why don't you tell us your story?"

Alexis shuffled in his seat nervously. "I will start at the beginning. We were in Ekaterinburg, prisoners of the Bolsheviks. We heard news that loyal soldiers were coming, so the Bolsheviks had to do something with us. We thought we would be moved."

"But you weren't," Appleton said.

Alexis nodded. "It was late at night and my whole family was awakened. We were all dressed in traveling clothes and sent to the basement of the house. I had a lot of jewels hidden in my clothing for if we ever found a way to get away. We waited for a long time before a number of men came into the room. One of them pulled out a page and announced we were to be executed. The guns came up and they started shooting. I was hit in the stomach, but the jewels stopped the bullet."

His eyes started to water, a lump forming in his throat. "You don't have to continue," said Elizabeth, putting her arm around the boy.

"But the exciting part comes next," Alexis said, sniffing up his courage to continue. "The door burst open and three men with guns stormed in, shooting the Bolsheviks."

Alexis paused to let his excitement calm down. No one spoke, waiting for him to continue. "A man stepped towards me. It was Count Raynykov."

Rainey sat up quickly. "You've said that name before."

"Yes, Captain," Alexis said. "You and he are from the same family line."

"Continue," Elizabeth said softly to Alexis.

"Only myself and my sister Anastasia were still alive, but she had been shot several times and was in a very bad way. The count took us out of the house and moved us to another one across the city. Yurovsky, who had been our jailer and whom I thought was a Bolshevik, was actually working for the count. Two or three weeks later, we moved to Chelyabinsk.

"I have been sick for a long time. Anastasia took a long time to recover, but she left with an agent of Raynykov's just before Christmas while an English man stayed with me. Later, in the middle of February, the English man went out and never came back. I was very worried until Mr. Clarke arrived and we moved to another house. We stayed hidden until you arrived."

"You said English man," said Rainey. "He wasn't American?"

"No, he was from England. He spoke Russian just like my English tutor."

"Why didn't your sister stay with you?" Elizabeth asked.

"She wanted to," replied Alexis. "We are very close. She did not want to go last Christmas, but I insisted."

Rainey leaned back on his stool. "So, instead of being murdered by the Bolsheviks, two members of the Russian Royal family got out with British help, one of whom is sitting here with us."

"There is no guarantee Anastasia got out," Appleton said.

Rainey shook his head. "I think what we have to understand is that Communist organizations are international and would hunt them wherever they went. Even if they do get out, they can never surface again. I'm beginning to understand your father's obsession with security."

"But the Bolsheviks would know that two Romanovs are still alive," Elizabeth said.

"Not necessarily," Appleton said. Rainey and Elizabeth looked at Appleton. He continued. "They'll believe whatever Yurovsky tells them."

"And since he's Raynykov's man?" asked Rainey. Appleton nodded. "I wonder what happened to stop Yurovsky from preventing the executions in the first place."

"One can only guess," said Appleton.

"You do not know of Anastasia?" asked Alexis.

"No," Appleton said. "Perhaps Jonathan may gain some information here."

* * *

As Rainey stepped off the train, he spotted the man in the long black coat watching him from the stationhouse. This was the second time Rainey had seen the man since they had arrived in Omsk, so it was time to find out what he wanted.

Rainey walked in among the tents, crouching a bit so he would not be visible from the stationhouse. He worked his way around out into the street on the far side, hugging the wall and moving toward where he had seen the man standing. As he reached the building, Rainey peered around the corner. The man was gone.

Rainey stepped around to where he had seen the man standing, looking out across at the train and the camp. It was a good vantage point. As he stood there, he saw Miller coming across the tracks towards him.

"What is it, Private?"

"Nothing, really, sir," Miller replied. "Just that the man you were tracking is in the stationhouse, looking at us from the window just behind you."

Rainey fought the urge to spin around. "You've seen him before, too?"

"No, sir, but when I saw you sneaking through camp, I thought I'd keep an eye on whoever you might be sneaking up on."

"Is he still there?"

"Yes, sir."

"Well, go in there and get him. I'll stay here for two minutes and then follow you in."

"Sir?"

Rainey sighed. "Go and make sure he stays there until I get there. He won't run from you."

Miller nodded. "OK, two minutes." Miller moved off, up the steps and into the stationhouse. Rainey began counting off the two minutes, and then followed Miller's path. He found Miller sitting on a bench, braced up against a door that was hinged to swing out.

"So where is he?"

"In here," said Miller, motioning towards the door.

"You sure he's still in there?"

"Oh yes, sir. He's in there. But you may want to prepare yourself. It threw me a bit when I saw him."

"What are you talking about?"

A heavy thud came from behind the door, with cursing in Russian. Rainey pulled out his Webley and signaled Miller to move the bench.

As the bench moved, the door sprang open to reveal the man in the long black coat. Rainey quickly brought the Webley up, but froze with surprise. He thought for a second he was looking in a mirror. Although the man had graying hair around his ears, the face was surprisingly familiar, with the same gray eyes, nose, and chin. It was uncanny.

The man stared back at him, then spoke in Russian. "We need to talk." The man's eyes shifted to the hilt of the sword on

Rainey's back. Then he spoke in English. "We definitely need to talk."

"Who are you?"

"I am Count Vasili Ivanovich Raynykov."

42

"Do not be so surprised, Captain," Raynykov said. "We are related, after all."

"Yeah, five hundred years ago, maybe," Rainey said. "You'd figure one of us would have different eyes or nose by now."

Rainey still had his Webley pointed at Raynykov's chest. They stood there, examining each other, marveling at the similarities. Raynykov was older by about twenty years and wore a bushy mustache in the Russian style. He wore his fedora jauntily tilted to the right.

"Is he your uncle or something, sir?" Miller asked.

"Or something," Rainey replied. He slowly lowered the Webley and returned it to its holster. After a second, he held out his hand. Raynykov took it and gave it one good shake. Then he smiled.

"May I see the sword more closely?"

Rainey nodded and lifted the sword off his shoulder, holding it out to Raynykov. He took it with reverence, examining the hilt and scabbard.

"May I?" he asked, sliding the blade slightly out of the scabbard. Rainey nodded. Raynykov pulled out the sword, feeling its weight, turning it gracefully as the light shone off the blade's surface. Miller subtly moved the barrel of his rifle toward Raynykov.

"It is a very fine weapon," he said, putting it back in the scabbard. "You and your ancestors have taken very good care of it."

"What do you know about it?" Rainey asked.

"Ah, the legend," Raynykov replied. "The Great Celt who saved Ivan the Great and helped him establish Muscovy as the leading principality. That led to the Tsars and the creation of Mother Russia. I have heard the stories because they are part of my family's history. But that will be for another time. Now we must discuss the present."

Rainey kept a straight face. "So you weren't following me just to get a closer look at the sword?"

Raynykov frowned. "You know what I am talking about." He glared at Miller.

"What?" Miller asked.

Rainey turned quickly on Miller. "Private, you're dismissed. Get back to the camp and wait for me."

Miller hesitated, but seemed to get the point that Rainey was trying to protect him. "Yes, sir," he said, and turned to leave.

Rainey grabbed him by the arm. "And no gossip. This is top secret. Understand?"

Rainey's eyes bore into Miller's to stress the situation's seriousness. Miller nodded, a little fright showing on his face. "Yes, sir," he said. "No one is to know."

Rainey let go of his arm and Miller quickly stepped out.

Rainey turned back to Raynykov. "Is there somewhere we can speak more privately?"

"Yes, of course,"

They walked in silence through the streets until they came to a hotel. Raynykov asked the clerk if he had any messages. Two, the clerk told him, one of which was from Major Slaughter. He stuffed the messages in his pocket without reading them and signaled to Rainey to follow him up the staircase to the third floor.

As they entered his room, Raynykov indicated a large comfortable chair for Rainey. He then grabbed a bottle of vodka from an icebox, filled two glasses and handed one to Rainey.

"Vodka is much better when chilled," he said and downed his glass in one gulp. Rainey did the same. Raynykov refilled the glasses, took the two messages out of his pockets and sat on the bed.

"The British secret service wants to know if the 'project' is still proceeding," he said. "And the American Mission says my 'package' is on board your train. So that answers my first question for you."

"Slaughter knows about Alexis?"

Raynykov frowned. "I am not used to hearing his actual name, but yes. After we had heard nothing for several months, we approached the major for any news about Mr. Clarke. But to get it, we had to tell him why we wanted to know. The sly dog then proceeded to tell us he had heard nothing, but would keep us informed if Mr. Clarke reappeared."

Rainey took a sip from his glass. "He's a good kid. Told me a bit about the legend. Showed me what a little gold disk on the sword's hilt meant. Said your family always supported the Tsars."

Raynykov smiled. "More supported a strong Russia. Hereditary rule has its . . . problems. We had to replace a few of them over the centuries." He gulped down his glass of vodka. "How is the boy?"

"He's pretty sickly, but he seems to be managing. He has some bleeding disease, right?"

"Yes. It has made it difficult for him to travel. I almost wished Rasputin was still around to help cure him."

"Any word about Princess Anastasia? I know Alexis will want to know if she made it out."

Raynykov's face turned grave. Rainey knew the story would not be good. "They were caught by a patrol east of Saratov. The Princess died there, shot through the heart. We brought her back to Ekaterinburg to bury her with her family."

Rainey could see the pain in Raynykov's face. "I'm sorry," he said.

Raynykov shook his head. "It is my failure. I tried to counsel Tsar Nicholas that slowly leading our country into a democracy would be his lasting legacy, but too many voices were saying no. I should have tried harder."

Rainey sipped his vodka again and got up from the chair. "Look around you. Slowly might have worked if there had been no war. But there was a war. All the monarchies fell, even England's to some extent. Do you think anyone follows the British aristocracy blindly anymore after they led vast numbers of their male population to slaughter?"

Raynykov got up and poured himself another drink. "The war. It destroyed all our efforts to make Russia better." He downed the vodka. "But mostly we did it to ourselves. What will the Americans do with the Tsar?"

"They're after the money in British and French banks."

Raynykov spat. "The money. It is always the money."

Rainey moved to the window. "Does the money matter to you?"

"Of course not," Raynykov exclaimed. "Only the Tsar matters. What will they do with him after they get their money?"

"I have no idea, but I'm pretty sure killing him is not on the agenda."

"Why, because they are Americans?"

"Actually, yes. They aren't after his throne. But whether they can keep his existence quiet and still get to the money is another story. There isn't a safe place for him anywhere if people know who he is."

Raynykov thought about that while Rainey glanced out the window at the crowded street. He became alert when he saw Appleton moving through the crowd. And farther up the street, he saw Sergeant Corelli. Glancing about, he was able to spot another seven soldiers from Clarke Company down in the street, spread out in a skirmish line.

"What is it?" Raynykov asked, noticing the sudden tension in Rainey's stance.

"I'm not sure, but I think I'm being looked for. I have to go down and see what's going on." He suddenly became curious. "By the way, have you ever met a man named Charles Appleton?"

The expression on Raynykov's face said it all. "Appleton is here?"

"He's been working with Jonathan Clarke for a couple of years," Rainey replied. "He told me I reminded him of someone. Guess it was you."

Raynykov moved to the window and looked out. He recognized Appleton right away. "It has been many years."

"Well, I best go out and see what he wants," Rainey said. As he moved from the window, Raynykov caught him by the arm.

"I need to be with the Tsar," he pleaded. He had a desperate look in his eyes.

"I'll see what I can do," Rainey replied. "Meet me at the train station in, say, two hours."

* * *

Rainey stepped through the hotel's doorway, right into Appleton's view. He crossed the street to meet him.

"What's going on, Charles?"

Appleton's hand stroked the handle of his Bowie knife. "Just looking for you. Jonathan's back and wants to talk to you."

"And you needed a squad for that?"

Appleton glanced over his shoulder, spotting Corelli closing in. "Dangerous place." He slowly slid the Bowie knife out of its sheath. "You meeting anyone at the hotel here?"

Rainey saw the shift in Appleton's balance, the slow movement of his right arm. "Charles, there's a perfectly good explanation . . ."

"I'm sorry, Captain." The Bowie knife flashed forward but Rainey was ready for it, blocking the thrust at Appleton's wrist with his right hand and twisting hard. He rolled into Appleton's body and brought his left elbow hard against Appleton's temple. Appleton snapped his head back and right to avoid the impact, but couldn't counter Rainey slamming his right foot down hard on Appleton's instep. The pain made him loosen his grip on the knife, which Rainey was able to wrench free with his left hand. Rainey then spun back to his left and held up the knife, its point inches from Appleton's face.

Corelli made it through the crowd, bringing his pistol up, not knowing who to point it at.

"Would someone like to explain what's going on . . . sirs?" he snapped.

The crowd was fading back, giving the adversaries room. The rest of the squad moved into the empty space, standing with their mouths open at the scene of Rainey pointing Appleton's knife right at Appleton's nose. Appleton relaxed and stood still, staring at Rainey.

"Clarke ordered me killed again?" Rainey asked calmly.

Appleton didn't reply. Corelli, however, did. "What?" The pistol moved toward Appleton.

"Stand down, Sergeant," said Appleton.

"Not if we are out here to commit an unlawful military act," Corelli said. Rainey smiled. Kennard had briefed him.

"Were you ordered to kill anyone?" Appleton asked.

"No."

"Were you?" Rainey countered. Again Appleton stayed silent. "I at least hope it was against your better judgment."

"Yes," Appleton answered flatly.

Rainey lowered the knife. Corelli moved the aim of his pistol back towards Rainey. "I'm sorry sir, but my orders do say I am to return you to camp, with force if necessary."

Rainey looked at Corelli, then slowly took a few steps back. "Sir?"

Rainey had gotten to the edge of the crowd and bolted in among them. Corelli didn't have a shot, and he lowered his pistol. He turned to the soldiers behind him.

"Well, what are you waiting for? Get after him," Corelli said sternly. The soldiers moved together into the crowd in the direction where Rainey had disappeared. Corelli turned to Appleton.

"And you, sir, return to camp. We'll bring him back without your help."

* * *

Raynykov watched the confrontation from the window. He admired the way Rainey moved, smoothly taking the knife from Appleton, how he dealt with the sergeant and made his escape. He got the feeling the sergeant had let Rainey slip away. There was discord amongst the members of the American group. That was not good for the Tsar.

He poured himself another vodka and downed it, then placed the bottle back in the icebox and prepared to leave. He had to get back to the station and look for a way in.

Back at the window to see if the way was clear, he saw only Appleton standing in the street with a sad look on his face. Raynykov was still at the window when Appleton looked up. Their eyes locked. Recognition flashed in Appleton's face. Raynykov jumped back from the window and pressed his back against the wall.

Charles Appleton. He hadn't seen the man in almost fifteen years. His mind whirled back to memories. Natalia. His young sister at an elegant ball on the arm of this plain-faced American.

Natalia. She had been a wild one. Courting the young American and getting involved with some unseemly political groups in St. Petersburg. Then, in January of 1905, she marched with the workers on the Winter Palace, where the guards opened fire. She was wounded in the leg, but it was Appleton who brought her home that night. Raynykov could see in his eyes that he loved her and was extremely worried about her. It was then that Raynykov began to trust him.

Then two months later, Natalia disappeared. Raynykov pulled as many strings as he could find to locate his sister, but learned nothing. Strangely, Appleton put distance between himself and the Raynykov family around the same time. Raynykov finally confronted the American in October by following him from the embassy to a small café.

"She's dead," Appleton said sadly.

"How can you know that?" Raynykov demanded.

"I just do," Appleton said coldly. "Accept it."

The mixture of anger, fear and despair emanated from Appleton as he slowly sipped his coffee. Raynykov was no longer angry. He felt sad for this lonely American in a foreign land. "You loved her very much."

Appleton didn't respond, placing his cup back on the saucer. He looked up at Raynykov before speaking. "It's best you not be seen with me. The Okhrana is watching."

Raynykov leaned forward. "The Okhrana? Why?"

Appleton picked up his cup again, took a sip and put it down. "They arrested Natalia back in March. I noticed people watching me afterwards because I was seen with her on Bloody Sunday."

"If the Okhrana had arrested Natalia, I would have known about it. I have the ear of the Tsar."

Appleton leaned right into Raynykov's face. "You think the Okhrana tells the Tsar everything they do?"

Raynykov leaned back. He was right. After arresting Natalia, the last thing they would do is tell the Tsar that a member of a very high-ranking family was in their custody for treason.

So many years had passed since then. His inquiries came up with nothing. He could not find out whether she had been executed or exiled. Either way, she was gone, never to be found.

There was a soft knock on the door. Raynykov reached for his pistol and slowly moved to the door. He knew who it was. What he didn't know was what was going to happen next. Reaching for the knob, he slowly turned it and opened the door just a little, looking through the crack for threats.

Appleton stood there, hands clasped in front of him, showing no signs of hostile intent. Raynykov opened the door fully and they looked at each other.

"Hello, Vasili."

43

Rainey sat in the corner behind the table, slouched in his chair, a glass of vodka in his hand. He had easily eluded the American patrol. As he stared at the clear liquid, he was confused as to what he should do with it. It was the first drink of alcohol he had thought he needed since that day in Rumania, when he thought he was dreaming. And the image that had gotten him off using alcohol to handle his misery was now threatening to put him back on it.

Elizabeth.

He feared he would never see her again and that just wouldn't do. He had to find a way to get back to the company, alive. He considered storming in and just killing Clarke. He was sure he could make it past the American sentries. Couldn't be any harder than sneaking up on a German trench during the war. He could slide in at night, slit Clarke's throat and then slide back out without anyone being the wiser. Even Elizabeth wouldn't know. But she would know. Besides, Rainey knew he wasn't a cold-blooded killer anyhow.

He was lifting the glass towards his mouth when a flash of a red coat appeared in the corner of his eye. He turned his head slightly to get a better view and saw a man in a red tunic standing at the bar. Two more men in red tunics stepped up beside him. Rainey stared at the three men, lowering the vodka back to the table. The memory of his father in uniform flashed through his mind. Red tunic, dark blue collar tabs, Sam Browne belt.

Rainey went to the bar. Tapping the left-most man on the shoulder, he asked, "Excuse me, are you three Canadian?"

All three turned. The tall man in the center wore a stern look that instantly burst into surprise. "Oh, my God, Robert?"

"Cecil, what the hell are you doing here?"

Cecil Crane gave Rainey a bear hug. "I could ask you the same thing. When did the Patricias get assigned to Omsk?"

"They didn't. Long story. But the last thing I figured I'd see in Siberia was a Mountie."

"Got myself assigned to B Squadron and shipped off to Vladivostok," Crane said. "Now we're just trying to make our way back." He motioned to his two colleagues. "This is Constable Mark Sturgess and this is Constable James Margetts."

"Pleasure to meet you. Captain Robert Rainey."

Sturgess's ears perked up. "Are you Superintendent Rainey's son?"

Rainey smiled. "One and the same."

"I'm sorry for your loss," Margetts said.

The image of the superintendent flashed through Rainey's mind again, sitting proud in his RNWMP uniform. "I got word as we were leaving Vancouver," Crane said. "A sad day."

"Thank you," Rainey said, trying to change the subject. "But now, tell me why you're here."

"Delivering horses, if you can imagine," Crane said. "General Elmsley sent six of us west to deliver our horses to Kolchak. Left

Vlad over two months ago. Everyone else shipped out back to Canada in early June."

"How are you getting home when you get back to Vlad?"

"Got to make Vlad first. There's supposed to still be an economic mission there that can arrange to get us home. Took us four weeks to get here. The British Mission isn't a big help. Got us doing provost duties."

"Well," Rainey said. "You are policemen."

"They're peeved that we pulled out of Siberia," Margetts added.

"Wanted you to fight the good fight against the Bolshies, did they?" Rainey asked.

"The Bolshies aren't even half the problem," Sturgess answered. "You need a program just to keep up with all the warlords."

"And the program changes daily," Margetts said. "Got shot up pretty good on the way here."

Crane scowled. "Yes, it was a nasty trip. Now you. What are you doing here?"

Rainey leaned in, the three Mounties leaning in as well. "Secret mission," he said softly.

Crane jovially pushed Rainey back. "Ah, you're pullin' ma leg."

"I'm serious," Rainey said, an idea germinating in his mind. "I'm attached to an American unit. Can't tell you much, but I could probably get you out from under the British command here."

"Secret mission or not," Margetts said, "if it can get me out of this hole, I'm in."

"That would be the consensus," Crane added.

Rainey nodded. "The American unit is heading for Vladivostok. It would just be a matter of getting you assigned to me so the Brits won't mess with you when you get home. I'll need some sort of official paperwork to make it happen."

A smile crossed Crane's face. "Like telegraph orders that never actually crossed a telegraph line?"

Rainey remembered. He had created a telegram at the wire office in Edmonton that effectively delayed Crane's departure for Frog Lake by a week so he could go to a dance with Mary Graham. The telegram had caused enough confusion that the fact Crane was AWOL for a week was forgotten.

"You have any official telegraph forms?" Rainey asked.

"Oh yes, real official lookin'."

"What are you two talking about?" Sturgess asked.

Crane winked at him. "A way home, son. A way home."

* * *

Clarke reached the boxcar and climbed in, his fury still not under control. He had seen Rainey leaving the train station with a Russian he didn't know and now Appleton had let him get away. Elizabeth was furious with her father for trying to have Rainey killed again. At least she knew Sergeant Corelli, who was still searching for the captain, wouldn't shoot him.

Appleton spoke first. "I'm sure the Captain . . ."

"Won't tell anyone?" Clarke snapped. "Are you willing to take that chance?"

"With him, yes," Appleton replied curtly.

Clarke's anger overflowed again. "After all these years in Russia, you have the gall to say to me that you actually trust someone you met only a month ago?"

"He's not Russian, Jonathan."

"And he's not American, either. And we don't know anything about who he met up with."

Appleton didn't reply. Elizabeth got up from her chair, anger in her eyes. "Father, he is an honorable man. I know him. He will not give us away."

"And you're blinded by love," Clarke retorted.

"Yes, I am," Elizabeth said sternly. "And if you hadn't sent Charles out there to hunt him, he'd probably be back by now with information about who that Russian is. Now he probably won't come back at all. What's happened to you? You used to be smarter than this."

Clarke spun around, raised his hand to slap her and froze. Elizabeth didn't flinch or step back, glaring at him. The silence was broken by a surprising source.

"He came to Russia for her and she came for you, not me," Alexis said from his chair in the corner. "I understand that. Perhaps, Mr. Clarke, you should try to understand that as well."

Elizabeth's head turned to Alexis and then to Appleton. She saw the three emotions: anger, calm and expectation, in that order. She hoped that her father would accept their arguments.

"Let's just get the hell out of Russia," Clarke said.

Appleton sat down and looked up at Clarke. "Jonathan, would you like to know about the Russian you saw with the captain?"

* * *

The telegram said Rainey had been sent to Omsk to collect the Mounties on orders from the Canadian Government. It looked official enough that no one from the British command could dispute it. It still took over an hour to get the paperwork cleared by General Knox, head of the British Mission, to assign the six Mounties to Rainey. Now they were making their way toward the train station, Rainey mulling over how best to get into the camp without a major furor. Rainey and Crane walked slowly together, two Mounties across the street, two trailing back about thirty feet and the fifth one fifty feet up ahead, on point. The red tunics were bright against the usual clothing worn by people in the street. Everyone knew these men were with the Provost Marshall and deferred to them as such. No one got in their way.

Rainey spotted Raynykov casually staking out the square in front of the station. He stopped and waited for Raynykov to spot him. He nodded. Raynykov nodded back. "Right now," Rainey told Crane, "you are still provost. Behave like it and pretend you don't know me." He strolled casually toward Raynykov.

"What's going on?" Rainey asked.

"They have sent another patrol out, I presume to find you," Raynykov replied. "Heavily armed. The patrol commander is over by that restaurant." He pointed at a restaurant four doors down the street. Rainey could see Corelli, cradling a BAR, watching the street. He must have missed seeing Rainey because Crane had been between them.

"Are you alone?" Raynykov asked.

"No, brought some help." Rainey cast his eyes around, noting the positions of the six Mounties as well as all the members of Corelli's patrol.

"Who are your friends?" Raynykov asked.

"Policemen from Canada. They're on our side."

"Very bright red. They do not hide well," Raynykov said.

"They're policemen. They're not supposed to hide."

"Then they are very successful."

Corelli stepped into the square, his squad right behind him. Rainey stepped back towards the building. The crowd in the square was not very big, so he had no chance of getting lost in it. Raynykov stepped back too. Rainey caught Crane's eye, signaling with his head towards Corelli and the squad. Crane nodded back.

Rainey turned to Raynykov. "I've got a plan. Follow my lead." He stepped into the square in plain view of Corelli, who quickly signaled his squad to advance. Rainey casually continued walking across the square until Corelli reached him.

"Captain," Corelli said, a tremor in his voice. "We've been looking for you. We need you back at the camp."

Rainey turned, looking at the well-armed squad surrounding Corelli. "Quite the squad. Planning an attack on someone soon?"

Corelli blinked rapidly several times. Rainey thought his nerves had just bunched up another notch. "No, sir, we just need you back. Right now."

"On whose orders?" Rainey asked calmly.

Corelli shifted uneasily. One of his privates started to angle his rifle at Rainey. Things could get out of hand in a hurry.

"Well, Sergeant?" Rainey continued. "May I remind you that I'm in the Canadian army and do not have to bow to the authority of the American military?"

Corelli was becoming confused and distressed, his men edgy. "Sir, please," he pleaded.

"Is there a problem here?" Crane's voice came from behind Corelli. All six Mounties appeared from around the squad, almost on cue.

Corelli recognized the British provost arm bands immediately, which seemed to make him even more edgy. "No problem, officer," he said. "We're just retrieving the captain here. He's wanted back at camp."

"And I have no intention of going to an American camp,"

Rainey replied.

A flash of confusion crossed Crane's face. He thought the idea was to go there. Since Rainey was playing the belligerent role in the current situation, Crane went into police mode on him. "What is your name, rank and unit?"

"Robert Rainey, Captain, Princess Patricia Canadian Light Infantry."

"And you, Sergeant?"

Corelli shifted uneasily. "Sergeant Enrico Corelli, 1st US Field Artillery Brigade."

Crane shook his head. "I may be wrong, but I don't believe either of those units have any personnel in Omsk. What, pray tell, would an American field artillery brigade want with a Canadian infantry officer? And why are your unit insignias missing from your uniforms?"

Rainey had to hold back a smile. This was working out well. Corelli was at a loss for words and the other Mounties stood watchfully, with blank, official looks on their faces. Crane continued with the interrogation.

"No answer? Well, then, perhaps we should proceed to this camp and ask a few extra questions there."

"I don't want to go there," Rainey said. "I'll be in danger."

Crane took Rainey strongly by the arm, his towering height dominating everyone. He had caught on to the ploy. "From Americans? Somehow I doubt that. Besides, they won't try anything with provosts present. Sergeant, lead the way."

Corelli wasn't too keen on bringing British authority into the camp. "It's OK, officer. We can handle this."

Crane stared down on him. "First, it's 'Constable.' And second, your story is pretty weak. Now let's go or I'll haul the lot of you in for questioning."

Rainey glanced over at Raynykov and gave him a quick smile. Crane noticed the look, just as Raynykov stepped down from the station platform. Crane returned his attention to Rainey. Their eyes met, Rainey's eyebrows lifting slightly, telling him to go with it.

"This way . . . Constable," Corelli said.

The mass of men, a knot of khaki ringed by red, began moving towards the station. Crane leaned over to Rainey's ear. "What the hell have you gotten us into?" he whispered.

"It'll be fine," Rainey whispered back.

44

"He has who with him?" Clarke demanded.

Elizabeth could hardly conceal her smile and noticed Kennard trying hard to do the same. Rainey was fantastic. He was magnificent. And he was back.

"British provost officers, Mr. Clarke," Kennard was saying. "Six of them with Sergeant Corelli and his men."

"What the hell . . ." Clarke mumbled. He turned to Appleton. "What should we do?"

"Go talk to them," Appleton said. "Can't avoid them now."

Clarke and Elizabeth joined Kennard and went to the camp's perimeter to meet with Rainey and his provost officers.

"Captain," Clarke began. "Good to see you again. We need to discuss some issues in private."

"Excuse me, sir," Crane interjected. "But this officer did not want to come here. I take it you know him?"

Clarke hesitated for a second. "Yes," he said tentatively. "I know him."

"He's my fiancé," Elizabeth piped up. All heads spun to look at her. "My father is a little too protective and made Robert angry. Thank you for finding him and bringing him home."

Crane gave a surprised look to Rainey, who just shrugged. "And you sent out a fully armed patrol to bring him back?" the Mountie asked.

"I'm sorry about that," Elizabeth said. "I got pretty upset when he left." Something in the back of her mind made her think something funny was going on. She'd never seen red tunics on soldiers before except in old paintings of the British army and their leader wasn't talking with an English accent. He sounded more like . . .

Rainey.

"I must warn you that fully armed patrols are only authorized by the Kolchak government and sending your own out could have sparked a dangerous confrontation. There was another man . . ." Rainey discreetly poked Crane in the side. Crane got the hint. "There was another armed group in the square, probably a regular patrol, that would have gotten involved if we hadn't stepped forward. In the future, may I suggest you contact our office and we can do a search for any of your missing personnel."

"Thank you for bringing him back," Clarke said curtly. "I will send my thanks to your CO. Captain, come with me." He turned to leave.

Rainey poked Crane again. "There is another matter," Crane said.

Clarke looked up at the tall Mountie. "And what would that be?"

"Apparently, both the captain here and your sergeant are from units that are not supposed to be in Russia. Can you clear up that little mystery?"

Rainey held back a smile. Crane was being the perfect detective and giving him the clout he needed over Clarke. Clarke just stared at the giant for a moment, then became obstinate.

"We're an American unit and are not disposed to discuss our mission with a foreign power."

That pretty well settled it. But Crane had one more card up his sleeve. "And the captain is a Canadian officer, so falls under command of the British Mission while in Omsk, and we are not about to leave him here if he feels endangered."

Clarke signaled to Rainey. "Captain, a moment alone, please." The look on his face signaled resignation. The two took several paces away from the group before speaking in hushed tones.

"Please, Captain. I know you feel in danger here, but that is not the case."

"You sent armed teams out to get me. What am I supposed to think, since you have ordered me killed before?"

"It was a security measure. Omsk is a dangerous place."

"So is your train. When I saw your patrol, I was sure I was still on your death list."

"I don't have a death list, Captain."

"Then why did Appleton try to skewer me with his big knife?"

Clarke sighed and looked over at Elizabeth. Arm still in a sling, deep worry lines on her face. "You still love her?"

Rainey hesitated a second. "Never stopped."

"And she loves you. There will be no living with her if I have you killed."

Rainey chuckled. "Now that is what I call leverage. OK, I'll come back, as before."

"So what do we do about the provosts over there?"

"That's easy." Rainey pulled out the orders from General Knox and handed them to Clarke. "They'll be coming with us."

"What?"

"Oh, and a Russian count will be joining us. I believe Charles and Alexis know him."

* * *

Raynykov stepped up into the boxcar, Rainey and Clarke close behind him. He inspected the inside, the dark and dirty walls, the only light coming in from the open doors, the two guards by the tarp at the car's end, a dim light glowing from behind the tarp. He turned to Clarke, apprehension on his face. Clarke nodded his permission to go forward. Raynykov turned to see the two guards stepping away from the opening in the tarp. Tentatively, he moved forward.

"This really complicates things," Clarke mumbled to no one in particular.

"For getting Alexis out of Russia or getting his money?" Rainey said quietly. Clarke gave Rainey a scowl. Both watched Raynykov pull the tarp back and step inside. "Since he was part of getting Alexis to you, it's probably for the best that he join us. For security reasons."

Clarke nodded slowly in agreement.

"Count Raynykov!" they heard Alexis exclaim.

"Your Highness." In the shadows, they could see that Raynykov had gone down on his knee.

"Get up, Vasili Ivanovich. There is no more Tsar. I am just Alexis now. And you are probably no longer a count."

Raynykov raised himself to his feet. "You are right, my Tsar. My lands have all been taken from me."

"I told you I am just Alexis now," Alexis said sternly.

"I will have to get used to that, my . . . Alexis Nicholaovich."

There was silence for a moment. No one moved. The moment was special.

"I'm so glad to see you again. Have you been treated well?"

Appleton stepped up into the boxcar. "So he talked his way in here without me, did he?"

"He had help from Captain Rainey," Clarke said. "And after what you told me about him, he definitely wasn't a security risk."

"So he's coming with us?" Appleton asked.

"Yes," Clarke said.

"The resemblance to you is uncanny, isn't it?" Appleton said to Rainey.

Rainey nodded. Then he took out Appleton's Bowie knife. "I keep giving this back to you. Promise not to try and stick me with it again?"

Appleton smiled and said nothing, accepting the knife and returning it to its sheath.

Clarke changed the subject. "Captain, Major Slaughter has secured us passage to Vladivostok with the Czechs. I will be meeting with them in the morning and they want you to be there."

Rainey nodded.

*   *   *

The next morning, Clarke and Rainey walked silently through the streets of Omsk to the American Mission. Tension vibrated between them, but both were resigned to the current situation in an effort to get Alexis, 165 American soldiers, Elizabeth, and now six Mounties and a Russian count out of Russia. They were ushered into Slaughter's office right away. Rainey was surprised to see the Czech general he had briefly met in Chelyabinsk, standing with his aide de camp behind Slaughter.

"General Syrovy, sir," Rainey said. "Pleasure to meet you again."

"Ah, I see you made it out of Chelyabinsk without my help,"

Syrovy replied.

"It was touch and go, but we managed."

"I am sorry we could not help, but once the artillery started up . . ."

"I understand. No apology required, sir," said Rainey.

"If we could get down to business," Slaughter said, attempting to gain control of the conversation, "General Syrovy, this is Jonathan Clarke with the US government and Captain Rainey, a Canadian officer attached to Clarke's mission. They are in a unique position to solve your particular problem, as you solve theirs."

Syrovy placed his hands on the desk and looked hard at Rainey and Clarke. "Our goal initially was for us Czechs just to go home. This has become difficult and we have ended up being involved in this Russian dispute. Due to that, my army has sustained considerable casualties and my wounded need to go home. Unfortunately, I cannot spare any able-bodied soldiers to accompany them, but I understand you can."

Clarke looked at Rainey. "Captain?"

"One hundred forty-nine able bodied, seventeen sick or wounded is our current complement," Rainey replied.

Syrovy stood back and clasped his hands together. "Excellent. Are you prepared to help us get our men home?"

"Yes," Clarke said, almost before Syrovy was finished. Rainey nodded.

"Let's outline some details," Slaughter said. "General Syrovy has about twelve hundred wounded soldiers to move. It will be a long train, which will attract attention. But it will be marked as a Red Cross train, so it shouldn't be much of a target. Your presence on the train is more of a precaution."

"Many of the wounded are capable of fighting from fixed positions on the train if necessary," Syrovy added.

"What weapons will the train be fitted with?" Rainey asked.

"Each carriage will have multiple machine-gun mounts on the roof," Syrovy said. "Steel plates have been attached to both sides for protection."

"We'll need a US command carriage separate from the rest of the train," Clarke added.

Syrovy eyed him suspiciously. "I must insist on a joint command structure. I have assigned Major Formanek to lead with your captain. Also, my aide here, Lieutenant Birosh, will be going since he can speak Russian, as your Captain does."

Slaughter spoke before Clarke could object. "Tactical command between us will not be a problem. The extra carriage is for Mr. Clarke's mission."

Syrovy still looked suspicious, but he nodded. "As long as this 'mission' does not endanger my men."

"I assure you, General," Clarke said, "no one knows enough about my mission to bother attacking an armored train over it."

"What happens once we get to Vladivostok?" Rainey asked.

Syrovy stepped back and sat in a chair against the office wall. "Major Formanek will have orders to take to General Gajda. They will outline what he needs to do. With any luck, that Serbian idiot will actually follow orders for once." He leaned forward toward Rainey. "Then it is up to you, Captain."

"Me?"

Syrovy smiled. "The wounded are to be put on a ship bound for Canada. They will be transported across Canada by train to a ship that will take them to Europe. I have arranged it with your government." He pulled some papers out of his tunic. "Take these to your country's economic mission in Vladivostok and they will find a ship for you."

Rainey nodded. "That I can do."

"I am not finished, Captain," Syrovy said. "I would like to request that you accompany my men all the way to their ship in a place called . . ." He looked down at the papers in his hand. "Montreal? I would feel better if a Canadian working directly for me escorted them across your country."

Rainey nodded. "It would be an honor, sir."

Syrovy's face became sorrowful. "Please, Captain Rainey. Get my men home."

* * *

As they were leaving, Slaughter held Clarke back. Once they were alone, Slaughter closed his office door and sat down.

"There is something else that needs to go with you," he said quietly.

Clarke nodded. "I suppose I don't need to know what 'it' is?"

Slaughter nodded back. "When you get to Vlad, go to the US headquarters and ask for Graham Compton. He's State Department and is in charge of the US shipping out of Vlad. He also works for me on the side. He'll take care of everything."

"Why are you telling me anything about this at all?"

Slaughter smiled. "Always best if someone on the train knows something, just in case. And I know I can trust you."

45

August 6-14, 1919
East of Omsk

It took two days before the train was assembled and everyone was on board. Sergeant Sutton smiled as he brought the steam locomotive on line and began the slow process of starting the train. This was a much newer engine, fresh out of a maintenance shop, Czech flags mounted on the front. Red crosses on white circles were painted on each carriage. Steel plating was attached to the sides and to the locomotive for protection, with machine guns mounted on the carriage roofs. This was a hospital train. No one expected any bandits or warlords to bother with a hospital train, knowing that such a transgression would bring a terrible wrath down upon them from the still formidable Czech Legion.

The Czech contingent's commander, Major Formanek, had lost his left hand in an explosion while manning a machine gun during the retreat from Ufa. Syrovy's aide, Lieutenant Birosh, turned out to know German, another of Rainey's languages.

They were only three hours out of Omsk when the assumption that the train would meet no resistance proved wrong. Twenty horsemen came out of the woods and tried to take over the engine. The machine guns on the front carriage made short work of them. The survivors bolted back into the woods. The next day, the train came across an unlinked length of track and had to stop to fix it. Rainey sent two large patrols into the woods before anyone got out to start the repair work. Bandits were waiting, but not enough of them to take on the patrols. Two bandits were captured as the rest were driven off.

The two bandits had their hands tied behind their backs. As they were forced down onto their knees, Birosh pulled out his pistol to shoot them. Rainey stopped him.

"They wanted to attack a hospital train," Birosh said. "They are despicable and deserve to die."

"Look at them," Rainey answered. "These aren't ordinary bandits. They're in White army uniforms. The same as the horsemen from yesterday. They weren't expecting resistance, but wanted our train. I think we should find out why."

Birosh paused, but didn't lower the gun. He looked at Rainey. "Then ask them."

"They will be more honest if they believe they will survive the interrogation."

Birosh lowered his gun. "Very well."

Rainey stepped towards the two men and addressed them in Russian. "I am the only one who can keep you alive, so answer my questions honestly. Why did you plan an attack on a hospital train?"

The two men stared up at him, fear clearly etched in their faces. Rainey smiled and nodded to them, encouraging them to talk. The one on his left spoke up first.

"We were told it would not be defended. We were told . . ."

His head exploded, the bullet carrying through his skull into the second man's head. Both pitched over onto their sides, dead. Rainey spun and found Clarke lowering a pistol.

"What the hell you do that for?" Rainey yelled.

"Security of the mission," Clarke replied. He turned and walked back towards the first carriage.

Rainey stormed after him, reaching him at the carriage as Appleton and Elizabeth appeared on the stairs. He grabbed Clarke by the shoulder and spun him around. Clarke brought his pistol up and pointed it at Rainey, who grabbed the barrel and twisted it out of Clarke's grip. They stood face to face, seething at each other.

"You would be wise to never shove a gun in my face again," Rainey said menacingly.

"This is my show, Captain," Clarke replied, "and I don't have to explain myself to the likes of you."

Elizabeth and Appleton were looking down from the train window. Elizabeth's look of horror said it all. Rainey looked back at Clarke. "You'll have to explain yourself to her. Good luck with that." He then turned and walked back towards Birosh. When he reached the Czech officer, he said, "You and I will need to talk a little later."

Birosh nodded.

* * *

Rainey sat by himself that night as the train rocked back and forth. His mind was compiling all the information and events he had taken in since leaving Omsk. Did word of Alexis leak out while they were there? Three days is a long time, but Alexis did stay in the old boxcar the whole time. The company's soldiers didn't know who he was. Besides, Jeremy Clarke had handpicked his men, all of whom knew that leaking information could get them killed. What if the information had leaked out just as they were leaving? Knowledge of a living member of the Russian royal family on their train would have made it impossible to get out of Omsk, even if the train had already started moving. And any group looking to claim Alexis would know he would have a strongly armed and trained American guard with him. They would have come out with a division-sized force and just demand that they turn him over. But the Russian solider Clarke shot was from a small White army unit that was sent to attack the train, which would have put the Tsarovich's life in danger. The man had said they had not expected resistance.

It wasn't adding up. The more he thought about it, the more it seemed that Alexis was not the target. A train full of wounded Czech soldiers made for a pretty poor target, as well. What were they after?

A shadow passed over Rainey. He looked up and saw Birosh standing in front of him.

"The Major wants to know what is so interesting about your mission that it endangers his," Birosh said. "I would like to know, too."

Rainey shook his head. "The more I think about it, the more I believe it is not my mission that's the problem, either. There's something else."

"What?"

"I don't know, but I think you and I need to start a search of the train. Just you and me. Best we find out what it is before we tell anyone, including the major."

* * *

So began the search, done on the QT. For three days, Rainey

and Birosh walked up and down the train, casually going about their duties, but also checking every part of the train for hiding places. Loose panels in the ceiling and walls, under the platforms between carriages, even checking the linings of the cots filled with the wounded.

After two days, Elizabeth came looking for Rainey as he had been avoiding the front carriage. She found him on a platform knocking his knuckle on a railing with great interest.

"Is it hollow?" she asked as she came up beside him.

"No," he replied. "It's a solid bar. All of them are." He lowered his hand away.

"You look disappointed," she said.

Rainey stepped back from the railing. "Why would you say that?"

Elizabeth put her hand on his arm. "Forget it. What I really want to know is why you have been avoiding me. I haven't seen you in two days."

Rainey turned to her and smiled. "You miss me?"

She slapped him on the chest. "Hell, yeah. Why haven't you come to see me?"

"I've been busy."

She looked up at him, unbelieving. "It isn't because of my father again, is it? After he calmed down, he promised me not to try and kill you again."

"Do you really believe if I came over there and he tried, he would be successful?"

Elizabeth saw a darkness in his eyes and it scared her. He was being Battle Man and she was distracting him. "What's wrong?"

The door of the next carriage opened and Birosh stepped out. He moved over to the railing and knocked it with his right knuckle. Only then did he notice Rainey and Elizabeth standing on the other platform. He looked up, the look on his face of being caught doing something he wasn't supposed to.

"I'm sorry, forgive me," he said as he quickly turned and left the platform. Elizabeth looked up at Rainey, whose face had not changed from the darkness she had seen a moment earlier.

"What's going on?"

Rainey remained silent.

* * *

On the third day of the search, Rainey entered a carriage where Birosh was talking with one of his wounded soldiers. As he walked down the aisle, he felt the floor sag a bit. He didn't think much of it until a step later it sagged again. He stopped walking and rocked his step back over the solid flooring to the sag he noted first. He then measured his steps and took five steps forward and stopped.

There was a pattern he hadn't noticed before. Slight, but definite. He looked up from the floor to see Birosh looking at him. He glanced quickly to the floor and back up. Birosh gave him a very slight nod.

For the next few hours, Rainey and Birosh went over each carriage nonchalantly checking out the sags in the floor boards for patterns. Each carriage had the same pattern. When they got together out on a platform, there was an air of excitement between them.

"It could just be cross boards in the construction of the carriages," said Rainey.

"But they would be even with the door, not raised up," replied Birosh. "And every carriage has the same deformation."

Rainey nodded. "That is unusual. If it was just the cross

boards, there would be more inconsistencies between the carriages. Did you see anything resembling a trap door?"

Birsoh shook his head. "We would have found those already."

"So we need to get under the carriages to take a look."

"How do we do that without attracting attention?"

Rainey stared out across the passing Siberian landscape. "We're going to need help and I know just where I can get it."

* * *

The next morning during a water stop, Rainey and Birosh stepped from their respective carriages and moved to one halfway down the train's length. They were met by the six Mounties. Birosh looked dubiously at them, but Rainey reassured him they would make good cover and were loyal to him, not to Clarke's mission.

The Mounties took positions on either side of the carriage, standing casually, keeping an eye out for anyone approaching. Rainey and Birosh ducked under the carriage and up to a spot they knew was under one of the floor's solid sections. Along the entire length of the carriage, a long steel box was welded to the underside of the floor. Rainey had not thought anything of it, not knowing anything about railroad car construction. But it did make an excellent hiding place. They were working at prying open a steel panel when a short whistle made them stop. Rainey looked out and saw a familiar pair of boots walking towards them.

"Good morning, Cecil. Have you seen Robert?"

Crane used his official police voice. "No, Miss Clarke. I am planning on having some breakfast with him in about an hour in carriage number three. Would you care to join us?"

"Yes, that would be lovely. If you see him before then, tell him I'll be joining you."

"Very well." And with that, Rainey smiled as he saw Elizabeth's boots turn and head back towards the front of the train. Then they went back at the steel panel. It wouldn't budge, but they were able to peel it back a bit. Birosh brought up a flashlight and aimed the beam into the crack.

"It's a small wooden crate," Rainey said.

Birosh shone the light down the length of the carriage. "To get this panel right off, you would have to remove almost fifteen feet of steel."

"Let's put this back up firm and get out of here." They pushed the loose section of steel back into place and crawled out from under the car.

"Thanks, Cecil," Rainey said as he stood up.

"Find what you were looking for?" Crane asked.

Rainey nodded. "Kind of."

As he walked away with Birosh, curiosity started to stir in the two of them.

"Care to guess what is in the crates?" Birosh asked.

"Something worth attacking the train for," Rainey replied.

* * *

At breakfast an hour later, Crane was regaling Elizabeth with stories of Rainey back in Canada from before the war, much to Rainey's embarrassment.

"It wasn't that bad," Rainey said to a particular quip of Crane's.

"It took them three days to get the police truck up and running again," Crane said. "They had to run around with that horse-drawn jail wagon from the old west to ferry criminals."

Rainey laughed. "Hey, a little public humiliation was probably good for the criminals."

The laughter calmed down as they continued to eat. As the

silence lengthened, Elizabeth casually said, "So, did you find anything interesting under the train?"

Rainey and Crane stopped cold, their forks in midair as Elizabeth kept eating. She looked up at them both. "Really Robert, did you think I didn't see you under there? Cecil's whistle actually gave you away."

Crane put his fork down on his plate and got up. "You two probably need to talk about something that I'm not supposed to know about, so I'll leave you to it." He bowed to Elizabeth. "Always a pleasure, Miss Clarke."

As he left, Rainey went back to his food. After a moment, Elizabeth asked, "Well? You know you can trust me."

Rainey stopped eating again and looked up. Her eyes seared into him, asking questions he thought might be dangerous to her if she got answers. But he also knew she was getting very good at taking care of herself in this chaotic world they had found themselves in. And he hated keeping things from her.

"If someone wanted Alexis exposed, would you send small army units to attack a hospital train he was on?"

"No," she said without hesitation. "I'd take the whole army and present my loyalty to him if he'd lead us. He would be a magnet for all White forces and an inspiration that could end the Revolution in their favor."

Rainey smiled at her. She really had a grasp of the geopolitical situation they found themselves in.

"So what else is on, or should I say under, the train?" she asked straight out.

"I don't know. We found a small crate, but there is no way to get into it without attracting too much attention."

"A crate. We are being attacked because of a crate."

"According to my calculation, there are 120 of those crates."
Elizabeth's mouth dropped open.

46

August 20, 1919
Lake Baikal

There was nothing to do but just travel on. Elizabeth told Rainey there was no point bringing it up with her father. First off, he wouldn't tell them anything anyway. Second, there was a good chance he knew something was on the train, but also a good chance he didn't know what it was. It would be under the same security procedures under which the company had travelled across Russia.

There were no more attacks on the train now that they were a reasonable distance from Omsk. That was where any security leak about the crates had obviously occurred. By the evening of day sixteen, the train was twenty miles short of Lake Baikal. It was pitch black out as the moon hadn't yet come up as a sliver over the horizon. Although Rainey would have preferred the train to run dark, it was safer for Sutton to have the headlight on. With the headlight burning, there was no point having the carriages totally dark either.

The train was moving at around ten miles per hour. Rainey

was in the carriage with Corelli's platoon. Corelli had been avoiding Rainey since the incident in Omsk and Rainey decided he wanted the old Corelli back. He found him out on the rear platform.

Corelli turned to see who was coming outside. When he saw it was Rainey, he quickly turned back to looking into the darkness. Rainey rested his arms on the railing next to him. "Good evening, Sergeant."

"Sir." Corelli's voice was so low Rainey barely heard him.

They stood side by side, listening to the constant sound of wheel on track, the breeze passing by, looking out at the blackness of night. Rainey was hoping Corelli would say something, but nothing was forthcoming.

"You didn't know what Appleton's orders were, did you?" Rainey asked.

Corelli's face went grave. "No, of course not."

"Then why are you avoiding me?"

Corelli turned to him. "Because I was there."

"And?"

Corelli didn't continue, turning back to the darkness. Rainey turned back to the night as well. "You recall I was holding his knife."

Corelli turned to face Rainey again. The intensity in his face was high. "It's not that, sir. It's MacGregor. It's Mr. Clarke, Mr. Appleton. It's like I'm back in the Bronx and wondering if my best friend was selling me out to a rival gang. I joined the army to get away from that. One enemy, over there, everyone on my side aimed in the same direction and not worried about being shot in the back."

"Is that why you joined the company?" Rainey asked.

"Yeah. I was hanging on as best as I could to hide from my past. The old Don of my neighborhood was pressing me to send munitions I was disposing of his way. The lieutenant and his mission gave me an escape before I got my legs broke, or worse."

Rainey nodded. "And you being sent out as part of a plot to kill me didn't sit well."

Corelli lowered his gaze. "It was double dealing. I've learned to trust you as a leader. We have each other's back. Then I let you down by getting caught up in this security crap, and that just drives me nuts."

Rainey reached out and put his hand on Corelli's shoulder. "You did have my back and I knew that, which is why I made for the crowd."

Corelli looked up. "Really?"

"Sure," replied Rainey. "Now if it was Garcia . . ."

They both laughed. Garcia was known to have a heavy trigger finger.

"I figured you were mad about that game I played on you with the Mounties," Rainey said.

"Nah. Once we got back and thought about it, I realized you couldn't have just asked me."

They both noticed the flash in the distance and recognized it for what it was. "A 75," Corelli said, "about a mile and a half out." The explosion was well short of the railroad. Two more rounds also fell short of the tracks. "They're not very good. From their position, they should know how far the tracks are."

Rainey looked down the side of the train. The train was speeding up. Sutton was accelerating as fast as the locomotive would let him to outrun the shelling. Another round fell short, but the next round smashed into one of the carriages farther up the train.

Rainey turned quickly on Corelli.

"I didn't say they weren't lucky," Corelli said.

They both bolted through the carriage. More shells were falling around the train. "Out of the way!" yelled Rainey as he traversed each carriage until he found Kennard on a platform, fighting a fire. Rainey's stomach dropped when he realized that the shell had hit the command carriage. Elizabeth. He stopped suddenly in the aisle, fighting panic. Corelli ran into his back.

"Sir, we have to help Sergeant Kennard," Corelli yelled in his ear.

Corelli's words shook Rainey loose from his freeze. He launched himself forward onto the platform just as Kennard was able to break down the door. A blanket landed on Rainey's shoulder. He grabbed it and moved into the carriage, using the blanket to beat at the flames. He discovered an opening that had once been fifteen feet of the carriage floor. He looked around furiously, but couldn't see anyone in the darkness at the carriage's far end. Some of the floor was still intact along the right wall, so he moved in that direction. It was then that he saw Raynykov, blood on his face, standing up along the gap in the floor on the other side.

Rainey turned, finding Corelli and Private Miller right behind him, each with a blanket. "Where's O'Hanlon?" he yelled.

Kennard was still at the door. "He's coming sir," he yelled back.

"I'm heading forward," said Rainey. Corelli and Miller nodded, swatting at the burning wood of the carriage. Rainey sprinted across to the other side, Raynykov grabbing his arm as he reached it to steady him.

"Are you all right?' Rainey asked Raynykov.

"I will live. Clarke is gone, everyone else wounded."

A vision of Elizabeth lying in a heap, slowly dying, flashed through Rainey's mind. To come this far and lose her now was almost more than he could take. He pushed past Raynykov into the darkness of the forward carriage.

"Elizabeth!"

"Over here." It was Appleton. Rainey found him leaning over Elizabeth, a large wood splinter sticking out of his right shoulder. Elizabeth was lying still, eyes closed. Appleton was tearing strips of cloth from his shirt and pulling splinters out of her body. He handed the strips to Rainey.

"She's alive. I haven't found any serious wounds, but she's bleeding a lot. Blast knocked her out."

Rainey sprang into action, applying pressure to a wound on her left leg. He checked her bullet wound, which seemed no worse for wear. *Where was O'Hanlon?*

Almost on cue, O'Hanlon appeared behind Rainey. "C'mon, Captain, let me in there," he said, gently pulling Rainey away by the shoulder. "Go get that big stick out of Mr. Appleton. I'll take care of the little lady."

Rainey hesitated, but relented and let O'Hanlon in. He turned to see Appleton looking very pale and wavering. Rainey grabbed him under his arm and sat him down on a bench. He now had something other than Elizabeth to focus on.

"Give me your knife," Rainey said.

"You get to actually stick me with it this time," said Appleton as he drew his knife from the sheath and handed it to Rainey. Standing up, Rainey looked at the piece of wood sticking out of Appleton's shoulder. Gently grabbing it with his left hand, he cut around the wound with the knife with his right, digging down so as to free the wood safely from the shoulder. Appleton grimaced, but remained very still. Rainey could feel the wood beginning to come free, so he gently started to pull it out, cutting with the knife where it snagged on flesh in the process. The wound was deep, but the bleeding did not appear too excessive. Rainey looked up to ask O'Hanlon for some bandages and found Miller holding out bandages and a canteen of water for him. Rainey cleaned and dressed the wound and leaned Appleton down onto the bench. Appleton's eyes were closed when Rainey turned back to O'Hanlon and Elizabeth.

O'Hanlon moved to Appleton to check Rainey's work. "How is she?" Rainey asked, his voice forced.

O'Hanlon smiled at him. "She's a tough one. Didn't take too much damage. Mostly just knocked out. Let her sleep and she'll be fine. Now let's see if you did up Mr. Appleton properly."

Miller was lifting Elizabeth onto a padded bench and propping her head up with a makeshift pillow. She'll be fine, O'Hanlon had said. The fear in his throat was subsiding. He walked over and looked down at her peaceful face, brushing away the hair that was covering it.

"Captain."

Raynykov called from a few benches back and signaled Rainey to join him. Rainey took the few steps back to find Raynykov holding Alexis tightly to him. The boy had what looked to be only superficial cuts, but Raynykov looked extremely worried.

"Alexis, how are you?" Rainey asked.

Alexis looked up at him. "Just some minor cuts. I will be fine."

"You know that is not true," Raynykov stated.

"I have survived worse."

Rainey wasn't following. "What are you two talking about?"

Alexis looked at Raynykov, who nodded, and turned to address Rainey. "I have a condition where when I'm cut, I bleed a lot."

"I've heard of that," Rainey said.

"He damaged himself back in Ekaterinburg," said Raynykov, "which is why he has been so weak for the last year and a half. Now, any cut could be fatal."

"I'll get O'Hanlon to look at him," Rainey said.

"The best doctors in Russia could not help him. Your doctor will not, either."

"So what do we do?"

Alexis sighed. "Wait to see if I can fix myself."

47

August 22-28, 1919
Lake Baikal to Vladivostok

The images flashing through her mind disturbed her, but she couldn't stop them. Elizabeth was standing next to a pallet filled with bundles of US currency while soldiers faded in and out, staring at her and asking *Why?* There was the young soldier on the bridge at Majaki, bullet holes apparent on his chest, the soldiers with the machine gun from Ekaterinoslav, their faces mutilated by bullets, the Cossack soldiers. Each image got more disturbing. Reinhardt. Jeremy, and then, lastly, Tom Bradley, who didn't say anything at all. With his blank face and eyes hanging over her, she heard her father's voice behind her saying *They are not important.* The last image was of Rainey, sadly shaking his head and walking away. She reached out to him, tried to scream his name, but no sound came out. Rainey's image slowly faded to nothingness.

She started to feel a rocking sensation. The noise of a train began to pierce the veil of her reality. But she was still frantic, searching the mists before her for any sign of Rainey. Then came a big yellow flash and she jerked awake with a cry. Her arms shot out. Someone grabbed her wrists and a voice called.

"Get the captain."

Elizabeth's eyes snapped open and she glared into the face of Private Miller. But her mind did not see Miller. She saw Kolochov with an evil sneer on his face. Panic-stricken, she fought his grip on her wrists, but she was not strong enough. Her wounded shoulder screamed in pain, making her cry out again.

"Miss Clarke, it's OK. You're safe," said Miller, a little panic in his voice as he struggled to hold her still.

Kolochov faded, revealing the private's familiar face. Her heavy breathing began to slow, the sense of panic fading. She stopped struggling and slowly lowered her arms down to her chest. She looked around to see the worry on a couple of soldiers' faces before she focused back on Miller.

"Where am I?" she asked.

"We're still on the train, somewhere in Siberia," Miller answered.

Elizabeth glanced toward the window next to her hammock. It was daylight, a deep blue sky visible through the opening in the steel plating. She tried to raise herself for a better view, but her shoulder wouldn't let her. Appleton appeared over Miller's shoulder, his arm in a sling.

"Good morning, young lady," he said. "About time you woke up. O'Hanlon was starting to worry about you."

"What happened?" Elizabeth asked.

"Artillery fire hit the carriage. You were knocked out. Been about thirty-four hours now."

Elizabeth began to remember. She had been talking to Raynykov when the explosions started. She had gone to a window to look out, and turned to see her father doing the same near the other end of the carriage. Then the big flash of yellow and . . .

"My father!"

Appleton slowly shook his head. Elizabeth made a short intake of air and her whole body began to shake. She lay back in the hammock. An enormous feeling of being all alone consumed her. First her mother, then Jeremy. Now her father. She was alone.

"We're all so very sorry, Miss Clarke," Miller said. "Can we get you anything? Food? Water?"

Elizabeth willed herself to regain her self-control. She was parched and hungry. "Yes, Private. Whatever's handy."

Miller held a canteen to her mouth, but Elizabeth took it from him and drank deeply. When she was finished, Miller had some army rations ready for her along with some bread. She quietly ate what was offered, canned corned beef, her sense of being alone in the world nagging at her. She still had Rainey, didn't she? When someone had said get "Get the captain," they'd meant Rainey, hadn't they? Although O'Hanlon was a captain, too, the men usually referred to him as "Doc." Doubt rose in her again. What if Rainey was gone too?

A commotion down the aisle of the carriage told her Rainey was making his way to the hammock. The worry on his face changed to a smile when he saw Elizabeth awake and eating.

"How are you doing?" he said softly.

Elizabeth smiled back at him. "You seem to ask me that a lot." Rainey was here. All feelings of loneliness disappeared in an instant and her confidence returned. No more panic. No more doubt. She was herself again. "Are we still feeding the men this ration slop?" she said bluntly.

A smattering of laughter came from among the men around the hammock. Rainey turned to them. "She's fine now, boys. Go find somewhere else to be."

Several soldiers got up, remarking to each other, giving her casual salutes as they walked down the aisle.

"You too, Miller," Rainey said. "They were here in shifts. You've been awake almost the whole time. Go get some sleep."

"I'm OK, sir. Caught a little extra shuteye along the way . . ."

"Private," Rainey said sternly.

Miller got the hint. "Yes, sir." He stood and moved down the aisle.

"And I'll leave you two alone as well," Appleton said as he followed Miller.

Rainey sat down beside the hammock. "I'm glad you're back with us."

"What did you mean 'they were here in shifts'?" Elizabeth asked, puzzled.

Rainey pushed the hammock gently to get it rocking a little more than the train's motion was doing. "It's heartwarming, really. Everyone wanted to spend time with you while you were out. They set up a schedule so two squads were up here with you at all times, one hour at a time.

"So I always had sixteen men watching me be unconscious for thirty-four hours?"

"Plus Miller. I assigned him full time when I couldn't be here myself. He set the schedule."

Elizabeth squirmed a little. "I find that a little more embarrassing than heartwarming."

"Hey, they care. That means a lot."

Elizabeth knew it did. "I truly belong to the company."

Rainey leaned over and kissed her on the forehead. "You always have. First, perhaps just a passenger. But as early as Majaki, the men saw you as special, one of them."

Elizabeth smiled coyly. "If you were wounded, would they watch you in shifts too?"

Rainey laughed. "No. There would have been consequences once I woke up and found out."

Elizabeth took another bite of the ration, thinking about being part of the company. It was her family now, the men of the company, who respected her, cared about her. Somewhere along the road through Russia, the gaping hole in her soul left by Jeremy dying had slowly been filled.

She grimaced at the food. "I definitely won't be missing this stuff." She moved to place the can aside, but Rainey pushed her hand back.

"You need to build your strength. It's not great, but it's the best we've got right now. We shot a couple of deer at our last stop, so there will be venison for dinner tonight."

Elizabeth took another bite, chewing quietly. After she swallowed, she asked, "How are Alexis and Vasili?"

Rainey's face fell, looking down at his lap. "Alexis died about six hours ago."

Elizabeth threw her ration can across the carriage. The mission. All the preparations. All the deaths. All for nothing. She thought very briefly about the money, but quickly dismissed that as totally irrelevant. She was not her father. She looked up at Rainey, seeing the sadness in his eyes, and a little doubt.

"I'm not concerned about the money," she said sternly. "For me, once we knew, it was about getting Alexis out of Russia so he could have a life free of fear."

Rainey smiled. "Alexis would have been the first to tell you that his life was not worth more than any of our soldiers."

"The count?" she asked.

"He left the train with Alexis's body at our last stop. He said he'd take the boy back to his family. He wished you . . ."

O'Hanlon appeared behind Rainey. "Good morning. How's my little patient?" he said with his light Irish lilt.

"Better now that I've woken up," Elizabeth said sullenly.

"Ah, wonderful," O'Hanlon said. "I was a little concerned because I really couldn't find any reason for why you were unconscious. It was like you just didn't want to wake up. That's psychological and I can't fix that if you're not awake."

Elizabeth knew O'Hanlon meant well by trying to be cheerful, but her mood wished he wasn't. "I guess I had some things to work out," she mused, remembering all the dead soldiers asking "Why?" in her dream.

"Well, I still have to look you over. Got a few extra cuts now to join the serious bullet wound from before."

Rainey got up. "I'd better get back to the men. But before I go . . ." Rainey reached into the breast pocket of the tunic that was hanging next to her and pulled out the locket. Elizabeth took it, watching it spin on the chain. "I found it on the floor of the carriage."

"I had it out when the explosion hit."

"You keep it with you at all times until you are safely back in New York. Understand?"

"Yes, sir," she said mockingly, rolling up the chain in her right hand and saluting.

"I'll check on you later," Rainey said, smiling.

After she watched him leave, she opened her hand and gazed at the locket. She could almost feel its power making her feel better.

"That locket has great magic," O'Hanlon said. "Keep it close at all times."

"I'm surprised at you," Elizabeth said. "A doctor and a man of science believing in magic."

"Magic is science that we don't understand," O'Hanlon replied. "Doesn't mean I can't believe in it."

* * *

Train traffic was lighter once past Lake Baikal. Control of the line was more in the hands of the Japanese and American forces and showed better track maintenance and fewer bandits. It only took another six days for the train to reach Vladivostok. It was not without incident, however. An American officer they met at one of their stops mentioned a warlord named Semyonov who was supported by the Japanese Army. Their train would be watched as they progressed through his territory. Without Japanese blessing, he would most likely leave the train alone without asking for a toll or other tribute. But the Japanese couldn't be everywhere.

Two days out of Lake Baikal, the train was halted by a very large armed party. As the locomotive braked to a stop, three officers approached. It all seemed so formal that Rainey decided to go out and talk with them.

As he was passing the first carriage, he saw Appleton coming down to join him. "Any idea what this is all about?" Rainey asked.

Appleton shook his head. "I guess we will find out shortly."

Rainey glanced behind him to find Birosh and Formanek trotting up to join them as well. The four reached the engine and stopped just short of the three Russian officers.

"Good morning," Appleton said brightly. "My name is Charles Appleton, United States State Department. We are escorting this hospital train of Czech Legionnaires to Vladivostok. How can we help you?"

The senior Russian officer looked the four of them up and down. "We are here to inspect your train. Allow my men access to search for contraband."

"This train is protected by the diplomatic status of the United States of America. We will not allow you to board," Appleton replied firmly.

"Diplomatic status carries no weight here. Get everyone off the train while we search it." The officer waved his hand and the sound of several rifle bolts slamming into place could be heard.

Appleton took a step back. "Please, give me a moment to confer with my colleagues."

"You have two minutes."

Appleton signaled the others to walk with him. He switched to German so the Russians couldn't understand them. "Any idea what they are looking for?"

If they wanted Alexis, they would have just asked for him, Rainey thought. He traded a knowing glance with Birosh before looking back at Appleton.

"Nothing but wounded Czech soldiers and us on this train."

"I know you were checking out the opposition. What are our chances?"

Rainey glanced at the trees. "It would be messy, but if they brought a little artillery along with them, we'd lose."

He looked at Appleton and wondered what could be so bad about letting the Russians on the train. With Alexis gone, there was nothing to find. He was confident the crates wouldn't be found. There was the chest of gold that the company had brought along to Russia, but that was a small price to pay to avoid a conflict.

"Good morning, gentlemen," a voice loudly in English, with a strong southern accent, called from the trees behind the Russians. "What seems to be the problem here?"

They turned to find an American officer approaching them, fully decked out for combat. The Russians showed signs of alarm, as he was followed by several American soldiers.

"That'll even out the odds," Rainey mumbled to himself.

The American sauntered past the Russian officers with barely a glance and greeted Appleton with a big smile. "Captain William T. Beauregard, 27th Regiment, at your service, sir."

"Charles Appleton, State Department. Glad to see you were in the vicinity."

"They've been sittin' here for two days waitin' for you. We've been sittin' up there watchin' 'em the whole time. Got some intelligence that the local warlord had an unhealthy interest in your train."

Rainey stepped up. "I'm Captain Rainey, the commander on the train. What's the military situation?"

Beauregard chuckled. "They brought some artillery, but their boys have been 'stepped back' from their guns at the moment. The rest you can see. None of 'em even bothered to hide."

"Well, thank you most sincerely, Captain," Appleton said. "If there's nothing else, may we be on our way?" He held his hand out.

Beauregard took his hand and gave it a firm shake. "Nope. Just shuffle on outta here and we'll keep the Russkies occupied. Glad to have been of service." And with that, he saluted. After Rainey, Formanek and Birosh returned the salute, he turned and slowly walked away, totally ignoring the Russian officers as he passed them.

* * *

There were no further incidents. The train finally rolled into Vladivostok to the cheers of everyone on the train. It had been a long and arduous ride for both American and Czech, both looking forward to finally going home. From the train coming out of the heights above the city, ships could be seen in the harbor, gleaming in the sunshine. They were a sure sign of a ticket home for every soldier. The city wasn't large, but the main buildings were very European. Only a few motorcars were visible in the streets. Most transportation still included horses and wagons or goods strapped to one's back.

Elizabeth was feeling queasy as the train eased into the station. As she tried to stand up, she stumbled.

Rainey was there and reached for her elbow to steady her. "Are you all right?"

Her face was flushed and she was sweating. "Just a little indigestion. I think the food is finally catching up with me."

"Either way, you should get checked out," Rainey said. "I'll send O'Hanlon by to see you."

"I'm sure it's nothing."

"And I don't care," Rainey said sternly. "O'Hanlon's going to check you out before we go traipsing around Vlad."

Elizabeth lowered her head and grinned. "Yes, sir."

The train came to rest on one of the rail yard's middle tracks. It wasn't the best location, but they didn't have control of the switches to get them next to a field or other more comfortable position. Most of the Czechs had never left the train during the whole trip due to their injuries. The yard was crowded with trains. One beside them began moving, clearing an area for the soldiers to disembark. Men stepped off the train and started mingling,

Kennard and a Czech officer taking command and organizing the men into the prearranged groups they would stay in, close to the train. For the next thirty minutes, Rainey did his rounds to ensure everyone knew the score and to take care of some little details that had cropped up. He finally relinquished command to Kennard and headed to the assembly point, where all would meet before entering Vladivostok proper. Private Miller fell into step beside him.

"Sir, Sergeant Kennard assigned me to your detail," Miller said.

Rainey looked Miller up and down, noting he was armed with a BAR as well as a Colt pistol. "Who gave you the BAR?" he asked.

"Sergeant Garcia," Miller replied. "He'll be leading the American part of the detail."

Garcia was standing by the command carriage with three other soldiers from his platoon. They were all armed with BARs as well.

"Expecting trouble, Sergeant?" Rainey asked.

"Unknown territory, sir," replied Garcia. "Always prefer superior firepower."

Rainey patted Garcia on the shoulder. "You keep your safety on, OK?"

Garcia grinned. "Always."

Rainey looked back down the track and saw Major Formanek, Lieutenant Birosh and five Czech soldiers hiking towards them. Formanek and Birosh were in their best uniforms, full medals, swords and all. Rainey looked down at his tunic, threads hanging out and dirt spots, and thought that perhaps he should start getting Private Miller to clean and press his uniform after all. Elizabeth and Appleton appeared on the carriage platform. Elizabeth was wearing her own clothes; a long skirt, boots, a blouse and vest. Her hair hung loose past her shoulders, a fedora on her head. She smiled at him and came down the stairs.

"You'll be happy to know that Brendan said I'm fine. I was feeling much better by the time he saw me."

Rainey took her hand to help her down to the ground. "Better safe than sorry."

Appleton was dressed up as well, with a black vest, long coat, clean spats, tie and a top hat Rainey didn't know he had.

Appleton surveyed the group as he came down the stairs. "Looks like we're going to war."

"Fear of the unknown, mostly," Rainey responded. "Nice hat."

"Thank you," said Appleton. "Been a while since I've had an occasion to wear it."

"Kolochov's dinner would have been appropriate."

Appleton's scowl made Elizabeth laugh. It sounded good to hear her laugh like that, Rainey thought.

"You two armed?" he asked.

Elizabeth tapped her holster on her hip. Appleton raised both sides of his coat to reveal a holster for a Colt on his right and his sheathed bowie knife on his left. Appleton glanced over at Garcia's detail.

"Not as well as our detail," he said, "but we can contribute."

"OK, Sergeant, form them up," Rainey said. Switching to Russian, he gestured to Birosh. "You take the left?"

Birosh nodded and proceeded to give commands to assemble his detail. Formanek stepped up beside Rainey while Elizabeth and Appleton fell in behind him. Rainey looked over at Formanek and gestured for the major to take a step forward and take overall command. Formanek smiled, nodded and centered himself up front on the detail.

The detail formed up. Formanek looked over his shoulder at Rainey, a quizzical look on his face. Rainey nodded, signaling that they were ready to go. Formanek smiled and faced back down the street.

"*Rameno Pusky!*" The Czech soldiers threw their rifles up onto their shoulders and Rainey smiled as he heard the BARs going up on the American shoulders a split second later. Formanek and Birosh pulled their swords from their scabbards, holding them straight up in their right hands. Rainey reached back and pulled his sword free, holding it the same way.

"*Vpred Brezna!*"

Everyone stepped off together, marching in time up around the locomotive, across the tracks, out beside the stationhouse and into the streets of Vladivostok.

48

August 28, 1919
Vladivostok

The American HQ sat on a hill in a large stone building with a gated courtyard. Originally the home of some count or duke no one could remember, it personified the grandeur of the Russian Empire from before the Great War. Apart from a few bullet pockmarks in the stone exterior, it looked much as it had back in 1850 when it was built. What was different was the military vehicles, the two artillery pieces with full crews and the several soldiers wandering around in the courtyard. A small guard house had been built to the left of the courtyard gate and two soldiers and an officer operated out of it. An American flag was draped over the entrance way to the house and the vehicles all had large five-pointed stars painted on them.

"It's almost like being home," Appleton mumbled to Elizabeth.

At the gate, they learned that a Lieutenant Colonel Morrow was in command at the time. More senior officers were either away or with General Groves was on his way back from Omsk.

Once Appleton presented his State Department credentials, they were ushered into the colonel's office without delay.

"Come on in," Colonel Morrow said. "Have a seat." Appleton and Elizabeth sat down beside one another across the desk from their host.

"So," Morrow continued. "I must also apologize for all the generals being out for drinks or something. Left me holding the fort and I'm not normally here at all."

"No?" Elizabeth asked. "Where are you normally?"

"I command the 27th Regiment. We're currently stationed . . . well, I can't really tell you that."

"We more or less already know," Elizabeth said. "Let Captain Beauregard know we made it the rest of the way and thank him again for his service."

Morrow smiled. "Yeah, ol' Beau likes to put the Russkies in their place when he can. I'll let him know." He addressed Appleton. "They said you're with State?"

"I am," Appleton said simply.

Elizabeth reached into her tunic and pulled out the charred remains of the orders. "Sorry about their condition, but we had a little incident on the way here. They are mostly intact. You can read the important parts and General Graves's signature." She handed them to Morrow.

Morrow read them quickly and then looked up at Elizabeth. "A ship to San Francisco. Let me see what's out there." He got up from his desk and left the room.

"He didn't scrutinize the signature very closely," Elizabeth said quietly.

"It's possible he's never seen it before," Appleton said. "In the end, not having Graves here is a bonus. By the time he gets back, we'll be back in the States."

The door opened and Morrow walked in with a man in tow. "This is . . ."

"Charles?" the man said.

Appleton looked at him with surprise. "Graham. What are you doing in Siberia?"

"Could ask you the same thing. Everyone at State thinks you're dead."

Appleton stood up and shook the man's hand. "You should know I'm too hard to kill."

The man laughed and embraced Appleton. "Damn it, Charles. It is good to see you. You'll have to tell me what you've been up to since you and that industrialist disappeared almost two years ago. What was his name?"

"Jonathan Clarke," Elizabeth said coldly.

"Graham, this is Elizabeth Clarke," Appleton said. "Jonathan's daughter."

Graham held out his hand. "Graham Compton, State Department."

"I figured that," Elizabeth stated, ignoring his outstretched hand.

Compton looked back at Appleton. "Why is she here?"

"Mr. Compton," Elizabeth said. "Do you not think it rude to ask questions about someone when they are sitting right next to you?"

Compton was lost for words. Appleton smiled and broke the tension. "Colonel Morrow. About a ship?"

Morrow sat again behind his desk. "Graham, you have the schedules. What's available?" He handed the orders to Compton. Compton read them over and a knowing look came over him.

"The 'Pacific Endeavor' is bound for San Francisco via Honolulu," he said. "Scheduled to leave tomorrow. That should be suitable."

"OK," Morrow said. "If I could leave this in your capable hands. I'm due to return to my regiment tomorrow morning."

"Not a problem." He turned to Appleton. "If you and Miss Clarke will follow me, I'll get you the information you need for passage."

Elizabeth stood up and reached out to shake Morrow's hand. "Thank you, Colonel, for all your help. Good luck with your regiment."

Morrow stood and took her hand. "I'll need it. After last winter, they're all cursing about coming here from the Philippines."

Elizabeth laughed, then suddenly felt light-headed. As her knees weakened, Appleton caught her under her arms.

"You OK, Miss Clarke?" Morrow said, coming around his desk.

Elizabeth regained her footing and stood up, letting out a sigh. "Yes, I'm fine. I'll be better when I can get back home."

"I can have a doctor take a look at you," said Morrow. "There have been instances of the Spanish Flu about."

"My doctor says I don't have that," Elizabeth replied. "Doesn't know what it is, but it comes and goes. I think it's the food over here, myself."

"That could be," Morrow said. "Well, take care of yourself."

"I will. Thank you again."

They followed Compton down a hallway to his office. He signaled them to sit while he took his place behind his desk. He continued reading the orders. The silence in Compton's sparse office dragged painfully on. Compton repeatedly looked down at the orders, then back up at Appleton and Elizabeth, then back at the orders. "Is there a problem, Graham?" Appleton finally asked.

Compton looked up at Appleton. "These are from Slaughter, aren't they?" It was more a statement than a question.

"They're signed by Graves," Appleton said.

"No, they're forged by Slaughter."

Appleton didn't show any change in his demeanor. Testing Elizabeth, Compton saw only her business poker face staring back at him.

Compton continued, matter-of-factly. "Don't worry. This isn't the first time he's forged the general's signature. I can tell because he can never get the 's' right. Had Graves even made it to Omsk when he wrote these up?"

Elizabeth glanced at Appleton. He didn't look worried at all.

"No, he hadn't arrived yet."

Compton looked down at the orders. "Probably good you and your little army were gone before he got there, but the date on the orders could be a problem later if it gets checked for some reason." He glanced up at Elizabeth. "You needn't worry, Miss Clarke. I'm on your side. Like Charles here, my duties tend to cross the boundaries of our State Department's jurisdictions. I'm by no means a master spy like Charles, but I do work for Major Slaughter on the Q.T." He looked back at Appleton. "You have the shipment with you?"

"Yes," Appleton said without hesitation.

"Do you know what it is?"

"No."

"Why isn't Jonathan Clarke with you?"

"He's dead."

The room went silent again. The interval was oppressive to Elizabeth. She wanted to burst out and demand an explanation for why this new intrigue had put her original mission at risk. But this was not the place to ask questions, as she knew she would get no answers. She wondered if this shipment was what Rainey had found.

All sat silently while Compton wrote out two notes. When he finished, he handed them to Appleton. "The first one is an introduction to Captain Howard of the 'Pacific Endeavor.' It'll get you and your little army on board. The second note is for Peter Langdon. He'll meet you in San Francisco and take possession of the shipment. Remember the code phrase we used in college?"

"Yes," Appleton replied.

"He will have a description of you and will use the phrase to make contact."

"Very well."

Compton leaned back in his chair and crossed his arms. "I'm glad you've made it out of this chaos. I should hope we can get together stateside when I get out of here."

"I would like that."

Compton spoke directly to Elizabeth. "I'm sorry for your loss, Miss Clarke. I'm told your father was very good at what he did and senior people at State spoke very highly of him."

Elizabeth still sat with her poker face on. "Thank you."

Compton got up from his chair. "I'll show you out."

* * *

"So, we have a shipment?" Elizabeth asked calmly as they exited the courtyard of the American HQ building. "I'm assuming he wasn't referring to Alexis."

Appleton nodded. "We can discuss this back at the camp."

"Did you know?" she asked, wondering if he had been in on it from the beginning.

"Not until the day we lost your father."

Garcia and the troopers were gathered outside the main gate and began to form up as Elizabeth and Appleton approached them. Elizabeth waved her hand at Garcia. "Don't bother, Sergeant. Let's just walk back normally. You can keep a better eye on our surroundings that way."

Garcia gave a curt nod. "Yes, ma'am." He turned to the soldiers. "You heard the lady. Greer, take point. Phillips and Kowalski, watch our backs." And so they made their way back to the rail yard at a steady walk, arriving without incident. Elizabeth found Private Miller waiting for her at her railcar, as per his captain's orders. He told her that Rainey and the Czechs were already back, so she ordered him to fetch Rainey for a meeting. Once in the railcar with some privacy, Elizabeth pushed Appleton down into a seat and sat down across from him. She wanted to know how much he knew.

"So when were you going to tell me about this shipment deal?" she asked.

"I was hoping I wouldn't have to," Appleton replied. "Compton must have thought you were privy to it."

"Well, it's time I was. Tell me what you know," she said.

Appleton remained silent for a moment, and then said, "Are you sure you want to know?"

Elizabeth leaned forward. "Charles," she said firmly.

Appleton sighed. "They were on the train before we even boarded, in the command carriage under the floor boards. I didn't know anything about them until after the shell hit. When we were emptying the carriage before we left it on the siding, I ran across them. Eight small crates, very heavy. I had Sergeant Kennard move them in behind the ammunition supplies in the cargo box-car. I told him to be discreet."

He thinks there are only eight crates. "So past Kennard and a couple of soldiers, who else knows?"

Appleton shrugged. "That's it."

Elizabeth leaned back. "You actually know what it is, don't you?" She hoped she will know in a minute, too.

"I can guess pretty accurately. There are not a lot of things that weigh that much that require secrecy when transported."

Elizabeth looked out the window. The crates contained gold. Kennard she could count on, but any men he picked would be able to guess their contents as well.

She looked back at Appleton. "So now they are parked pretty much beside our own little stash."

Appleton grinned. "It is the best hiding place."

"Don't be flippant," she scolded. "Any idea where it's from?"

Appleton stroked his chin. "There are theories around Russia that Kolchak came into possession of the Russian treasury's gold reserve. It had been shipped east during the war for safe keeping. The Bolsheviks were mighty angry when they went into the treasury building in Moscow and found it empty. It's thought that Kolchak has been using it to finance his war. But now that they are in retreat, my guess is the decision was made to get it out of Russia to a safer place."

"Eight chests can't be all of it," Elizabeth said.

"No," Appleton replied. "There will be a lot more, but shipping in small amounts can be done discreetly. Kolchak doesn't have control of the Trans-Siberian Railroad or a full trusting relationship with the Czechs, who do. It would be too risky to ship it all out at once. No doubt another shipment will come through with General Graves when he returns and he probably won't be privy to it either."

"So now we're here with eight crates, which is why it seems that a ship has been waiting just for us. It also explains much that happened to us since we left Omsk, including Captain Beauregard's appearance. Seems like a lot of effort for eight crates of gold." Elizabeth glanced at Appleton, hoping to get an indication that he might know about more crates. But she saw nothing.

"Do you think my father even knew?" she asked.

"He would have had to, although perhaps not what it was. Otherwise Graham would not have asked me about it." It was Appleton's turn to lean forward. "You cannot tell Captain Rainey."

Elizabeth shrugged. "He is already suspicious."

"That doesn't change the fact that he doesn't need to know."

"Good luck with that," she said with a knowing smile.

49

Rainey, Formanek and Birosh came into the carriage for the meeting. Rainey sat down beside Elizabeth. "How did it go at your HQ?"

"Actually, it went very well," she answered. "We're off to see a ship captain tonight. How about you?"

Rainey looked over at Formanek and Birosh, both standing in the aisle. "We're off to the Canadian Economic Mission tomorrow to look for a ship. We've picked up some additional wounded to take with us and some extra food and medical supplies, but it cost me."

Elizabeth frowned. "Cost you what?"

Rainey grimaced. "I agreed to let General Gajda have your weaponry."

"You what?" Elizabeth said coldly.

"Once you're away on your ship, you won't need them."

"That's not the point," Elizabeth retorted.

"Then what is?" Rainey responded firmly.

Appleton stood graciously. "While you two have your . . . discussion, I'll take the major and the lieutenant here out for a drink." He waved in the direction of the door. Formanek and Birosh, sensing the tension, quickly moved through the door, followed by Appleton. The carriage went silent, with only the muted sounds from the rail yard. Elizabeth had turned to look out the window while Rainey sat down across from her and looked into his lap. They stayed that way for a few moments. Then Rainey spoke.

"It's not about the weapons, is it," he stated.

Elizabeth continued to look out the window. "We'd probably just end up dumping them all overboard once we were at sea. I really wanted to get you alone."

Elizabeth looked up into Rainey's eyes. Thoughts of her brother swelled up her emotions, mixing with those that made her snap at Rainey in the first place. She swallowed, trying to drive them back down into her core.

"So, tell me what's up," Rainey said softly.

A tear formed in Elizabeth's right eye. She reached up to wipe it away. She had the locket in her hand and the chain slapped against her face. She brought her hand back down and opened it, staring at the locket again. She was thinking it needed a good polishing and some work to take out the dent the bullet had caused. She was trying to get her mind on anything but what was troubling her the most.

She looked up at Rainey. "What was it all for?"

Rainey wrapped his arm around her shoulders, pulling her close. He kissed her on the top of her head. "I don't know. Someday, we may figure it out."

"We'll be shipping out tomorrow," Elizabeth said quietly. "That ship we're seeing tonight is destined for San Francisco and we'll be on it."

"That was fast."

"Yes. About time we had a little luck, I guess."

Worry creased Rainey's brow. "No questions about what a mercenary unit was doing running around Russia?"

Elizabeth's face was blank. "Major Slaughter made the arrangements."

"But without Alexis," Rainey began. He paused for a moment before continuing. "You're shipping out with the crates." Elizabeth nodded. "Does Charles know?"

"He thinks there are only eight crates, or at least that's what he wants me to think. Says he found them in the bombed carriage."

"Where'd he put them?"

"Next to my gold box."

Elizabeth said it in a way for Rainey to figure it out. "Do the crates contain gold?"

She nodded. "Charles said they were heavy enough. I can't believe my own country painted a target on our train. Because of that, we lost my father and Alexis."

"Don't think like that," Rainey said. "That artillery crew may have just been shooting at every train that went by. Whether the gold was on the train or not, the result could have been the same."

Elizabeth sat silently, emotions rising up in her. They were going separate ways as early as tomorrow morning and it all finally pushed her over. Rainey wrapped his other arm around her, holding her tight. She turned into his shoulder and wept openly.

"I'll miss you too," he said softly, then kissed her on the top of her head. They sat for quite a while, Rainey slowly rocking her back and forth while the occasional sob or sniff came from Elizabeth. Finally, she looked up at him.

"This time tomorrow I'll be gone, and I'm afraid that I won't see you again."

Rainey smiled down at her. "I'm surprised you think you could get rid of me that easily. I know where you live."

Elizabeth grinned. "Thank you." She reached up and kissed him, and then held the locket out to him. "I plan on giving this to you when you get to New York. I expect you to come get it."

Rainey closed his hand over hers. "With bells on."

Elizabeth nodded and placed her head back on his chest. It was getting dark and the visit to the ship still had to be made. She pushed Rainey away and got up.

"Charles and I have to meet the ship's captain. I'll see you when I get back." She leaned over and kissed him on the lips, then turned and left the carriage.

Rainey sat there for a minute, thinking about what tomorrow would bring. But first, there were the crates to deal with. He and Birosh would have to move fast.

* * *

A team came by from the American base to take the train away just before midnight. Several hours later, it was still dark as the camp broke up, the company getting ready to march to the ship. Kennard had the men lined up, each with his own kit on his back. Each was armed with only Colt pistols, the rest of their weaponry having been handed over to the Czech contingent.

Elizabeth had wanted to fall asleep in Rainey's arms after returning from the ship, but Rainey said he had something to do during the night.

As she stepped from her tent, she spotted Rainey talking with Appleton and Kennard next to Rainey's tent. She went to see what they were discussing.

". . . and you're sure it's not only under lock and key, but very few people know about it?" Rainey was asking.

"Even the ship's crew was unaware they were moved on board, sir," Kennard answered.

"Don't worry, Captain. The ship will not be a target over eight crates," Appleton said.

"Unlike the train, Charles?" Elizabeth said as she came up beside Rainey. She looked calmly at Appleton. "How did the captain find out?"

Appleton nodded toward Rainey. "He was wandering the camp last night."

"So it's already aboard?"

"Yes, and secure. You agreed not to tell him."

"And she didn't," Rainey broke in. "I figured it out after too many attacks on the train."

Appleton turned to Rainey. "So, were you just wandering the camp waiting to see what it was?"

Rainey shrugged. "I suppose."

"Gentlemen," Elizabeth interceded. "The shipment is on board and secure and I trust Captain Rainey won't be telling anyone about it. His concern is for our welfare." Kennard and Appleton looked at her doubtfully. "OK, my welfare. Captain, are you satisfied with the arrangements and 'need to know' list?"

Rainey was grinning. Somewhere along the way, he had developed a certain adoration of Elizabeth when she took charge. He remembered that his father had mentioned more than once that his wife's take-charge attitude was why he married her. Was Elizabeth starting to remind him of his mother?

"Captain?"

Rainey didn't realize he was standing there with a stupid grin on his face. "Yes," he stammered. "I think we're good."

"Then that's settled," Elizabeth declared. She turned to Kennard. "How are we with getting everyone on board?"

"Only a couple of squads from Corelli's platoon left, Miss Clarke," Kennard replied.

"Then tell him to get over his attachment to the machine guns, hand them over to the Czechs and get his ass on the ship." She leaned toward Kennard. "And make sure you use those exact words."

Kennard grinned. "Yes, ma'am," he said, saluted, turned sharply and marched off.

"Mr. Appleton," Elizabeth continued, "you can board now. Captain, you're with me."

"Yes, ma'am," Appleton and Rainey said simultaneously.

* * *

They sat quietly in each other's arms, watching as the light of day slowly grew stronger with each passing minute through the window of a hotel room near the train station. Elizabeth had wanted to clean up before heading for the ship. They had been together for a couple of months now, but very rarely alone like this. She was thinking back to when she first met Rainey, slouching in a chair, cap pulled down, drunk. And then he'd had the gall to call her "Lizzie." But even then, she didn't despise him. Something about being called Lizzie had brought back words in the letters from her brother, talking about this man who had befriended the inexperienced lieutenant, taken him under his wing, and became attached to a tiny picture of her in the silver locket she had given him. Elizabeth knew who he was before Kennard introduced him. This was the man her brother had held in such high regard. The man he had insisted she must meet some day.

And now she had. But at what cost? The mixture of guilt and

love was confusing her and Rainey could sense it. He squeezed her a little harder and turned her face up to his.

"Penny for your thoughts?" he asked.

She smiled at him and lowered her eyes, but said nothing. When she brought her eyes back up to his, she stopped short, bothered.

"What is it?" she asked.

"You've never been in love before, have you?" he asked.

"Have you?" she replied.

"Don't avoid the question."

Elizabeth gazed into his eyes for a moment longer, then answered. "No, but that's not it." Rainey said nothing, giving her time to continue. "I don't know if I deserve you," she said quietly.

Rainey frowned. "Excuse me?"

"What do any of us deserve?" she began. "I was born into wealth, but what does that mean against the lives of so many people? Why do I deserve your love when viewed against Jeremy's death, my father's death, Tom Bradley? Why am I alive and they're not?"

"Whoa, whoa, whoa," Rainey stopped her. "You're thinking about this way too much."

"That's what I always do. You know I have to know every detail about everything. Help me understand this. I need to understand the meaning of it all."

"Observe, learn, dominate," mumbled Rainey.

"Where did you hear that?" asked Elizabeth. But she already knew from whom. Rainey just smiled at her.

He looked at the ceiling before continuing. "This is a little deeper into philosophy than I've ever gone," he said. "You're pretty well asking for the meaning of life. That's more O'Hanlon's area."

He looked back into Elizabeth's eyes. He took a big breath, let it out and gave another try to answer her question. "OK. I joined the Patricias because I had a sense of how devastating the war would be. I wanted to help other soldiers survive it."

"That gave you meaning?" Elizabeth asked.

"At first, yes," Rainey said. "but over time, with all the soldiers I saved who ended up dead a day or two later, I came to know there was no meaning to it, to the world, to anything. All you had to do is find something to live for and you'll do all right. There's no deserve or not deserve. There is just what fate deals you, how you handle it, and help where you can."

Elizabeth remained quiet. Rainey looked into her eyes. "Does that help?"

Elizabeth matched his look. "So you're saying that looking for meaning in life is a wasted exercise?"

Rainey thought for a moment. "Kind of a simple summary, but yes. How an old friend worded it was, 'Find meaning in your own life. There is none in the world in general.'"

"Quite a philosophy, Doctor. I would like to meet this old friend of yours."

"Can't. He was killed in action just before I left for your brother's regiment."

"Oh, I'm sorry."

"Me too." They sat quietly for a few moments. "Feeling better?" Rainey asked finally.

"Yes," Elizabeth replied softly, "and I'm starting to understand why my brother had been changed so much by the war."

"Do you feel changed?"

"Yes," Elizabeth said. "I'm not sure how I can just go back to my old life now."

Rainey smiled knowingly. "You don't. You make a new one. Hopefully with me."

* * *

All was aboard. Elizabeth could hear the ship's engines starting up as the gangway was raised. She was at the rail up near the stern, looking down at the pier where Rainey stood with Major Formanek and Lieutenant Birosh, all looking up at her. Standing back against a warehouse was Private Miller. He had asked to stay with Rainey, still not feeling comfortable among the men after what had become known as the "MacGregor Incident." Everyone agreed it was for the best. Miller could set out for wherever he wanted to go once he arrived in Vancouver.

The ship slowly began moving forward and away from the pier, the engine sounds rising to a heavy throb. Elizabeth waved at Rainey and blew him a kiss, an action that immediately embarrassed her. She had never been a girly girl. She ran a company, for God's sake. Company presidents didn't blow kisses. But then again, she had never been in love before, either. A lot had changed for her and she had adapted. She immediately blew Rainey another kiss.

Rainey waved back as big as he could. She was already missing him. At least he still had a job to do. Elizabeth's was done. Nothing to do but sail home. She watched from the railing until the ship had left the harbor and the pier was no longer visible. Rainey had stood there the whole time as well. She turned and found O'Hanlon behind her.

"Miss Clarke," O'Hanlon said. "I've been thinking about your . . . condition, and I'd like to check something if you have a moment."

Elizabeth sighed. "Very well. I'm sure it's just the food."

* * *

Back on the pier, Rainey looked over several pallets of medical supplies that Birosh and Formanek had acquired for the trip home to their new country. Intermixed with them, he could spot some of the sixteen crates he, Birosh, Crane and the other Mounties had liberated from the train before it was taken away. He smiled to himself as he walked away.

Fair payment for putting the wounded at risk like that.

Part 4

50

September 16, 1919
Edmonton, Canada

Standing across the street from the large wood-frame house, Rainey thought he would feel different. Everything was familiar. The front porch still had the two rocking chairs where his parents used to sit in the evenings, watching the sun go down. The large kitchen window made for bright dinnertimes in the summer, and the thick shutters kept out the cold northwest winds in the winter. It also looked like his brother, William, had recently put a fresh coat of pale yellow paint on the walls. Other than that, the two-story structure wasn't much different from other houses on a lot of streets in Edmonton. This was where he had grown up. It was home. At least it had been. It was William's home now. He hadn't been here in over five years and only returned for brief periods for six years before that. It was part of the tradition. He was the Rainey who had gotten the sword, so he was expected to build a life somewhere else, somewhere his adventures would take him.

Rainey smiled just thinking about it. Elizabeth would have a welcoming home for him now.

Elizabeth. He saw her face in his mind as clear as day, smiling at him. He missed her so much. Then came visions of his journey home. The "Empress of Russia" had sailed from Vladivostok to Vancouver in twelve days. There wasn't much to do on the ship during the crossing. Rainey spent much of the time walking the deck or in his cabin. Private Miller followed him around until he got more comfortable with the Mounties. By the time they made Vancouver, Crane had persuaded Miller to apply for Canadian citizenship and join the Force.

In Vancouver, they had been met by a general superintendent of the Canadian Pacific Railroad, who took control of the operation. The Canadian government had agreed to get the Czech legionnaires home and had promptly passed the buck, literally, to the CPR. The train was already in Vancouver, waiting to be loaded. A flexible timetable had been set up, as the company's regular trains would have precedence in the use of track. It was harvest time and many trains carrying wheat were heading west. When they arrived in Calgary to begin a three-day layover, Rainey and Crane arranged to catch a local train the next morning up to Edmonton. Now here he was, standing across from his childhood home, not knowing what to do next.

The front door opened and a young girl stepped onto the porch. Her blond locks were braided down both sides of her face and she wore a simple dress with an apron. As she made her way down the steps, she saw Rainey staring at her and she stopped suddenly, a look of confusion on her face. Rainey almost didn't recognize her. *Could this be Sarah, William's daughter?* She would be about eight by now, he thought. He was about raise his hand to wave at her when recognition sparked and she drew a big surprised grin.

"Uncle Robert!" she exclaimed loudly.

Rainey smiled and trotted across the street as Sarah careened down the stairs to the gate. As they reached each other, Sarah flung her arms around Rainey's waist with a laugh.

"How's my favorite niece?" he asked.

Sarah looked up at him with a mischievous grin. "I'm your only niece."

"No, not anymore," Rainey replied. "I have two others from your Aunt Millie and Uncle Richard."

"They don't count," Sarah insisted. "You've never met them."

"I see, but then you were only three when I last saw you. How did you recognize me?"

"Your picture is still up on the mantel," Sarah said knowingly. "What took you so long to come home? I missed you."

"I'm sorry, Sarah. Army business."

"But the war's been over for a year."

The door to the house opened and a woman stepped onto the porch. She was small, her brown hair up in a bun, with a heart-shaped face and a full dress and apron on. "Sarah, who are you . . ." She saw Rainey, and her hand came up to her mouth in surprise.

"Hello, Margaret," he said.

"Robert," she said, releasing a big breath. She stood, hand up by her mouth, staring.

"Mom, Uncle Robert's home," Sarah said matter-of-factly.

The spell was broken and Margaret recovered. "Yes, dear," she said. "I can see that. Why don't you invite him in for some tea?"

Sarah looked up at her uncle. "Want to come in for tea? Or maybe something stronger?"

"Sarah!" Margaret exclaimed.

Rainey laughed. "Can tell which side of the family she's from."

Margaret smiled. "You Raineys. All the same. Come on in, then. I'll see if William has any of that good stuff he brings in from Scotland."

They entered the house, Sarah tugging on Rainey's hand, and settled at the kitchen table. After Margaret poured some tea, she slid a half-empty bottle of Macallan's twenty-year single malt and a shot glass in front of him.

"William saves this for special occasions," she said. "I would guess you coming home is a special occasion."

Sarah sat across from Rainey, hands and chin on the table, watching him with a smile. Rainey poured himself a shot and sipped it. It had been a while since he had tasted a good Scotch and his brother William always had the best. "William and James at the store?" he asked.

"Yes," Margaret replied. "They should be home after closing up around six. You'll be staying for dinner?"

"I was hoping to stay the night. I'm catching the train back to Calgary tomorrow morning."

"What's in Calgary?"

"Fifteen hundred Czechs making their way home."

"What's a check?" Sarah asked.

Margaret patted Sarah on the head. "They are soldiers from Europe."

"What are they doing here?"

Margaret looked at Rainey with a knowing look. "Sharp as a Rainey, too. Honey, Uncle Robert can tell you all about it later at dinner when your father and brother are here. We don't want him to have to repeat himself."

Little Sarah scowled, but stayed silent.

"How is William?" Rainey asked Margaret.

"Daddy's mad at you," Sarah said.

Rainey looked over at Sarah. "And why is that?"

"Sarah, don't be talking about things you don't understand," Margaret said.

"But I do understand. Uncle Robert should have come home sooner because of Grandma and Grandpa."

Rainey and Margaret looked at each other. From the look on Margaret's face, Rainey could tell that his niece was only part right.

"There are some things your father left for you," Margaret said. "They are a little odd and they bother William. He wants them gone and you taking so long to get here hasn't helped."

Rainey was curious. "What things?"

"A box containing things William says have something to do with that sword of yours."

Rainey subconsciously glanced back at the hilt of his sword. He understood why William would have been upset. William was a family man. A pillar of the community. He had no time for the sword legends and didn't want his children getting interested in it. Having to sit on this box until Robert finally came to get it would not have sat well with him.

"I guess dinner will be an interesting meal," Rainey said.

* * *

William Rainey and his son had come home just before six. Where James was happy to see his uncle, William remained aloof and cool to his younger brother. Few words passed between them through dinner, with Margaret steering the conversation for her two curious children. James wanted to hear about battles while Sarah's main concern was whether she was going to get a new aunt soon. Once Robert mentioned Elizabeth in passing, Margaret raised her eyebrows and joined her daughter in asking questions. James went silent. He would have to hear about his brave uncle's war exploits later.

After dinner, William and Robert retired to William's study. William immediately collected a wooden box and a package wrapped in brown paper off a top shelf and brought them to his brother. "The box was found in Dad's office at Headquarters, with your name on it. The package arrived a week ago from Germany." He dropped them in Robert's lap.

Robert looked at the paper bundle first. He could tell right away it was from Dietrich. He could deal with that later. He picked up the box and looked up at his brother. "What's in it?"

"Look for yourself."

Robert slowly opened the box to find an old rolled-up parchment, a thick leather-bound journal, an old coin depicting two men on a horse, and an envelope, unopened, with his name written in his father's flowing script.

Robert looked at William. "Did you read any of this?"

William hesitated before answering. "I glanced through the journal. There's a story in there about how Mom and Dad met."

Robert picked up the journal to examine it. "You have the right to read it all, you know."

"Was never interested," William said. "It pertains to your life, not mine."

Robert placed the book back in the box and picked up the letter. It remained unopened. As he started to open it, William got up and headed for the door. "Don't you want to know what it says?" Robert asked.

"You know I don't. It's that part of our family that involved only you, Dad and that sword. I don't want it to be part of my family."

Robert nodded slowly. This was Robert's legacy to continue, not William's. Robert thought back to Count Raynykov and how a younger son of the "Great Celt" must have moved on from the family way back when. Now it was his turn to drift from his family. It wouldn't be very hard, considering how far he had already drifted. With their parents gone, it was William's family now, not his.

"My train leaves tomorrow at one."

William nodded. "When James asks, and he will, please don't fill his head with glorious stories from the war."

"Don't worry. There wasn't much glory to be had there."

"I know. I have some veterans working in the mill for me. They stick together, away from most people, and say nothing about their experiences. It's like they are helping each other forget a nightmare."

Robert nodded. "They are. In time, they may speak out about it, but now they need time to settle their minds. It was horrible in France." Robert's voice petered out, his eyes getting a faraway look.

William's face showed concern as they looked at each other in silence. Finally, he asked, "Are you OK?"

Robert's eyes had seemed to glaze over, visions and noise of battle washing over him. But then, the image of Elizabeth's face appeared. Everything in his body began to calm.

"Robert?"

His eyes cleared as he saw his brother frowning from the doorway. "I will be," he said. "I have someone to hold on to now."

William nodded. "Then I will bid you goodnight." As William

left the room, Robert moved to a chair where a lamp was lit. He took the letter out of the box, examined it, and opened it, finding a single sheet of paper with the RNWMP crest at the top. He looked at his father's flowing script and began reading.

October 15, 1914

Dear Robert

If you are reading this letter, it means that I have died before I could give you the contents of this box and explain more of our family legacy to you. It was my intent to do so after you returned from France. I always knew you would. You had the sword with you.

As your Grandfather passed these on to me when it was my time to leave, I now hand them over to you. You are my son with the wandering spirit, the same spirit my father saw in me and his father saw in him. Our history with the sword goes back centuries. How far, I will let you read for yourself, because my journal, and the one you are keeping, are continuing chapters that have been written by Raineys since we first came into possession of the sword. The other journals you will find in France. Take the sword, the coin, the rolled parchment and my journal to 12 Rue de la Boucherie in Limoges and you will find our full legacy through the centuries. Leave my journal there when you leave and remember to make arrangements for your journal to be sent there as well when your adventure ends.

I said you had a wandering spirit, but I would be remiss if I did not tell you that someday, as history does seem to repeat itself in this area, you will meet a woman. This woman will be strong-minded, fiercely loyal, smart, and will love you with a passion you will never be able to properly describe. Basically, she will be some version of your mother and she most likely won't like you very much in the beginning. But when she does love you, you will find you will not want to wander away from her. Then it will be time to settle down and build your new family.

My last advice to you is to live your life to the full values of your Masonic teachings, stand upright and always do right. Protect the downtrodden against evil and injustice wherever you find it and fight for the good in the world. This is how I raised you and you'll find it is our legacy.

I love you, my son. Your adventure is continuing. Have a good life.

Dad.

Robert folded the letter and placed it back in its envelope. He wiped a tear away from his cheek as he remembered times with his father. Even in discipline, Thomas Rainey always had a knowing look in his eyes that was reserved only for his son, Robert. Thomas knew very early in Robert's life where his son was headed. He must have seen a lot of himself in the young boy.

Robert placed the envelope back in the box. *Guess I'm going back to France*, he thought. *Now how do I tell Elizabeth?*

51

October 12, 1919
Limoges, France

Rainey stood across and down a few doors from 12 Rue de la Boucherie, watching the doorway for any signs of activity. He had been standing there, leaning up against a building, for almost thirty minutes, watching people walking up and down the narrow street doing their daily business. But no one approached the door at No. 12. The name plate said Financiere de Molay. Rainey noted the Masonic connection with the name de Molay. It had raised his curiosity significantly.

The address was just a doorway, jammed between a flower shop and a butcher, part of a row of houses in the style common through Europe. It had three floors. Rainey suspected all of No. 12 was on the upper floors.

He had not come directly to Limoges after landing at Cherbourg. He had taken the train to Paris with the Czech soldiers. There, he bid goodbye to Lieutenant Birosh and Major Formanek. Birosh insisted that he find the time to come to Plzen to visit, where he would be offered the best beer he had ever tasted. Formanek had been brought into the gold crate conspiracy while on the ship and had guaranteed the gold would be put to good use helping the wounded. Rainey found two gold bars in his duffle bag when he reached his hotel.

He did a little shopping in Paris. He had shipped his uniform to New York from Montreal and had only a few pieces of civilian clothing to wear during the Atlantic crossing. He had spent much of that time reading his father's journal, fascinated by the stories from a man he had only seen at home or behind his desk at the RNWMP post in Edmonton. By the time Rainey was ten, his father was a superintendent and no longer made long rides to police the west. What shocked him most was the story of his mother and how she had met his father. William had been right; it was quite a story.

While in Paris, Rainey realized how close he was to the battlefields where he had fought. For the next two weeks, he journeyed up and down the old front lines. Frezenberg, Vimy, Ypres, Passchendaele, the Argonne. It had only been a year, but he already saw signs of the landscape recovering from four years of destruction. That helped him face his demons. The world would recover and so would he.

While looking up at the ridge at Vimy, he made a promise to himself that he would do whatever he could to prevent such a travesty from happening again. On his last night in Paris, he sent a coded letter to Peter Dietrichs saying as much and reaffirming his offer of assistance with whatever intelligence Dietrichs felt needed to get out to the greater world. He hoped it wouldn't be too hard to find Appleton for his help.

He took the train down to Limoges, arriving the night of October 11. He checked into a small hotel close to Rue de la Boucherie. The next morning, as he found himself watching the door of No. 12, a level of nervousness countered his curiosity. He finally shook his head and decided just to go find out what was behind the door.

With his sword on his back, his father's small wooden box under his arm and a shoulder bag, Rainey stepped into the doorway and reached for the knocker, giving it three short raps. He took a small step back to wait for someone to come to the door, ensuring they could see him clearly through the spyhole. It took about a minute before he heard locks disengaging. The door opened a crack. An old man with stark white hair stared at him through the gap.

"*Oui?*" the man said in a raspy voice.

"*Mon père m'a envoyé, Thomas Rainey,*" said Rainey.

"*Et vous êtes?*"

"Robert Rainey."

The old man looked him up and down. "*Avez-vous la documentation?*"

Rainey held out the small box. The old man took it.

"*L'épée ainsi,*" said the man.

Rainey hesitated, but his father's letter had said to bring the sword. He lifted it off his shoulder and passed it to the man.

"*Un moment.*" The old man closed the door and Rainey heard the locks re-engaging. He hoped he had not just been robbed. He had nothing left to do but wait for everything to be authenticated.

He stepped back onto the street and looked down towards the small square he had come through on his way there. He could see the corner of an outdoor café where the street joined the square, with two people conversing at a table. It was not a warm day, but it was sunny and pleasant. He pulled his coat closed and turned back to look down the other way. The street ended at a cross street. It was narrow with a brickwork surface and very narrow sidewalks.

This was an old part of Limoges. The buildings dated from the late 1700s, built of brick and stone from the quarries nearby. The quarries would have been in operation since medieval times. It all seemed a rather odd location for a financial house, especially one that his Dad, who as far as he knew had never been to France, would have dealings with.

Rainey turned at the sound of the door locks being disengaged again. The door opened and the old man stood in the entrance.

"*Suivez-moi s'il vous plaît.*"

Rainey stepped through the door and saw what he expected. A small entryway led to a staircase up to a second floor landing. The old man moved slowly, Rainey following close behind, cresting the landing and continuing towards the third floor. They climbed in silence, Rainey not wanting to bother the old man as he wheezed his way upward. At the top, on the left, was a solid, ornate door with a name plaque on it, saying simply *Directeur.*

The old man rapped with three very slow knocks. He reached for the knob and opened the door. Stepping back, he signaled Rainey to enter, then closed the door behind him.

The room did not fit with the nondescript front door. It was much more elaborate, with what looked like mint-condition antiques, a great canvas painting on the wall and a large Napoleon desk in the middle of the room. Another table had a telegraph key and receiver on it. Rainey judged that the room extended out over the next address on the building's street level.

A man was standing by the window looking down at the street, sweeping his gaze back and forth like he was looking for something. Then he turned abruptly with a big smile of his face.

"Monsieur Rainey," he exclaimed in English with a flowing French accent, arms wide in greeting. "It is such an honor finally to meet you. It has been almost a year since I had heard of your father's passing. I was beginning to worry." He came around the desk, his hand stretched out. Rainey took his hand and noted the masonic grip that the man used. Rainey returned it.

On the desk, Rainey observed, his father's box lay open, its contents lying beside it. The sword lay across the desk as well. He looked back up at the man. He noted the slicked-back hair, the fine suit and the mustache that curled up at the corners. The man appeared to be in his late thirties or early forties. "You know me, but I have no idea who you are or why my father insisted I come here."

"Of course, of course," the man said, circling back behind the desk and sitting down. "You have been in the war and your father wrote this letter in 1914." He picked up the letter and held it out to Rainey. "He was obviously making sure. But forgive me. I must introduce myself. I am Jacques Louis Monteux, *Directeur* of Financiere de Molay. We have much to discuss."

Rainey stepped forward and took the letter, folded it and placed it in his coat. "Yes, I suppose we do. Let's start with why I'm here."

"Please sit down, sir." Rainey took a seat across the desk from Monteux. "You are here so the account can be transferred."

Rainey looked confused. "What account?"

Monteux had an amused smile on his face. "I suppose my father had a similar conversation with your father. I was not born yet and by the look of you, neither were you."

"When was that?"

"March of 1873."

"That was before he joined the North West Mounted Police."

"Yes, it was," Monteux said knowingly. "I believe he went off to Canada right after he came here."

Rainey cocked his head to one side. "He was the son of a Hungarian count."

"Actually, your grandmother was a countess. Your grandfather just married her."

Rainey smiled. "That's right. You seem to know a lot about my family."

"I should," Monteux said. "Our families have been working together for centuries."

Rainey leaned back in his chair. "So, where do we start?"

Monteux reached over and picked up a file. "First, we will need your signature on these documents. Then, if you are interested, I can show you the journals chronicling your family history."

Rainey looked surprised. Then he looked down at his father's journal. "The other journals are here?"

"Of course," said Monteux. "This is where they are the safest. My family have been guarding over them and your wealth since the beginning. It is my family's tradition. But first, sign the papers. I will leave you to read through them." Monteux got up and crossed the room to what looked like a blank wall. But he patted the surface and with a soft click, a section of the wall popped open and he exited.

Rainey sat for thirty minutes going over the documents. They were in English and covered how the *account* operated and who had what authority and exclusive access to it. Basically, Rainey owned the account and directed where funds would go while Monteux and his firm would carry out the actual transactions. The documents said nothing about what was in the account. They appeared to be simple and direct, unlike any bank documents he had ever signed before.

After signing, he stood up walked around the room. He took note of a few Masonic symbols on the walls and smiled knowingly. Monteux was a Mason and seemed to know Rainey was one as well. He stopped at one painting he recognized and looked at the plaque on the frame. *War, the Exile and the Rock Limpet* by William Turner.

"You like the painting?" Monteux said from behind him.

"Yes," answered Rainey. "It's about Napoleon. My father had a postcard of this painting. You have a marvelous reproduction."

"That is an original."

"Then what's hanging . . ."

Monteux chuckled. "That is an original as well. Your great-grandfather actually knew William Turner. He liked this painting so much that Turner made another one. I have never been able to determine if this one was the first or the second one produced."

Rainey paused, slowly taking in the information. "So the painting is part of the account."

"Yes," Monteux replied.

"Really."

"There is story behind this painting, but I will let you read about it in time. Also, since no one knows of this version's existence, it hangs here in my office. I have valued it, but selling it would cause a stir in the art world."

"I can imagine."

Monteux moved to his desk and checked the signatures on the

documents before putting them back in the file folder. He looked up at Rainey with a bemused smile. "Being very interested in history, especially the untold stories, I have read all your family journals. They are very entertaining. I can't wait to read your father's. Now that you have signed the documents, the account belongs to you and I can give you access to the journals. But first," he picked up two pages from his desk, "you will want to know what is in the account in total." He handed the pages over to Rainey. "This is just a summary. I can provide details if you wish."

The pages contained bank names, account numbers and amounts, along with a list of company stocks, land titles, and art. A total was listed near the bottom of the second page. When he saw it, he stopped breathing and slumped down into his chair.

"Is that number real?"

"Based on current stock prices, the auction value of the art, the land and amounts in the bank accounts, yes. I compiled it up just two weeks ago, something I do once a quarter. You are, quite possibly, the richest man in the world."

Rainey looked at the number again. "And this is in pounds sterling?"

"Yes."

"Where did it all come from?"

Monteux sat down. "Smart investments for over five hundred years. I have the records of everything since my family began its association with yours."

Rainey was still staring at the number on the page. "That's nine figures."

"Yes, it is." Monteux let Rainey have a moment to let it all sink in before continuing. "Our family association dates back to 1371.

Henry had just deposed Peter as King of Castile and he encouraged riots against the Jews that killed hundreds. Twelve knights, one of them your ancestor, Fredrick, escorted my family and the riches we controlled from Najera to Limoges where we were set up as before as a money house. The twelve knights all signed similar agreements as the one you just signed, making our money house the repository for their wealth. In their honor, we named the house De Molay."

"After the last Grand Master of the Templars. Were they Templars?"

"No. There were no Templars by 1371. But they were descendants of those knights. They came from all over Europe as mercenaries to fight for Edward, the Black Prince, during the Hundred Years War. After winning the Battle of Najera in 1367, they stayed on with King Peter."

A realization hit Rainey. "You're Jewish."

Monteux frowned. "Is that a problem?"

"No, of course not," said Rainey. "You seem to keep that quiet."

"After centuries of anti-Semitism, it has become a family trait. Limoges has been a quiet backwater for centuries. It was easy to stay hidden here."

Rainey nodded. "So there are other families?"

Monteux shook his head. "Over the centuries, the other families have died out. Yours is the last one."

"What happened to their accounts?"

"From the beginning, it was decided that if a family died out, their wealth would be evenly divided among the remaining accounts. The last family line died out in 1815, at Waterloo I believe.

It is all yours now. I suspect the unique transfer method your family used helped in its longevity."

"How so?"

"All of the other families passed the chit down to their first born and tried to establish some hereditary link to the account. That turned out to be unwise as fools could get control or, after the last hundred years, nobility developed some disadvantages. We lost three of the families in quick succession during the French Revolution. Your family passed the account down to a son with a certain character while any hereditary wealth acquired by the particular ancestor went to another sibling."

Rainey nodded, thinking about William and his family. The store had originally been founded by their father.

"What's a chit?"

Monteux lifted the parchment out of Rainey's father's box. "This method of identification dates back to the Crusades. It is a little more elaborate now, but it is still a coded letter to prove the bearer's identity and give access to the wealth stored for him by our firm. It was a Templar banking technique. And now," he said, getting up from his chair, "let us look at your library. I am sure you would like to learn more about your family. I suggest you start with the first journal. Angus Rainey. That story will tell you much about your unique sword."

He went to the wall with the hidden door and clicked it open again. Rainey followed him through to find a small reading room with a large, comfortable chair, a small table with a new electric lamp, and two walls of bookshelves.

"On these shelves, you will find your family history," Monteux said. He pointed to a volume on the end. "This is Angus, dating from the late thirteenth century. He was a Templar. I always feel it is best to start at the beginning."

Rainey was looking at another shelf. Monteux noticed what book he was looking at. "Ah, the Bible. Take it down and look at the inscription on the first page."

Rainey took the volume off the shelf and carefully opened it up. On the first page, in fine script and in an old German dialect, was written:

To Ivan,

For all your efforts to protect me, I give thanks to you and to the Lord for bringing you to me. May God bless you always.

Rainey couldn't make out the signature.

"The Bible dates from 1455," said Monteux, "and is believed to be one of the original 177 copies Gutenberg first produced. It was given to your ancestor Ivan by Martin Luther himself in the early 1500's."

Rainey chuckled. "Of course, I would have an ancestor named Ivan."

Monteux smiled. "Ivan, born in Russia . . ."

"Son of the Great Celt," said Rainey, finishing the sentence.

Monteux looked surprised. "Yes, Connor Rainey. Your father told you the story?"

Rainey shook his head. "I was in Russia recently and ran into someone from that branch of the family."

"How unusual."

"Yes, it was." Rainey stepped over to Monteux. "Are all these books mine?"

"All but the three shelves over there. My family collects books as well."

Rainey placed the Bible back on the shelf and took down the journal of Angus Rainey. He sat and opened the book to the first page. The swirling letters were dark against the old parchment. "It's in Latin."

"Remember, it was the late thirteenth century. Just about everything was written in Latin then." Monteux paused. "Can you read it?"

"It's been a while, but it will come back to me," Rainey replied. Now he realized why his father insisted he learn a dead language.

Monteux smiled. "Then I will leave you to your reading. If you need anything, I will be in my office. When I am ready to leave, I will let you know."

"Before you go." Rainey reached into his shoulder bag and took out the two gold bars. "I suppose I should deposit these with you?"

52

Dec 21, 1919
Long Beach, NY

The sun was shining bright, high over the horizon. It was mid-morning on Long Island with a fresh, cold winter breeze blowing along the coast. The sound of the breeze among the bare branches of the maples was soothing. It felt biting against Elizabeth's face, but still comforting, a reminder that she was home and safe. She appreciated these times much more than she used to. Before, she had taken the place for granted as she left on a Monday for the city. But those days were in a distant past. This was home. A place of peace. A place of renewal. The tall maples, the shoreline, the stables, the horses, and the veranda on the big old house her grandfather had built. And a place of beginnings.

Elizabeth's thoughts drifted back to eight months ago. The men were still arriving then. Equipment being stored out in the open under tarps. Rows of tents as living quarters across the front yard. The appearance of organized chaos as the men prepared equipment and trained. Her misgivings were strong then, but slowly she had begun to accept that the mission had a purpose. If not for her father, then for the men who were looking for a purpose. Now that she was home, her new purpose was to remember the many names and the grim faces of the men who never made it back from Russia.

It was the blank stare of Tom Bradley and the dead eyes of her brother Jeremy that were forever burned into her subconscious. The nights were still filled with horrific memories of the mission, but they were fading as Rainey had said they would. He had also said that those memories would never completely go away. Standing on the veranda, the contentment she felt made her wonder if maybe, just maybe, he was wrong. But the faces of the dead continued to reappear in her mind, and she knew Rainey was right. Like him, she would be haunted by ghosts, too.

It had been months now since she had seen Rainey. There had been a cable from him in late October from Limoges, saying he wanted to go back to a café in Sedan where he and her brother had been the day after the Armistice went into effect. Then it was back to Canada to get officially discharged from his regiment. Something always seemed to be keeping him away and she was afraid he would never come back to her. But he did keep her posted on his whereabouts. That was a good sign, although he never stayed in one place long enough for her to send him any replies.

A movement in her stomach made her jump, bringing her back from her musing. The baby was beginning to move around, just as doctor had told her. She reached for the locket around her neck, stroking it with her thumb for comfort. Five months along now, the bulge in her belly was becoming quite prominent. A gust of wind blew across her face and she began to feel the chill. She stepped back from the doorway and closed the door, but lingered there, looking out the window, waiting.

With the ship still within sight of Vladivostok, O'Hanlon had broached the subject that Elizabeth might be pregnant. He chided himself for not seeing the signs earlier, but Elizabeth had forgiven him. She spent most of the journey to San Francisco in her cabin.

Once back in the States, all had gone smoothly. The government man came and got the Russian gold without anyone being any the wiser. Appleton had been surprised to find there were more than eight crates. But he also understood. Not every day did an American military unit leave Omsk with Czech blessings. It was later that someone came by the house to ask about the shipment being a bit short. Of course, no one wanted to admit that there was a shipment. She suggested that the man talk to her lawyer if he didn't believe she had no idea what he was talking about. And that ended that.

She wondered what some of the men of Clarke Company were doing now. Some were working for her, but many had just disappeared once they were paid. No one tried to stop them as they left to find their own futures. She had boarded the Union Pacific Trans-Continental alone, ready to put the mission behind her.

Rainey was totally unaware that he was going to be a father, but he would be finding out soon. His last cable was from Ottawa, telling her he would be arriving in New York late yesterday. He fully expected to get up to the house today, which is why Elizabeth was spending time watching the driveway.

The baby made another small move, coinciding with an automobile turning into the drive and approaching the house. Elizabeth gulped in some air in anticipation that this was her Robert. Two men were in the car, however, making Elizabeth wonder if it was someone else altogether. As the car came to a stop in front of the house, she could clearly see that Rainey was in the passenger seat. To her surprise, Charles Appleton was driving. She flung open the door and stepped out onto the veranda.

Rainey jumped out of the car with a big smile, but stopped dead in his tracks when his feet hit the ground. He had spotted Elizabeth's belly sticking out from her coat. Elizabeth could only describe the look on his face as one of complete shock.

"Charles," said Elizabeth, watching Appleton get out of the car as if nothing odd was happening. "How wonderful to see you. I haven't seen you since San Francisco."

"I've been pretty busy," he said nonchalantly.

The baby moved again. Elizabeth was thinking that it didn't like the cold. Smiling, she turned back to Rainey, who still had the look of shock on his face. "Robert, help me back into the house," she ordered matter-of-factly.

Rainey still hadn't moved from the side of the car. Elizabeth encouraged him again. "Robert."

Rainey took a tentative step forward. "When . . .?" was all he could get out.

Elizabeth frowned at him. "Really? You've already forgotten the night in Chelyabinsk?"

Rainey continued slowly up the stairs to stand in front of Elizabeth, his eyes lowered towards her belly. He slowly raised his hand and stroked it lightly. He raised his face, smiling, to look into Elizabeth's eyes.

"Kiss me, you idiot," she said.

Rainey moved in for the kiss. It was long, deep and seemed to go on forever, rekindling the love that had fired so strongly so many months ago. Neither of them wanted it to end, but the baby had other ideas. Rainey felt it move, surprising him and breaking the moment. Rainey looked down at her belly again, but didn't say anything.

Appleton cleared his throat. "I take it Robert didn't know?"

"If he would have stayed in one place long enough for me to have gotten a message to him," Elizabeth said.

Rainey smiled. "I'm here now. Charles, why didn't you tell me last night?"

"I assumed you knew," Appleton said.

"Is this why you were feeling ill those last days in Russia?" Rainey asked.

"Of course," Elizabeth replied, smiling. "Poor Brendan was baffled by my case, but what would he know about women's issues? Come into the house. Miranda will bring us some tea."

They entered the house and went through to the sitting room, Rainey helping Elizabeth into a chair. Elizabeth waved him away. "I'm not an invalid. When I get to eight months, you can help me into chairs." She looked to Appleton. "So, how did you two meet up? Robert only got into New York last night, didn't he?"

Appleton leaned forward. "I was in the lobby of the Waldorf after some meetings and there he was, checking in."

"The Waldorf?" Elizabeth said, surprised, turning to Rainey "You rob a bank recently?"

"No," Rainey replied. "Apparently, I'm richer than you are. I'll tell you all about it later."

Appleton continued. "Remember in San Francisco when I got that update from the State Department about the closing of all clandestine operations?"

"Yes. You were very upset."

Appleton snorted. "The world is still a very dangerous place and the government is sticking its head back in the sand. So I've left State. I have been visiting a number of corporate contacts I made through your father and subtly developing an intelligence network around the world. I was wondering when I could get ahold of Robert here, when there he was."

Elizabeth frowned. "Intelligence network. Like spying."

"Yes. That is what I do."

"For whom?"

Appleton leaned back in his chair. "No one, really. And everyone."

Elizabeth looked perplexed. She turned to Rainey. "I don't understand."

Appleton nodded at Rainey. "Why don't you continue from here? It was your idea to take this out of US control."

Rainey took a deep breath. Elizabeth sensed he was now having doubts, most likely because he was now going to be a father. She nodded encouragement for him to continue.

"Remember Peter Dietrich?" he asked.

Elizabeth thought for a moment. "Your German friend. We met him in Russia."

"Yes. That night when we went off talking alone, he told me he had been assigned by the German General Staff to become a Bolshevik so he could report on their activities. He was able to get close to Kolochov, but as it turned out, after the Armistice his bosses disappeared or had more pressing issues than Russia. He had been gathering a considerable amount of intelligence on the top leadership and their operations abroad through the Comintern. He realized that they were turning the Comintern into an international intelligence network.

"Peter's notes contained very valuable information. But he had no one to send them to. He wanted me to take them, hoping that through my connections with Charles, they could be put in the right hands. I agreed. I was never really sure what I would do with it. Running into Charles last night and seeing what he was trying to accomplish gave me the idea. I convinced Charles to forget about working for the US behind the scenes and start working for the world."

Rainey paused, looking into Elizabeth's eyes for any indication of what she was thinking. But he saw nothing. *Small wonder she was so good in boardrooms*, he thought.

He continued. "Did you get the package I sent from Edmonton?"

"Yes," Elizabeth said. "It's in the safe, unopened as you requested."

Rainey nodded. "That package is the first step in building our network. We have Peter in Germany, running the Communist operations, keeping tabs on all other political groups and keeping his people from overthrowing the republic. He will have a new boss in Moscow. There are some interesting contacts in Czechoslovakia and France to develop further. Through you and Clarke Steel, we can gain better access than Charles can to industrialists and politicians all over the world. We expect to find among them the right people who can feed us intelligence from the countries they operate in. In essence, our intelligence network is already operating. It just needs some central leadership, so to speak. A group that can put all the information together and work it."

Elizabeth didn't move or even acknowledge what she was hearing. She just stared at Rainey. When it became apparent Rainey had nothing left to say, she finally spoke. "Is there a goal for this intelligence network?"

Rainey looked at Appleton. Appleton turned to Elizabeth.

"The world fell all too easily into war back in 1914. Much of that was due to egos, nationalist fervor, and just downright poor intelligence about the other side's capabilities. It is a sad statement that the royal heads of Germany and Russia, two monarchs with absolute authority, tried to bring their countries back from the edge and couldn't. I believe that the proper information placed in the right hands, regardless of country or allegiances, could have prevented the war from starting."

"So you want to spy for the world," Elizabeth said. "Rather grandiose, don't you think? It takes a lot of money to fund a private intelligence network on the scale you're talking about. You expect Clarke Steel to fund it? I'd never be able to hide it from the board for very long."

Rainey smiled at her. "Clarke Steel will be a conduit for accessing the right people. Funds will come from me."

Elizabeth's head tilted to one side. "You said you were richer than me. Perhaps this would be a good time to explain how a simple army captain from a policeman's family could possibly be worth more than twenty million dollars."

Rainey put his hand on Elizabeth's shoulder. "I came into an inheritance that was established several centuries ago. It's a long story that will take me several days to tell you about. So for now, if funding isn't a problem, what do you think?"

Elizabeth pondered for a moment. "We would be the central clearinghouse for the intelligence?"

"Yes."

"And we would decide what to do with it? Who to approach with it?"

"Yes."

"And I am considered one of the 'we'?" That was more a statement than a question.

Appleton leaned forward. "We wouldn't be telling you this if you were not going to be a major part of it. We both trust you explicitly and require your excellent business acumen and contacts when deciding which paths to take."

Elizabeth turned to Appleton. "Are you trying to flatter me? I still don't fully trust you."

Appleton smiled. "I would be disappointed in you if you did."

Miranda appeared at the door with a tray of tea and cakes. Everyone stayed silent while she put it down on the small table in front of the chairs, turned and left. Elizabeth gazed out the window across the yard in front of the house. "We'll have to discuss it further. It will generate a lot of power, and that will be corrupting. We will need safeguards in place against that. As for the mechanics of the network, it'll need a basic business structure to operate with and a way to keep the money hidden. Some support staff will be needed and vetted, investigators hired, and a blind to operate behind so we can mask what we are doing."

"You sound like you've done this before," Rainey said.

Elizabeth looked at him like he was a child. "How do you think a fully equipped two hundred-man army made it to Russia without anyone noticing?" she asked.

Rainey looked at Appleton and smiled. Elizabeth was on board, even though she didn't come right out and say it. Appleton only had one thought.

The adventure continues...

Epilogue

October 12, 2007
St. Petersburg, Russia

The light coming through the window was waning fast. She watched her boss reach over and turned on the desk lamp, throwing incandescent light across the pages.

Dr. Igor Valenskaev placed the pages back down on his desk when he was finished. An air of finality set in as a historical mystery was finally put to rest. The DNA analyses were conclusive. The remains found outside Ekaterinburg were those of the Tsarovich Alexis and either Maria or Anastasia Romanov.

"So, that is the end of it," Valenskaev said. He put the report back in the file folder and reached it out to his assistant. "File this and send the summary to all the names on the list on the top page."

"Yes, Doctor," his assistant answered. "I'll get it done before I leave today."

"Evgenia, they died almost a hundred years ago. It can wait until tomorrow. Go home."

Evgenia Raynykova looked down at the file, debating whether

to get the email out tonight or not. It might take about thirty minutes to set it all up. But then, another thought entered her head.

"I wonder why their remains weren't with the rest of the family's?" she asked.

Valenskaev sighed. "What does it matter? That is for conspiracy theorists to ponder. We just do the analysis. Now go home to your husband."

Evgenia smiled. Her husband would be home from the office already. The decision was made. She would do the email tomorrow.

"Goodnight Doctor. You should consider getting home to your wife as well."

Valenskaev waved his hand at her as she left, his nose already in another file. She passed by her desk and placed the file in the top drawer. The lab was empty, the rest of the staff having already gone home after a busy day. She grabbed her coat and headed for the door. She was looking forward to telling her husband about the file. He and his father had shown great interest in the DNA results.

The remaining Romanovs had been found, but the nagging question was still in her mind.

Why were they buried away from the others?

Author's Notes

Although this is a book of fiction. I have attempted to maintain a certain level of historical accuracy and add actual historical figures into the story. The more common figures that everyone would know about, like Stalin, Trotsky and Makhno, were placed in the story if their timing and location corresponded to the "company's". I added some lesser known historical figures that I discovered through research; men like Major Slaughter, the Czech Generals, and there were six Mounties in Omsk at the time.

There are several sources I would like to thank. Wikipedia was very handy for general information. I'd also like to thank James Carl Nelson for his book *The Remains of Company D,* about the 28th Infantry Regiment during the Great War.

There are several people who have contributed, supported and taught me a lot about writing and publishing. Lorraine Patton reviewed my first draft and gave the story the focus it needed. John Meyer of Cape Fear Publishing did an excellent and entertaining editing job, making the novel as good as it could be. The gang at IBPA (Terry, Mimi and Patti) for marketing guidance and Peter Skagen for great advice on how to approach self-publishing and marketing. Grady at Damonza, worked with me to create the great cover for the book. And I can't forget my brothers from St. Mark's Masonic Lodge #118 for their encouragement for this project of mine.

And, of course, I must thank my wife, Carmen, for her support over the last year and a half as I took all my little pieces of *The Locket* and created the finished book.

B.G. Cousins
Calgary, Alberta

Made in the USA
Charleston, SC
07 August 2016